Perfect Match

ALSO BY JANE MOORE
FROM CLIPPER LARGE PRINT

The Second Wives Club

Perfect Match

Jane Moore

W F HOWES LTD

This large print edition published in 2008 by
W F Howes Ltd
Unit 4, Rearsby Business Park, Gaddesby Lane,
Rearsby, Leicester LE7 4YH

1 3 5 7 9 10 8 6 4 2

First published in the United Kingdom in 2008
by Century

A CIP catalogue record for this book is available
from the British Library

ISBN 978 1 40741 951 0

Typeset by Palimpsest Book Production Limited,
Grangemouth, Stirlingshire
Printed and bound in Great Britain
by MPG Books Ltd, Bodmin, Cornwall

FSC
Mixed Sources
Product group from well-managed
forests and other controlled sources

Cert no. SGS-COC-2953
www.fsc.org
© 1996 Forest Stewardship Council

For Paul Duddridge

ACKNOWLEDGEMENTS

A big thank you to Dr Mohamed Taranissi of the Assisted Reproduction and Gynaecology Centre for giving up his valuable time to talk me through the process of pre-implantation genetic diagnosis, a procedure in which he has been, and continues to be, a pioneer in this country.

Thanks also to my agent Jonathan Lloyd and all at Curtis Brown; to Susan Sandon, Georgina Hawtrey-Woore, Rina Gill and all at Random House; my husband Gary and daughters Ellie and Grace for putting up with me being locked away in a room; and my mum Pat for endless babysitting.

And finally, thank you to Paul Duddridge whose 'What if . . . ?' in the pub started the whole thing off.

PROLOGUE

'Are you sure it's safe?' Joe hovered beside her, his face decidedly reluctant. 'I mean, shouldn't we be . . . you know, *careful*?'

'*Safe*?' scoffed Karen. 'Of course it's safe. I'm hardly going to get bloody pregnant, am I?'

She made a loud harrumphing noise and rolled on to her side, gently easing herself into the upright position, the weight of her bloated belly making her wince with discomfort.

Joe poked out his tongue playfully. 'I'm just worried about the baby. This is a mighty weapon you know.' He grinned and peered down at his misshapen boxer shorts.

'Well it can stand down,' she giggled, 'because I've gone off the boil now.'

She lowered her swollen ankles to the floor and gingerly attempted to stand up, hastily grabbing her dressing gown to shield her bulbous shape.

Joe was constantly telling her how attractive she looked, admitting it turned him on to know she was carrying his child. He would rain kisses on her belly whilst squeezing her rapidly expanding buttocks as if comparing a pair of over-ripe peaches left on the supermarket shelf.

But Karen didn't share his fondness for her distended abdomen. She felt unwieldy, sluggish and deeply unsexy, particularly as her due date had come and gone six days previously. It's fully cooked, she thought. All it's doing now is sitting in there, growing bigger and bigger by the hour, biding its time before it squeezes out of a very small space. The mere thought prompted her eyes to fill with water. For the umpteenth time, she glanced downwards and wondered how her body was going to cope with the ravages of childbirth.

'It'll be *fine*,' soothed Joe, raising his eyes heaven-ward. He recognised her expression from the many other times when she'd actually voiced her fears. He stood up and walked around the bed, cupping her face in his hands, his kind brown eyes staring in to hers.

'Stop worrying,' he urged. 'Women have babies all the time . . . they say it's no worse than trying to push a medicine ball through the eye of a needle.'

She took a couple of seconds to computer what he'd said, then burst out laughing and shoved him with enough force to make him tumble back on to the bed.

'Bastard.'

He lay there grinning, then started writhing around, his hands fashioned as if clutching a large, spherical shape between his splayed legs. When he realised the joke was wearing thin, he propped himself up on his elbows for a few seconds.

'Right, come on.' Grabbing his jeans from the floor, he hopped up and down as he tried to put them on. 'Let's get serious and coax this little sod into joining us in the big, wide, scary world. If sex is off the menu, perhaps a takeaway chicken biryani will do the trick.'

'Jesus fucking Christ!'

Karen closed her eyes tight shut and pushed downwards with a strength she didn't know she possessed. Her face was puce from the effort, her hair matted to her forehead.

Joe's hand was clamped over hers, anxiety clouding his face. He had never felt so surplus to requirements.

He and Karen had attended only one antenatal class, at which they'd disgraced themselves with a fit of giggles when the men had been instructed to deep breathe in rhythm with their partners. Joe was the first to crack, emitting a snort of such velocity that the teacher stopped her own breathing display to inquire after his welfare. A few seconds later, Karen went, her face contorted with the strain of trying not to laugh. When the teacher misinterpreted her efforts as emulating the expression of childbirth and complimented her, they lost it completely, shedding tears of mirth.

So that, and the hospital's sheet of A4 entitled

'What Dad Can Do', were Joe's only instruction in matters relating to childbirth.

Reaching down to a small black bag at his feet, he pulled out an Evian atomiser and pressed the top to release a fine mist of cool water on Karen's perspiring face. Her ensuing head-swivel made Linda Blair look angelic.

'*What* are you doing?'

Joe held up the spray by way of explanation. 'Cooling you down?' he ventured tentatively.

She looked at him with naked derision. 'Do you *seriously* think that's going to make me feel better?'

He studied the canister carefully, not wishing to make eye contact with the flared-nostril bed monster. 'Erm, no, not really. It was just on that list of things the hospital suggested I bring.'

'That's to make you feel useful,' she snorted, her lip curled, 'because once we're pregnant there's not much else for you to do . . . *aaaaaaaargh*!'

A contraction kicked in again and her whole body spasmed in agony. Joe grabbed her hand and glanced across at the midwife for reassurance. She was a West Indian of about fifty, with twinkly eyes and a broad, open smile you couldn't help responding to.

'Don't worry.' She flashed her teeth at Joe. 'This is all entirely normal. The abuse too.'

Positioned between Karen's knees, she peered downwards. 'I can see a lovely rim of hair, so keep pushing. One more big one and I'd say we'll get the head out.'

'*Uuuuuurrrmmmggghh*!' The strain was etched on Karen's clenched, sweating face as she made yet another gargantuan effort. She was squeezing Joe's hand so hard, parts of the pinky flesh had turned white.

'That's it, that's it,' the midwife coaxed. She took a slight step back and gave a gentle sigh. 'There! The head's out. The hard bit's over. Now for the rest.'

'I can't, I can't.' Karen was crying slightly, rolling her head from side to side. 'I'm too tired.'

'Yes you can,' the midwife chided gently. She looked at Joe. 'Tell her she can.'

He was utterly terrified at the prospect of telling Karen *anything* to do with childbirth, so simply smiled in what he hoped was an agreeable and supportive fashion.

'Fuuuuuuuucccccking *hell*!' she screamed, her head jerked forward with the effort of pushing. Her neck was so elongated that she resembled a tortoise emerging from its shell, but as soon as the thought popped into his head, Joe dismissed it. Now probably wasn't the time to mention the comparison.

Suddenly, there was a small squelching noise and a spray of fluid hit his face as the midwife seamlessly jerked the baby into the air. It was bloodied and slightly blue, its face contorted with rage but no sound emerging. She carried it to the far corner of the room and laid it on the scales, making a note of the weight. An ear-piercing cry punctured the silence.

'Is everything OK?' asked Karen, looking anxious.

'You want to worry when he *doesn't* cry,' said the midwife over her shoulder.

'He. It's a boy!' Karen turned back to Joe who was now sitting down, his face level with hers.

'You did it,' he smiled.

'*We* did it. Sorry I shouted at you.'

He shrugged it off and stroked her hair, moving a wet strand away from her eyes. 'I don't know why they bother giving fathers a list of things to bring,' he grinned. 'It should say in bold capitals "You are simply there to be blamed for everything and be shouted at". At least then we'd *know*.'

She was about to reply, but instead she squinted at his face and rubbed her finger down the side of his nose. 'You've got blood on your face.'

'I'm not surprised.' His expression was faux grim. 'That was unbelievably hard, painful work for me.'

Forming her thumb and forefinger into a pincer, she squeezed his cheek and made a clucking noise like a mother to a child. 'Diddums. You poor thing.'

The midwife returned to the bed, carrying the baby wrapped in a blanket. She placed it across Karen's chest, its dark, currant-like eyes peering out at its mother.

'Meet your little boy,' she said. 'I'll leave you alone for a minute.'

'It's a boy.' Karen looked up at Joe and smiled.

'I know. You already said.' He couldn't stop

grinning. Using his forefinger to part the blanket slightly, he studied the child's face intently.

'Who does he look like?' she asked.

Joe was thoughtful for a couple of seconds then pursed his lips. 'If I'm honest? Mr Magoo.'

'Rude sod.' She peered at her little boy. 'You're beautiful, aren't you? You take after mummy's side of the family.'

The door creaked open and the midwife re-appeared with a trolley bearing a bowl of water. She nodded at Karen's nether regions. 'Time to get you cleaned up.'

Joe extended his arms and scooped up the little bundle from Karen's chest, nestling the baby's head in the crook of his left arm. Walking over to the window of the delivery suite, he tilted his arm so the child was more upright, then studied the rooftops of London for the first time since he and Karen had arrived in a panic. With its riverside view of the Houses of Parliament, he marvelled how the hospital hadn't yet been flogged to the richest penthouse developer and relocated to some backstreet wasteland.

Joe looked down. His son was staring back at him, a frown furrowing his already wrinkled brow, his shock of mousy hair still matted to his head. He made a small gurgling sound and moved one of his hands, a tiny finger emerging from beneath the blanket and curling round its edge.

Joe had never felt such a rush of pure and uncon-ditional love for anyone in his life. When his friends had spoken of their experience of becoming a father, he'd smiled benevolently, secretly hoping they'd soon shut up and move on to the football.

But now he got it. Absolutely. That powerful rush of protectiveness and the deep-seated panic that someone, somewhere, might take advantage of his child or try to hurt him. It was all-consuming: the world had shrivelled in size, with only Karen and their son truly mattering to him, even other family members slipping to the periphery of his mind. All his hopes of one day travelling the world or owning a supercar were gone, channelled solely into his desire that his son should always be safe and happy. Here was a brand-new human being, blank computer software to be programmed by him and Karen. Responsibility, he mused, doesn't come greater than that.

Tilting his head forward, he placed a gentle kiss on the boy's slightly crumpled forehead.

'Hello, son. I'm your daddy. And I'll never let anyone hurt you.'

CHAPTER 1

Ben held on to the sofa and tried to pull himself up, his little legs wobbling with the sheer effort. He resembled a Saturday-night drunk stumbling home.

'Good boy!' Karen made a small clapping noise and he tried to copy her, waving his hands back and forth and falling on to his bottom in the process.

'Oops, thank goodness for padded nappies,' she laughed, grabbing him under the arms and gently levering him back in to position.

She glanced at the clock. Six p.m. Her happiness evaporated, replaced by a familiar tight knot of dread. Time to start the bedtime routine soon.

In most houses, this consisted of splashing happily in the bath, followed by a vigorous towel rub and tickle session, warm jimmy jams and a milky drink. But for Ben, the word 'bedtime' held a more sinister undertone.

The door swung open and Joe walked into the living room, a troubled but determined look on his face.

'Look at this, Daddy!' Karen pointed at Ben who had worked his way round to the side of the sofa.

'I know. He was doing it yesterday.' Joe moved purposefully towards his son, scooping him in to his arms. Ben looked up and smiled briefly before his body instinctively went rigid.

Within two seconds, he was writhing from side to side in a desperate bid to escape his father's clutches, his eyes black with fright, his face turning instantly pink with the exertion of his struggle.

Ben was only eight months old, but he had the stubbornness of a toddler, letting out a piercing wail that consistently made his parents feel they were being repeatedly stabbed in the head.

'Leave it for a bit, eh?' Karen's face was chalky white as she watched her son try to battle against the inevitable.

'You *know* I can't do that.' Joe's expression was mutinous. Tightening his grip, he turned away and walked through the living-room door into the hallway, leaving her alone.

She stood like a statue, staring at the open doorway, then fell into the armchair with an air of hopelessness. She could hear Ben's screams fading as Joe climbed the stairs, then increasing again as they reached his bedroom above her head.

Knowing the torture his small body was about to endure, she couldn't bear to listen. Jamming her fingers into her ears, she rocked backwards and forwards on her elbows as tears started to course down her cheeks.

Half an hour later, Karen tentatively pushed open the door to Ben's bedroom and peered in to the gloom.

The only light came from his illuminated Thomas the Tank Engine lamp, but it was enough for her to make out the shape of Joe sitting next to the cot. The collapsible side was half down and his arm was hanging over the top, stroking his son's hair.

'I'm not sure I can do this much longer,' he murmured, not looking at her.

'How is he?' She tiptoed her way to the end of the cot and looked in. Ben was curled into the foetal position, his knees drawn in to his chest, his face puffed from crying.

'The painkillers have kicked in.' His voice was low but his tone was slightly brusque. 'He fought it but he fell asleep about five minutes ago.'

A wave of sadness washed over her. 'Poor little mite. Eight months old and all this trauma.'

Her eyes had adjusted to the half-light by now and she could see Joe looked shattered. His eyes were heavy with strain and his hair mussed up, a sure sign he'd been running his fingers through it as he often did during times of high stress.

'And how are *you*?'

'As well as can be expected.' He gave a quick smile that didn't reach his eyes.

They lapsed into silence for a few seconds, both staring into the cot as Ben now snored gently, oblivious to his parents' concern.

'Bloody injections.' She let out a long sigh. 'Still, they have to be done.'

Joe shifted awkwardly in the hard, plastic chair she'd used for breastfeeding until three months ago. His brow furrowed. 'Yes they do. So please stop telling me to do them later and start backing me up, will you?' he muttered. 'It's bad enough having to stick a huge needle in my son every night, without you playing bloody good cop all the time.'

'I'm sorry. He just gets so upset.'

His expression softened slightly. 'I know. Weird isn't it? He's still only a baby yet he instinctively knows when it's time for his injection. Otherwise, he's pleased to see me.'

Joe stood up and walked around the cot until he was standing so close she could feel his hot breath on her cheek. He placed a hand on her arm. 'Come on, he's fine now.'

Following him down the stairs, Karen studied the back of his head, with his smooth, tanned neck and the broad shoulders she'd always found so appealing. The shoulders that could bear anything, including the burden of having to inflict pain on the son he adored.

He was thirty-six and in great shape for his age, a combination of good genes and an active lifestyle, pounding the pavements for an hour a couple of times a week. He was a 'proper bloke', as her friend Tania described masculine men, but he'd surprised her with his tenderness towards Ben from the second he was born. She knew his inherent kindness would make him a caring father, but his hands-on approach, his enthusiasm to become involved in the day-to-day minutiae of his son's life, set him apart from other fathers she'd encountered at the doctor's surgery where she worked as a part-time receptionist.

Joe was an accomplished graphic designer, but work these days was hit and miss, so occasionally he took painting and decorating work when he could get it. The rest of the time he was happy to be seen pushing the buggy to the local shops and preparing the majority of Ben's home-cooked meals.

Karen, by contrast, was the ready-meal queen. Her job meant that she rarely cooked the evening meal and when she did, he'd often quip: 'What are we heating tonight?'

He'd already prepared tonight's dinner, a lamb stew with dumplings, thrown in the slow cooker six hours earlier. Over a bottle of wine, he told her about Ben seeing a little boy at the playground with the same teddy and how he'd tried to wrestle it from his grasp.

As Karen laughed, she reflected how much their conversation had changed since having Ben. Pre-children, they'd talked avidly about films, favoured or loathed, and shared gossip from each of their offices when Joe had worked full-time as a graphic artist for an advertising agency.

Now they were as likely to talk about Ben's bowel movements, or the revelation that he'd tried a new vegetable. They were both fascinated by their son, but knew better than to drone on endlessly about him to others. Unlike some who thought their child's every utterance and act would be of interest to the outside world, Joe and Karen knew there was nothing drearier and were happy to restrict such child eulogies to within their own four walls.

Ben's illness aside, she thought as she sipped her wine and smiled at Joe, life couldn't be better.

Nick and Stella Bright sat at their dining table, both silently watching a tourist boat glide past the window, its searchlights scanning the banks of the river for buildings of interest.

Nick raised a hand and waved. 'If you come back in ten minutes, I'll be having a shit.'

'They can't see you,' said Stella matter-of-factly, raising her eyes heavenward and feigning a yawn. This was a regular battle cry of his.

'Feels like it. Can't we get some curtains or something?'

'*Curtains*?' She spat the word as if he'd just suggested they paper the walls with images of Hitler. 'The whole *point* of having a riverside penthouse is to see the view.'

'What? A shitty old tourist barge, a couple of old tyres and God knows how many used condoms floating by? Nice.' He smiled to show he was joking. Sort of.

Stella loved modern, minimalist living. He'd have preferred a tall, traditionally decorated Georgian house in one of London's many picturesque squares, but as Stella had reminded him, he was at work most of the time and *she* was the one who ran their home and spent most time in it, so her preference took precedence. She also liked the extra security of an apartment block and the fact that a concierge took in parcels if they were out. She'd had enough of queuing at post offices with a 'while you were out' card clutched in her hand.

So here they were, having dinner in front of a plate-glass window, with Nick feeling as exposed to public scrutiny as a gorilla at London Zoo.

He popped a piece of bread in his mouth, made a couple of grunting, monkey-like noises, and looked up to see if Stella was laughing. But she was lost in a world of her own, staring down at her abdomen, her left hand resting on it.

Nick watched her for a while then let out a resigned sigh. 'I really *am* sorry. But what can I do?'

'I know, I know. I just wanted you with me . . . to see the first scan.' Her tone was conciliatory but weary.

Leaning forward, Nick squeezed her arm reassuringly. He kept his expression caring, but inside he was a little jaded, as if everyone wanted a piece of him. Not for the first time, the image of his clothes neatly folded on a beach flashed into his mind, the police milling around, searching for his body whilst he sat on a plane to Buenos Aires, off to start a new, uncomplicated life under an assumed name. But he knew he'd get bored after a couple of days and, besides, he loved Stella too much to ever leave her.

'I want to be there but I can't do that time because of Prime Minister's Questions,' he murmured. 'Can't you change the appointment to early morning instead?'

She smiled weakly. 'As Health Secretary, I think you need to do your homework on the NHS appointments system. The next available one would probably be when I've *had* the baby.'

He smiled, relieved the mood had shifted to being more light-hearted. 'Just as well I've got you to put me right then. Though in my defence, I *have* only been in the job for three months. But ask me anything about the rail networks and I could bore for Britain.'

'Don't remind me.' She crossed her eyes and grimaced.

Flicking her a playful V-sign, he wolfed down the last vestiges of pasta from his plate. 'Maybe I could pull a few strings at the hospital?'

'You will *not*!' She was horrified. 'Can you imagine if that got out? The press would murder you . . . and rightly so.'

Nick smiled resignedly and rubbed his hand back and forth across the top of his cropped hair.

It was a habit of his since childhood, his comfort blanket when life felt turbulent or even slightly uncertain. Standing, he kissed the top of her head, inhaling so that her scent, a mix of musk and lemon verbena, filled his nostrils. It always calmed him. 'It'll be fine, you'll see.'

'God, I hope so.' She sighed heavily. 'I couldn't bear for something to be wrong.'

Nick had already taken a couple of paces away from the table, but turned and walked back, his expression one of mock chastisement. 'Now come on, what did the doctor say?'

'Think positive,' she answered flatly. But it's bloody hard after five years of trying, she thought. She was sick of the positive-thinking platitudes uttered by everyone involved in her pregnancy. She didn't blame Nick, he couldn't understand, but when her GP and gynaecologist took the 'smile, it might never happen' route she felt they were no better than the builders who bellow it from scaffolding at every passing female under thirty-five. Worse even, because the doctors *knew* the extent of her suffering. Nick's voice punctured her thoughts.

'Now, talking of swotting up on the NHS, I'd better go and do some.'

He wandered off in the direction of his study, leaving her sitting alone among the debris of empty dinner plates. Nick rarely did anything around the house, but Stella didn't push it as she didn't work. He earned the money; she ran the house. That was the unspoken deal.

17

Yet occasionally, when he needed to raise his political profile via the media, he would give interviews in which he'd yabber on about what a modern man he was and how his wife had to practically beat him away from the dishwasher.

These days, to be seen as even slightly old-fashioned and traditional was political death, despite the fact that behind the closed doors of Nick's rural constituency, the majority of the electorate had the same deal. Trouble was, she mused, the middle-class intelligentsia of media commentators seemed to run the country and politicians had to jump to their liberal, progressive eco-tune.

She smiled at the thought of what an unreconstructed male Nick was and whimsied over the money her memoirs would make, blowing the lid on government spin of the marital kind.

Letting out an unintentionally long sigh, she started to clear the table.

Karen lay in bed, flicking through *Hello!* magazine and wondering where all these celebrity women, whose relationships always floundered because they were 'too busy', found the time to look so well groomed. They must have manicurists on call 24/7, she thought, glancing down at her own chipped fingernails.

At thirty-two, she was still, as Joe put it, 'in good nick'. But she was aware that Ben's illness had taken its toll on her appearance through worry and lack of sleep. Her blue, almond-shaped eyes were striking, but the faint, dark circles under them betrayed her constant exhaustion. After years of having a dental hygiene routine drummed in by her mother, plus a couple of her formative years spent wearing an orthodontic brace, her teeth were impressively straight and white, producing a killer smile that illuminated her face. Trouble was, having a seriously ill child meant it wasn't put to much use anymore.

Once a fanatical cleanse-and-moisturise girl, now it was barely all she could do to run a wet wipe over her face before bed. Beauty routines faded into insignificance when your child was fighting a life-threatening illness.

Similarly, her trendy wardrobe of clothes had morphed into one of practicality, consisting mostly of T-shirts, jeans and her trusty old pair of pink Converse trainers. The only time she had to dress remotely smart was for the surgery reception from one till six p.m. most days.

Joe pottered around the bedroom, putting his clothes away and changing the batteries in the television remote. She marvelled that, physically, he hadn't changed much since the day they'd met: slightly less hair perhaps, if you looked *really* closely, with a chiselled but kind face that only seemed to improve with age. Emotionally, though, she knew Ben's illness was destroying him. With every bone and muscle in his body, he wanted to protect his boy from life's ills, and yet here was this dreadful disease, eating away at Ben, and his father felt impotent to do anything about it. Worse, he was the one having to administer the drugs that caused Ben to scream out in raw, searing pain every night as the medication hit his bloodstream.

Consequently, a lot of her husband's natural joie de vivre had left him. Always the life and soul of any party prior to Ben's birth, now he was too drained by exhaustion, a shadow of his former, ebullient self. Out socially, he would still laugh a lot, but it was reacting to others rather than playing the clown himself. And Karen noticed his smiles rarely reached his eyes, which harboured a deep sadness and pain no pub anecdote could overcome, not even for a second. Not long ago, he'd told her that his favourite moments of the day were waking up, when for a few blissful seconds he felt everything was right with the world. Then his brain would click into gear and fill his mind with the unpalatable reality of Ben's wretched disease and the momentary reverie would evaporate. She knew what he meant: she felt the same way.

Closing her magazine, she threw it to the floor beside the bed. 'Hurry up with the light. Big day tomorrow.'

Joe nodded silently and walked over to the bed, his striped pyjama bottoms resting on his lithe hips, his chest bare. Sitting on the edge of the bed, he swung his legs under the duvet and rested his head on the vast bank of pillows he claimed he couldn't sleep without. Karen stared unblinkingly at the ceiling, waiting for him to flick the light switch. When he did, the light from the landing threw a hazy glow across the bed.

The weight of their pain and feelings of hopelessness bore down on them in the darkness. Karen's mind was full of it and she knew Joe's would be too, leaving no room for any of the relaxed frivolity that sustained so many couples through the often mundane patches of married life.

She started as he suddenly shifted on to his side, turning to face her as he gently began kissing her mouth. Instinctively, she recoiled awkwardly. 'We need to sleep.'

He flopped back on his pillow and stared intently at the damp patch above their heads, a reminder of last summer's water-tank leak. 'It was just a goodnight kiss, that's all . . .'

They lay in silence, both as rigid as statues. Karen closed her eyes tight shut, knowing she should try and make amends but struggling to make the move. She loved Joe deeply and couldn't imagine being with anyone else, but the burden of having a sick child consumed her so greatly that there was little or no energy left for working hard at marriage too. Eventually, she turned over and snuggled in to his chest, placing a quick kiss on it.

'Sorry.'

He peered down at her for a moment, then moved an arm to stroke her shoulder, perfunctorily kissing the top of her head. 'Don't worry about it. Come on, let's get some sleep.'

Grateful the awkwardness had passed, she turned on her side and closed her eyes, desperate to succumb to her sensation of sleepiness. But as ever, her mind had other ideas, whirring through what might happen tomorrow and analysing every possibility. She and deep sleep had been strangers for some time, and she was too wary of Ben needing her in the night to take the sleeping tablets offered by her doctor.

Joe had turned over too, so they were back to back. But she knew, like her, he would only sleep fitfully, tormented by the worry and guilt of their son's suffering.

CHAPTER 2

Robert Pickering flicked through the medical notes in front of him and pursed his lips. He was a grey-haired man with a careworn face and half-rimmed glasses, an archetypal picture-book image of a doctor, something that reassured Karen. She knew he'd worked at the hospital for at least twenty years and, last-chance saloon as it was, had probably become inured to delivering bad news to countless parents.

Joe and Karen were sitting on uncomfortable, high-backed chairs in front of his desk, their expressions rigid with apprehension. Oblivious, Ben played with a small wooden train set, repeatedly pushing the engine back and forth across the linoleum-tiled floor.

Finally, after what seemed an eternity, Pickering removed his glasses and looked up at them. 'I'm afraid no one on the bone-marrow register is a close enough match.'

Karen shut her eyes tight as she struggled to control the well of nausea in the pit of her stomach. There were thousands registered, so she'd had high hopes of someone matching. She heard Joe clear his throat.

'And us?' His voice was cracked and he coughed again.

'I have everyone's DNA results here.' Pickering put on his glasses and pulled a sheet of paper out from the file, his expression impassive. 'All grand-parents . . . no, I'm afraid.'

He placed it back and pulled out another, his pale blue eyes fixed directly on Karen. 'Mrs Eastman? Close, but unfortunately not close enough for this level of procedure. And Mr Eastman . . .' He faltered slightly and stopped speaking, studiously examining the piece of paper in front of him. He blinked a few times then placed his glasses on the desk and massaged the bridge of his nose with his thumb and forefinger. 'That's a no too. Sorry.'

Joe, who hadn't taken his eyes from Pickering's face, puffed out his cheeks and made a loud exhalation of air. Karen had turned deathly white. They stared at the consultant as if he was about to announce he'd been mistaken and that one of them could save their son's life after all.

'Maaaaaaaaaaaa!' It was Ben, trying to get their attention. He was holding a little plastic man in his chubby hand, waving it delightedly, blissfully ignorant of the life-or-death conversation taking place above his blond, curly head.

'That's lovely sweetie,' smiled Karen, her face flushing with emotion. She turned back to Pickering.

'So what now?' She could hear her own voice speaking but felt disembodied. She wanted to get up and run, back to her younger years of no responsibility or heartbreak. She felt Joe's arm snake round her back and start to rub reassuringly between her shoulder blades.

'Diamond Blackfan Anaemia is very rare, as you know . . .' Pickering paused and waited for their acknowledgement, which they duly delivered with a sombre nod. 'And in Ben's case, it's also impossible to cure without a bone-marrow transplant from a perfect match.'

They nodded again, having researched it so thoroughly on the internet they felt they could almost perform the procedure themselves.

'What's happened in other cases?' asked Joe. He and Karen had read about the experiences of others but wanted the generic, professional overview.

'Some have found a donor from the register and because it's one of those random conditions and not hereditary, one couple I know of are trying for another baby in the hope that it matches.'

Karen's spirits lifted, thinking that if he'd bothered to mention it then perhaps it was a viable option for them. She turned to Joe and saw his eyes were alight with optimism.

'We could do that,' he urged.

She nodded back, her expression softening slightly.

But Pickering was pensive. 'There's only a one

25

in twelve chance that a baby conceived naturally would match an older sibling, so it's a hell of a lot to go through for no guaranteed result.'

Joe's face clouded over again. Karen looked shell-shocked.

'So it's preimplantation genetic diagnosis then?' Her voice was barely audible.

Pickering gave a half-smile. 'You've done your research then.'

'Yes, to a point. But there's a lot of scare stories out there.'

'In that case, let me give you the down the line, medical version.' He sat back in his chair and pressed his fingertips together. 'We put you through the IVF process, fertilise several eggs, then choose the one that's the closet genetic match to Ben before implanting it for a normal pregnancy.'

Karen leaned forward earnestly. 'And that the baby's bone marrow will help cure him? No more blood transfusions or injections?'

He shook his head slowly, clearly recommending caution. 'There's no absolute guarantee. But it's the best chance he's got.'

Nick Bright lifted his red box from his knees and placed it in the seat well at his feet, making room for the large green file James Spender had handed him. He flipped it open and stifled a sigh so it escaped from the corners of his mouth. 'God almighty, does this shit ever end?'

'That's the trouble with being Health Secretary,' said James matter-of-factly. 'It's bad for your health.'

A mobile phone rang, a polyphonic version of Prokofiev's *Romeo and Juliet*, filling the air with its doom-laden notes.

'Hello?' James's tone was tetchy. He'd specifically asked not to be disturbed whilst he was briefing Nick on the way to the House of Commons and no one but the office had this number. Even his mother had to go via his PA. 'No. Tell him I'm in a meeting and can't be disturbed. Which is what I fucking told you to say to anyone who calls, so why you're bothering me with this is beyond me.'

He flipped his phone shut with such ferocity that Nick flinched.

'They don't listen,' he offered by way of explanation, smiling thinly. 'Now then, let's crack on.'

Nick had been working with his 'spin doctor' for only three months since getting the health job, but already he was daunted by James's brutal manner. And, if he was honest, more than a little impressed by his thick skin that made rhinoceros hide seem diaphanous. If a security guard would take a bullet for his employer, James took the verbal brickbats, swatting away persistently awkward, off-message journalists as if they were annoying bugs.

This wasn't the good cop, bad cop routine. This was angelic choirboy and serial killer. The deal was that Nick could pretend to be Mr Affable, seemingly willing to answer any question a journalist chose to throw at him, whilst James was the boot boy, stepping in with his size elevens and announcing that the Health Secretary couldn't shed light on that particular inquiry for 'security reasons'. James was in his early thirties and of average height, but he was heavily set and a look in his eye suggested he shouldn't be messed with.

'Right, first things first.' James opened his copy of the *Post*, turning immediately to page eight and a glaring headline that read: 'New poll says Labour's future is not Bright'.

'Shit!' Nick stared down at it, shaking his head slowly. Poor poll results weren't the end of the world and a policy announcement could tip the scales the other way, but the opinion pieces that often accompanied them could easily sway public opinion, with the line between news and comment becoming increasingly blurred.

'It's written by that little turd Jake Thompson,' muttered James. 'Correction. Giant turd.' He tapped his phone. 'That was the office telling me he'd called to get a reaction from you.'

'Am I going to give one?' Nick already knew better than to imagine it was his decision. 'Why have a rottweiler and bark yourself,' James had retorted the first time his boss had suggested he would deal with a media inquiry himself.

James shook his head. 'No. If we respond to every half-baked story now, it'll be a hard habit to break if you end up going for the leadership when the PM bows out. Let's keep our powder dry.'

The way he spoke, if a premiership happened it was going to be a joint one. The car slowed down and edged its way towards the security check at the House of Commons car park. James peered out of the window, scanning the area whilst showing the security guards his face. Woe betide any of them who didn't consider it an identity pass.

'We're aiming for the dignified statesman approach,' he said, as he withdrew back into the car. 'So bear that in mind if anyone shoves a microphone in your face and asks a question.'

Nick nodded compliantly and opened the door to get out.

Pickering looked at his watch and closed the file in front of him, indicating in no uncertain terms that time was pressing and he had other patients waiting outside.

'I suggest you both go and think about what you want to do.'

'Think?' Joe had a look of tetchy derision. 'What's there to think about? This is our son's life we're talking about, not an order for a new kitchen.' He bent down and prised the plastic man from Ben's fingers, dropping it back into the toy basket. The boy started to grizzle, his face screwed up with the injustice.

Joe fixed Pickering with a definite stare. 'We've talked about nothing else in the few weeks since he's been officially diagnosed, so we've had plenty of time to think. The decision is already made. Come on, son, let's go home.'

He scooped Ben into his arms and headed out of the door, not looking back. Karen started to follow him, then paused and turned round. She was faintly embarrassed by Joe's tone, even if inwardly she too reckoned Pickering's bedside manner could do with tweaking.

'He didn't mean to be so abrupt.' She smiled apologetically. 'He and Ben are very close.'

Pickering nodded. 'I can see that.'

'I work every day so he's the main carer.' Karen didn't know why she was telling him this, but she felt compelled to defend her husband in case Pickering thought ill of him. 'He does work though,' she burbled. 'It's just that his work is more flexible than mine. We muddle through . . . you know?'

He doesn't know at all, she thought to herself. Aside from his NHS work, he probably has a private practice earning hundreds of thousands from parents with equally sick children but more money to jump the queue. And undoubtedly Mrs Pickering, assuming that was the identity of the matronly woman pictured on his desk, had been a stay-at-home mother who baked fresh bread every day and darned all her children's socks rather than chucking them away and buying more

30

at Primark like Karen did. Pickering's voice broke into her thoughts.

'Mrs Eastman, preimplantation genetic diagnosis is a long, stressful process with no guarantees. I know your husband says the decision's made, but you *should* discuss it a little more.'

'We will. Thanks.' She smiled gratefully and shook his hand. They walked towards the door, his arm extended in a 'there's the way out' gesture, like a waiter keen for you to pay your bill so he could usher in the next paying customer. His hand resting on the door frame, with Karen safely deposited in the corridor, he cleared his throat awkwardly. 'And I'm afraid it's not available on the NHS, so you could be looking at up to twenty-five thousand pounds for the whole treatment.'

Karen's eyes widened with shock. 'Twenty-five *grand*. Where are we going to find money like that?' She knew it was a rhetorical question but paused anyway, in the faint hope he might make a suggestion. But apart from a fleeting look of sympathy, his face remained impassive.

'It's a child and he's *desperately* ill,' she muttered, feeling a swell of anger. 'We've paid in to the NHS all our lives.'

'I'm afraid I don't make the rules, Mrs Eastman.' He let out a long sigh that suggested he had heard this entreaty from furious and desperate parents many times before.

'OK, well thanks for letting me know. It's just quite a shock to find you have to *pay* to try and make your son's life normal.' She mustered a brave smile and expected one back, even if it was one of the chilly seen-it-all-before professional ones. But he was rubbing his eyes wearily and looked pensive.

'There's something else I need to tell you . . .'

'Kaaaaaaren! Come on.' Joe's impatient voice could be heard further down the corridor.

She shouted back: 'Just coming!' then turned to face Pickering. 'Sorry. Carry on.'

The professional smile finally materialised. 'Don't worry. It can wait.'

CHAPTER 3

Stella sat in the waiting room of St Thomas's Hospital in South London, flicking through an old copy of *Country Life* magazine and practically salivating at the sight of some of the grand houses for sale. She knew many of them were photographed with a fisheye lens from the middle of the perilously close motorway, or cropped strategically to omit the adjoining property inhabited by squatters, but she didn't care. They triggered her escapist fantasies anyway. Ever since she was a little girl, and despite her socialist tendencies, it had been her dream to marry a wealthy country 'squire' with a family seat somewhere in the Home Counties, complete with orangery, orchard and a stable block. Stella was a keen rider, and she could see herself in head-to-toe Barbour, galloping across the estate whilst her four beautiful children were given breakfast by 'Nanny' and waited for Mummy to return and take them off to buy freshly picked produce at the farmers' market in the local village. At the weekends, she'd have a variety of fascinating friends to stay and they'd dress for dinner with fine food and scintillating conversation.

Instead, she had met Nick – working-class lad and lowly MP for a northern factory town – most definitely not a squire and unlikely to want to be one, judging by his curled lip every time he encountered someone he considered to be even faintly upper class. She'd met him at a local government seminar where she'd been booked to talk about charitable trusts and he'd been circling the room, schmoozing businessmen whilst, as he later told her, admiring her from afar. In those days, Stella Bower, as she was known, was a high-flyer in charge of the charitable causes division for one of London's top banks, working there since she'd left Oxford with a first in economics. She was highly professional and well thought of, her chairman soon calling her in to the inner sanctum to mark her out as destined for greater things.

That was ten years ago and, up to then, her boyfriends had been cut from the same cloth – Home Counties, hardworking, financially success-ful and, if she was honest, a teensy bit dreary. Dating was something she felt she should do, as a flag to the outside world that she was a normal, hot-blooded female and not a career-obsessed automaton who was going to wake on her forty-fifth birthday and shriek, 'Christ, I forgot to have a personal life'. In truth, her heart wasn't in it: dating was a mere time-filler outside work hours.

Then Nick had blown in to her busy but predictable life like a whirlwind, coaxing her out

34

for furtive weekday lunches and hiding the mobile phone she kept close by her at all times. He'd taught her to relax a little, to enjoy life.

Initially, her parents had been horrified by this brash, outspoken man who seemed to have disrupted their daughter's ordered world. Of course they were thrilled to bits now he was a cabinet minister, but the early days of long hours, little money and his rough and ready approach to life had made relations between them rather strained. Stella smiled at the memory and looked up from her magazine, stealing furtive glances at all the other women in the room, many in the advanced stages of pregnancy. With the exception of herself and one other woman, they had their partners with them and she watched wistfully as one man gently rubbed his wife's distended belly. Even if he was here, she couldn't see Nick being so touchy-feely, certainly not in public.

A nurse appeared from a side room and shouted into the middle distance. 'Mrs Bower?'

From the outset, she'd kept a low profile as Nick's wife, refusing all media interviews. She was happy to be a supportive spouse in the home, but didn't see why that should extend to being wheeled out for various photo shoots and having a torch shone into the private corners of her own life. Consequently, she was rarely recognised, and today in the waiting room was no exception, particularly as her hair was scraped back and she wore no make-up. She'd used her maiden name as a precaution, but no one batted an eyelid as she stood up and followed the nurse down the corridor and into the consulting room.

Settled on the bed, she recoiled as the cold gel hit her abdomen. With all the advancements in modern medicine, she thought, couldn't they invent a self-heating version? The consultant noticed her wince.

'Sorry. Cold, isn't it?'

And my child's life is in these capable hands, she thought ruefully. He dragged the ultrasound device backwards and forwards across her abdomen, never taking his eyes from the screen. Every so often, he'd stop and push it in a little further, peering more closely at the image it projected. Each time he did this, Stella's heart leapt in to her mouth, anxious something might be wrong. Finally, he spoke again.

'There's a nice strong heartbeat. And look, there's baby's head.'

Stella lifted her head to look at the screen but all she could see was a collection of grainy blobs. The section he was describing as the head resembled a photocopy of someone's partial thumbprint.

'So it's all looking good?' she ventured, not daring to contemplate the alternative.

He removed the device, switched off the monitor and swivelled his chair round to a table where he made a couple of notes.

'So far, yes.'

'So far?' It struck her as an odd thing to say. Or perhaps it was a necessary evil of the mushrooming blame culture, a catch-all vague remark that couldn't be claimed against. 'What does that mean?'

'It means that it all looks as it should at this stage,' he replied matter-of-factly before clearly sensing her apprehension and breaking into a smile. 'That's a good thing.'

Slightly mollified, she sat up as a nurse handed her a tissue to wipe off the gel. Rearranging her clothing, she reached for her handbag on a nearby chair.

'Your husband couldn't make it today?' The consultant didn't look up from his notes.

'No. Something came up.' She was taken aback by his remark in these politically correct times. What if she'd been a single parent wearing a wedding ring for appearance's sake?

He smiled knowingly. 'Politics is a demanding business.'

'Ah.' She raised her eyes heavenward. 'And I thought I was here incognito.'

He shook his head. 'Someone rang from your husband's office to make sure you weren't kept waiting too long.'

Stella scowled, unsure whether he was joking. His expression told her he wasn't. 'They what? Jesus Christ!'

The consultant laughed. 'No, James Spender.'

*   *   *

Joe pushed Ben's buggy through the doors of the hospital and out into the cool air. His face was taut with poorly suppressed anger.

'Smoked all your life and got cancer, sir? Yes, no problem, of course the NHS will do your life-saving operation,' he spat to no one in particular. 'Sorry, sir?' He cupped his hand to his ear, feigning listening to someone. 'Oh, your child is being destroyed by Diamond Blackfan Anaemia through no fault of his own, is he? No, sorry, we don't cover that. Goodbye!'

He booted the base of a wall, sending shards of dry brickwork flying into the air.

Karen stooped down and buttoned the top of Ben's coat, her face impassive but her chest tight with tension.

'There's no point getting upset about it,' she said pragmatically. 'Life's hard enough without pouring on more woes we can't do anything about.'

The dynamic of their relationship had always been that Joe was more inflammatory, with Karen cast in the placatory role, calming him down with reasoned argument.

'But twenty-five grand?' His face was screwed up with frustration. 'We don't have that kind of money. We don't have *any* money other than what we need to survive from day to day.'

'Then we'll just have to find it.' Karen stood up and started to push the buggy away from the hospital, away from Joe's anger. She understood it might sate his immediate feeling of rage, but she didn't see the point: it would alter nothing about what they might face in the future. After a couple of seconds, Joe started to follow.

'I'll find it,' he said through gritted teeth. 'Even if I have to kill someone.'

They walked a few metres in silence, both deep in thought. Eventually, she spoke. 'Don't forget I'm meeting Tania tonight.'

He nodded wordlessly, then stopped at a café with chairs and tables outside. He went to sit down at one, but despite the clear skies and temperate climate, Karen visibly shivered.

'It's summer.' He raised his eyes heavenward, his eyes mocking her kindly.

'Actually, it's May,' she countered, 'which, strictly speaking, is still spring.'

Their widely varying body temperatures meant they rarely enjoyed the same climate, which made booking holidays tricky. But at night, they were very compatible, with Karen enjoying a double thickness duvet thrown across from Joe's side of the bed.

'Besides,' she added, nodding at Ben anxiously, 'shouldn't he stay in the warm?'

His pale skin and faintly blue lips reminded her of the first two months of his life when, constantly snuffly and listless, he'd shown little of the energy displayed by other thriving babies. Given her job at the surgery, Karen had mentioned her concerns to one of the doctors who had conducted some initial tests but concluded that perhaps he was just a 'sickly' child.

But when the listlessness worsened and he developed breathing problems, they had been referred to a respiratory specialist who, after more tests, had suspected some form of anaemia. Eventually, when Ben was seven and a half months old, they had ended up at Great Ormond Street Hospital for Sick Children where their son was finally diagnosed as having a condition so rare it was suffered by only 125 in the UK.

At first, he'd been prescribed a course of steroids, often effective in controlling it. When he hadn't responded, the injections and transfusions had become the next option and their lives had changed forever.

Joe's voice broke into her thoughts.

'A bit of fresh air doesn't hurt him, but as you wish . . .'

He dutifully took hold of the buggy and pushed it inside the café, grabbing a window table as two solemn-faced, middle-aged women left. Ben started to whinge, never taking his eyes off his dad.

'Yes, yes, hang on a minute. Your apple juice is coming.' He rummaged in a bag hooked on the back of the buggy and pulled out an Anywayup Cup with teeth marks embedded in the spout.

Karen smiled hesitantly, feeling like an outsider. 'You two have your own special language.'

He shrugged. 'Not really. That's just the noise

40

he makes when he's thirsty.' He handed the cup to a grateful Ben. 'There you go, mate. Baby beer.'

Smiling indulgently, she went to order their coffees at the counter and, not for the first time, marvelled how Joe managed to make the whole house-husband thing incredibly sexy. A lot of women in the same situation were torn between feeling grateful their partner was so supportive and battling against a sense that it somehow emasculated them, but not Karen.

She found Joe's strength and capability incredibly attractive. The only problem was that most nights, she was too exhausted to act on it.

Stella placed a plate of shepherd's pie in front of Nick and sat down opposite him at the table. He noted her portion was half the size of his. 'Not hungry?'

She shook her head. 'I've been chomping all day.'

'Not least on James Spender's testicles I hear,' he grinned delightedly.

Stella tried to look cross but couldn't help laughing. 'I can't believe he rang the hospital. I was furious and told him so. It's absolutely none of his bloody business.'

Nick held his hands out in front of him in a gesture of surrender. 'Nothing to do with me. First I knew of it was when he came into my office, quivering from your monumental bollocking.' He laughed heartily at the memory. 'I said "My wife is a ferociously independent woman who, despite seeming a posh blue blood, is an all-things-should-be-equal Labourite. Forget that at your peril."'

'I doubt he'll do it again,' she smiled, flushing slightly.

'So, talking of the hospital, more detail please.' He'd rung her earlier to establish it had gone well, but they hadn't discussed the finer points. Stella wasn't given to telephone small talk, preferring the face-to-face option.

'He said I have the ovaries of a twenty-two-year-old.'

Nick widened his eyes and swallowed the large chunk of potato he'd just jabbed. 'Any chance of getting the body to match?'

She laughed and poked her finger in his upper arm. 'Sadly for me, I think he was joking. It was amazing to see the baby though . . .'

She was about to elaborate on the wonder of the scan but faltered as she noticed Nick's attention drift to the television in the corner. He picked up the remote and hit the volume button, twisting his body to watch a news reporter talking excitably about the day's Prime Minister's Questions.

'. . . that small blob that'll become a little human being,' she continued lamely.

'Uh-huh.' He was still turned away from her, his eyes glued to the screen. Suddenly, the reporter introduced footage of Nick leaning on the lectern in the main chamber of the House of Commons.

'The NHS is improving each day, with more

investment than ever,' he boomed, careful not to catch the eye of Opposition Leader John Tucker sitting directly in front of him. The House erupted in a cacophony of boos from the Tories and less convincing cheers from his own back-benches. The footage showed Nick waiting until the noise had subsided, a patient smile on his face.

'And today I'm proud to announce the start of a multi-million-pound awareness campaign aimed at lowering the rate of sexually transmitted disease amongst the under-twenty-fives in this country.'

The chamber erupted again and he sat down on the jade-green leather bench with a triumphant air, Prime Minister Harold Maynard slapping his back as he did so.

Nick half swivelled to face Stella, his eyes shining. 'Did you see that? Harry loved it.'

Stella opened her mouth to answer, but Nick had turned away again, leaving her high and dry. She knew politics was important to him, but she wished he could pretend something else occasionally took precedence, like the forthcoming birth of his first child.

'And then,' she continued, 'the consultant threw me on the bed and we had passionate sex . . .'

'Uh-huh,' he said distractedly, flicking the off switch before they could show John Tucker driving a well-rehearsed verbal juggernaut through his announcement. He winced as Stella punched him playfully on the arm and turned back to face her.

43

'Now where were we? Oh yes, you were shagging the doctor . . .'

Karen stretched her legs out in front of her and studied her feet. She had to admit her shoes had seen better days, with scuffs at the front and the heel pads wonky with wear, but on the basis that they were tucked under a desk at work and she had more important things to worry about, she hadn't got round to buying new ones.

She was in Great Ormond Street Hospital, back where she and Joe had waited nervously earlier that day for their appointment with Pickering.

Curiously, his secretary had phoned to say the consultant needed to speak with her alone. She'd assured Karen it wasn't more bad news about Ben's health – he'd specifically told her to say that much – but she had no idea why he wanted to see her.

Karen looked at the clock. It was now 6.10 p.m., ten minutes after their meeting was supposed to start. Christ, she thought, chewing the skin down the side of her thumb, I'm apprehensive enough without piling on the agony.

Her attention was diverted to a commotion behind her, and she turned her head to see Tania Fletcher sprawled on the floor, surrounded by a scattering of brightly coloured wooden bricks.

'Who the effin' hell put those there?' she muttered, straightening her skirt and removing a strand of Titian curls from her eyes.

44

'It's a children's hospital, love,' drawled Karen. 'Just as well it wasn't a patient you squashed.'

'It's a bloody death trap more like.' She grimaced and plonked herself in the chair next to Karen, taking in the surroundings. 'Anyway, mine's a nicely chilled white wine please.'

Karen winced. 'Yeah, sorry about this, but it shouldn't take too long and there's a nice pizza place around the corner with more wine than even you can drink.'

A subdued polyphonic version of Abba's 'Dancing Queen' suddenly permeated the air, coming from the briefcase on the floor. Tania flicked the catches and opened it, making the mobile phone loud enough that a passing nurse scowled in their direction.

'Switch it off!' Karen hissed.

'I'm trying. This may be red but up here . . .' Tania tapped a finger on the side of her head '. . . I'm very much blonde.'

She switched it off and threw it back into her briefcase.

'It'll be bloody James Spender. The second I leave the office, he's on my case. I wouldn't mind, but I've worked for Nick way longer than he has.'

Karen raised her eyes heavenwards. 'Why don't you two have sex and get it over with?'

'With that reptilian reject from the *Star Wars* bar?' She pulled a retching face. 'No way. I'd rather have sex with a tramp who's just completed the

45

Tour de France in tight Lycra shorts on a hot summer's day.'

Karen didn't bat an eyelid, used to her friend's theatrically lurid descriptions.

'With such an overactive imagination, no wonder you're so well suited to politics.' She paused a moment. 'Does he have a girlfriend?'

'Did. She shagged someone else. And frankly, who can blame her?'

'Ah,' said Karen ruefully. 'We've all been there.'

'Yes, but when you discovered Joe's little indiscretion, you didn't use it to make everyone else's life a misery, did you?' Tania looked at her questioningly.

'No, just his.' Karen smiled sadly.

Tania was about to reply when a door opened to their left and a nursing assistant poked her head into the waiting area. She looked at Karen and jerked her head backwards, presumably to indicate that Pickering was finally ready to see her.

He was at his desk, though this time he was wearing an overcoat, suggesting he was about to go home. Clearly, he'd squeezed Karen in at the tail end of a busy day. He looked weary but the constant drumming of his fingers on the desk made him seem apprehensive about something.

'Sorry if it all sounded rather mysterious when my secretary rang you, but I needed to see you face to face and alone.'

His grave expression scared her.

'You said it's not about Ben.'

He shook his head. 'It isn't. Not about his health anyway.'

'Something else?' She didn't take her eyes from his face.

He nodded then tapped the beige file on the desk in front of him, the same one he'd been studying at their earlier appointment.

'There's no easy way of saying this, Mrs Eastman, so I'll come straight out with it.' He leaned back in his chair and sighed heavily. 'The DNA tests show your husband can't possibly be Ben's father.'

CHAPTER 4

Gloria Eastman was immensely proud of her house. Granted, it was modern and very small, but it served her needs and she liked the quiet cul-de-sac inhabited by only three other families, all of whom seemed 'nice' people, which, in Gloria's book, meant they didn't play loud music and spring-cleaned their homes regularly.

It was what successive governments had described as 'affordable housing', one of those ubiquitous new-build estates that were springing up outside towns and cities, all clean and aspirational on the architect's plans but, ten years on, looking frayed around the edges.

At first she had dreaded moving there. Before Joe's father Roger had died unexpectedly eight years ago, she'd been used to the grander surroundings of their large Victorian house near to the city centre, with its sixty-foot garden and close proximity to a Waitrose.

But now she'd got used to a modern house, she felt liberated. No leaky roof or cracking walls, no rotting, draughty window frames or wobbly guttering. This was far more manageable and, best of all, easier to keep tidy. Neat-and-tidiness was Gloria's 'thing' and she filled her largely lonely days by wiping, dusting and rearranging furniture that had been wiped, dusted and rearranged only the day before.

The only time she could bear to see the place looking less than perfect was when Ben came round to play and scattered his toys everywhere, and even then she had to fight the urge to stash them away in a cupboard, blissfully out of sight. Today, he was banging away at a drum, having already tipped a Thomas the Tank Engine jigsaw on the floor. It was only four pieces but to Gloria it looked like four thousand.

'He's not as breathless today,' she said to Joe as he picked up the pieces and chucked them in the box.

He stopped what he was doing, as if her remark had filled his head with unpleasant thoughts. Then he sighed long and hard.

'But he'll still have to have that bloody injection later.' He let out another sigh. 'It's relentless.'

She scowled, her naturally creased brow furrowing deeper. 'Why does it always have to be you? Can't *she* do it for once?'

Joe stretched for the drumstick that was slightly out of reach and handed it back to Ben. 'Mum, don't start . . . please.'

They lapsed into an uncomfortable silence, Gloria staring out of the window at her tiny patio garden with its bistro-style table for two and the colourful hanging baskets she tended as though they were two babies. She turned back and gazed down at her son.

'So are you two set on having another baby then?' she asked flatly.

'If we *don't*, Ben probably won't see thirty.' He didn't mean to sound so snappy but wanted to end that particular line of questioning because he knew it would lead down the same rocky, dead-end path.

His mother's sigh rippled the crossword page lying on the table in front of her.

'What a *mess*.'

Throwing the last piece of jigsaw into the box, he stood up, his face impassive.

'Let's not have yet *another* conversation about my marriage.'

Joe knew she only had his welfare at heart, but sometimes he wished she'd keep her opinions about his personal life to herself.

She raised her eyebrows. 'You've got to admit it's always been volatile, particularly since you had that . . .' She paused with a faint look of disapproval, as if she could barely bring herself to utter the word.

'*Affair* is the word you're looking for,' he said, faintly bored of her Hyacinth Bucket pretensions. If it wasn't insisting on milk being in a jug and taking her own cutlery to restaurants, it was pretending she was sullied by hearing about life's harsh realities. Most of the time it amused him, but on occasions he found it tiresome.

She screwed up her face. 'No, I was going to say dalliance. Affair sounds so sordid.'

'They tend to be. All furtive, sweaty and *deceitful.*'

He was overwhelmed by a desire to teasingly shock her and it seemed to work, her mouth puckering in distaste as if a foul smell was assailing her nostrils.

'And now here you are about to have another child together.'

'As I *said,* unavoidable really.'

Rubbing his hands over his face, he felt dog-weary of her intransigence. 'Marriage is never easy, Mum. Christ knows you and Dad had a few fallings-out in your time, but you came through them.' He looked at her and smiled sadly, anxious to return to more mundane subjects like what was on TV or how the postman was delivering later than ever before. 'Besides, we're getting on really well at the moment. I think Ben's problems have helped us gain some perspective.'

Gloria returned the smile but he could tell she wasn't convinced. 'Oh Joe, I can't remember the last time I saw you really laugh together.'

'Not much to laugh about when your son's crying out in pain every night, is there?' he replied bleakly.

Walking across to the armchair in the corner of the room, he grabbed Ben's coat from the back of it, noting with surprise that it hadn't been hung neatly in a cupboard. 'We'd better go.'

She looked dismayed and he instantly felt bad for her.

'Already? But you've only just got here and I haven't seen him all week! At least stay for one cup of tea.'

Standing in the neat, sterile living room, he knew that his and Ben's visit was the highlight of her day, if not her week. She could irritate him, but he loved her and couldn't bear to think of her feeling lonely.

He closed his eyes in defeat. 'OK. Just one. But can we please talk about something else?'

Karen was sitting on a park bench, looking at the ground and twisting a wet tissue in her shaking hands. She was deathly pale, shock distorting her features. Tania snaked an arm round the back of her neck and squeezed her shoulder comfortingly.

'It's a mix-up,' she murmured. 'Joe's test results have been confused with someone else's. You read about that sort of thing all the time, we'll be laughing about it one day.'

Karen carried on staring downwards, her foot scraping backwards and forwards and making a rut in the mud.

'Call the consultant now.' Tania held up her mobile phone in front of Karen's face. 'Tell him it's a mistake.'

Straightening her back, Karen rubbed her eyes and glanced uneasily at her friend before facing forward again. It felt as if a hidden force was systematically thumping her abdomen. 'There hasn't *been* a mistake.'

Tania frowned. 'But that means you must have slept . . .' She paused and drew back from Karen, trying to get a better look at her expression. '*Did you sleep with someone else?*'

Karen nodded miserably but said nothing, the thumping moving to her head now. She looked up at the overcast sky and studied the blurred line left by a long-departed plane, whisking people away from whatever they were escaping – the lousy weather, their lousy life, whatever. She had a sudden urge to be sitting among them, a silent, solitary stranger heading off to start again some-where new, with none of the emotional baggage of *this* life.

Like a patient recovering from an anaesthetic, she was vaguely aware of a voice calling her name. It was Tania's, dragging her back to unpalatable reality.

'Who is it?'

'It's not ongoing.'

'I didn't ask that.'

She saw a shadow of faint hostility cross Tania's eyes and wondered whether their friendship was about to be stretched to its limits. Or even beyond them.

Karen groaned. 'It was a reckless, bloody *stupid* one-night stand.'

They sat in silence, the air thick with awkward-ness. Eventually, Tania turned and looked at her.

'I'll ask again. Who is it?' Her tone and determined jaw suggested she'd keep asking until she got a straight answer.

'Do you swear you won't tell a soul?' Karen felt panicked, as if her toes were curled over the edge of a precipice and she was about to jump into the oblivion of uncertainty.

'Christ, is it someone I know?' Her eyes revealing naked intrigue, Tania crossed her fingers and held them in front of her face. 'Lips sealed. Brownie's honour.'

Deep breath. Jump, thought Karen.

'It's Nick.' She watched her friend carefully, waiting for the explosion. But none came.

Instead, realising that Karen wasn't going to expand further, Tania widened her eyes to suggest she was still in the dark.

'Nick Bright.' Karen winced as she said it.

Tania looked at her intently, then gave a puzzled smile. 'Odd thing to joke about.'

'It's not a joke.'

This time, there was an explosion, albeit a small one in the form of bulging eyes and a choking noise. She clamped a hand over her gaping mouth, speaking through her fingers.

'This is a fucking nightmare.'

Karen nodded, her expression pleading forgiveness.

A bag of shopping in one hand and Ben in his other arm, Joe shoved the living-room door open with his foot, before gently placing his son on the floor and easing off his blue anorak, lobbing it in the direction of the sofa.

'Now then, how about a bit of Teletubbies?'

Ben started to kick his legs excitedly at the sight of the four brightly coloured figures on the cover of the DVD being waved in front of him. Joe pushed it into the machine and pressed play.

'But for God's sake, don't tell your mother. She thinks we should be studying algebra all day.'

Standing up, he looked down at his son and smiled warmly at the sight of Ben's blond hair and its particularly unruly patch at the back where he slept on it.

Since he'd started walking round the furniture, his legs were less tadpole-like and developing greater muscle definition. To the casual observer, he might have seemed a strong, thriving child, a rugby player in the making. But they didn't see the breathlessness and fatigue caused by the hidden disease eating away inside him.

Just the thought of it made Joe emotional, biting his lip to counteract the telltale pinprick of potential tears.

Ben looked up at him, his chubby arms extended towards him. 'Dada!'

Stooping down and enveloping him in a long hug, Joe closed his eyes and savoured the moment.

'I love you too.'

★   ★   ★

'When? *Where?*' Tania was looking at Karen as if she didn't know her anymore.

They were still sitting on the park bench, the sky darkening over with ominously grey clouds. Consequently, there were only one or two hardy types remaining, walking their dogs.

Karen buttoned up her coat and tucked her chin behind the collar.

'You remember the local election night, when you invited me down to celebrate with you and the rest of Nick's canvassing team?'

Pursing her lips, Tania nodded wearily. 'But I don't remember you and him even speaking to each other, except for the usual "Hello, pleased to meet you" stuff.'

'We didn't really. There were a couple of, you know, *looks*.' She smiled ruefully, one woman to another. 'But nothing more. Then we ended up looking for a cab at the same time and he suggested we share one . . .'

'You had sex in a *cab*?' Tania looked horrified.

'Don't be daft.' She raised her eyes heavenward and smiled thinly. 'I have a little more style than that.'

'But not enough to say no to sex with him.'

'Cheap shot.'

She scowled at her friend, who nodded almost imperceptibly.

'You're right. Sorry.'

'He invited me in for coffee . . .' She stopped speaking and distractedly returned to rubbing her foot up and down, covering her shoe with flakes of mud.

'I was a bit pissed and, I suppose, flattered that someone found me attractive – even if it was just for sex.' She paused and glanced quickly at Tania, trying to assess how her explanation was faring. She still looked faintly disapproving.

'I'd just found out about Joe's affair if you remember . . .'

By the way Tania raised her eyebrows, Karen knew she wasn't impressed by the mitigation. 'Where the hell was Stella?' she muttered.

'I didn't ask.'

Silence again. Her mind miles away, Karen was subconsciously aware of two smartly dressed, middle-aged women sauntering in front of her, exercising their matching Westies. She wondered how they would react if she rushed over and told them her revelation. Would they be sympathetic? Or would they judge her as harshly as she was now judging herself? A stupid, irresponsible woman whose reckless act stemming from her insecurity was about to ruin so many lives? She was consumed by a deep sense of shame and looked at Tania whose face was tilted downwards, her stillness eloquently showing her disbelief. Clearly, the enormity of the situation was beginning to sink in.

'That was . . . *is* . . . my boss,' she said eventually. 'What a bloody mess.'

'Sorry.' Karen's voice was so small it was barely

audible. She jumped as a plastic ball hit her feet and bounced up towards her face, narrowly missing it. A girl of about five or six appeared at her side.

'Sorry,' she panted, her voice muffled behind the chunky woollen scarf knotted round her neck.

'That makes two of us.' Karen smiled and handed her the ball. 'Don't worry, have fun.'

She watched as the little girl ran back to her mother in the distance, then turned to look at Tania whose expression was now hard and challenging.

'Why didn't you tell me?'

'I don't know. Shame I suppose.' She smiled briefly at no one in particular. 'I'm not proud of it. In fact, I've probably been in denial ever since. I figured that if I didn't tell anyone about it, then I could pretend it hadn't happened.'

'And it's never crossed your mind before now that Ben could be his?'

She nodded. 'Once or twice, but I always shut it out. I still can't believe it now.'

She felt a rush of sadness. It was true, the question of Ben's paternity *had* only popped into her head a couple of times and she'd dismissed it instantly, telling herself that the boy looked so much like Joe he couldn't possibly be anyone else's child. But what *were* the physical similarities now she knew the unpalatable, biological truth about the blood coursing through her son's veins? Ben had blue eyes, Joe's were brown, but her son's features were so chubby and ill-defined it was hard to make any other comparisons. Had she suspected and simply buried her misgivings?

But her pregnancy aside, if she was honest, the sex with Nick had flashed through her mind hundreds of times since, like a scene from a porn film, something she found a turn-on but didn't associate with herself. It was a harmless fantasy she kept in her head for the days when the drudgery of real life became too much and she wanted to indulge in a spot of escapism.

She felt Tania's hand on her leg, squeezing it reassuringly. Karen was relieved to see her face had softened.

'And you're absolutely *sure* Ben is Nick's child?'

She nodded miserably. 'He's one hundred per cent not Joe's and Nick is the only other man I've slept with during our marriage.' She tilted her head towards the sky, watching a bird soaring above her head. '*Fuck.* This is going to break his heart.' Her eyes filled with tears.

'Do you have to tell him?' Tania rubbed Karen's back to try and calm her.

'Of course I do.' She ran her forefingers under her eyes.

'Perhaps you should weigh up your options first.'

Her brow furrowed at the suggestion. 'There aren't any. I have to tell him. I can't live the lie *and* help Ben.'

Tania considered what she'd said for a moment, nodding sympathetically. Then realisation dawned and her eyes widened.

'Oh my God! You're not seriously going to drag Nick into all this?'

'Don't be daft, of *course* I am. What choice do I have?' Holding her hands out in front of her, she moved them up and down like weighing scales. 'Save the life of my son . . . worry about someone's political career . . . hmmm, that's a tough one.' She pulled a face to suggest it wasn't a tough choice at all.

Tania's head was in her hands and she was shaking it from side to side. 'So let's get this straight . . .' She sat bolt upright. 'You're going to call Nick, tell him that the drunken one-night stand he had eighteen months ago resulted in a child . . . and that now he should have *another* child with you to save the life of the one he didn't even know he had?'

'If his bone marrow doesn't turn out to be a perfect match, then yes, something like that. But all he's got to do is donate some sperm.'

'*All?*' Tania looked incredulous. 'Karen, do you have *any* idea of the repercussions this is going to have?'

'I know it's not an easy situation, but what else can I do?' she replied defiantly. 'He doesn't have to tell anyone.'

Tania snorted with sarcastic disbelief. 'I can't believe you're being so naive.' She looked around her, but no one was nearby. 'We're talking about a high-profile politician here, possibly even a future prime minister.'

'We're also talking about *my son*,' hissed Karen, feeling a rush of anger at her friend's insensitivity. She knew Tania didn't have children herself, but surely it was basic common sense that a child's life took precedence over politics. Or perhaps she had misjudged her friend all these years? 'He's eight months old and he's having blood transfusions every couple of weeks and injections that make him scream out in pain every single night . . .' She took a deep breath to calm herself, deliberately softening her tone and talking more slowly. 'I have a chance to make it all stop and I'm going to take it. What mother wouldn't?'

Tania puffed out her cheeks. 'I know, but once you pull the pin on this hand grenade, it's going to explode in the middle of several people's lives and there'll be no going back.'

Karen smiled thinly. 'But I would do anything . . . and I mean, *anything* . . . including giving up my own life, if it would save Ben. When you have kids, you'll understand.'

'Maybe.' Tania shivered slightly and pulled her coat tighter at the front.

An old lady sped past them with two sausage dogs straining on a double lead, pulling their owner this way and that.

'Who's walking who?' whispered Karen, anxious to lighten the atmosphere. But her friend was in no mood for idle chit-chat.

'So how are you going to approach Nick?' Tania's tone was business-like.

'I was hoping you'd do it for me.'

'No *way*.' She looked appalled at the mere suggestion.

'Just get him to meet me, that's all.'

Tania let out a hollow laugh. 'Oh by the way Nick, remember that friend of mine you had a one-night stand with? Well she wants to meet up. Sorry, can't tell you what it's about though.' She shook her head. 'Yes, that'll work.'

'So don't tell him it's me.'

This time the hollow laughter was even louder. 'He doesn't go round having impromptu meetings with mysterious members of the public. His security is cast iron, every *second* of his day is accounted for.'

'You'll think of something.' Karen was highly irritated at having to practically beg for help from someone who had been a pivotal part of her son's life since birth, someone she assumed would be as driven and passionate as she was to facilitate Ben's recovery, whatever the professional cost to others.

But Tania was shaking her head. 'Sorry, no can do. I slogged my guts out to get that job.'

Frozen with disbelief, Karen hardly dared trust herself to speak. Finally, she turned to face Tania, taut with woefully suppressed anger. Jerking her handbag on to her shoulder, she stood up and looked down at the woman with whom she'd shared so much in life. Every secret, every teenage angst, every adult heartache. Yet right now, she didn't know her at all.

'Exactly when did you become so bloody self-centred?' she spat, before turning on her heel and walking away.

CHAPTER 5

The changing rooms of the gym were deserted except for an Elle Macpherson lookalike bouncing around in a towel so tiny it was best described as a flannel.

'Do you think she's paid to do that, to make the rest of us keep coming here until we look like her?' Stella whispered to her older sister Judy.

Judy pursed her lips. 'I could come here ten hours a day for the rest of my life and never look like her.' She peered down at her stocky, unstretchable legs. 'Sadly, my favourite machine at the gym is the one that dispenses crisps and Mars bars.'

Stella laughed and started to towel-dry her naturally dark blonde hair, then peered in the mirror. All her life she'd struggled to find the right style because it was so flyaway and fine, settling for a structured, shoulder-length bob to give it some shape and texture. It succeeded in that respect, but had a tendency, she felt, to make her look schoolmarmish. She was hoping her pregnancy hormones might thicken it up, but no sign yet.

Anyone meeting her and Judy for the first time would never have guessed they were sisters. Stella was tall and slim with a quite masculine face, while Judy was petite but pretty, with thick, glossy brown hair cut short and spiked on top. There were only three years between them, but Stella's formality against Judy's 'rock chick' chic made Stella seem at least ten years older.

'You coming Sunday?' asked Judy idly, as she rummaged in her locker. When Stella didn't reply, she emerged from behind the door and dropped her shoulders in blatant exasperation.

'Mum will be so disappointed. She wants us *both* there to honour Dad's memory.'

'It's been four years now. Life goes on.' Stella didn't mean to shrug so dismissively, but sometimes she couldn't help herself, irritated by her family's penchant for the theatrical, drawing the last vestiges of drama out of any situation.

'Yours might, *hers* doesn't,' said Judy defiantly. She eyed her sister suspiciously: 'Nick's kicking up about it, isn't he?'

Stella rolled her eyes. 'He doesn't even know about it.' Sitting on a bench, she rubbed a towel between her toes. 'Our Sundays are sacrosanct, you know that. The man deserves *some* time to relax . . .'

'Oh let's cut the crap. He ponces about making speeches and doing a bit of paperwork, yet everyone has to tiptoe round him and his bloody precious career. It's hardly the night shift down a mine.'

'No, but it's not a nine to five job behind a desk

65

either. It's relentless.' She began to rub her arms so vigorously with the towel that they turned bright pink.

A highly charged silence followed, then her sister softened her expression. 'You were so good at your job, don't you . . . you know . . . fancy going back to it?'

Stella bent down to tie up the laces on the supposedly cellulite-busting trainers that, so far, had only given her leg cramps. 'If I was still flying all over the world dealing with charitable private clients and their offshore accounts, then we'd never see each other. It's better this way.'

Judy looked doubtful. 'Hardly a good use of that industrial-sized brain of yours though, is it?'

Tying her Abercrombie & Fitch sweat-top around her waist, Stella peered into the mirror again and winced at the sight of her hair, brushing it behind her ears to try and make it look neater. 'Besides, when this little one comes along . . .' She patted her stomach '. . . it's better if I'm living the quiet life.'

'How are you feeling?'

She nodded slowly. 'Fine. In fact, I have so few symptoms that I sometimes forget I *am* pregnant.'

'Lucky you. Remember my plum pudding ankles?' smiled Judy. 'And my arse expanded to the size of Norfolk.'

'It still is,' teased Stella, eyeing her sister's petite backside. 'Anyway, I reckon my effortless pregnancy is payback for having to wait five long years to conceive in the first place.'

'I *told* you it would happen in the end. You worried far too much about it.'

'Easy coming from the old woman in the shoe.' She smiled wryly.

'Oi, less of the old, thank you. And I've only got three kids . . . well, the last time I counted anyway.' She picked up her handbag. 'Which reminds me, I've left their father in charge. I'd better get home and see what the damage is.'

They walked out of the changing room and into the main foyer of the private, riverside gym where Stella was a member and often booked Judy in as her guest. She went at least three times a week, doing power aerobics and a light-weights circuit prior to pregnancy, a more gentle yoga session since. Her sister, however, mostly swerved the exercise part, hanging out in the sauna and making use of the free lotions and potions in the changing rooms.

As they reached the car park and prepared to say goodbye, Stella looked pensive. 'It's taken me so long to get pregnant I'm not sure it would happen again.'

Judy gave her a hug then took a step backwards, her hands clasping her sister's arms. 'There's more to life you know. Being knee-deep in shitty nappies and a lifetime of responsibility isn't the be-all and end-all.'

'I know you mean well by saying that.' She gave her a quick smile. 'But it's not true. Your kids are your world.' She aimed the key remote at her Fiesta and the unlock mechanism fired into life. 'And despite Nick pretending he doesn't mind either way, I know he wants to become a father.'

Nudging her way into the steady, slow-moving stream of rush-hour traffic, Stella switched on Radio 2 and resigned herself to a journey home taking at least half an hour. The music and commentary washed over her as she contemplated Judy's well-meaning but disingenuous assertion that having children wasn't all it was cracked up to be. She'd met plenty of childless women 'of a certain age' who'd vociferously maintained it was their choice, favouring an existence of weekend lie-ins and spontaneous, last-minute foreign travel. Some she'd even believed.

But then there were the ones whose eyes told a different story, showing a deep longing that would never be sated. Some had convinced themselves it was what they wanted; others had married men who didn't want children and had sacrificed their own desires at the altar of their husband's.

What would *I* tell people, she mused, subconsciously edging towards the car in front. Would I too join the women who told the outside world they felt thrilled and unhindered to be childless, whilst secretly feeling unfulfilled? Or would I be honest and watch people's expressions wither to dismay as they realised their well-meaning question had tapped a raw and bitter nerve?

As she automatically indicated to go left, the

loud clicking noise dragged her thoughts back to reality.

'Think positive, Stella,' she murmured under her breath.

It was five o'clock by the time she arrived home, having struggled round Marks & Spencer's food department with what felt like half of West London. She was a fantastic cook, having applied the same level of perfection to it that she did everything else, but she'd lost count of the hours she'd spent slaving over everything from homemade puff pastry to hand-made butter balls, only to have Nick wolf it all down in five minutes flat, one eye on the evening news and oblivious to the time and effort it had taken to prepare.

So these days, particularly since becoming pregnant and feeling drained by the evening, she often bought pre-prepared food from the supermarket. Once or twice, she'd even buried the packaging deep in the bin and claimed credit for it, with Nick swallowing it in every sense.

Emptying one of the bags into the fridge, she turned back to the counter separating the kitchen from the living room and held up a packet saying 'Steak and Guinness Pie'. That, along with McCain's crispy oven fries and garden peas, was Nick's favourite meal of all time. You can take the boy out of Fleetwood, but you can't take Fleetwood out of the boy, she thought wryly.

She'd given up trying to convert him to healthier

food, accepting that if his preference made life easier for her, then why complain? Though, of course, in interviews he lied and said his top dish was the less carbohydrate-heavy roast chicken and fresh vegetables.

Her handbag started to vibrate and she rifled through it, searching for her mobile.

'Hi darling.' She watched the rain lashing the window, pleased they weren't going to a dreary political function tonight. 'Yes, I feel fine thanks. I've bought dinner and there's a new crime series starting at nine, so it's our favourite kind of night . . . OK . . . love you too.'

She chucked the phone back in her bag and smiled to herself. Nick's busy schedule meant he was unlikely to see the rest of the series, but at least they'd manage one episode together. Their Sky+ was rammed full of programmes he was going to watch when he got the time. Which was never.

She knew he wouldn't have minded going to her mother's for the 'memorial' lunch on Sunday, but the truth was she saw so little of him during the week that she cherished and fiercely protected any quiet time they had together.

When her father Ralph had died suddenly of a heart attack four years ago, she and Nick had organised everything when her mother Francesca had spiralled into depression, barely able to function let alone plan a funeral. Judy had young children to deal with, so Stella had taken it all on board with Nick as a sterling back-up, drawing up lists of attendees and mapping out the service, as well as the distressing task of choosing the coffin.

Since then, they had dutifully attended the first, second and third anniversaries of his death, marked with a sombre dinner at her mother's house during which Francesca would sob loudly, Stella and Judy would comfort her, and Nick would spend most of his time in the garden on his mobile phone trying to help sort out the latest government scandal exposed in the Sunday newspapers.

She didn't want to appear harsh, but she'd had enough and, besides, she didn't want to expose herself to any unnecessary stress during this critical time in her pregnancy. So she'd used Nick's workload as the excuse not to attend, although it was as good a reason as any.

Flicking on the kettle switch, she reached for a mug from the overhead cupboard and felt a shooting pain in her abdomen, strong enough to make her catch her breath.

Narrowly avoiding dropping the mug, she carefully placed it back in the cupboard before rubbing her stomach. The other hand was clamped on the worktop to steady her.

Seconds later, the next pain came, so sharp that it caused her to cry out and grab the high stool next to her. Placing both hands on the seat, her arms ramrod straight, she leaned forward and tried to find a position that would alleviate the pain, but nothing worked.

As the next wave hit her, her whole body flinched and she felt the unmistakable trickle of something wet running down her upper left thigh.

'Oh God,' she whispered, her eyes screwed shut, her head thrown back.

She eased her hand inside the elasticated waist-band of her tracksuit bottoms and moved it down to her groin area where her fingers found the wet patch.

'Please don't be blood, please don't be blood . . .' she chanted quietly as she slowly moved her hand out again. She held it up in front of her face then opened her eyes.

Her fingers were bright red.

The smell of the Great Ormond Street Hospital ward always made Karen feel sick because she associated it with her son's pain. They were surrounded by seriously ill children but there was nothing like the crying of your own to pierce your heart.

Once every two weeks, Ben had to have a full blood transfusion to help him fight the anaemia and here they were again, with him looking so small and pale in the bed, his little body wired up to machines. The first few times he'd fought it. But now, even at his tender age, he'd learned that it was less painful to succumb, that resisting was pointless.

Karen was standing at the end of the bed, her shoulders rigid with tension, watching Joe as he stroked Ben's hair. She felt swollen with nausea, both for her son's predicament and the life-shattering secret that was festering inside her. She wanted to scream it out, to fall at Joe's feet and beg his forgiveness, to share her pain with him, as they had done through every step of Ben's diagnosis and treatment. But this, of course, was different.

Ben made a whimpering noise and Joe leapt to his feet, readjusting the pillow behind his head.

'Daddy's brave little soldier, aren't you?' he murmured.

She bit her lip and closed her eyes, struggling to control herself. When she opened them, he was watching her with concern. 'Are you all right?'

She nodded, tears welling in her eyes at this small consideration. Gripped by the feeling of remorse that hadn't left her since she first heard the bombshell, she didn't trust herself to speak.

'He's had a transfusion loads of times before, love.' He looked puzzled. 'This one's no different.'

Knowing now was not the time to unravel in front of him, she felt overwhelmed by an urge to leave the room and jerked her head towards the door. 'I need some air,' she mumbled.

Out in the corridor, the tears began to flow, blinding her as she walked hurriedly away, nearly colliding with a young couple and their sallow little girl in a Barbie nightdress. 'I'm so sorry.'

'That's alright,' the woman reassured her. 'Is everything OK?'

She nodded firmly, gave them a quick smile and carried on walking at a brisk pace, glancing in to each room she passed. A pressure cooker of emotion was building in her chest and she wanted its release to be out of sight.

About four doors along on the left, she found one that was empty and darted in, pushing the door closed. Her back against the door, she sank to the floor, legs splayed out, her head lolling to one side as loud sobs engulfed her.

Joe glanced at his all-singing all-dancing diver's watch that had never been to a greater depth than the washing-up bowl. Karen had been gone about ten minutes and he'd stuck his head out into the corridor a couple of times, but no sign. He hoped she was alright, but he couldn't leave Ben to venture any further.

Hearing the door open, he looked up expecting to see her, but a nurse walked into the room. She was very pretty, probably in her mid-twenties, with white blonde hair in an elfin cut.

'I'm just going to check his blood pressure.' She smiled warmly at him and he sensed the flash of flirtation in her eyes. A couple of years ago, he would probably have responded, enjoying the kind of fleeting frisson that made him feel alive. Despite being married, Joe had been the flirtatious type, but not a man who followed it through. He liked women, they liked him, and it never went beyond a bit of harmless banter. With the exception of Sally.

They'd shared a cramped, untidy office at the ad agency and, over time, an office flirtation had gone deeper. With depressing predictability, they had stepped over the line at a particularly boozy office Christmas party, sneaking away from the prying eyes of colleagues for a snog in a nearby alleyway. Then, thanks to their daily close proximity, it had developed from there. Joe hadn't been looking to have an affair; it had just happened and he had been too weak to stop it.

Inevitably, the rumours had started, but they both denied it around the office and there was no tangible evidence to prove otherwise. But then the agency had held its annual summer party, with spouses and children invited, and Karen had come along to meet his colleagues, including shaking the hand of the woman with whom her husband shared an office.

Karen had been uncharacteristically quiet in the taxi on the way home, waiting until they'd walked into the hallway before asking quietly: 'How long's it been going on?'

'Sorry?' He'd genuinely had no idea what she was talking about at that point.

'How long have you been seeing Sally?'

His mind had raced with the possibilities of how she knew. Had someone said something? If so, who? Or perhaps Sally had been consumed with jealousy at finally meeting his wife and confessed all? He'd quickly dismissed both options, leaving him with Karen's intuition.

'It's so bloody obvious,' she'd added, appearing to read his mind. 'You sit within a few feet of her every day and yet there was a terrible awkwardness about your body language. She could barely look at me, which I assume must be guilt, and when you topped her drink up she didn't say thank you. That's a real sign of intimacy.'

'It is?' He had always been baffled by a woman's ability to read something in to the most mundane gestures.

The determination of her delivery made him realise it was pointless denying it. Besides, he didn't want to insult her any more than he already had. So he'd confessed all and blown both their lives apart.

Since then, the old, harmlessly flirtatious Joe had been buried for good, knowing he owed it to Karen to never make her doubt him again. Now he'd betrayed her trust, she'd be watching him like a hawk, wondering if the late night at the office was genuine or a cover, flinching every time she heard a text arrive on his mobile phone. He'd known he would have to throw open every aspect of his life to her, to account for his every move whether she asked him to or not. And most of all, he'd known he would have to leave the agency, and Sally, behind.

Joe had reflected about that period in his life, going over and over in his head why he'd betrayed the woman he adored and had only been married to for just over a year when it happened. Perhaps it was the finality of 'tying the knot' that had prompted his bad behaviour: a juvenile over-reaction to the reality that he was now expected to stay with his wife for the rest of his days? It couldn't be anything else because, despite a few teething problems and run-of-the-mill arguments, he and Karen's relationship had been strong enough for them to continue making love whilst, as he now saw it, he was having sex with Sally.

'Has he been ill long?'

Dragged away from his flashback, he started slightly. The young nurse was looking questioningly at him whilst pumping the pressure monitor.

He smiled sadly. 'Pretty much all his life. He's not long been diagnosed . . . it's Diamond Blackfan Anaemia. His body doesn't produce enough red blood cells.'

She raised her immaculately plucked eyebrows, enhancing her large, pale blue eyes. 'It's the first time I've come across it.'

'It's very rare. And very hard for him. A twelve-hour drip injection five nights a week, this every two weeks . . .' His head throbbed at the thought. 'I just want to swap places with him.'

Removing the pressure band from Ben's arm, she scribbled the result on the pad at the end of the bed and smiled warmly.

'He's very lucky to have a dad like you.'

★　★　★

White with tension, Nick let himself into the flat and strode purposefully through to the living room.

Stella was lying on the sofa, with the doctor in an adjacent armchair, placing his stethoscope and blood pressure monitor back in his bag.

Grabbing Stella's hand, Nick fell to his knees next to her and placed his cheek gently against hers. 'Are you OK?'

She opened her mouth to reply but nothing came out. A solitary tear ran down her face.

Standing up, the doctor cleared his throat, his expression one of discomfort. 'She'll be fine, but I'm afraid she's lost the baby.'

Stella started to wail loudly, like a wounded animal.

Nick was a forthright, dynamic man capable of creating and implementing social policy to help transform the lives of millions of people, but when it came to dealing with his wife's pain he felt totally impotent, kneeling by her side with a look of abject despair. He was disappointed and sad that she'd lost the baby, but this depth of feeling for a small blob he'd never known felt alien to him.

'All you can do is comfort her,' said the doctor, sensing his feelings of hopelessness. 'I'll be off now. Make sure she takes it easy for the next few days and call me if you need anything.'

Nick nodded, feeling shellshocked. He'd have given anything to follow the doctor out of the door and lose himself in some dreary government white paper, returning home only when his wife was mended and smiling again.

Hearing the front door close, he placed his palms either side of Stella's face and looked into her eyes that were red raw from crying. 'Darling, I'm so, so sorry.'

'My baby!' she sobbed. 'I wanted it so much.'

He held her tight, rocking her back and forth. 'I know, sweetie, I know.'

CHAPTER 6

The pub was packed out with a sweating mass of men, all craning their necks towards the large plasma screen on the far wall. Joe noted the score was Manchester United one, Arsenal nil, with just five minutes to full time. As this was a pub in North London, it wasn't going down too well.

Ignoring the scowls and various curses, he pushed his way through the crowd to find Andy sitting in isolated splendour on a leather, two-seater sofa right in front of the screen.

'Thank fuck you're here,' Andy bellowed above the loud, collective groan as an Arsenal player hit the bar. He removed his jacket from the seat next to him. 'About eighty-four thousand people have tried to nick your place.'

'I'm impressed.' Joe settled into the comfortable prime location, trying to ignore the envious scowls. 'What time did you get here to secure *this* view?'

'Lunchtime.' Andy's face was deadpan.

Joe wasn't sure if he was joking: his brother did spend an inordinate amount of time in pubs. He was supposed to be a self-employed computer engineer, but whenever Joe rang him on his mobile he was in some bar claiming to have just finished work.

Quite how he coped financially was anyone's guess, but he'd bought his 'bijou' – meaning minuscule – flat when London property prices were still realistic and only had a bijou mortgage to match. Equally, he had only himself to fund.

Andy was two years younger than Joe, but it looked the other way round. He would be the perfect guinea pig for one of the ubiquitous TV makeover shows, with a pleasant face hidden under a mop of tangled hair and unkempt beard. His slim, athletic body was swamped by holey, oil-stained jeans and one of the only two sweatshirts he was ever seen in, either with 'If you can't beat them, have them beaten' written across the front, or 'Practise safe sex: use an airbag'.

When challenged about his dress sense, Andy described his style as 'biker chic', except he hadn't saved up enough for the motorbike to finish the look off.

A loud groan filled the room as the match ended with an Arsenal defeat and the pub started to empty on to the street. A disgruntled fan switched the TV off in disgust, leaving Joe and Andy alone at their end of the room.

Andy pushed a pint of lager towards him. 'Here's one I made earlier.'

Picking it up and draining half of it in one go, Joe held it aloft. 'Cheers.'

'Cheers.' Andy tapped his glass against his brother's. 'And here's to the next baby.'

Smiling wearily, Joe shook his head in wonderment. 'Radio Mother I presume?'

His brother winked. 'The fastest known means of communication. Makes broadband look like the days of carrier pigeon.'

'Well, she's right.'

'Wow.' Andy's eyebrows shot up. 'That's a big deal.'

'Yes it is.' He nodded slowly, looking thoughtful. 'But of course I didn't tell Mum that.'

'She also said you told her that you and Karen are getting along quite well at the moment.'

'Because I can't stand the lecture otherwise.' Protruding his bottom lip, he sighed so heavily his fringe rose up. 'Let's face it, Mum's never been that keen on Karen as it is. They're both strong characters who think their point of view is the only one.'

Andy pulled a face of mock horror. 'Aaargh, you married your mother!'

Joe smiled distractedly. 'I think the problem is more that because Karen's parents emigrated to New Zealand when she was twenty-one, she's spent most of her adult life doing what she wants, when she wants, without someone close commenting on her daily life. They only know what she chooses to tell them, so I think it was hard for her to have our mum around, putting in her two penn'orth on life, love and the universe.'

'Why didn't she go with them?'

'They wanted her to, but she was old enough to make her own choice and when she said no, it would have meant them giving up their lifelong dream to move there. So they went anyway. She's been there a couple of times, but it's more an email relationship now.'

'Hmm, only conversing with Mum via email. I can see the attractions,' joked Andy, but his brother didn't respond, his expression wistful.

'Do you remember when we went to that party at Eamonn's . . . where I first met her? She was so outgoing, so bloody sexy. I thought we were indestructible.'

His brother frowned. '*Thought*? Is everything OK with you guys? I thought there was just the occasional rough patch?'

'Kind of.' Joe shrugged. 'It varies from day to day really.'

'As a sad fuck who could sit dead in his own detritus for weeks on end before anyone would find out, I'm not an expert on relationships as you know, but . . . isn't that normal?'

'Probably.' Joe sighed softly. 'And even if it isn't, it doesn't alter the fact that we have to do whatever it takes to save Ben's life. But I find myself thinking . . . or should I say fantasising . . . about how uncomplicated life is when you're single, never having to account for someone else's wants or needs.'

He felt guilty even verbalising it, but Andy seemed unconcerned by the revelation.

'Believe me, being single isn't all it's cracked up to be,' he sighed wearily. 'You're suffering from the old grass is greener syndrome. If you left, you'd miss it all within a month, if not sooner . . . guaranteed.'

'You're probably right.' He nodded towards a couple snogging at the bar. 'But I'm struggling to remember when we were like that, if we *ever* were.'

'Hellooooo!' Andy pulled a 'duh' face. 'You were so intertwined the first year you couldn't have put a bloody credit card between you.'

Joe afforded the remark a quick smile but his mind was on more serious matters. It felt good to voice his feelings because he so rarely did. He couldn't talk to his mother about Karen because she'd store every negative utterance in her mental Rolodex and regurgitate it when things were going well in a 'but you said she was . . .' kind of way. What Joe needed was a sounding board against which to vent spleen but never hear of it again. Andy fitted that role nicely.

'It seems that we had so little time when things were really happy, you know? Like constant, unadulterated happiness.'

His brother smiled ruefully. 'I guess your affair put an end to that.'

Joe grimaced. 'God knows what I was thinking. It kind of just happened and before I knew it, it had become complicated.'

'Oh puh-lease. Accidents *just* happen, affairs don't.' Andy was nothing if not forthright and painfully honest in his views, never sugaring a pill. His derisive expression made it clear he regarded his brother's plea-bargaining as downright pathetic.

Joe decided to take the blow on the chin and move away from a subject that made him uncomfortable and – if he was honest – irritable. As far as he was concerned, it had been a brief aberration that meant nothing and was never likely to be repeated with Sally or anyone else. Yet other people, particularly Karen, had seemed intent to dwell on it, as if it had been a passionate, unfinished love affair he'd sacrificed for the sake of his marriage and had regretted ending ever since.

He'd understood that, for a few months afterwards, she would need to throw it back in his face and thrash it out, over and over, in her bid to understand and reconcile it in her mind. Then she'd fallen pregnant and her hormones had gone haywire, prompting her to burst in to tears over something as simple as dropping a plate on the carpet. The combination of seesawing emotions and growing insecurity because of her expanding shape had sparked many tense exchanges where Karen had screamed at him to return to Sally and he, feeling guilty at being the source of his pregnant wife's stress, had tried to calmly reassure her that she was the love of his life and no one else.

But when, after Ben's birth, she was *still* bringing it up during arguments – an emotional hand grenade she knew would always hit its target – his tolerance had worn thin. In between the occasional flashes of their old selves, their relationship in the last six months had become increasingly strained. On top of all that, Ben's illness had reared its ugly, soul-destroying head and added yet more pressure. In his darkest moments, Joe wondered if Ben's illness was some kind of punishment for the affair.

Joe leaned back on the sofa to let a barman collect the empty glasses from their table.

'Right!' Andy stretched his arms in the air. 'Time for one last swift one, then back home for some late-night porn and sex with myself.'

'Join the club, mate.'

'What?' his brother scoffed. 'You've got a gorgeous wife waiting for you at home.'

'Gorgeous, yes, but waiting for sex? I fear not,' he said wistfully. 'In fact, I *know* not. Her last words before I left were that when I got home we needed to talk.'

Andy gave a theatrical shudder. 'Words to strike dread into a grown man's heart.' Standing up, he turned towards the direction of the bar. 'Forget all your problems and just have a damn good shag. I know I would.'

Joe grinned. 'You know what? You're right.' He drained his glass. 'Brace yourself love!'

Karen put her book down on the side of the bath with a heavy sigh. She had now read the same page five times and couldn't concentrate. Every time she heard a car door slam, her heart would leap into her mouth, then she'd hold her breath to hear if it was followed by the sound of the front door opening. But it was now 11.30 p.m. and there was no sign of him.

Before he'd left for the pub, she'd deliberately kept her tone light when she'd said they needed to talk: she didn't want him to suspect the severity of what she had to say. Now she was wondering if he was deliberately staying out late to avoid what he probably suspected might be another conversation that descended into her dragging up his affair.

The water was turning cold around her so she sat up and twisted the hot tap to full, noisy flow. She jumped as Joe sauntered casually into the bathroom, carrying a bottle of white wine and two glasses.

'Oh, I didn't hear you come in.' She smiled uncertainly, her heart racing with the adrenalin of nervousness.

'I always thought I'd have made a good cat burglar.' He placed the glasses on the toilet lid and filled them up, handing one to her.

'Thanks.' She took a sip, trying hard not to show her anxiety. 'This is nice.'

He nodded. 'We don't do it enough.'

'I meant the wine.' There was an awkward pause before she added: 'But you're right, we don't.'

She took a gulp this time, hoping it would numb her. He rapidly topped up her glass, a slight smile on his face as he glanced down to her breasts.

'How was Andy?' She couldn't think of anything else to say.

'On good form.'

'Look, I . . . I . . .' Karen felt she had to instigate *the* conversation or she might burst.

But suddenly, Joe was swaying from side to side.

'I . . . I . . . I'm just a love machine . . .' he sang, his bare feet twisting the bathroom rug into a messy heap. Shimmying over to the bath, he took the wine glass from her hand and placed it on the floor. Then he knelt next to the bath, still singing.

'. . . and I don't work for nobody but yoooooo . . .'

He kissed her neck, butterfly kisses that set her already stimulated nerve endings into orbit. Her whole body shivered, goosebumps rising on her arms. Chin resting on his shoulder, she studied the toothbrush holder and tried to keep a grip of her senses, but the more urgent the kisses became, the more she visibly relaxed, giggling at a ticklish bit.

'I take it you've been drinking,' she murmured.

'Irrelevant. I fancy you rotten,' he whispered, now nibbling her ear, knowing it got her in the mood. 'I always have.'

He climbed into the bath fully clothed, the water spilling on to the floor as Karen shrieked with laughter. They started to kiss with a passion that had been missing from their relationship for some time. Knowing that what she had to tell him might destroy it forever, she closed her eyes, savouring what she feared might be their last ever act of intimacy.

Dog-tired, Tania looked up from her desk and noted it was eleven p.m. Switching off her computer, she gazed blankly into the distance, mulling over her argument with Karen. They'd fallen out many times when they'd been at school together, about trivial matters such as borrowed and lost jewellery or vaguely fancying the same boy who, inevitably, only ever returned the compliment in Karen's direction. But this was different. This was their first ever grown-up row and Tania didn't like the feeling one little bit.

She was still reeling from Karen's revelation, not only because of Nick Bright's involvement, but because her friend had never confided in her about the fling. She always thought they shared every little thing, that there *were* no secrets between them. Yet here was the mother of all secrets and Karen had seen fit to keep it to herself.

Did that mean she didn't trust her? If so, it had implications for the strength of their friendship.

Brow furrowed, she jumped slightly at the sound of a door opening from the gloom of the far side of the room.

'Fuck me.' James Spender appeared from the shadows, displaying his usual charm. 'Has your boyfriend kicked you out?'

She closed her eyes wearily, then opened them again. 'I don't have a boyfriend, as you well know.' She let out a heartfelt sigh at the thought of the tumbleweed blowing across her sex life. 'For the same reason that you don't have a girl-friend – we're married to our rotten, ungrateful jobs.'

He made a disapproving sucking noise through his teeth. 'Oh dear, time of the month is it?'

'I haven't heard that since I was in school.' She shook her head in amazement. 'Boy, you really *are* an arsehole.'

'But a cute one.' He walked closer, his shadow falling across her desk. 'Come on, I'll take you to my club for a cheer-up tipple.'

My club was a private member's bar round the corner that he and dozens of senior Westminster figures frequented when they were avoiding going home to their wives by pretending to be taking part in some late-night vote. It would have been easy for the wives to check if the vote even existed or, if it did, whether their husbands had actually voted, but Tania presumed few of them bothered. Perhaps it suited them to have their husbands away a lot, she mused.

'I really don't . . .' she faltered, but James stuck his fingers in his ears and started singing. 'La la, la . . . not listening . . .'

She raised her eyes heavenward and gave him a tired smile. The alternative was going home for a Horlicks and a couple of late-night digestives, which, as her mother always reminded her, were 'a moment on the lips, a lifetime on the hips'.

Grabbing her handbag, she stood up and followed him out of the door.

Joe pottered around the bedroom, hanging his wet clothes on the radiator and humming joyously to himself, his spirits lifted immeasurably by having had sex. What's more, it had been the passionate, spontaneous sex he spoke so fondly of from the days before their marriage became bogged down by the complications of his infidelity and, subsequently, Ben's illness.

It's that easy to make him happy, thought Karen, sitting in bed and watching his every move. And now I'm about to destroy him.

Hopping in next to her, he turned and smiled as she leaned in to him and placed a gentle kiss on his shoulder. His expression screamed 'game on'.

'You do know that I love you, don't you?' Her voice was soft and calm, but inside her heart was pounding against her chest with the ferocity of engine pistons.

Joe's expression changed to one of curiosity. 'Of course I do. We have our moments, but I don't ever doubt that.'

'Good.' She smiled, her eyes sad.

He extended an arm to turn out the bedside light, but she placed a hand on his shoulder.

'Hang on . . . I need to tell you something.' She

felt her throat tighten. 'I was going to wait until the morning . . . but I just can't . . .'

He looked at her, his hand hovering near the light. 'Blimey, that *is* a serious face.' He dropped his hand and turned to face her, his forehead suddenly creased with worry lines.

'Is Ben OK?'

'He's fine.'

Slapping his hand against his chest, the worry lines evaporated. 'What is it then?'

Karen felt the chemical rush of adrenalin pumping up her heart rate. She studied him for a couple of seconds, savouring the kind, open face looking back at her inquiringly. In one second, the softness would be gone.

'I've been unfaithful to you.'

The words hung in the air between them, echoing in the silence.

'*Seriously?*' His eyes were searching hers, hoping for a sign that this was some kind of wind-up.

She nodded miserably.

Joe gasped. His eyes, shining with happiness a few minutes earlier, filled with incomprehension and pain. She hated herself.

'Is it still going on?' A muscle in his jaw was twitching.

'God no,' she replied hastily. 'It was a one-night stand ages ago.'

'Who with?' he rasped, the words seeming to stick in his throat.

She shook her head vehemently. 'No one you know.'

He nodded slowly but had the look of someone who hadn't a clue what was going on.

'Well you got away with it, so why the big confession now?'

'I felt you deserved to know.'

'*Deserved*?' He looked perplexed by this declaration and waited for her to answer. Picking at a loose thread on the bedspread, she looked at him apologetically. 'I don't know . . . I guess I thought it might help redress the balance a bit . . . you know, even things up between us.'

He shot out of bed, an incredulous look on his face. 'What? *I* had an affair, then *you* had a one-night stand . . . and now we're *quits*?' he said, pointing at himself and then her.

She had the grace to look sheepish. 'Something like that, yes.'

Joe paced up and down the room, his back to her. Suddenly he spun round and glared at her.

'Your timing stinks, do you know that?'

She looked confused. 'Sorry?'

'We've just had the best sex in ages . . . just for *once* forgot about our bloody problems and now . . . now *this*,' he spat.

'I was going to tell you as soon as you came in,' she said apologetically, 'but we . . . well, you know.'

Shaking his head in disbelief, he walked to the

bedroom fireplace and turned to face her, his features twisted.

'You are fucking unbelievable. When I think how you've put me through hell because of my infidelity and now, *only* now, when you've grown tired of your own sanctimony, do you see fit to tell me that you aren't the bloody angel you've made yourself out to be.'

She bristled. 'I'm not making excuses for it, but my drunken one-night stand was a direct consequence of your sober, long-standing affair with a woman you worked with every day of the week.'

'Right, so now it's *my* fault you had one shandy too many and dropped your pants for some lucky bloke, is it?' he muttered contemptuously.

Karen took a deep breath to calm herself, anxious it didn't descend into mud-slinging. 'All I'm saying is that I was emotionally vulnerable at the time and acted completely out of character.'

Her voice was quiet but it had no impact on Joe who was still angry. His eyes were like granite, his jaw slowly moving from side to side as if he was grinding his back teeth.

'And now you're so torn apart by guilt that you want to tell me all about it?' He looked at her challengingly. 'Sorry Karen, I just don't buy it.'

He was right to doubt her reasons, of course, but she wasn't ready to pile on the extra agony. She wanted to isolate the revelation of her infidelity so she could assess his reaction, not sure why it mattered but suspecting that it was because she hoped he'd forgive her for it. If it was tangled up in the mêlée of her further bombshell, she'd never know. She smiled ruefully.

'Marriage is tricky, isn't it?'

'Yep, sure is,' he replied evenly.

'And I just figured that it was time to acknowledge that . . . to lay our cards on the table and do some honest *talking* rather than arguing.'

He didn't respond, but considered what she'd said. Leaning against the fireplace, his body seemed less taut and a bit of colour had crept back into his cheeks. Eventually, he made a muted sighing noise and walked back to the bed, perching on the edge.

'I suppose you're right. Fire away.'

Relief washed over her; she was grateful for this gesture of possible forgiveness.

'I was devastated about you and . . . Sally.' She could hardly bear to utter her name. 'Even when you said it was over, I tortured myself with the thought that you were still working together, perhaps meeting in your lunch break for clandestine snogs and angst-ridden little chats about how much you were missing each other . . .' She smiled apologetically.

'I know.' He didn't return the smile. 'That's why I left my job . . . to put your mind at rest, remember?'

'But it wasn't enough. I felt so betrayed.'

He ran a hand through his hair, then rubbed his eyes so hard she feared he might damage them.

'So you took your revenge by sleeping with another man.' It was a statement not a question.

He lifted his legs on to the bed and sat with his back against the pillows, staring at the window. The curtains were closed, but through a gap Karen could see that it was a fantastically clear but cold night, the moon nearly full. She wanted nothing more than to snuggle down and fall asleep in Joe's arms, but she knew she had to go on.

'It was someone I met at a party. He wasn't my type really.' She paused, faintly nauseous at the memory of her recklessness. 'But I'd had a lot to drink and wasn't thinking straight.'

She looked at him for a response, but none was forthcoming. Feeling adrift, she longed to press her cheek against his shoulder and wrap her arms around his waist, hanging on for dear life.

'I never saw him again,' she added, as if that made it better.

Joe's tormented eyes searched her face. After a while he got out of bed again, letting out a long, deep breath. 'Forget it.'

Walking across to the window, he pulled back the curtains and looked out.

'People say that having a sick child puts the rest of your life into perspective and now I know what they mean,' he said softly. 'Somehow, your drunken one-night stand seems utterly trivial by comparison.'

From this point, Karen thought, they could get their marriage back on track. They had both made mistakes, but with a commitment to better communication they could rebuild absolute trust.

But it was all immaterial, because she knew that what she was about to tell him was an admission of such magnitude that they might never recover from it. Not for the first time, the possibility of not telling him crossed her mind. She fantasised about hushing the whole thing up, about letting Joe continue to believe he was Ben's father, about going ahead with the PGD pretending it was her husband's sperm, not that of a virtual stranger.

But it was pie in the sky for two reasons: first, Pickering had made it quite clear that if *she* didn't tell Joe then he would, but most of all because her deep and shameful remorse meant she could never keep such a life-shattering secret from the man she considered her best friend, lover and confidant.

Tell him she must. She felt sick to her soul.

James was so close that Tania could feel his breath on her cheek, could smell his aftershave that was everything he wasn't – subtle and pleasant. They were sitting on a low-level, slouchy sofa with a vast dip in the middle that propelled her towards him whether she liked it or not. But she had to admit that through the 'beer goggles', he was growing on her.

It wasn't that James was unattractive physically, in fact in a certain half-light he resembled a young Harrison Ford. It was just that she only ever saw

97

him at work, where his features were always contorted into a sneer or curse as he berated some hapless colleague or off-message journalist.

Tonight, he seemed different, appealing even, as he nursed a whisky on the rocks in his left hand and his right lay idly on the back of the sofa behind her head.

She hadn't planned to come to his flat, but predictably the club had been full of men either avoiding their own wives or furtively escorting someone else's, and it had made her desperately uncomfortable. Not least because most of them knew James and had smiled knowingly when they'd seen the two of them together.

'Ah, late-night briefs eh? The best kind,' leered one, as if referring to the zipped-crotch variety.

So here she was, back at James's flat for a 'coffee' that had yet to show its face among the surfeit of white wine.

'Come on, why the glum face earlier?' he asked, jerking his head backwards in reference to when he'd found her working late in the office.

Shaking her head, she felt a hot flush rise through her at the thought. 'Nothing. It's personal.'

Topping up her glass, he swiftly returned to lounge lizard mode, flashing her a lazy, languorous smile.

'Boyfriend trouble?'

'I don't have one. I told you that.'

'OK, *lack* of boyfriend trouble?'

Almost imperceptibly, he moved closer, his hand

now resting on the back of her head, one finger idly caressing her hair. Her spine tingled, but she wasn't sure if it was from excitement or terror. Anxious to detract from the overbearing, seductive atmosphere, she figured it wouldn't hurt to tell him part of what was troubling her. 'I've fallen out with my best friend over something, that's all.'

'Steal your shampoo in the school showers, did she?' he grinned, moving closer still. She could feel his leg pressing against hers.

'No.' She smiled quickly to show she wasn't lacking in humour. 'It's a little more serious than that.'

Shifting herself forward, away from his hand, she sat with her knees clamped together and sipped her wine. Her head was starting to feel woozy.

'Any chance of that coffee?'

But he ignored her, his hand nestled in the small of her back.

'I know you think I'm a big mouth, but I'm actually very discreet,' he murmured. 'You can tell Uncle James anything.'

A combination of his soothing tone and the alcohol finally forced her to relax slightly. Loosening her leg muscles, she allowed herself to slip backwards, turning so she could look at him.

'You know, maybe you're not the utter shit I've always thought you were,' she smiled.

'I'll take that as a compliment,' he murmured, nuzzling her shoulder with his chin.

'In fact,' she added, 'you're actually quite nice.'

'Naughty but nice. That's me.' He slipped his hand up the back of her shirt and ran a finger up and down her lower spine. 'Now then, about that problem of yours.'

Her mind was very foggy now and she shook her head slowly. 'It's not my secret to tell.'

James positively quivered. 'Oooh, a *secret*, eh? Well, you've really whet my appetite now.' He grabbed her waist and pulled her back into the comfortable dip of the sofa. 'Come on, don't be a bore. Cough up.'

Pained, she wished the conversation could return to the safer territory of who they liked or disliked at work, but knew any diversionary tactics would be fruitless. He was like a dog with a bone.

'I can't, seriously.' Her head was really pounding. 'If it gets out, we're all up shit creek.'

As soon as the words had left her mouth, she regretted the lapse of concentration. James reacted as if he'd been stung, his back ramrod straight, his eyes black with the whiff of intrigue.

'*We*? Is it to do with someone at work?'

'No,' she blustered quickly and unconvincingly. 'OK, *yes*. But that's all I'm saying. Don't ask me any more.'

He narrowed his eyes. 'Well, taking into account your mention of shit creek, there's only one person with the power to put us all there . . . it's Nick isn't it?' He raised his eyebrows questioningly.

'I'm not saying who it is.' Her tone and expression were defiant, but inside she was the psychological equivalent of a duck treading water. He was so close she could feel his hot breath on her ear, a not altogether unpleasant sensation. Wondering if he was about to kiss her, she forced herself to move away, but when she looked at him, his expression was more ominous than amorous.

'If it *is* something to do with Nick, and I discover I could have done some damage limitation in advance, *your* neck will be on the line.'

He didn't quite do the Hannibal Lecter tongue rattle but it was close enough, causing the hairs on the back of her neck to tingle. She let out a long sigh.

'God, me and my big mouth. Get me another drink. I think I'm going to need it.'

CHAPTER 7

Taking hold of her hand, Joe stared down at it, distractedly twisting her wedding ring round and round.

'Let's draw a line in the sand,' he said, looking at her earnestly. 'From now on, we move forward. No more recriminations from you about what I did, and none from me about what you've just told me. Agreed?'

'Brownie's honour.' She placed three fingers against her forehead, feeling like a lying, prize shit as she did so. Already she was beginning to doubt the wisdom of separating the two revelations. Now Joe had forgiven her for the one-night stand, it seemed cruel not to have told him everything at the same time. It was as if she was deliberately withholding the final bombshell so she could see him start to recover from one before piling on yet more agony, deriving some twisted pleasure from it. God he was going to hate her.

He emulated her salute. 'Let's hope we stick to it or that way lies madness.' Visibly relaxing, he turned towards her, propping himself up on one elbow. 'Funny isn't it? You've told me you had a one-night stand, yet I feel as if a weight has been lifted from my shoulders.'

'I know what you mean.'

Except that she didn't. The weight of what she had yet to say was bearing down so hard that she felt leaden.

Joe stretched and yawned, his well-toned arms rising above his head. 'We've got a tough few months ahead of us. Ben will need us to be strong.'

'He will.'

She longed to stretch across and caress his arm, but nodded slowly instead, biting her lip and trying to show a strength that she seriously felt was beyond her. When the tears fell, it was silently at first, building up into loud, inconsolable sobs.

Grabbing her shoulders, he tried to get eye contact with her, but she kept her head hanging low, reflecting the shame she felt.

'Don't cry, love.' Reaching for a box of tissues on the bedside table, he tugged one out and handed it to her. 'I know you're scared for him but he's a tough little sod.'

'It's not that.'

Dropping his hands from her shoulders, he looked perplexed. 'What could be worse?'

'I'm so, so sorry,' she mumbled through the soaked tissue.

He looked faintly annoyed now. 'Sorry about what? For fuck's sake, Karen, you're scaring me now.'

With a Herculean effort, she lifted her head and

looked directly into the familiar, loving face she was about to pulverise with her confession.

'You're not Ben's biological father.'

She watched his expression morph into puzzlement, his eyes searching hers. 'What do you mean?'

'He's not yours.' She didn't know what else to say.

Sitting bolt upright, he swivelled his legs out of bed and sat with his back to her, his head in his hands. 'Is this some kind of sick joke?'

'No. It's the truth.' Bile rose in the back of her throat.

Her unequivocal words hung in the air between them. Neither spoke or moved. Eventually, Joe started to shake his head.

'I don't get it. How can he *not* be?' Twisting slightly, he looked at her from the corner of his eye. 'Are you sure?'

She nodded miserably. 'Yes.'

'How long have you known?'

Now he looked totally destroyed and she wanted to wrap her arms around him, reassure him that everything was going to be alright. But she couldn't because she knew it wasn't. The truth, however hurtful, had to be told.

'The consultant rang me after we'd left the hospital this morning.'

'The DNA tests . . .' His face drained of colour. Jumping to his feet, he ran through to the bathroom, reaching the sink just in time to retch up the last vestiges of that night's supper. Like her, he now knew the evidence was incontrovertible.

Rushing to his side, she gently placed a hand on the back of his neck. 'Are you OK?'

As soon as she made contact with his flesh, she felt him flinch, arching his body away from her. He wiped his mouth with a towel and gave her a look of raw, naked hatred. 'I'm not going to even dignify that with an answer.'

Exiting the bathroom, he walked over to their pine double wardrobe on the far side of the bedroom, his hands resting on the door handles, his head and shoulders bowed.

She leaned against the bathroom door frame, watching him and feeling helpless. 'They say anyone can be a father but it takes someone special to be a daddy.'

The snort was loud and contemptuous. 'You've just destroyed me and you're quoting some embroidered cliché from a fucking novelty cushion?'

Anxious to calm things down, she waited before answering. 'It may be a cliché, but it's true. Ben calls you dada, you *are* his daddy.'

'A fucking useless daddy who now can't help save his life,' he spat. Angry tears fell down his face and he hastily wiped them away. Yanking the wardrobe door open, he began rifling through his shirts then abruptly stopped moving, his back rising and falling with the exertion of heavy breathing.

'I told Ben everything would be OK.' His voice was so choked she could only just hear it.

'It will be. We just have to contact his . . .' She trailed off, looking uncomfortable.

Joe swivelled round with such ferocity, he had to put his hand out to steady himself. 'His *father*. That's what you were going to say, wasn't it?'

There was no point denying it, so she nodded miserably and sat down on the end of the bed with a heavy thud and even heavier heart.

'It's the one-night stand, isn't it?' His face was hard. 'Or are there any others you've forgotten to tell me about?'

'Yes.' She felt a deep, corrosive shame as she admitted to it.

'Fucking great. So *that's* why you told me, not because of any guilty moral dilemma.' His face twisted into a sneer. 'Jesus, you're a piece of work.'

'It's not like that. I didn't tell you before because it meant nothing and it would only have hurt you. You *have* to believe me,' she urged.

'Right now, Karen, I doubt I'll ever believe anything you say ever again.' Pinching the bridge of his nose with his thumb and forefinger, he looked so desolate she wanted to run over and gather him in her arms, to take the hurt away. But she was the cause of it and knew nothing she could do or say would console him.

Suddenly, the desolation turned to anger again, his eyes blazing with the injustice. 'You must have fucking *known*.'

'Truly, I didn't,' she beseeched.

'Suspected then. You'd have to be a complete moron not to. Yet all this time you watched me building a relationship with Ben and you never said one fucking word. Not *one*, Karen. What kind of mother are you?'

'I thought he was yours.' Tears were pouring down her face now and she made no effort to wipe them away.

'You mean you *wanted* to think it,' he spat. 'Because it suited your needs. Fucking hell, what a mug I've been.' He clenched and unclenched his fists, trying to resist the urge to punch a wall.

She was about to protest but he was on a roll, pacing the carpet and muttering to himself, a coiled spring of tension and anger.

'I feel like such a fucking fool,' he raged. 'Is everyone laughing at me? Am I the only fuckwit still in the dark here?' He looked at her challengingly and she started to shake her head, but then he turned away, raging again. 'Months and *months* of deceit, that takes some fucking doing.'

'The only deceit was on that one night,' she interrupted miserably. 'Nothing more.'

But again, he didn't seem to be listening, falling to his knees with a heavy thud and drawing his arms into his chest. With head bowed, he stared down at the carpet.

'Injections, transfusions, no fucking sleep for eight months, wiping arses and snotty noses, bathing cut knees,' he ranted. 'You let me do the fucking *lot* knowing he wasn't even mine.' He stayed motionless before another thought struck him and set him off again.

'Christ, my *mother*,' he raged. 'And Andy. Their lives are going to be devastated by your lies too.'

'I haven't lied,' she said quietly, knowing it was fruitless.

'What a fucking nightmare.' He looked at her with pure hatred then stood up and walked back to the wardrobe. Resting his hands on the sides of the doors, he stared ahead of him into the dark recess.

'What's his name?'

Her pulse quickened. 'It doesn't matter right now.'

She flinched as something whistled past her and landed with a loud thwack against the wall to her right. It was one of Joe's trainers, and his hand was still extended from the throw.

'It matters to *me*,' he bellowed, his eyes blazing, teeth bared. 'His fucking *name*!'

'Nick,' she fired back. 'Nick Bright.'

He froze, his expression momentarily changing to one of puzzlement. 'What, the one Tania works for?'

She nodded.

Throwing his head back, his laugh was theatrically loud and resoundingly hollow. 'You always did have delusions of grandeur. I've never been good enough for you, have I?'

'Joe, don't . . .'

She walked towards him, her hand outstretched. But he swatted her away.

'Don't *touch* me.'

Turning back to the wardrobe, he pulled down a holdall from an overhead shelf, stuffing a couple of T-shirts and jumpers inside.

She felt a swell of panic. 'You're not leaving?'

'Just watch me.'

'I know you're hurting, but please stay. Ben adores you.'

He dropped the bag to the floor for a moment and closed his eyes, his face tight with obvious distress. 'Ben, my wonderful boy. God, I love him.'

She smiled sadly through a wall of tears. 'That won't change.'

'Don't tell me what to feel,' he hissed viciously. Shooting her a murderous look, he zipped up the bag and flung it over his shoulder. 'I can only make one guarantee and it's that I will never, ever forgive you for this.'

He walked purposefully towards the door that led out on to the landing, and, she feared, out of her life.

'*Where* are you going?' she wailed.

'Away,' he spat. 'From *you*.'

Seconds later, she heard the front door slam. There was no sound of a car starting up, so wherever he was going, he'd obviously set off on foot.

Falling on to the bed, she buried her face on his

side, where the pillow smelt of him. By the time she raised her head a minute or so later, it was soaked with her tears.

Nick punched the pillow behind Stella's head, making a crevice for her to sink into. Perching on the edge of the bed, he took her hand.

'OK?'

She nodded listlessly. 'Just a little tired, that's all.'

'I'm more worried about what's going on in here.' He gently tapped the side of her head with his forefinger. 'You have to stay positive.'

That phrase again. Tears welled in her eyes. 'Sorry, but it's hard.'

He pulled her towards him and she rested her face on his chest. His fingers began idly stroking the back of her neck, sending a pleasurable shiver down her spine. Nick wasn't a particularly affectionate person, his kisses and hugs usually restricted to the bedroom and categorised as foreplay. It felt good to have him caress her like this, for no other reason than comforting her.

'I'm never going to be a mother.' She sighed rather harder than she intended.

'Come on,' he chided gently, upping the pressure on the back of her neck. 'You will.'

She wished it was that simple, a case of knowing it *would* happen if she persevered, so in the interim she could relax about it. But it had taken her five years to even get pregnant, and if it was going to prove that difficult again, it was time she didn't have.

For two years prior to getting pregnant, she'd taken to staring longingly at babies, wondering if she would ever enjoy the experience of motherhood herself, of nurturing her very own child.

'It's my age, I know it is.'

Nick sighed. 'Don't start about that again. You might have had these problems anyway.'

'We should have tried ten years ago . . . when *I* wanted to.' She knew she was going over old ground, but she couldn't help it.

'Well we didn't.' He closed his eyes in quiet frustration. 'So there's no point torturing yourself about it.'

'I should have come off the pill without telling you and had one of those happy accidents everyone talks about.' She paused and smiled wistfully at the thought. 'We'd probably have a couple of kids by now.'

'Stella, please don't . . .'

'But no. I did as I was asked . . . sacrificed my own needs and desires on the altar of my husband's ambition. Heaven forbid that a few sleepless nights might hinder the onward march of your political career . . .'

She smiled at him to show she didn't mean it bitterly, she was just sad that her golden years of opportunity to become a mother may have passed. Gazing over his shoulder, she pondered what might have been. If only she'd listened to her biological clock and ignored her husband.

He said nothing, his head bowed to the inevitability of another conversation about Stella's sacrifices.

'And now, now you actually *want* to have a child . . . your wife's ovaries have shrivelled to the size of sultanas.'

He shot to his feet. 'Stop it.' His tone was calmly firm, his face belying a quiet fury.

'Come on, lie down and get some sleep. You'll feel more positive in the morning.'

She slid under the duvet and turned away from him.

'God I hope so,' she murmured.

Head pounding, Tania winced as a sliver of morning sunlight came through the blinds and seared into her eyes. Lifting her hand to shade her brow, she squinted and waited for the room to come into focus.

When it did, she sat bolt upright. It wasn't hers. And she was naked.

Gathering the sheet around her chest, she scanned the minimalist room. There was the bed she was sitting in, one contemporary wardrobe in mahogany, a matching chest of drawers and one little side table with a photograph of two men dressed in cricket whites. One was about fifty-five with grey hair and a cheerful face, the other was . . .

'Shit!' she muttered, peering at the image of James Spender with the man who was presumably his father.

Tentatively, she glanced out of the corner of her eye at the other side of the bed. Had it been slept in? Or had he been a gentleman and taken the sofa instead? She knew the answer already because James had never been chivalrous in his life and, secondly, vague flashbacks of them ripping each other's clothes off were now seeping through the fog of her hungover brain. She closed her eyes in a vain bid to shut them out.

Noticing a dark blue towelling dressing gown hanging on the back of the door, she reached for it, careful not to make any noise. Despite the clothes-ripping flashback, she was still harbouring the faint hope of finding him fast asleep next door. After all, last night he'd shown he wasn't the unfeeling brute she'd always thought he was . . . hadn't he?

Walking out in to the narrow corridor, she turned left in to the small kitchen, her heart pumping with anxiety when she saw a fully dressed James at the window, a cup of cold, film-covered coffee on the table in front of him. She was hoping he'd turn and smile at her, make an effort to put her at ease in this strange place. But he didn't even acknowledge her presence.

'Morning,' she said brightly. 'Any chance of a cuppa?'

'Kettle's there.' He pointed towards it, but carried on looking out of the window.

Smiling fixedly, Tania flicked the switch and helped herself to a mug from the shelf. Any faint hope that the revelatory Mr Nice Guy of the previous night would have made it through till morning was starting to fade dramatically. With a creeping horror, she realised she'd been played like an old piano. Not only had he charmed her in to bed, she remembered that she'd told him Karen's secret, the one she'd promised faithfully not to divulge to anyone. She felt her neck flush with shame at the thought of such a betrayal, even if she had told him because she genuinely thought he might help.

Clutching her tea, she walked over and lingered awkwardly by his side, hoping, in vain as it turned out, that he'd invite her to sit down. On the table was a black notebook with 'Karen Eastman' underlined at the top of the page and various scribblings underneath. Proof, if she needed it, that the truth was now out there.

She let out a low groan. Noting two empty bottles of red wine on the drainer, her head throbbed excessively and she needed to sit down. In the absence of an invitation, she squeezed into the chair opposite him, but he still didn't look at her.

'You can't tell him,' she urged softly.

Finally, he looked at her, his mouth twisted with contempt. 'Just fucking watch me. This is going to ruin him.'

She felt a flutter of panic but was determined to keep her cool, knowing any sign of weakness meant James would crush her like a small bug.

'Not necessarily.'

He didn't answer, but shot her a disparaging look that suggested he thought her comment was ludicrous.

'Whatever,' she countered irritably. 'My point is that *she* should tell him, not you.'

'What, some two-bit tart he poked once after a few drinks? No fucking way,' he drawled. 'This needs serious controlling.'

'She's not a tart,' she bristled. 'She's a lovely, intelligent woman who is trying to save the life of her son, that's all.'

But James wasn't listening. He was already standing up, grabbing his mobile phone from the table and checking it for the umpteenth time.

'I'm going to walk to Westminster to clear my head. Then I'll decide what to do.' He didn't look at her as he spoke. 'In the meantime, you position yourself alongside this *intelligent* friend of yours and tell her she's to say absolutely nothing to no one until I call you. Got that?'

'You can't tell her what to do.'

He fixed her with a steely glare. 'Yes I fucking can. And I am. And if she wants any help at all on this, then I suggest she does *exactly* what I say. That goes for you too.'

Whatever the rights and wrongs of the situation, two unavoidable facts stood out for Tania. James probably had the authority to fire her for insubordination if he so chose, and besides, she needed him to get to Nick. So on that basis alone, she decided to do as he demanded.

'Yes, OK.' She knew that despite his claim to be thinking things through, his decision was already made and it was 'protect Nick at all costs'.

Watching him walk briskly out of the kitchen, a ruthlessly determined man on a mission, she knew she didn't have long.

Red-eyed and exhausted from lack of sleep, Karen was perched on the edge of the sofa, staring into space. Ben was at her feet, playing with the wooden train set they'd bought him for Christmas.

'Ma!' He looked up at her, his arms outstretched.

'What is it, pumpkin?' Bending down, she lifted him on to her knee, burying her face in his hair and inhaling his scent, a mix of banana porridge and baby oil. It was like a drug to her. She held him close, wanting to shut out the world and stay that way forever, but he became irritable and struggled to be put down.

Placing him on the floor, she studied his face. The irony was that even though the possibility he might be Nick's child had crossed her mind a couple of times since his birth, she had dismissed it because Ben looked so much like Joe. They had the same almond-shaped eyes, albeit different colours, and sandy hair, and Ben slept with one leg tucked into his chest, the same way Joe did. But now she wondered if she had imagined the similarities because she wanted to believe it herself.

Unconsciously, she let out a long sigh, but the leaden knot of despair in her chest showed no sign of dissipating. Ordinarily, pre-confession, she'd be looking forward to another night at home with Joe and Ben, predictable, yes, mundane even in parts. But familiar, comfortable, *reassuring*, all the things she valued and wanted from a marriage. If Ben wasn't ill, perhaps she and Joe might have had the occasional drunken night out, dancing until the early hours before hurrying home for a passionate fumble and waking the next day with hangovers that reminded them why they didn't do that kind of thing much anymore. She knew they were capable of going out and having fun as a couple, but their circumstances dictated otherwise. So instead they'd invariably settled for having fun at home, enjoying conversation over dinner or sharing jokes about a woeful TV show. Her heart ached at the memory of what they'd had, fearing it was now gone forever.

The sound of the doorbell disturbed her thoughts. Walking to the front window, she peered through the curtains and stiffened. It was Tania.

Deliberately keeping her expression impassive, she opened the door. 'Hello,' she said flatly.

117

'Hi.' Tania smiled sheepishly. 'And sorry. Truly, truly sorry.'

Karen had never been one to hold a grudge and her halfhearted sulkiness evaporated immediately. She grinned broadly and stepped to one side. 'Forget it. I'm sorry too. I should never have put you in that position.'

They hugged then walked through to the living room, where Tania rushed across to Ben and enveloped him in a big hug before putting him back down again. Turning to Karen, she winced. 'You told him then?'

Karen nodded miserably.

'Thought so. The bloodshot eyes and red nose are a bit of a giveaway.' She paused to stoop down and put Ben's train on the track. 'What did he say?'

Karen shrugged, biting her lip at the memory. She'd cried so much through the night she felt utterly spent. 'Not much. Then he left.'

'He must have said *something*.'

'He was baffled, hurt, angry . . . everything you'd expect really.' She blew her nose.

'And where is he now?'

'Not sure. I doubt he'd have gone to his mum's because she'd drive him mad asking questions. So probably Andy's. But I daren't call, I'm so ashamed.'

She tailed off and started to whimper. Taking her arm, Tania led her to the sofa, gesturing that she should sit down. She appeared nervous.

'I've told James Spender.'
'You've *what*?'

'He was being nice to me for a change and I was pissed. It seemed like a good idea at the time.' She had the grace to look guilty. 'But you know what? It actually might be.'

'Really?' Karen's imagination was in overdrive, trying to guess how James would handle it. None of the possible scenarios were good.

'Yes,' said Tania earnestly. 'Look, if Nick so much as goes for a shit, James is right there behind him . . . if he could he'd do a Gillian McKeith and actually inspect it. So even if I had managed to get to Nick alone he would have told James anyway.'

She paused, waiting for Karen's response but none was forthcoming. 'So I figure that confiding in him beforehand, and asking for his help, might make him a little more sympathetic to what needs to be done.'

'And has it?'

She pursed her lips. 'Hard to tell at this stage.'

Karen got to her feet and paced agitatedly back and forth. 'I have a bad feeling about this. What does he actually know?'

'That Nick is Ben's father, that Ben needs a bone-marrow transplant and that you want Nick to have a test to see if he's a close enough match.' Tania answered as if reciting a shopping list. 'That's it so far.'

Karen felt slightly mollified. 'And what did he say to all that?'

119

'That he's thinking it through and we shouldn't do anything until he contacts us.'

Karen thought about it then crouched down and stroked the top of Ben's head.

'God, I hope you've done the right thing.'

CHAPTER 8

James was sitting in Nick's office, drumming his fingers on his knee. He glanced at his watch, then the door, repeating the process several times a minute.

At 8.45 a.m. precisely, the door banged opened and Nick appeared looking distinctly pissed off, his hair still wet from the shower.

'This had better be good,' he growled. 'Stella lost the baby last night and I'm in no mood for trivial bollocks.'

James was genuinely shocked and showed it, his mouth falling open. 'God, I'm sorry. I had no idea.'

Throwing his briefcase under his desk, Nick sat in his chair with such force that it shot backwards a couple of metres. He folded his arms and scowled.

'Now what's so bloody important that it couldn't have been dealt with on the phone?' Dragging his chair closer to the front of the desk, James rested his elbows on his knees, looking intense.

'Does the name Karen Eastman mean anything to you?' He studied Nick's face for even a flicker of recognition, but there was none. He looked completely blank.

'Nope. Who is she?'

'She's an old friend of Tania Fletcher's.'

Nick concentrated for a moment, then a shadow of naked fear crossed his face. 'Jesus. She's not doing a kiss and tell is she?'

James heard the thump of the tabloids hitting the street. 'It's true then. You did sleep with her?' He sat back and rearranged his tie. 'I was hoping it was some sort of windup.'

Nick shuffled his chair forward and gave him a fixed stare. '*Is* she doing a fucking kiss and tell?'

James shook his head, prompting Nick to expel a rush of air through his nose, relief flooding his face. 'Thank Christ for that.'

'I'm afraid it's worse.'

'Worse? What do you mean?'

James hadn't mentally rehearsed this bit, so he made an on-the-spot judgement that this was no time for coy prevarication.

'She had your child.'

Nick's jaw dropped and he blinked rapidly.

'How old?' he asked, spreading his fingers on the desk as if for support.

'Between eight and nine months.'

He looked up at the ceiling, doing the maths. 'That would figure,' he mumbled.

Standing up, he turned his back to the room and stared out of the window. 'So if it's not a kiss and tell, how do you know about it?'

'Tania told me. Apparently, the boy's ill and –'

'It's a boy?' Nick interrupted, looking back over his shoulder with an interested expression.

'Yes, and apparently he has a life-threatening illness which could be cured by a bone-marrow transplant from a perfect match. She wants you to be tested.'

'I see.' He narrowed his eyes. 'How do we *know* the child's mine?'

'We don't. But if the story about the boy's illness is true . . . and Tania says it is . . . then I can't imagine the woman would be wasting time making up stories about his parentage. She must be pretty sure.'

'But how sure?' Nick scrutinised his face.

James shrugged. 'I don't know. But Tania says DNA tests have shown that the woman's husband isn't the boy's father and that you're the only man other than her husband she's slept with since she got married.'

Walking across to the bookcase, Nick stared at the rows of classic novels and political biographies, his breathing sounding laboured. Then he slammed his hand against the edge of the case. 'Fuck!'

Spinning round, he marched back to his desk where a photo of a smiling Stella had pride of place. 'Just suppose that it's proved I *am* the boy's father, what else does she want from me?'

'As far as I know, just a DNA test to see if you match,' James replied carefully. 'Then if you do, some of your bone marrow to transplant.'

'That's it?'

'So far.' James never made promises he was unsure he could keep.

Nick suddenly looked a decade older than his forty-two years, his eyes deadened by the onset of deep worry. It was the only outward sign that he had been affected by this undeniably massive shock. James found himself wondering what kind of man he worked for.

Politics was full of ambitious types who would sell their own grandmother for a place on the front benches, but Nick had struck him as being in touch with life's priorities, in particular, his marriage. For someone who adored his wife as much as he did, it was odd that he was now so unemotional about the existence of a child, *his* child, particularly as the boy was battling with a life-threatening illness. James could only conclude that the emotions were in there somewhere and Nick wasn't the type to display them in front of colleagues or strangers.

'First of all,' Nick continued quietly, 'I want you to check and check again that this woman isn't pulling a fast one. Then, *if* we find she's telling the truth, I want you to pull out all the stops to keep the lid on this.' He put his head in his hands. 'If not, we're all fucked.'

James stood up and straightened his cuffs to show he was on the case. 'Don't worry, even if it is true, we will handle it so it doesn't damage you politically.'

Nick shook his head slowly. 'I don't care about that.' He picked up the photo of Stella and tapped the glass. 'It's the potential hurt and damage to her that I'll do anything to avoid.'

Joe sat motionless in the armchair, his mug of tea untouched on the table at his elbow. Andy was on the sofa looking shellshocked.

'Jesus, what a mind-fuck. You love that kid.'

Joe nodded, overwhelmed with a pain he feared might destroy him, such was its intensity.

'Sorry I didn't tell you last night. I just couldn't face it.' He hastily wiped away a tear. He hadn't cried in front of his brother since Andy had accidentally broken his new Chopper bike when he was twelve years old.

He murmured, 'I was hoping I'd wake up this morning and find it had all been a bad dream.'

'What are you going to do?'

It was a question he'd been asking himself all night, as he'd tossed and turned on the sofa, veering wildly from intense sadness to raw anger and back again. 'I don't know. I feel like packing a bag and going on that world trip I'm always fantasising about. But I couldn't leave Ben.'

'You could leave *her* though, and see Ben whenever you wanted . . .' Andy paused, uncertain. 'If she'd let you . . .'

Joe picked up his tea but couldn't bring himself to drink any. He was sick to his stomach. 'Believe me, right now I'd like to be as far away from her as possible.' He placed the mug back on the table. 'But who'd do Ben's injections? I'm the only one who really knows how to calm him down when he's in pain.'

Tears filled his eyes again, but this time he didn't attempt to disguise them, which was a relief, albeit a small one.

'I know exactly how milky he likes his hot chocolate, I can tell what he's thinking just by looking at him, and I'm word bloody perfect on the Teletubbies.'

He smiled at the memory, rubbing his eyes which were also stinging from exhaustion. He may have nodded off for half an hour in the night, he wasn't sure, but that was all.

'So I don't think I *can* leave,' he added.

Andy walked through to the kitchen and returned with a piece of kitchen towel, handing it to him.

'I know how you feel about Ben, but what about her?'

Joe's mouth hardened. 'I hate her.'

His brother winced. 'In a love-hate way, or just hate-hate?'

'Hard to tell at this point.'

Andy raised his eyebrows and puffed out his cheeks. 'You loved her once. Sickeningly so.' He smiled encouragingly. 'Surely that has to count for something?'

He stopped speaking, hoping for a reply, but Joe had nothing to say. If he actually voiced his darkest

126

thoughts, he feared they might come back to haunt him. In his absolute lowest moment, he had even fleetingly envisaged strangling her, watching her as the life ebbed out of her eyes and she finally slumped in death.

'I always hoped I'd find a relationship like yours,' Andy continued. 'You had a real spark. I know you argued, but I thought it was because you *cared*. People think married couples who don't fight are the happiest, but I sometimes wonder if it's just because they've kind of given up on each other, have settled for safe mediocrity.'

He lay back in the sofa and extended his legs, his battered trainers centimetres from Joe's bare feet.

'It was a good marriage, mate, before it got buried under your affair and Ben's illness. If he gets better, you might find it again.'

Joe's face was wet from tears and he made no attempt to use the scrunched-up ball of kitchen towel in his hand. His brother's uncommonly perceptive view of his marriage only made the pain more intense, his feeling of loss greater.

'I have been loving . . . I *still* love,' he corrected himself, 'another man's child. I'm not sure I can ever forgive her for that.'

Nick shifted some papers from one side of his desk to the other and glanced at the clock on the far wall. It was now four p.m. and he'd spent the past few hours trying to do some work, but his mind kept wandering back to that morning's bombshell. Nursing his head in his hands, he tried to ignore the tight knot of panic in his chest.

At first, the sheer shock of hearing he had a child had numbed him to the extent that he'd gone through the bureaucratic motions with James earlier feeling nothing except an instinctive urge to try and control the situation, as if it were just another political damage-limitation exercise like the dozens they dealt with each week.

But after James had left, the force of the news had hit him like a speeding train, leaving him panting for breath, his heart racing erratically. Now he knew what a panic attack felt like, but the reasons for it weren't so easily read. He knew it was partly down to worrying about the effect on Stella, particularly given her miscarriage the previous day, and of course his political career was a factor too. But buried deep down, in an emotional place he rarely tapped into, he knew he was reeling from the discovery that he had a child.

Son, he thought. Such an emotional word to a man, and he'd often wondered about the day he would hold his for the first time and embark on his journey as a father. But he'd never imagined it like this, a child who was already several months old and whose mother he had encountered only once. That hadn't been the plan at all and he had to admit he felt cheated of his right to experience fatherhood on his own terms.

He also knew that if and when the news leaked out, there would be a huge expectation on him to 'do the right thing', as society described it, and show an interest in being part of the child's life. Whether he would or not, he pondered, would be a bridge he'd have to cross when he came to it. Right now, he felt nothing but shock and it was hard to fathom whether, buried underneath, there were any feelings for the son he hadn't even seen.

A knock at the door startled him and he sat bolt upright, anxious not to give the impression there was anything wrong.

'Come in.' It took a great effort to keep his voice steady.

James walked in and closed the door behind him.

'Oh, it's you.' Nick slumped again. 'In which case I can go back to my look of abject despair. Any news?'

'Tania finally called me back and she was at the woman's house. But the woman won't bloody see me –'

'Karen. Her name's Karen . . .' he interrupted wearily.

James shrugged, as if her name was as irrelevant as her shoe size in the grand scheme of things. 'She says she'll only speak to you.'

'Fuck.' Nick banged his hand down hard on a pile of receipts stacked on his desk. 'Still, can't blame her I suppose.'

He swivelled his chair and looked out of the window at the rain, his thoughts racing. He had never felt so out of control in his entire life, and he hated it.

'I don't want to be seen skulking around wine bars or private houses, so let's look like there's nothing to hide and get her to come here.' He turned round again and looked directly at James. 'If anyone asks, we can say she's from one of the charities I support.'

James looked as if he'd suggested they stand on the balcony of Buckingham Palace and declare their undying love for each other. 'Have you lost your fucking mind?'

Nick was irritated by this outburst. But he rapidly deduced that under the current circumstances his aide's blatant lack of respect was probably a side issue.

'Absolutely *no* way.' James made a slicing motion across his throat. 'She might have already done a deal with a tabloid and you'd be walking right into it by granting her a face-to-face meeting.'

Nick considered what he'd said, then shrugged. 'What choice do I have? If I *don't* meet her, she could go to the papers anyway. I'll have to take the risk.'

They lapsed into silence, Nick staring at the picture of Stella, James studying his shoes intently.

'Bizarre, isn't it?' mused James. 'You and Stella had such problems conceiving . . .'

'Her problems, not mine,' he replied flatly, despite his racing pulse. 'Clearly mine are the bloody SAS of the sperm world.'

★   ★   ★

'Did he *seriously* think I was going to speak to the monkey rather than the organ grinder?' Karen paced her kitchen then swivelled on her heel to look at Tania. 'And saying he wanted to verify the *story*, as he put it. The bloody cheek of it.'

Tania smiled wryly. 'That's James for you. Ever the diplomat. Far be it from me to defend him, but he's only doing the job he's paid to do.'

'He's still an arrogant shit.' Karen stopped pacing and looked anxiously at her watch, biting her lip. It was six p.m. 'He's not coming.'

She was talking about Joe. She'd thought about little else since he'd walked out the previous evening.

Tania pulled a doubting face. 'He will. What time does Ben usually have his injection?'

'About seven, but there's a routine he goes through first to try and calm him . . . you know, a bath and so on. Joe always does that because I'm usually on my way back from the surgery.'

The muted sound of a door slamming sent a shock wave of expectation through her body. Then she heard Ben shriek 'Da!' from the next room. Rigid, she looked fearfully at Tania and mouthed 'It's him.'

Seconds later, Joe walked in carrying Ben in his arms, his lips pressed against his cheeks. His eyes looked faintly puffy, with black circles under them. Seeing they had company, his expression hardened.

'No prizes for guessing what you two have been talking about.'

'She's going to help us get to Nick Bright,' said Karen earnestly. Her insides were churning with the pressure of everything she wanted to say.

'*Us?*' he replied sarcastically.

'Us. Me. Whoever,' she countered. 'We need him on side.'

He looked at her coldly. 'Well he's screwed you once. I'm sure he won't mind doing it again.'

'Joe, *please.*' She nodded towards Ben who was happily chewing the toggle on his dad's sweat-shirt.

'He's eight months old, Karen. If he knows what I'm talking about then he's a genius.'

He turned away and looked Tania directly in the eyes for the first time since entering the room.

'Your boss, my wife. Quite the little matchmaker aren't you?'

She said nothing, but looked extremely un-comfortable.

'Stop it,' said Karen angrily. 'She knew nothing about it. She's as furious with me as you are, so leave her alone.'

Joe's scowl diminished into perplexity. 'Sorry. I shouldn't have a go,' he said begrudgingly.

'Don't worry about it.' Tania gave him a weak smile. 'I think we're all feeling a little tense at the moment.'

He gave a tetchy sigh. 'Right. Now we're all *friends* again, I'll get on with what I came home to do.'

He left the room and Karen waited until she

heard the telltale creaking of floorboards above her head before sitting opposite Tania at the table and putting her head in her hands.

Through the long, restless night, she'd imagined many things she wanted to say when she saw Joe again, but the exchange that had just taken place hadn't been one of them. Although she'd felt comforted by Tania's presence earlier, she was regretting it on Joe's return, wondering if it had somehow influenced his mood or prevented him saying his piece.

She wanted to run upstairs screaming 'I'm sorry,' then cling on to him until he agreed to forgive her. But she knew Joe well enough to know that it would backfire enormously, that his anger with her was so deep-rooted that it might always be there, wrecking everything.

'What a *mess*.'

Tania reached across and placed her palm on Karen's head, trying to lift it. 'Come on, you can't fall apart now. Ben needs you.'

Karen lifted her head and nodded slowly. 'I know. But what about Joe's pain? How am I ever going to cure that?'

CHAPTER 9

Stella had managed to choose a matching bra and pants, but beyond that she was at a loss what to wear. Staring wearily into her wardrobe, all she wanted to do was wrap herself in her soft, oversized dressing gown and crawl back under the duvet, to be lost in sleep where she was protected from the thoughts that tormented her.

Hearing the creak of floorboards, she swivelled her head as Nick walked into the bedroom, his hair damp from the rain pelting down outside. He looked tense as he kissed her cheek.

'The office has just taken a call from the *Post* asking if you're pregnant. I've told them to say no.'

'Well, not anymore.' She smiled sadly.

'How do they find these things out?' He removed his shoes and threw them angrily to the corner of the room. 'It makes you wonder if they're watching every time we have a shit.'

She shrugged. 'It was probably someone from the hospital waiting room. Everyone's out to make a fast buck these days. Don't worry about it.'

Deciding she wasn't in the mood for anything

new or colourful, she pulled a favourite old black cocktail dress from the wardrobe and stepped into it. Nick sat on the end of the bed and watched her.

'I can easily go alone tonight if you don't feel up to it.'

'What?' She pulled an expression of mock horror. 'And miss out on all the other wives' scintillating conversation about the Rotary club and their latest manicure? No, we'll endure it together.'

He smiled and sighed simultaneously. 'Dreary bunch, aren't they? Luckily, *my* wife is the exception.' He walked over and stood behind her, wrapping his arms around her waist. They were both facing the mirrored wardrobe, looking at their reflections.

'You look great,' he murmured. 'But then you always do.'

She smiled in thanks. Now that Nick was a cabinet minister, he exuded the kind of power many women found compelling, and she knew he could easily attract a 'trophy wife', one several years younger than her and probably able to conceive children at the drop of a Dutch cap. But despite her age and fertility problems, and despite the fact that running off with a younger woman wouldn't bode well for her husband's political career, she knew that he stayed with her because he genuinely loved her. Through everything, she found comfort in that.

He nuzzled his head into the curve of her neck.

'Whatever happens in our lives, you do know I'm crazy about you, don't you?'

She frowned slightly, puzzled that he felt the need to justify himself. 'Of course.'

An hour later, they were working their way across the crowded function room, the consummate networking couple pressing the flesh for all they were worth. Tonight it was a 'Women Mean Business' night sponsored by several major companies and the Prime Minister had put his cabinet on a three-line whip to attend, to bolster the party's assertion that it cared about the all-important female vote.

Nick had always been in awe of Stella's ability to chat to complete strangers as if she'd known them for years. Equally, her skill at looking fascinated throughout the most dreary of anecdotes. The latter, in particular, was an art he had yet to master, often finding his gaze wandering halfway through someone's inexorably long story.

One of the hardest things about being a politician, he had decided long ago, was the expectation that you had to be nice to everyone.

It was happening now, as Stella gave the impression she was utterly spellbound by the ramblings of a large, rotund woman with bright red cheeks that clashed with her green taffeta frock. Her anecdote about her son's school seemed to have no beginning, middle or end and Nick started smiling beatifically whilst desperately searching the room for a reason to excuse himself. When it came, he was unsure whether he'd rather have stayed where he was.

'Hello, Nick.' It was *Post* reporter Jake Thompson with the trademark idle grin that masked a deadly serious, not to mention dangerous, inner core.

'Jake. What an unexpected pleasure,' he replied dryly. This man had given him many causes for displeasure in recent years, not least the recent feature headlined 'Not Very Bright' and listing, as Jake saw it, Nick's political failings.

'All mine, all mine.' Jake took a swig of his beer. 'How are things?'

Nick looked round the room distractedly, anxious not to bed in for a tête-à-tête with this man, particularly whilst Stella was otherwise engaged and not able to act as a witness to the conversation. He had been misquoted too many times.

'Dandy, just dandy.'

Moving a little closer, the journalist's voice dropped to a murmur. 'That's good to know, because we'd heard that things were a little . . .' He paused and looked over to where Stella was still talking '. . . you know, *difficult* at home.'

Nick stopped looking round the room and focussed sharply on Thompson's face, his nose just inches away from his. His heart was thumping against his ribcage. 'I don't know who told you that but it's utter bollocks,' he hissed. 'And if you print anything that even *suggests* it my lawyers will make sure you pay heavily. Clear?'

Thompson flushed, looking faintly bemused. 'Very clear indeed.'

Nick strode off, powered by the adrenalin of panic and fear. A man with a mission, he ploughed his way through the crowd, scanning every face and giving quick smiles to those trying to speak to him, but stopping for no one.

Then he saw him, leaning nonchalantly against the wall in a dark corner, chatting to a striking blonde in killer heels.

'Sorry.' Nick smiled quickly at her then turned his head and stared intently at James, desperate to convey the urgency of his purpose. 'I need to speak with you. *Alone.*' Grabbing his sleeve, he tugged him away from the woman and over to a quieter recess where the only thing lurking was a potted palm that looked in dire need of water.

'I've just spoken to Jake Thompson. He fucking *knows*,' he hissed.

'Knows what?' James looked momentarily baffled.

'About Karen Eastman.'

'He can't possibly know.' There was a flicker of mild surprise in his eyes.

Nick's mind was racing, flicking through a mental Rolodex. 'Tania?'

'No.' James shook his head. 'She wouldn't dare.' Pausing, he rubbed his chin, his brow furrowed. 'What did he say exactly?'

'That he knew things were difficult for me at home.'

'Ah.' He visibly relaxed. 'In which case, I think you'll find he's referring to Stella's miscarriage.'

Looking over his shoulder, he turned back and moved his mouth closer to Nick's ear. 'As you know, he rang earlier and asked if she was pregnant. But what I didn't tell you is that he also insinuated that they knew she'd already lost it. I think he has some contact at the clinic.'

Nick's throat tightened. 'Christ, they're not going to *print* that are they?'

'Relax! It's hardly in the public interest and besides, we denied she'd even been pregnant, remember?' James stared at him intently. 'Get a grip will you? If you don't, you're going to blow this whole thing wide open.'

Stella fell back on to the pillow, her face flushed with post-coital glow and a surfeit of white wine. She'd been abstaining from alcohol for at least a year, firstly to enhance her chances of falling pregnant, then, when she did, keeping off it for the sake of the baby. Now there *was* no baby, the few glasses she'd consumed had gone straight to her head, and she'd wanted to be close to Nick, despite her loss.

Nick tumbled off her and on to his back, reaching for the glass of water by his side of the bed. Glugging back several mouthfuls he wordlessly passed it to Stella who did the same.

'God, that was dull wasn't it?' she panted.

'Gee, thanks.'

She poked out her tongue playfully. 'The party, stupid.'

He nodded. 'Aren't they always? The collective noun for politicians and their wives should be "a drone".'

They both lay down, his arm encircling her shoulders, her head lying on his chest. His free hand idly stroked her hair.

'Nick?'

'Hmmm?' His eyes were closed.

'What if we don't ever have a child?'

'We will,' he murmured sleepily.

'But what if we don't?'

Shrugging slightly, he kissed the top of her head. 'Then we'll deal with it.'

'But will we?' She stared into space, wondering how on earth *she* was going to handle the loss of the dream she'd harboured since she was a young girl. It was different for Nick, she mused. He could seemingly take or leave having a child. She *wanted* one with a desire so strong it felt all-consuming. She was in danger of becoming a no-baby bore.

'You've always said how much you'd like a son one day,' she added, knowing she was stretching the truth slightly. What Nick had *actually* said, when pressed, was that he didn't care whether he had a boy or girl, although a son would probably enjoy it more when he dragged him off to see his beloved Man Utd play.

Nick opened his eyes, then closed them tight

shut again, looking slightly pained. She could feel his breath on the top of her head.

'If it doesn't happen then it doesn't happen,' he replied, his tone light. 'What matters most to me is having you.' He shifted slightly, indicating that he was now uncomfortable and wanted to lie down properly. 'Come on, let's get some sleep.'

She lay on her side facing him, her eyes open. Nick closed his but she could tell he was struggling to fall asleep. His eyelids were fluttering and a muscle twitched almost imperceptibly in his cheek, both symptoms of restlessness she'd seen before, the night prior to a big election.

Stella smiled sadly to herself. He's more worried about me than he's letting on, she thought, and her heart swelled with love for him. Perhaps, baby or not, it was going to be alright.

Creeping up the stairs, taking care to avoid the creaky fifth step, Karen stopped on the top landing, trying to assess where Joe was. She peered into Ben's bedroom, but it was empty, so she moved across the landing to the main bedroom.

Pushing the door gently, she peered into the half-darkness and saw a sight that made her insides hit spin cycle.

Joe was lying on his side on their bed, with Ben curved into his stomach. The boy was fast asleep but still making the involuntary gulping noises from the sobbing fit that usually followed each injection. Joe was softly stroking his wispy hair.

'Do you need anything?' she whispered into the gloom.

He shook his head and started to slowly extract his arm from under Ben's head, trying not to wake him. Then he stood up and positioned himself above the boy, scooping him into his arms in one fluid motion.

Ben stirred slightly and made a small whimpering noise, but then went quiet again, his head lolling in the crook of Joe's arm.

Karen opened the door wide so they could walk through. When Joe emerged into the slightly brighter light of the landing, she could see the flesh around his eyes was red and swollen.

He laid Ben in his cot and gently pulled the door so it was almost closed, peering through the gap for a last-minute check. When he'd established all was quiet, he finally spoke, his eyes looking everywhere but at her.

'Has Tania gone?'

'Yes. About half an hour ago.'

'I'll do his bottle for later,' he said, his foot already on the first stair.

Watching him walk away, she had no idea if he was staying at home tonight or disappearing back to Andy's. All she knew was that she *wanted* him to stay and try to work things through. The alternative was too frightening to contemplate.

With her ear cocked for any sign that he had returned upstairs, she spent the next ten minutes pottering around the bedroom, trying to busy herself. Perhaps, she thought, if I behave as if nothing has happened, it will become a self-fulfilling prophecy and we'll just slip back in to normality. She knew it was unlikely but it didn't stop her hoping.

Sitting on the bed fully clothed, she extended her legs in front of her and started reading a book. Well, holding a book whilst the words swam across the page in front of her. Her heart-rate quickened as she heard the telltale creak of the fifth stair then the bathroom light click on and its interminably humming fan.

After a while she heard the loo flush and the door open. The fan stopped whirring but her mind started. She felt as apprehensive as a Victorian virgin on her wedding night. Not wishing to appear anxious, she stared studiously at the page in front of her, in preparation for when he entered the bedroom. But after several seconds had passed, she gave up and stared blatantly at the door, willing it to open whilst straining to hear any noise outside.

After a couple of minutes, it became clear he wasn't coming. She toyed with the idea of just settling down for the night and worrying about it in the morning, but she *had* to investigate, knowing otherwise she wouldn't sleep a wink.

Padding quietly across the carpet, she peered out on to the landing. The bathroom was in darkness and Ben's door was as they'd left it, so her eyes moved to the door of the spare room where a small put-me-up bed wrestled for space with the interminable amount of junk they both hoarded in the unrealistic expectation that one day it might just come in handy.

She poked her head around the door but could only make out the indeterminate swell of various pieces of stored furniture, with old suitcases stacked on top. Flicking on the light switch, she was greeted by the sight of Joe lying on the camp bed with his back to her. He squinted over his shoulder.

'Isn't it a bit early for sleep?' she asked meekly.

'I'm exhausted.'

'Oh.' She felt the flutter of a palpitation in her chest. 'Why are you in here?'

'You work it out.' His voice was cold.

'We should try to keep things normal for Ben.' She knew it was the only straw she had to clutch at.

'He's a baby. He doesn't think like that.' He turned back to face the wall, as if to indicate the conversation was over.

'So you're staying here then?'

'Yep,' came the muffled reply.

'Can't we at least talk?'

'There's nothing I want to say. Or hear.'

Fighting back tears, she switched off the light and returned to the lonely expanse of their marital bed.

CHAPTER 10

James was in danger of wearing a hole in the carpet as he paced up and down, brow furrowed, Montblanc pen jabbing the air every time he made a point. 'I have a bad feeling about this.'

'So you've said. *Many* times now,' replied Nick wearily. 'I take full responsibility for inviting her here and whatever happens afterwards. Does that make you feel better?'

'No, not really. But she's on her way and there's nothing I can do about it now, so let's deal with it.' He let out a critical tut-tut. 'Right. She's made it quite clear that it's to be just you and her . . . though quite why she feels she can call the fucking shots is beyond me.'

Walking over to Nick's desk, he pulled out the top drawer to reveal a state-of-the-art digital recording machine. 'So I'm recording the conversation to be on the safe side.' He pushed the drawer in, leaving a one-inch gap.

'Be pleasant as we don't want to rub her up the wrong way, but not over-friendly as we don't want her to think you're going to be popping round for Sunday lunches *en famille*.'

He started pacing again whilst Nick sat motionless. He still couldn't believe it was happening, it all felt so surreal.

'Just listen to what she has to say and for Christ's sake don't admit *anything*. If she even mentions that you once had a cup of tea together, don't corroborate it.'

'We didn't anyway.'

'What?' snapped James.

'Have tea. It was the euphemistic coffee.' He made quote marks with his fingers.

James shot him a look of naked irritation. 'You had fuck all, euphemistic or otherwise. Got it?'

Nick nodded his agreement, deducing that trying to lighten the sombre mood was not the route to go with his in-a-spin doctor right now. He jumped as the buzzer sounded on his phone and his PA's voice crackled: 'A Mrs Eastman is here. She says you're expecting her?'

James stopped pacing and stood directly in front of the desk, staring intently at his boss. 'Right. All set?' His sense of gravitas suggested they were about to attempt a moon landing.

'Yes.' He felt overcome by a sense of fatigue but knew it had to be done. 'Send her in.'

Nodding, James left the room, closing the door gently behind him. Nick placed his elbows on the desk and put his head in his hands, peering through his fingers at the photo of Stella. All he could think about was her desperation to have a baby. Mother Nature can be a cruel bitch, he thought bitterly.

There was a tap at the door and his chest pounded with apprehension. Straightening his back, he smoothed his tie and tried to look as unruffled as possible.

'Come in.'

He remembered her instantly. She was still attractive, with her dark blonde hair and heart-shaped face, but the wide-set pale blue eyes that had once flirted so briefly with him now looked haunted. Whether it was because of the conversation that was about to take place or having a sick child, he didn't know.

'Hello again.' She gave him an uncertain smile.

He was careful not to return it, merely gesturing towards the chair in front of his desk, his expression non-committal. 'Please. Sit down.'

Settling herself on the chair, she clutched her handbag to her stomach as if her life depended on it. Her back was ramrod straight, like a particularly nervous job interviewee.

'So what can I do for you?' he asked lightly.

She looked thrown. 'I thought James had told you?'

'Vaguely. But it all sounds rather far-fetched. I need to hear more detail.'

'*Far-fetched*?' She scowled, leaning forward as if she hadn't heard correctly. 'I can assure you, Mr Bright, that my son's illness is horribly real.'

Her formality took him by surprise, considering

their history. The memory of her naked breasts flashed across his mind and he examined Stella's photograph until he regained control.

'I wasn't referring to his illness.'

'Ah.' She raised an eyebrow. 'You mean his paternity?'

He nodded but said nothing. Feeling like a prize shit, he didn't trust himself to.

'The DNA tests prove my husband isn't Ben's father, and you . . .' she looked him straight in the eye '. . . are the only other man I've had sex with. You work it out.'

'I don't remember,' he lied, his mind filling again with thoughts of their passionate encounter. He shifted uncomfortably in his chair as he felt his penis stiffen.

'We weren't *that* drunk,' she said derisively.

Again, Nick said nothing, leaning back in his chair and slowly rotating his thumbs. When the silence became unbearable, he looked up as enlightenment filled her face. 'Oh, I get it. You've been told by that slimeball . . .' she jerked her head over her shoulder to the outer office '. . . not to admit anything in case I'm taping you. Haven't you?'

'Don't be ridiculous.' He did his best to look misjudged.

'Well let me put your mind at rest . . .'

Standing, she dropped her handbag on to his desk and pointed at it. 'Feel free. You'll find nothing.'

Then she started to unbutton her pink cotton shirt.

Now he was on his feet, feeling distinctly uncomfortable. Instinctively, he looked over his shoulder to the window, half expecting a line of paparazzi lenses trained on him, momentarily forgetting his was a third-floor office.

'What the hell are you doing?'

She continued to undo her buttons, slipping off her shirt and letting it fall to the ground. Taking a couple of steps forward she stood in front of his desk, dressed only in bra and jeans. 'No wires.'

Never taking her eyes from his face, she started to undo her jeans as Nick simultaneously lunged forward, his arm extended in a 'Stop' gesture. 'Don't. *Please.*'

She considered what he'd said then stooped down to pick up her shirt, slowly putting it back on. 'It's nothing you've not seen before.' She sat back down on the chair, but left her handbag on the desk.

Nick sighed resignedly. 'OK, I *do* remember that night . . .'

She looked relieved.

'. . . but it was a drunken mistake . . . on *both* our parts,' he added hastily. 'I thought you were on the pill.'

'You mean you *assumed.*'

He felt irritated and showed it, his face hardening. He hated all this feminist shit, being of the opinion that a woman who didn't want to get pregnant should be the one to ensure it didn't happen. Not that he'd ever dare air such views in a press interview.

'Alright, I *assumed* that an intelligent, married woman having a one-night stand might take precautions.'

'And what about an intelligent, married man?' she countered quickly.

He felt out of control again, a state he didn't like one little bit. It took him back to his school years, when he'd been forced to swim in the icy depths of the outside pool, with no say in decisions relating directly to him.

An awkward silence descended. Nick could hear the subdued sound of the busy office outside and would have done anything to be out there, just an ordinary, anonymous worker for whom damage limitation wasn't a priority. He let out a loud sigh that would have left her in no doubt he was tiring of her presence.

'So what do you want from me?'

She tucked her hair behind her ears and shifted in her seat. 'A DNA test.' The words came out as if she'd just asked to borrow a pen.

'Is that it?'

It sounded innocuous enough and, more to the point, he mused, something that could probably be achieved anonymously and kept out of the papers.

'For starters, yes. Then if you match we'd need some of your bone marrow. You'd be in hospital overnight at the most . . .'

150

His mind raced. It was still manageable, though less so. 'And if I don't match?'

Now she looked transparently nervous. 'Then pre-implantation genetic diagnosis is the only option.'

'English please . . .' he scowled. He might be Health Secretary but most procedures beyond a tonsillectomy were beyond him.

'You'll probably know it as a designer baby.'

He looked at her intently, computing the information. Then it registered. 'Absolutely *no* fucking way. Not ever.' He leapt to his feet and started pacing the floor behind his desk. 'No, no, no.'

Karen remained seated but looked at him beseechingly. 'He's in terrible pain a lot of the time . . .'

Shaking his head in despair, all he could think about was having to tell Stella and how she might react. 'Sounds like a no-brainer doesn't it?' he muttered bitterly. 'Just do this medical procedure and you can save a young boy's life.' He stared out of the window, his back to her. 'But now you're asking me to have *another* child with you . . . on top of the one I didn't even know about in the first place.'

James hadn't mentioned this and Nick could only assume it was because Tania hadn't told him in the fearful assumption he would block all paths to his boss.

'He's still a baby yet he has to be injected in his stomach nearly every night. If you agree to this,'

151

she pleaded softly but urgently, 'then there's a chance he can have a normal life.'

Nick felt a swell of anger and spun round to face her. 'My wife has recently miscarried . . . we'd been trying for five years.'

She looked as if she was about to reply, but he talked over her, desperate to make this go away. 'This would destroy her. Not to mention my political career.'

There was a fleeting flash of sympathy in her eyes, and he felt a surge of hope. But it was gone almost as soon as it appeared, replaced by a look of persistent determination.

'I know it's a lot to ask, but perhaps your upset over the miscarriage will help you understand how desperate *I* feel about my son.'

Rummaging in her handbag, she pulled something out and held it up to him. He could see it was a photograph of a smiling blond child. His heart lurched slightly, but he convinced himself it was a symptom of panic rather than emotion.

'Look at him,' she urged.

'No thanks. This is hard enough.' He closed his eyes tight shut, determined not to become emotionally involved, even on the smallest level. Looking at the photograph would mean showing an interest, which would then inevitably lead to a conversation about the boy and, before he knew it, an agreement to take him to the park on Sundays. It was easier for him if he blocked all attempts to engage.

She stayed where she was, with the picture face upwards, so he spanned one hand across his forehead with two objectives. He couldn't see the child and she couldn't see his eyes.

'Look, I understand how difficult all this must be for you,' she persisted. 'And truly, I'm not here to make trouble, I only want to save my son. I'll sign whatever you want . . . a contract saying I promise we'll never contact you again, never ask for money . . . that sort of thing. Whatever it takes to get you to help us.'

He heard her open her handbag and, from the corner of his eye, saw her put the photograph away.

'I don't see how you can refuse,' she added ominously.

He removed his hand and glumly stared at it. What she said was true: he was damned if he did and damned if he didn't. There was every chance Karen could expose him and, besides, he wasn't sure if he could live with himself if he didn't help. Lifting his chin, he looked directly at the virtual stranger who had his balls in her hand for the second time.

'I'll do the DNA test. I'm not promising anything else.'

Tania watched James as he walked back and forth to Nick's office, occasionally lingering a little too long by the door.

'You won't hear anything,' she said. 'God knows

153

I've tried enough times when you two have been hatching plots.'

He glared at her, unsure whether she was joking.

'Sit down,' she frowned. 'You're making me nervous. Besides, you can always listen to the tape afterwards.'

'What tape?' He knew she didn't have to be a behavioural expert to know he was being disingenuous.

'Oh please, don't pretend you're not recording every word in there. That really would be pathetic.'

'What do you take me for?' He affected a wounded expression, but secretly he was rather pleased she seemed to have returned to their old ground of barbed banter.

He'd felt horribly awkward waking up next to her the other morning, quietly creeping off to the kitchen to deal with one problem, leaving the other one sleeping peacefully. Alcohol and subsequently lust had got the better of him and he feared their brief intimacy might change their working relationship forever, perhaps forcing him to consider transferring her to another department. But now, he thought with relief, that might not be necessary.

'I take you for a duplicitous, Machiavellian, scheming toad. Have I missed anything out?' she demanded.

Hovering by Nick's office, he was about to answer her when the door opened. He sprang to attention looking for all the world as if he'd had a glass pressed to the wall the entire time.

154

'Karen!' he boomed, with all the enthusiasm of someone meeting a long lost relative at Heathrow. 'How did it go?'

She ignored him, walking straight to Tania's desk, puffing out her cheeks. 'That was tough, but he's agreed to the test.'

James made a spluttering noise. Surely Nick hadn't been so bloody stupid?

'Don't be ridiculous,' he said lamely but, deep in whispered conversation, neither of them were listening to him.

Without knocking, he strode purposefully into the office where Nick was still sitting at his desk, his face expressionless.

'Ah James, to what do I owe the pleasure?' he said dryly.

'Please tell me she's taking the piss.' He knew she wasn't but he needed to hear it from the ass's mouth. That was the trouble with bloody politicians, he thought mutinously, they never did as they're bloody told.

'If you're referring to the DNA test, what choice did I have?'

'Complete fucking denial, like I told you.'

Nick yawned, clearly wearied by James's relentless aggression towards anyone or anything that he perceived might get in the way of politics. But as James saw it, he was paid to guide and protect Nick, come what may.

'She's a decent woman, and I do have *some* responsibility.' Nick opened the desk drawer that housed the digital tape recorder and hit the delete button. 'This really isn't necessary.'

James slumped on to the chair Karen had sat on just minutes earlier, his head in his hands.

'Jesus Christ,' he muttered. 'Game over.'

CHAPTER 11

Joe walked back across from the window and sat next to his mother on her cream damask sofa, placing a reassuring arm round her shoulders and drawing her in to him. He handed her a crumpled, slightly dusty tissue extracted from his sleeve.

'It's clean.'

Gloria took it and dabbed her eyes, but they filled with tears again almost immediately.

'I don't believe it,' she sobbed. 'First his illness, and now . . . now, *this*.'

He'd waited until after lunch to tell her about Ben, not wishing to spoil the effort she'd made with a home-made fish pie. Then there'd been the vanilla ice-cream with chocolate sprinkles to sit through, Ben's favourite, before they'd adjourned to the sitting area and he'd come straight out with it.

'Karen told me that I'm not Ben's biological father.'

At first, she'd seemed to take it well, but he now realised she had probably been in shock. She'd asked a succession of matter-of-fact questions about the finer details of when Karen had told him, how long she'd known, how did he feel and what had been the circumstances of Ben's conception. When Joe had answered 'one-night stand' her lip had curled in abject disgust. Now, an hour or so later, she'd run the gamut of emotions and settled on distraught.

His thoughts were interrupted by the sound of her blowing her nose loudly. 'This would have killed your father.'

Behind her back, he rolled his eyes wearily. 'He's been dead eight years.'

But his mother was off again, wailing gently. Whether it was in memory of her husband Roger or the news about Ben, he wasn't sure.

Gloria and Roger's marriage had been a tumultuous one which, in more modern times, would probably have ended up in the divorce courts. They put up an appearance for the outside world of being a typical married couple, but behind closed doors the reality was sharply different, and Joe and Andy had frequently felt impaled by it.

Roger was an enthusiastic drinker, always had been. But the witty, gregarious man who had first attracted Gloria when they were in their early twenties had descended into a bitter middle-aged curmudgeon who felt life had passed him by and who sought solace in the best part of a bottle of vodka a day. Consequently, his health suffered, making him even more miserable.

When Joe and Andy were young, they had

adored the father who would often arrive home late, in a flurry of activity, bearing little gifts for them. They'd always assumed he'd been working late at the office, striving to provide for his family. But once they became adults, they'd realised during several brotherly pub confessionals that his generosity to them had been a weapon against their mother, invariably furious because he was returning from yet another all-afternoon drinking session in the local pub, rather than selling the insurance policies they needed the commission from to pay next month's rent. But with her boys grinning so broadly at the sight of their father, how *could* she spoil the atmosphere by starting an argument?

Watching her now, sobbing on the sofa and looking every one of her sixty-five years, Joe realised how difficult it must have been for her, bringing up two young boys and getting so little emotional support from her husband. He loved his mother dearly, but there had been many times in recent years when he'd wanted to tell her to lighten up and enjoy life, to go with the flow. But he knew that the years of coping with a difficult marriage had taken their toll and losing the residual inner misery was easier said than done.

He wondered if Gloria would still be with Roger had he survived this long. After all, once he and Andy had left home, there'd have been no reason to stay. Society didn't exactly frown on divorce anymore.

As it was, she'd come home from the supermarket one day to find Roger lying in his own vomit on the bathroom floor. He was so drunk he'd fallen and cracked his head on the toilet bowl.

The hospital said he'd died of a head injury, but the coroner pointed out that cirrhosis of the liver was well advanced and would have killed him before long anyway.

For Gloria, it had almost been a release. She could play the grieving widow to great effect, without, as she saw it, losing her respectability through divorce.

She'd told Joe she was looking forward to moving on with her life, exploring countries she'd always wanted to visit but Roger had been reluctant to accompany her to.

But as the months and then years had progressed, little had changed about her routine, with the exception of moving house. Every time Joe had suggested she go abroad, she'd found excuses not to. Eventually, he'd surmised that perhaps Roger hadn't stopped her doing anything and that her dreams had been just that . . . dreams.

Over time, she even started romanticising the marriage, describing a husband that no one who knew him in life would have recognised. It was as if she'd deliberately chosen to forget Roger's shortcomings so she wouldn't have to admit to herself, or anyone else, that her marriage had been a failure.

So when Ben had been born, Gloria had thrown herself wholeheartedly into the role of doting grandmother, filling the imagined void left by her long-dead husband. She often commented to Joe how Ben was so like his grandfather, an observation that seemed fanciful now.

She placed a hand on Joe's forearm. 'You adored that little chap.'

He smiled and looked across at Ben who was playing with some building bricks. 'I still do. My feelings haven't changed . . . and neither should yours.'

She didn't answer the question, looking past him towards a walnut bureau covered in family portraits.

'I rewrote my will the other day.' Her voice was small. 'And one of my requests was that my gravestone be inscribed with the word "Grandma".'

She dabbed her eyes again, though there were no tears this time. In fact, her face had clouded. 'You must hate her.'

'I don't like her too much right now, but hate her? No.' He sighed deeply. 'After all, if you think about it rationally, she stuck with me after my affair, and all she had was a one-night stand . . .'

'And another man's *baby*,' she whispered under her breath.

He winced. 'Yes, that's the bit I'm struggling with.'

An awkward pause kicked in. Then Gloria stood up, smoothed down her skirt and walked across

161

to the dining table, opening a small drawer in one end of it. Pulling out a large buff envelope, she folded it in half and held it out to him.

Joe didn't open it, simply looked at her quizzically.

'I remortgaged the house,' she explained. 'House prices have risen quite a bit in the past couple of years so there's a lot of money sitting in it . . .' She trailed off, smiling ruefully. 'There's ten thousand pounds in there, my contribution to Ben's medical bills.'

Her eyes filled with tears again. 'What you've just told me makes no difference. Use it . . . please.'

He walked across to where she was standing and wrapped his arms around her, pulling her so close he could smell the faint vestiges of that morning's Yardley Rose, the perfume she'd worn for as long as he could remember. They hadn't embraced like this for at least ten years and, at first, he felt his mother tense up. But then she relaxed and they stood there, saying nothing but holding on to each other for comfort.

Eventually, he broke away and tucked the envelope under his arm.

'Thanks,' he whispered. He felt dreadful accepting money from her.

'It's not like I need it.' It was as if she'd read his mind. 'What am I going to spend it on . . . gambling and nightclubbing?'

She smiled but her eyes still looked sad. 'So.' She closed the drawer and brushed away a speck of dust from the tabletop. 'Who *is* Ben's biological father and how on earth are you going to find him?'

Joe flinched slightly. 'We won't have to look far. It's Nick Bright, the Health Secretary.'

Tania stood in front of the cracked mirror in the office toilets and placed a palm on her forehead. It felt clammy. She'd had a slight headache all morning; even the thought of her usual almond croissant made her feel nauseous.

'Shit!' she muttered aloud, confident all the cubicles were empty. Aside from eating a dodgy prawn the night before, which she hadn't, there was only one thing she associated with morning sickness.

Please God, she thought, don't let me be pregnant. Not only was she not ready for such a life-changing event, but the thought that James would be the father was enough to heighten her feeling of nausea.

Despite the surfeit of alcohol they'd consumed that night, she remembered that he'd used a condom and the thought reassured her now. Perhaps she was just feeling generally exhausted.

Throwing cold water on her face, she widened her eyes and gently slapped her cheeks a couple of times, trying to bring some colour back. Then she walked back out in to the corridor and through to the hum of the office, slipping back behind her desk unnoticed. Or so she thought.

'Ah, Fletcher,' boomed James from several metres away. 'So glad you could join us.'

'I've just been to the bloody loo,' she hissed furiously. 'Surely even someone as dedicated to their job as *you* has to answer the call of nature.'

He ignored her, fussing around his desk and picking up various documents, officiously sorting them in to some sort of order. James was a past master of what Tania called 'presenteeism'. He was always in the office, making lots of noise so everyone knew he was there, but it was unclear whether he actually got any more done than someone who worked quietly from nine to five. James filled his day with plotting, subplots, networking and generally knowing everyone else's business.

If he put as much effort into his own job as he did monitoring everyone else's comings and goings, his productivity would be doubled, she thought mutinously, though in fairness she acknowledged his effectiveness in protecting Nick was 100 per cent. So far.

Since their night together, any faint assumption she'd had that, consequently, their working relationship might improve slightly had been dashed. If anything, his obvious awkwardness over what had happened between them had made him even more bullish and unpleasant than before. Neither of them had broached the subject, but the fact he visibly bristled whenever he saw her made it clear he harboured no desire to repeat the experience, which was fine by her.

'Right.' He was standing in front of her desk now, clutching a piece of paper to his chest proprietorially. 'Come on. Nick's office pronto.'

His tone made her feel uneasy, as if she was about to be fired for some imagined misdemeanour. Then she remembered that they needed her on board right now, as a close link to Karen. After that, however, she knew it was back to job uncertainty again.

Nick was on the phone when they walked in to his office. As Tania closed the door behind them, he pressed his finger to his lips, indicating they shouldn't make a noise.

'I know, I'm sorry darling, but there's no way round it,' he said, the receiver cupped between his cheek and shoulder. 'The meeting shouldn't take too long then I'll be home as quick as I can. Love you. Bye.'

'God, I hate lying to her.' He slammed his fist down on the desk.

Tania thought about uttering a platitude, but came to the conclusion she might get her head bitten off, so kept quiet. James moved forward, holding out the piece of paper he'd brought in.

'It's a medical history thing. You need to fill it out before the doctor gets here.'

Nick stared at it. 'Nick Burton?'

'False name,' James replied briskly. 'The sample has to go off to a clinic so we can't be too careful.'

Tania nodded solemnly, as if she knew what the hell everyone was talking about. James, with his customary man-management skills, hadn't bothered to tell her. So far, she'd deduced that a doctor was coming in to get Nick's sample for DNA testing, but still wasn't sure why she had been dragged into the room by James.

'Now then,' he intoned, doing a Wimbledon spectator routine from her to Nick and back again. 'Outside of Karen Eastman and whoever she chooses to tell . . . something I *can't* control . . . we are the only three people that know what's really going on here.' He stopped moving his head and stared directly at Tania. 'So if I hear the faintest whisper even *alluding* to it in the office, I'll hold you personally responsible.'

'Me?' Aghast, she slapped her palm against her chest. 'I can assure you that, other than telling you so you could discuss it with Nick, I'll be saying nothing to anyone. What about *you*?' She stared back at him pointedly.

'Don't be ridiculous,' he replied dismissively, turning back to Nick and raising his eyes heavenward. 'Now then, back to business. The doctor will be here in about half an hour. If anyone asks, he's been told to say you've asked him to collaborate on a forthcoming report about stem-cell research.'

'Ah, another person who knows the truth. Have you given him your little speech?' She raised a questioning eyebrow.

'He's a private doctor with very high-profile clients, so he's watertight. Plus he's signed the Hippocratic oath.'

As opposed to the hypocritical one of politics, she thought to herself.

'By the way, how many people has Karen told?' Nick asked her.

She shrugged. 'As far as I know, no one apart from her husband.'

Nick stiffened. 'How did he react?'

'As you might expect. He was devastated.'

He nodded solemnly and cleared his throat. 'Look, I don't want to put you in an awkward situation, but if you *could* have a quiet word with them and ask if they could keep it to themselves, it would be much appreciated.'

He paused and sighed, a little melodramatically she felt. 'I really want to help them, but it will be so much harder if it gets out. Do you understand?'

Tania nodded compliantly but had absolutely no intention of even mentioning this conversation to Karen and Joe. Who they chose to tell was their business, and she knew that even suggesting they keep quiet would only worsen what was already an inflammatory situation.

Nick opened his mouth to say something else, but was interrupted by the sound of James's hands clapping together. 'Right, let's get this show on the road. Fill out the form . . .' he tapped the questionnaire on Nick's desk '. . . and I'll get it in a sealed envelope as soon as possible. Then all you have to do is the sample and that, hopefully, will be the end of the matter.'

Nick put his head in his hands. 'Jesus, could my life *get* any worse?'

CHAPTER 12

'Choo choo! Oh no! Mind out of the way, I'm going to craaaaaash!' Joe rolled over on to his back, lifting the toy train into the air and bringing it down again to the floor with a thump. Ben shrieked with delight.

Karen watched them both with a sad smile. Joe was as much in love with Ben as ever, but his attitude to her had changed markedly. He put on a good show of being friendly in front of their son, but alone it was a different story. He wasn't blatantly hostile, just cold and seemingly scathing of everything she said. She didn't blame him. Right now, she probably hated herself even more than he did.

She had spent hours now worrying about when to tell him about her meeting with Nick Bright, whether to tell him beforehand, whether to tell him last night. But in the event, he'd put Ben to bed then shut himself in the bathroom for an hour, before announcing he was going to watch a movie on the small portable TV in the spare room.

The irony didn't escape her that whilst she was having yet another sleepless night worrying about her crumbling marriage, he was watching *Love Story* a few metres away. So she'd left it until now to broach the thorny subject of Nick Bright. Opening her mouth to speak, the words wouldn't come out. She had played it over in her head so many times she felt she was going mad with the stress.

'I went to see Nick Bright yesterday,' she blurted suddenly, studying his face closely for a reaction.

'Really?' His tone was indifferent but his expression told another story. A muscle in his cheek twitched sporadically. 'Why didn't you tell me you were going?'

Because you've shut me out, she wanted to scream. 'I thought it might upset you.'

'Bit late for that,' he countered derisively, replacing the train on the track in front of Ben.

She decided to let the remark pass. 'He's agreed to do the DNA test.'

She saw Joe's chest rise and fall as he let out an almost imperceptible sigh of what she guessed was relief. Shifting sideways so he was closer to Ben, he lifted the boy's T-shirt to reveal the angry red mark where the needle went in every night. Studying it, his face was tight with contained emotion.

'And what about the implantation? Has he agreed to that if it comes to it?'

'Not yet. He wants to take it one step at a time.'

'Does he now?' He snorted. 'I wouldn't have said he's in any position to call the shots.'

She shrugged philosophically. 'Unfortunately, we need him. But he needs us like a hole in the head.'

Letting Ben's shirt drop, Joe stood up and walked across to the sideboard where a hammer and spirit level lay and picked them up. 'I'm going to finish that bookcase in his room.'

'Thanks.' She attempted a weak smile.

'You don't have to thank me. He's my son.' His tone was brittle.

Frowning slightly, she sighed with exasperation, tired of walking on eggshells. 'I didn't mean it like that.'

He started to walk past her towards the hallway door, but her hand rested on his arm, urging him to wait a moment.

'I'm sorry, Joe, I really am. But I don't know what to do to take away your pain.' She noticed he had at least stopped walking, but his body was still facing forwards, his face set hard.

'I know you're hurting like hell, but I didn't plan it this way. I wish Ben was yours. I *thought* he was . . .'

She looked at him plaintively, but he didn't betray any emotion, simply moving his arm away from her grasp.

'We have to find some way of dealing with this,' she continued. 'I know Ben's young but children can sense when there's an atmosphere.' She knew any plea on her own part would fall on stony ground.

Joe held up the hammer and she instinctively flinched. 'As I said, I have a bookcase to attend to.'

He left the room, leaving Karen staring rigidly at the empty door frame.

Nick was looking in Stella's direction but not really focusing on her. She was sitting in the chair opposite his desk, rummaging through her vast handbag and muttering something about her lost glasses.

He glanced at his in-tray and winced. He had so much work to get through that even the thought of it induced a small panic attack, but his mind kept coming back to the damned DNA test and its possible impact on his future. Instinctively, he knew already that Karen wasn't lying about her son's parentage and the child *was* his, but it was the possible stages beyond that were causing him sleepless nights. If he was a perfect match, he pondered, then there was a faint chance he could get away with giving bone marrow without Stella ever knowing, assuming he went into a private hospital under cover of darkness and was tended to only by senior staff working under a strict confidentiality clause.

But preimplantation genetic diagnosis? Not a chance. Too many complications, too many people involved. He felt sick again. Stella's voice made him start.

'It's your mother's birthday next weekend so I thought I'd get her a cashmere scarf.'

Nick read some documents on his desk, the words swimming before him. 'Great.'

'I think I'll just go straight to Harrods and be done with it.'

'Great.'

'And then I thought I'd jump under a bus.'

'Lovely.'

'Nick! You're not listening to me . . .'

He smiled weakly. 'I'm teasing. You said you were going to jump under a bus.'

There was a loud knock at the door. Without waiting for an answer, James strode in but stopped in his tracks as he saw Stella.

'Oh sorry, I didn't realise . . .'

'Don't worry, I was just leaving.' She stood up and blew a kiss in Nick's direction. 'Bye darling.'

She didn't attempt to even shake hands with James, a man she had made it clear to Nick that she loathed. A casual 'Bye' in passing was all she could muster.

James smiled stiffly, waiting until she was out of sight then closing the door gently. He looked apprehensive. 'That doctor's holding on line two.'

Bile rose in Nick's throat. Gulping it back down, he took a couple of long, deep breaths. 'Sit down.'

James did as he was told, watching Nick's face as he held the receiver and listened to the voice on the other end.

'OK, thank you,' he said finally, ending the call and staring disconsolately at the phone. 'I'm not a good enough match.' His voice was so quiet it was barely audible.

James leaned forward, his elbows resting on his knees. 'But you *are* the boy's father?'

Nick nodded, his face impassive for a couple of seconds. Then he let out a frustrated gasp and put his head in his hands, rolling it from side to side.

'Christ, what a fucking nightmare.'

Karen stared out at the dark evening sky then pulled the living-room curtains close, shielding herself from the outside world. Right now, she felt she could easily never leave the house again, comforted by its warmth and familiarity.

Returning to the sofa, she kicked off her shoes and put her feet up, reaching down to pick up the bowl of microwave popcorn she'd made. Joe was out, she hadn't dared ask where, and she planned to make the most of it by watching one of the weepy old movies she recorded frequently but never seemed to get round to watching. She needed the excuse to have a damn good cry without it being obviously self-pitying for the mess she'd brought on herself.

Just as she picked up the remote, the doorbell chimed and she let out a grunt of frustration. She wasn't expecting anyone so she stayed where she was, assuming it was yet another of the ubiquitous dishcloth salesmen who seemed to turn up every other night. How much washing-up could one woman do?

The doorbell rang again, more prolonged this time. Whoever it was clearly wasn't giving up easily and another bout of noise could wake Ben. Huffing, she hauled herself up from the sofa and walked into the hallway, opening the door with a glare.

'Hello.' It was Gloria.

Her glare weakened to a slight frown. 'Joe's not here.'

'I know. I've come to see you.'

'Oh.' Karen's shoulders visibly slumped as she saw her precious 'me time' evaporate. From past experience, it was now going to be Gloria's 'me me me' time.

'Tea?' she said over her shoulder, walking back into the living room with a heavy heart and switching off the old movie that hadn't even made it past the opening credits.

'No thanks.' Gloria's expression suggested she thought her daughter-in-law might poison it.

She sat down on the sofa, exactly where Karen had been languishing just two minutes earlier and glanced down at the bowl of popcorn.

'My little treat,' Karen explained, marvelling how her mother-in-law managed to make her feel guilty for even *trying* to enjoy herself.

Gloria pursed her lips disapprovingly. 'Is it microwave popcorn?'

'Yes.'

'Then it's stuffed full of trans-fats. You really shouldn't you know.'

Because Gloria had little else in her life, she was an avid viewer of daytime television. Consequently, there wasn't much she didn't know about diet, exercise, fashion, flower arranging, medical matters and every other subject so tirelessly covered by mid-morning magazine shows.

'I'll bear it in mind,' said Karen stiffly. 'Anyway, nice to see you!' she added in a let's-move-on-shall-we tone, anxious to get on with the bollocking she suspected was coming. Gloria wasn't given to popping in for little apropos-of-nothing chats.

'I thought you'd come and explain yourself . . .' She made a coughing noise, a symptom of her obvious discomfort.

Karen sat down, a tetchily bemused expression on her face. 'To *you*?'

'He's my grandson . . . or was,' she faltered. 'Surely I deserve some sort of explanation?'

'I thought Joe . . . your *son* . . . had told you everything.'

'The details, yes. But not the reasons. I felt only you could explain those . . . you know, woman to woman.'

Not for the first time, Karen felt herself bristle at the thought. Given the physical distance between her and her own mother, it had inevitably become an emotional chasm too. Beyond a weekly catch-up call, she'd become used to ploughing her own furrow without having to justify every move to an involved parent.

176

In fact, when it had come to telling her parents that Joe wasn't Ben's father, she'd bottled it and put it all in a letter posted the day before, too filled with shame to make the call.

'With all due respect, Gloria, I only have to try and justify those to my husband, and I have done. If he's chosen not to pass my reasons on, that's up to him.'

'*Justify*?' said Gloria emphatically. 'How in God's name do you justify having another man's child?'

'I hardly think –' Karen began, but Gloria interrupted her.

'How?' The look on her face suggested she wouldn't be leaving until she'd secured an answer.

Karen sighed resignedly. 'I was feeling vulnerable after Joe's affair.'

'You mean you wanted *revenge*.'

'It didn't feel like that at the time.'

Gloria sighed heavily. 'Well you certainly got it, didn't you? Making him bring up a son that wasn't his.'

'Hang on a minute!'

'Oh come on, Karen, you *knew*.' She looked at her with sorry disbelief. 'What mother wouldn't?'

A surge of anger propelled Karen to her feet and towards the door. Opening it, she waved an arm towards the hallway and said flatly: 'You'd better leave.'

Gloria stayed resolutely where she was, watching her unblinkingly. 'The truth hurts sometimes.'

The two women stared defiantly at each other

for several seconds before Karen broke the tense silence.

'You know, it's funny, Gloria, but I don't remember you being quite so judgemental about Joe's affair.'

She shook her head. 'It wasn't the same. Besides, you'd been having problems.'

'Oh puh-lease.' She let out a hollow laugh. 'There were a few teething problems, that's all, just like millions of marriages go through. But not everyone feels the need to go and shag a work colleague. *Several* times.'

But Gloria was already shaking her head before Karen had even reached the end of her sentence. 'It was only sex, it always is with men. You shouldn't have got yourself so worked up about it.'

Speechless with indignation, Karen took a couple of theatrically deep breaths to show she was trying to rise above it.

'Look. You think your son's shit is spun gold. This is pointless.' She gestured towards the open door again. 'Go . . . *please.*'

She looked reluctant to do so, but Gloria finally stood up, hooking her handbag on to her shoulder. She walked towards Karen until their faces were just inches apart.

'It pains me to say this, but I rue the day he met you,' she said quietly.

She walked out and Karen slammed the door firmly shut behind her, feeling sick to her stomach in the aftermath of such an ugly confrontation.

But deep down, she saw her point of view, knowing that if her son found himself in the same situation she'd have reacted in exactly the same way.

Gloria was a mother protecting her child, just like she was trying to do with Ben.

CHAPTER 13

Karen stared out of the window, pulling her cardigan across her chest and hugging her own arms for comfort. The sky was china blue, a welcome respite from the recent rain, which made everyone walking past seem to have a slight spring in their step.

She was feeling more optimistic about life, particularly because Joe had been in an easier mood with her this morning. She wasn't sure if he'd known about Gloria's visit, but he hadn't mentioned it and neither had she, fearing it might make things more awkward again. But she was still churned up about it.

The two women merely tolerated each other because of their mutual love for Joe. Karen invariably kept her at arm's length, knowing that given an inch she'd meddle a mile. Gloria was labouring under the misapprehension that her two sons were highly eligible, fantastic catches able to have their pick of the nation's single women. Consequently, she also thought no woman would ever be good enough for them.

'She acts like you're bloody Prince William or

something,' Karen had grumbled to Joe after meeting his mother for the first time. 'She obviously thinks you could do better.'

'She has a point,' he'd grinned, shortly before she'd pummelled his head with a cushion.

She smiled to herself at the memory of happier days. Perhaps given time, she mused, they'll return.

The telephone rang, sending a wave of shock through her, such were her nerves.

'Karen speaking,' she said casually. 'Oh. Hello.' She felt her back stiffen with apprehension. It was Mr Pickering calling from the hospital.

'It's bad news I'm afraid.' His voice sounded distant and crackly, as if he was on a mobile phone. 'Mr Bright isn't a close enough match for the transplant.'

He stopped speaking, waiting for her to fire lots of pertinent, pre-prepared questions at him, but her mind had gone blank.

'So perhaps you should discuss things with your husband and let me know what you want to do next,' he continued in a tentative voice.

'Yes . . . thanks,' she managed, before adding, 'I'll call you tomorrow.'

Replacing the receiver, she went back to staring out of the window. Although Pickering had described the news as 'bad', if she was honest, it was what she had expected and already prepared herself for. After all, if she wasn't a perfect match as Ben's mother, she knew there was every chance it would be the same story with his biological father.

In the distance, she could see Joe and Ben on their way back to the house, a laboured approach delayed further by their son dropping his toy train in a muddy puddle.

As they got closer to the house, Joe saw her standing at the window and waved. He was unsmiling, but his acknowledgment that she was even on the planet was a small gesture which made her chest rise with hope that things might return to some semblance of normality.

But almost immediately, her spirits sank again as she remembered what Pickering had just told her. If the preimplantation went ahead, she would spend nine months carrying another man's child, her ever-growing belly a daily reminder to her husband of her betrayal.

Even if it *was* for the benefit of saving Ben's life, what man could possibly tolerate seeing his wife like that?

Walking out to the hallway, she opened the front door and stooped down so she was at eye level with Ben in his buggy.

'Hello sweetie. How were the ducks?'

'Fat and distinctly underwhelmed by our mouldy offerings,' replied Joe succinctly.

Unclipping Ben's straps and lifting him out, she repeatedly kissed his cold cheeks as she carried him into the living room. Joe followed and flopped into the armchair, stretching his legs out in front of him and letting out a long sigh.

'We came back earlier than I planned because he kept saying "Ma". He missed you.'

She smiled sadly. 'He misses you too when you're not around.'

Joe didn't respond, kicking off his shoes and picking up the local newspaper lying on the table next to him. She cleared her throat nervously, knowing there was no easy way to say this.

'Pickering rang. Nick Bright isn't a good enough match.'

He instantly stiffened, his mouth setting in a firm line. The atmosphere between them was palpably awkward again, any rapprochement now a distant memory. 'So it's the pre-implantation then.'

'Provided he agrees to it.'

Lips pursed, he stared blindly at the newspaper for a few seconds, folded it and placed it back on the table.

'Well, there's only one way to find out.' He picked up the phone and held it out towards her. 'Call him.'

Tania was sitting at her desk, trying very hard not to throw up the chicken sandwich she'd consumed only minutes earlier. The trouble with such old-fashioned, airless buildings, she thought, is that you sit all day breathing in other people's bloody germs, so it was hard to tell if her malaise was down to an office lurgy or, something far worse, a broken condom.

She hadn't felt right for a couple of weeks, but finding a moment to slope off to the doctors was a virtual impossibility and, besides, you had to make an appointment so far in advance that she'd be cured, or at full term, by the time she got to see them.

Karen had just called to give her the news that Nick wasn't a good enough match – something James had neglected to pass on to Tania himself. Her nausea, she hoped, was probably nerves connected to the fact that she had to go into Nick's office, at Karen's request, and ask if he would agree to the preimplantation.

Waiting until she saw James heading in the direction of the men's toilets, she swiftly moved across the room to tap gently on Nick's door.

'Come in,' said a muffled voice.

'It's me,' she said sheepishly, popping her head round the door. She wasn't accustomed to entering without James alongside.

'Hi.' Nick smiled. If he was surprised to see she was alone, he didn't show it. 'OK?'

'Fine thanks.'

She sauntered in, closing the door behind her as a barrier to try and thwart James, and stood in front of his desk, smiling like an idiot. He in turn smiled back, waiting for her to declare the purpose of her solo arrival.

'Please, sit.' He gestured to a chair. 'Or is it only a flying visit?'

'Flying, really,' she simpered. 'Awkward too.'

'Oh?' He looked expectant.

'It's about the preimplantation.'

'Ah.' His face fell. Taking a deep breath, he closed his appointments diary and pushed it to one side. 'What do you want to know exactly?'

'Whether you'll agree to it,' she replied bluntly, relieved the question was now out in the open.

He opened his mouth to speak but paused when there was a knock on his office door. He frowned and bellowed: 'Who is it?'

James walked in, clutching a folder under one arm. He half smiled then stopped in his tracks as he caught sight of Tania, his expression changing to undisguised fury.

'What are *you* doing here?' he growled, with all the venom of a jealous husband finding his wife with another man. He was very territorial about Nick.

'She was just asking me if I'm going to do the pre-implantation.'

'And what did you say?' He looked at Nick expectantly, instantaneously changing to murderous when he swivelled to face Tania.

'You walked in so I didn't get a chance to say anything.'

James's relief was palpable. 'In that case, the answer's no,' he muttered in her direction, his eyes firmly fixed on something over her shoulder.

'Hang on a minute.' She put her hands on her hips, then looked pleadingly at Nick who immediately averted his eyes and fiddled with his diary. 'Can't you make your own decisions?'

But Nick was still refusing to look at her, instead looking steadfastly at James who once again took the initiative. 'He did make the decision. We discussed it last night when we heard the test result. We just hadn't got round to telling anyone yet.' He looked at her defiantly.

Tania pointed at Nick: 'I don't believe you. I want to hear it from Nick.'

By now, James had hold of her elbow and was trying to steer her towards the door, but she wriggled free and stepped closer to the desk, tilting her head so she could try and catch Nick's eye.

'Is this true?'

He raised his head and looked at her. His face was clouded with shame, but he started to nod.

'*Why*?' she gasped.

'Because I've been online and researched it myself and it seems there's absolutely no guarantee it will work,' he answered quietly. 'Believe me, Tania, I didn't get a wink's sleep last night, playing every scenario over and over in my mind. If someone could tell me a hundred per cent that it would work, I'd do it. But as it is, it will undoubtedly end my political career, probably kill off my marriage and *destroy* Stella who has done nothing wrong . . . and for what? A procedure that might not solve anything. It's too much of a gamble.'

'Ben has done nothing wrong either,' she interrupted. 'And he's only a baby. A baby who will probably *die* if you don't agree to at least give this a try. Yes, it will devastate Stella, but she'll live. And if you place your political career above the life of a child . . . *your* child for God's sake, then you're not the principled man I thought you were.'

Nick looked away again, but James was less shame-faced, grabbing her arm more tightly this time.

'Come on, I want a word outside,' he muttered, propelling her towards the door.

'Stop. Wait a minute.' Nick held his hand up and looked directly at James. 'I've got a really bad feeling about this.'

James shook his head. 'We've already been over this with a fine-tooth comb. It's the right decision. If you do that preimplantation, the press will be on to it and *murder* you.'

Nick shrugged. 'Not necessarily. They might see it as me doing the right thing.'

'Get real,' James scoffed. 'You're always banging on about how kids should use condoms, so what is this . . . "Do as I say, not as I do"?'

'And what if I don't do it and the boy dies?' Nick stared defiantly at James. When James didn't reply, Tania saw her chance and leapt in.

'You're right. Who could blame you for trying to save a child's life? It might even heighten your popularity in a "flawed ordinary man trying to make amends" kind of way.'

James scowled at her and strengthened his grip on her arm. 'We can't count on that.' He paused and gestured around the office with his free hand.

'So, ten years of hard slog to get here, thrown away for a process that might not even work.'

'But it's morally wrong to not even *try*,' pleaded Tania, trying to catch Nick's eye again.

'Fuck morals,' said James, manhandling her through the open door. 'This is politics.'

He was about to close the door in her face when Nick shouted out, his hand making a 'Stop' motion.

'It's not a yes, but it's not a definite no yet either. Tell your friend I need a little more time to think about it.'

Tania mouthed 'Thank you' as the door clicked shut, confident she'd done everything she could.

A sliver of sunshine broke through the ominous cloud and illuminated Ben's face as Joe pushed him back and forth on the garden swing. Shrieking with delight, his feet soared in to the air, then back again.

Karen watched them from the kitchen doorway, smiling fondly and nursing a cup of tea in her hand. Looking at Ben right now, she mused, you wouldn't know there was anything wrong with him. He looked happy and pretty robust, just like he could look forever if the preimplantation was a success.

Her insides churned over, as they'd done countless times since she'd made the call to Tania over an hour ago, persuading her to get Nick alone and ask him the killer question.

Glancing at her watch, she walked back inside to check the phone was on the hook. As she touched it, it rang. She felt nauseous, letting it ring three times for imagined good luck.

'Hello?'

She knew it was bad news as soon as she heard Tania speak. It was there in the tremor of her voice, obvious from her delay in getting to the point. People with good news always blurted it out immediately.

'Hi, it's me. I've been in to see him.'

'And?'

'It's a maybe. He needs more time.'

'OK, thanks. I'm sure you tried your best,' she said numbly, aware that Joe was walking in from the garden with Ben. 'I'll call you later, OK?'

She replaced the receiver and smiled at Ben, his face cherry red from exertion. 'I think someone needs a little drink,' she said brightly.

Filling his plastic Thomas the Tank Engine cup with diluted apple juice, she followed them through to the living room and gave it to Ben who glugged it noisily.

'It's a maybe,' she said quietly.

'Sorry?' Joe looked puzzled.

'Nick Bright. He says he needs more time to decide about the preimplantation.'

'What's to decide?' He looked incredulous. 'He *has* to do it.'

She shook her head. 'But that's just it. He doesn't, does he?'

They were both silent for a moment, contemplating that thought.

'How long does he need?' asked Joe eventually.

She shrugged. 'He didn't say.'

'I see.' He looked quietly angry now. 'So in the meantime Ben has to suffer God knows how many more injections and transfusions because he can't make up his mind whether to help stop the suffering of his own son . . . what kind of man *is* he?'

'A politician,' she answered bitterly. 'Let's face it, they never make snap decisions about anything.'

Joe didn't respond, deep in thought as he watched Ben playing happily with his building bricks. Karen had seen that look before, and it usually spelled trouble.

CHAPTER 14

Tania twirled her hair around her left index finger, the other hand holding the phone to her ear. She looked furtively around the office to check no one was in earshot.

'Joe, I'm *trying*. But James is like bloody Satan at the gate.'

She paused and listened, eventually letting out a long, quiet sigh.

'There's a press conference at the Mandela Centre later today and they're busy preparing for it. I *can't* barge in there again. I'll probably get sacked and then I'll be no use to you at all.'

As she put the phone down, the door to Nick's office opened and James strode out, eyeballing her to make sure she didn't try anything funny. Using his back as a shield, he practically wrapped himself around Nick as he walked out, blocking him from sight as they headed for the corridor.

With a laboured sigh, she picked up her handbag and headed in the same direction. But instead of taking the lift, as they had done, she carried on down the corridor towards the door marked

'Ladies', pushing it hesitantly and peering inside. The three cubicles were empty.

Opting for the nearest, she went in and closed the door behind her, double-checking the lock. Rummaging in her handbag, she pulled out a slim rectangular box with 'Predictor' emblazoned down the side. She'd nearly died of embarrassment when she'd gone to the chemist to buy it, but then reminded herself that they didn't know she'd had a drunken one-night stand with a man she was barely on speaking terms with. She'd consoled herself with the thought that the woman behind the counter might have presumed she was a happily married mother of one who was desperately trying for her second, adorably angelic child to make her nuclear family complete.

Holding the plastic paddle in the right position, she whistled to herself in the hope it might prompt some action, but nerves had clearly made her so tense that nothing came. She flushed the loo and the sound of the cistern refilling did the trick.

Balancing the paddle on top of the loo roll, she pulled up her trousers and sat back on the toilet seat to wait the required one minute, which, right now, felt like a lifetime.

Tania tensed again as she heard the main door open and someone walk into the next cubicle. She didn't want to look at the result until she knew she was alone again, and it seemed an eternity before the woman did her business, washed and

192

dried her hands and spent another few seconds doing God knows what before leaving the room.

Picking up the plastic paddle, she looked at it then leaned back against the cistern and closed her eyes, feeling first her stomach turn over, then the unmistakable slump of depression.

It was positive.

'Right. *Focus*.'

James flipped open the file on his knee and turned towards Nick in the back of the ministerial car. Whenever they were stuck in a traffic jam, he made the most of it. There was no down time on Planet James.

'Bill Adler from *The Times* is likely to ask why it's taking so long to slash waiting lists – his mother had her hip operation cancelled the night before . . . and Jake Thompson is *bound* to bring up that *Post* exclusive about the girl with appendicitis who was taken to three hospitals before they found her a free bed.'

Nick nodded, giving the impression he was listening intently, but really his mind was whirring with guilt about asking for more time to think about the pre-implantation.

After Tania had left his office, James had spent another half an hour trying to railroad him into saying a definite no, again citing the unpredictability of the outcome and the loss of everything he held dear. But after another sleepless night, Nick knew that what he held most dear was his integrity, and that ultimately, saying 'No' to even *attempting* to save a child's life was a decision he could never live with.

So, in the small hours of the morning, he had come to the conclusion that, whatever the consequences, he would agree to it. But first, he had this important press conference to get out of the way. Clearing his throat, he made a desperate effort to concentrate on the task in hand.

'Anything else?' He looked inquiringly at James.

'Yes, I've teed up Ferguson from the *Journal* to ask a soft question on midwives so you can announce that new recruitment drive.' He patted Nick on the back. 'Nothing can go wrong.'

Joe stood some way back from the entrance to the Mandela Centre, surveying the scene. There were a lot of people, presumably journalists, flashing their passes at the two security men before being allowed to progress to the bag scanners inside. In such tinderbox times, he knew that no amount of bluff or blagging would get him past them.

Walking away, he kept himself parallel to the building until he was out of sight of the entrance, before darting down the side where it looked even more impenetrable. It was a solid mass of brick with one emergency-exit door which was resolutely locked shut, with a keypad for entry.

Sighing, he leaned his back against the wall and pondered what to do next, twisting round as he heard a noise behind the door. There were two wheelie bins alongside the wall and he ducked between them just as the fire exit banged open and two men wearing blue overalls sauntered out with cigarette packets in their hands.

They walked only a few feet, but their attention was focused towards the front of the building and the collection of TV vans, so Joe took his chance and darted inside before the door could close.

Breathing heavily, he stood stock still against the inside wall, checking he hadn't been spotted. He deduced from the bare brick walls and metal ceiling tubes that he was in some sort of maintenance corridor. It seemed to be deserted, presumably because the only two workmen were outside having a fag break. Thank God for the smoking ban, he thought to himself as he walked towards a door marked 'Main building'.

Slipping through it, he found himself in a general area with two people running backwards and forwards with pieces of camera equipment, but neither of them gave him a second glance. When he turned his head to the left, he could see the security men and scanning machines, but he was well behind them and an angry cameraman was diverting their attention with a rant about how their jobs would be on the line if they didn't let him through in time for his next news bulletin.

Straightening his jacket, Joe followed a sign saying 'Conference hall' until he could hear the unmistakable sound of an orator in full flow at a microphone.

As he walked into the vast, square room, the voice stopped and he could see Nick Bright seated centrally on the stage, behind a long desk with three other men. One of them – whom he presumed from his confident demeanour was James Spender – was scanning the room and inviting more questions.

Joe crept noiselessly down the central aisle and found an empty seat about halfway back, edging his way to it past several scowling faces. Settling down, he studied the room.

There was a bank of television cameras along the front, interspersed with press photographers, all lenses pointing towards Nick. In front of him were at least twenty microphones, all bearing the logo of their respective TV or radio stations.

The press chairs were lined up in rows, with several he recognised from the television news sitting in the front row. Behind them were presumably the newspaper journalists, mostly scribbling notes in pads though some were using tape recorders.

Nick finished a short answer about NHS waiting lists and James was back on the prowl, scouring the raised hands. He lifted his arm, about to point at one of them, when Joe leapt up from his chair waving both hands in the air.

'I have a question!' he shouted, so loud and undignified that everyone turned round to see who it was.

James scowled at him. 'Sorry, I don't know your

name, but that's not how we do things around here.'

'I don't care. I'm not a journalist,' Joe shouted, anxious that he could be heard by everyone present. He knew it was now or never. 'I'm here on behalf of a little boy called Ben Eastman, a boy whose life might possibly be saved by him.' He pointed at Nick. 'Yet he's still undecided whether to help. So my question is this . . .'

He paused and looked directly at Nick. 'How on earth can you live with yourself?'

There was a stunned silence then James rose to his feet, pulling Nick up with him and pushing him towards a door at the side of the stage. The pair of them disappeared without another word, the room exploding into a riot of noise and flashbulbs.

Joe turned his head to the back of the room where the two security guards from the front door were now advancing towards him with a resolute look on their faces. When he turned back towards the front of the room, he realised that all the cameras were now pointing in his direction.

A man about his age appeared at his side, proffering a business card which Joe instinctively reached out and took.

'Jake Thompson from the *Post*,' he said quickly, glancing at the security guards who were now edging their way along the row of chairs. 'Who's Ben? Has he had an important operation cancelled or something?'

The security guards finally reached Joe. Positioning themselves either side of him, they manhandled him towards the door, his feet actually leaving the ground.

'No,' he shouted, as he was propelled towards the door, 'Ben is Nick Bright's illegitimate son and he's very sick. Only his biological father can save his life.'

As he was bundled through the double doors and back into the reception area, Joe could hear the room he'd just vacated erupt with the sound of journalists shouting to their photographers and cameramen and chairs being knocked over.

By the time he'd been dragged through the scanners and literally thrown through the front doors, he felt like the Pied Piper with a trail of rats following his every move.

In the few seconds it took him to regain his composure and smooth his clothes down, he was surrounded by bellowing journalists, being shoved this way and that as large, unwieldy camera lenses jostled for prime position.

'How old is Ben?' shrieked one woman, thrusting a radio microphone so close to his face that it struck his lip.

'Where do you fit in?' yelled a permatanned man he vaguely recognised from a local television news programme.

Joe raised his palms in the air, gesturing for them to quieten down. It seemed to work.

'I am going to make one quick statement, that's all . . .'

'Speak up!' said a voice at the back of the crowd, now at least six deep.

'My name is Joe Eastman and my wife Karen has a nine-month-old son called Ben.' He paused, giving the reporters time to scribble it all down in their notebooks.

'He has a rare condition called Diamond Blackfan Anaemia.' He paused again, ignoring someone's request to spell it. 'Nick Bright is his biological father and unless he agrees to a procedure called preimplantation genetic diagnosis, Ben's health will get progressively worse and he could easily die.'

He tried to leave, starting to push his way through the crowd, but a wall of pressed flesh prevented him from moving more than a couple of steps.

One of them was Jake something, the reporter who had introduced himself earlier. Unlike the others, his face was impassive, his eyes never leaving Joe's. 'How long has Nick Bright known about his child?' he asked.

'Sorry, I've said all I'm prepared to say at this point.' Joe fixed him with a steely look. 'Now if you don't mind, I'd like to get past.'

They stood facing each other like two gunslingers swamped by a circle of spectators, then Jake stood to one side and barked at the others: 'Let him through.'

As Joe sprinted across the concourse and hailed a passing black cab, an explosion of noise erupted as the journalists and photographers compared and double-checked notes and made frantic calls to their newsdesks.

Joe stared through the cab's rear window, watching the throng get smaller and smaller as he retreated away from it and headed into the unknown.

Stella stopped in her tracks and placed the shopping bags on the ground, stretching her pinched, aching fingers. Her feet were suffering as well, encased in a pair of unyielding new leather court shoes.

'I knew we should have brought the car,' she grimaced.

'Or . . . radical I know . . .' said Judy with her usual sisterly sarcasm, 'but you could have bought less.'

Stella poked out her tongue. Judy had always been the more frugal of the two, taking after their mother Anne who was so penny-pinching she insisted on using every tea bag at least twice and was recycling wrapping paper long before it was trendily 'green' to do so. Usually, Stella preferred to shop alone rather than having Judy tut-tutting at every purchase, but today they'd been scheduled to have lunch and she was combining the two.

The circulation returning to her fingers, she

clasped the carrier bags again and was about to walk off when Judy snorted and pointed at the window of Currys. 'Look, it's Nick. We can't bloody escape him.'

Stella turned to see several huge flatscreen TVs showing Sky News and a shot of Nick addressing the press conference.

'He made some big health announcement today.' She yawned and started to walk off, but Judy grabbed hold of her arm and yanked her back.

'Hang on. What's happening now?'

They both stared through the window as a man stood up and yelled something and the press conference seemed to descend into chaos. The next shot showed Nick being dragged from the stage by James, and reporters and photographers jumping over chairs to reach the man in the middle of the room.

'It's obviously some bloody nutter,' said Stella, relieved Nick appeared to be out of any danger this man might have posed. 'I'm afraid they're an occupational hazard. You should have seen some of the fruit loops who used to turn up at constituency meetings.'

She frowned slightly because, in these inflammatory times, anyone likely to cause trouble – be it even a relatively harmless protest about a local issue – was refused entry for the old, catch-all chestnut of 'security reasons'. So the fact this man had managed to penetrate such a high-profile *national* press conference beggared belief.

'Perhaps he's one of those Fathers for Justice people,' mused Judy.

The picture flickered slightly as the presenter crossed to a reporter standing outside the Mandela Centre, with the word 'Live' in the corner of the screen.

Underneath, a bright red caption popped up saying: 'Health Secretary's alleged love child.'

'Oh my God.' Stella reached for Judy's shoulder just as her legs buckled from under her.

CHAPTER 15

'Fuck, fuck, *fuck*!'

With each word, James thumped his forehead against the car window. His face was pinched with anger.

'I *knew* I should have agreed to it,' said Nick quietly, staring ahead of him but seeing nothing.

He sounded calm, but inside he was struggling to control a rising sense of anger, with James for trying to bully him into saying no, but mostly with himself for not having the guts to override his aide and agree to the pre-implantation from the outset.

Now his prevarication had cost him dearly, forcing the issue out into the open in wildly uncontrolled circumstances. Worse, he looked like a hard bastard who had needed time to decide between his political career and a child's life. It hadn't been as straightforward as that, of course, but he knew that was how tomorrow's papers would portray it.

'I must call Stella,' he said heavily, reaching into his inside pocket and pulling out his mobile. Between being unceremoniously bundled off stage then virtually thrown into a waiting car at a side door, he hadn't yet had the time. Everything had moved so quickly, it had felt like an assassination attempt. In many ways, it had been, he thought ruefully. A verbal one.

He felt gut-wrenchingly sick as he started to dial Stella's number, but James placed a hand on his arm to stop him.

'She knows already. We're on our way to her sister's house,' he said briskly. 'Leave your explanations until then.' He tapped a finger on the phone. 'You never know who's listening in.'

'Isn't it a little late for damage limitation?'

James ignored him, leaning forward to tell the driver to avoid the obvious main roads, which would doubtless be teeming with paparazzi on motorbikes, and favour the lesser-known back routes.

'Did you speak to Stella?' asked Nick, wondering how James had found the time.

'No. I got Ged to do it.' Ged was James's much maligned assistant. 'But she'd already seen it on the news.'

Nick pressed the button for the electric window and stuck his head out. The sudden blast of cold air cleared his head momentarily before it rapidly refilled with torturous thoughts of his wife hearing such devastating news, not from the man she had trusted to love and respect her, but from a news bulletin. He felt overwhelmingly wretched and close to tears for the first time since the age of nine when John Kinnear had been made football captain instead of him.

His eyes watering from a combination of emotion and the stinging cold, he withdrew back into the car and rubbed his face vigorously, trying to focus on what he was going to say to Stella. But James had other ideas.

'Who the fuck was that arsehole anyway?' he spat. 'And how did he get in?'

'I'm guessing Karen's husband . . . the boy's putative father. And in answer to your second question, I have absolutely no idea.'

James's mobile rang and he sat bolt upright. 'Shit. It's the PM's office.'

He took the call. 'Hi David . . . yes I know, it's all rather unfortunate I'm afraid . . . OK, I'll put him on.'

He pressed his finger over the tiny receiver. 'He's about to put you through to the Prime Minister on a secure line. He wants an explanation.'

Robotically, Nick pressed the phone to his ear and waited.

Blinking rapidly as she emerged from the tube station into the daylight, Karen put her hand in her pocket and took out a shopping list: 'Milk, bread, cheese and nappies'.

Hurrying into the small 'No Cost' store on the corner, she smiled to herself for the umpteenth time about its misleading name.

'So does that mean I can choose what I like and take it without paying?' she'd asked the owner, Rami, a few months after she and Joe had moved to the area. Rami had patiently explained, no doubt as he had done to many other customers, that it was a figure of speech in that when something is cheap people say, 'Oh, it's no cost at all.'

As she picked up a basket, her mobile phone found a signal and beeped to indicate she had a message. Hunching her left shoulder, she clamped the handset to her ear and walked towards the dairy section, where she grabbed two litres of semi-skimmed. The message was from Tania.

'Karen, it's me. Where the bloody hell are you? When you get this message call me . . . urgently.' Tania sounded frantic. She had always been a drama queen, but Karen knew with a sickening certainty that this was something serious.

'If you don't know already, Joe has turned up at Nick's press conference and blurted out about Ben in front of all the cameras. It's running on TV even as I speak. *Call* me.'

Karen's whole body turned cold, small pimples erupting on her forearms.

'Shit.' She dropped the basket and its contents on the floor with a loud crash and sprinted towards the exit as Rami looked on wide-eyed.

Ducking in and out of the stream of commuters, she reached home in record time. Her phone had already rung several more times, all from friends who had presumably seen the news, but she had let every one of them divert to mailbox. She wanted to see the damage for herself before speaking to anyone.

Ben was at Gloria's and there was no sign of Joe when she reached home, throwing her handbag on to the sofa and flicking on the TV.

'Eh-oh.' Po was dancing across the screen with the other Teletubbies.

'Fuck,' she muttered, punching in 501 on the remote. Living with a news junkie like Joe, she'd grown used to having Sky News or News 24 on in the background and marvelled at how he could watch the same stories going round on a loop all day. Now she was grateful for it.

'News at the top of the hour,' intoned the presenter, 'is that Health Secretary Nick Bright has been accused of having a love child. That child is in dire need of a bone-marrow transplant and the question the whole country is asking is: "Will Nick Bright try and help save his life?"'

It cut to footage of the press conference, with Nick on the podium and cameras swivelling to film Joe as he started shouting from the back of the room. It felt surreal to be watching her husband's face fill the screen and to hear him being talked about by studio 'experts'.

Karen wondered about the validity of a supposed medical 'expert' who could drop everything and be at a television studio within one hour of a story breaking. Surely they had more important things to do, like a life to save perhaps? She shook the thought away and heard Joe's voice booming through the TV speaker: 'Sorry, I've said all I'm prepared to say at this point.'

Karen put her head in her hands and peered at the screen through her fingers.

'I think you've said quite enough already, you bloody fool.'

As the black Jaguar rolled quietly into the cul-de-sac, a small group of children gathered on the pavement to stare at it.

'Christ, it's like the bloody Midwich cuckoos,' muttered James. 'Haven't they seen a car before?'

'Only Fiat Puntos and Honda Civics,' replied Nick. 'This is suburbia, mate, there's nothing too flashy here. They'd consider it vulgar.'

James opened the door gingerly, eyeing the children suspiciously as if he expected them to morph into paparazzi at any moment.

'Is that your car?' asked a lad of about twelve.

'No, it belongs to Justin Timberlake. I've just borrowed it.'

'Really?' The children stepped forward for a better look, blocking Nick as he tried to get out of the car.

'Oh, it's you,' said the twelve-year-old as he saw him. His disappointment was palpable. 'He's related to *her*,' he said to the others, jerking his head towards Judy's neat 1930s semi. 'My dad says he's one of those idiots who run this country.'

'Ah, the discerning future electorate,' smiled James through gritted teeth. 'Thank Christ I'll have retired by then.'

'Count yourself lucky.' Nick walked towards the

house. 'I'll probably have been sacked by tomorrow.'

'Oh?' James's eyes narrowed. 'Did you get that impression from the PM?'

'Not as such,' he shrugged, pressing the doorbell with a heavy heart. 'He wasn't so much bothered about the existence of the boy, more that we'd tried to cover it up.'

'*We*? Did he actually mention my name?' James looked anxious.

'Yes, a couple of times actually.'

He hadn't, but Nick wanted to make James squirm. He was a typical civil servant, quick to take responsibility for life's victories but rarely to be seen when bollockings were being handed out.

The door was opened by a stern-faced Judy. She and Nick had never really got on and he knew this would present her with ample opportunity to perfect her range of disapproving expressions, from quiet disappointment through to naked hatred. Now, it was most definitely the latter.

'You'd better come in,' she said begrudgingly, stepping to one side. 'She's in the living room.'

Nick was about to walk through the door on the righthand side of the hallway when he noticed James was following. He stopped in his tracks, causing him to crash into his back.

'I want to see her alone.'

'Are you sure that's wise?'

'It's my *wife*, for fuck's sake.'

James held his hands up in surrender. 'No

problem. I'm sure Judy won't mind making me a cup of tea while I wait.' He flashed a smile at her, but it wasn't returned.

'No.' Nick shook his head. 'Take the car and go back to the office. I'll call when I need you.'

'I don't think –'

'Go. *Now*,' Nick interrupted, in no mood to be contradicted.

Not waiting for any further answer, he turned back to face the living-room door. He was about to knock, but decided that was too formal and instead gently pushed it open. Stella was sitting on the floor doing a Noddy jigsaw with Judy's youngest child, four-year-old Oliver. She had always enjoyed a close relationship with her nephew and the boy was leaning against her with an ease that came from knowing her all his short life. The painful irony of the little scene was not lost on Nick and he felt a stab of pain in his temple.

She looked up as he walked in, her friendly expression giving way to one of obvious distaste. Rubbing the top of Oliver's head, she tilted his chin towards her and smiled.

'Go and tell Mummy how well you've done with the puzzle. She might give you a biscuit!'

The child stood up and ran to the door, glancing nervously at Nick as he passed. They'd met before at a couple of family functions, but not enough to form a bond.

There were two large, comfortable sofas in the

room but Stella immediately moved to sit in the hard-backed leather chair Judy's husband Mike used when his back was playing up. She sat ramrod straight, her hands resting in her lap, her face showing the blotchy pink puffiness associated with sustained crying.

The television was on Sky News. The volume was turned down, but the garish headlines running along the bottom of the screen were still predominantly about Nick and his 'alleged' illegitimate child.

He walked across and switched it off, his face pained. Turning back, he knelt on the floor in front of Stella's chair, resting his arms on his knees and looking up at her. He took solace from the fact she didn't leap up and move away from him.

'Are you OK?'

Up to now, she hadn't even acknowledged his presence in the room, simply staring ahead of her in a daze. But the sound of his voice seemed to break her reverie.

'Is it true?' she said measuredly, not looking at him.

He nodded silently, his expression belying his inner feelings of guilt and shame.

When it came, the slap was fast and hard. He recoiled in shock, clutching his stinging cheek.

'I guess I deserved that.' He stood up, edging backwards towards one of the sofas. Perching uncomfortably on the edge, he faced her.

Almost instantly, her anger seemed to dissolve

and she started to cry, wiping her face with the back of her hand. She was looking at him now, her eyes heavy with sadness.

'How long have you known?'

He wanted to take her in his arms and reassure her that everything was going to be alright, but how could he? He didn't even believe it himself.

Nick had always been the most outwardly confident in their relationship, the one who could stand at a podium and effortlessly address thousands of people. But Stella was the quiet powerhouse at home, the person who anchored him and provided an invaluably mature and sensible sounding board for his political ideas, harnessing his excesses where necessary. He knew she could undoubtedly survive without him, but he couldn't imagine his life without her.

'How long, Nick?' she repeated miserably.

'Just a couple of days.' He rubbed his hand across his hair. 'If it hadn't been for the lad's illness, I doubt I'd ever have known.'

'Why didn't you tell me?' The tears were running down her face now and she made no attempt to wipe them away.

It was the killer question and one he knew he'd struggle to answer with any conviction.

'Because I wanted to verify it first . . . because I wanted to find the right time to tell you, particularly because you'd just lost . . . our baby . . .' he faltered, feeling a swell of emotion at the thought.

'And not because you and James were working

out whether it could all be kept quiet and I'd be none the wiser?' she asked pointedly, her eyes boring into him.

'No, it wasn't like that,' he countered lamely, flushing with shame at the knowledge that she had nailed him like she had on so many other occasions when, to a far lesser extent, he'd tried to pull the wool over her eyes. He wasn't sure whether she truly believed him, but she seemed satisfied with his answer for the time being.

'So who is she?' Her face was etched with pain.

Nick wanted to swat the question away, like a tiresome fly. But he knew that however irrelevant Karen Eastman was to him, at this moment she was incredibly important to Stella who'd want to know every last detail about her. Details that he probably didn't even know himself, such had been the brevity of their sexual encounter.

Again, he was seized with the urge to comfort his wife, to feel her flesh against his, to rock her in his arms and tell her how much he loved her, as much for his benefit as her own. He found it almost unbearable to feel this distance between them.

Instinctively, he stood up and moved towards her, his arms outstretched. But she visibly shrank from him, her misery twisting into a look of disgust.

'Don't touch me,' she said flatly.

He noticed she had stopped crying and seemed harder now, her eyes darkened by poorly suppressed anger. She stared at him challengingly, waiting for an answer.

'She's a friend of Tania Fletcher. I met her just once, the night of the local elections when we'd had that ridiculous argument about politics and you'd gone off to stay at your mother's.'

'It was pre-arranged.'

'Sorry?'

'The trip to my mother's. I had *arranged* to stay there. You make it sound like I went there because we'd argued.'

Nick blinked a few times, his brow furrowed. He couldn't believe she had interrupted his explanation with something he regarded as so trivial, but it was typical Stella. She was a very methodical, straight-talking person for whom the chronology and finer details of events were just as important as the emotions involved. She was also ferociously clever and he knew she was making sure he couldn't use their argument and her subsequent absence as an excuse for his infidelity.

'Fine, whatever,' he said distractedly, trying to refocus on what he'd been saying. 'We'd done well in the elections, I'd had far too much to drink and well, one thing led to another.'

She watched him unblinkingly, as if hoping he would say something else. But as far as Nick was concerned, there was little left *to* say. In his mind, that was a comprehensive description of what had happened and his recollection didn't extend much further.

'Is that it?'

He nodded then shrugged.

'Pathetic.' She shook her head slowly. 'If the boot was on the other foot, are you seriously suggesting that you'd be happy with that scant and, quite frankly, downright insulting explanation of the highly public mess we have now found ourselves in?'

'Probably not, no,' he admitted shamefacedly, marvelling at Stella's ability to seem calm and controlled in a crisis. But he knew her sadness and disappointment weren't far from the surface and it crushed him.

'Right. So let's start at the beginning. What's her name, how old is she, and how long has she been married to him?' She nodded towards the now darkened television where just minutes earlier Joe's face would have been filling the screen.

'Karen Eastman, she's in her early thirties and she was married to him when I met her but other than that, I don't know anything about them,' he muttered, feeling as if the walls were closing in on him.

'Yet the both of you were clearly so unhappy in your respective marriages that you felt the need to shag each other within hours of meeting?' Her eyes were granite hard.

'It wasn't like that.' He shook his head slowly and stared at the floor. 'I can't excuse it, but I was euphoric about the results, had had too much to drink and felt as horny as hell. I could hardly turn up at your mother's with my dick in my hand, and she . . .' He faltered and stopped.

'She *what*?'

'She happened to be there,' he shrugged. 'That's all. It meant nothing, Stella, I can't stress that enough.'

'Unfortunately, Nick, I also appeared to mean nothing when it was going on.'

An angry silence descended, with Stella glaring at him whilst he stared intently at a wedding photograph of Judy and Mike on the nest of tables beside him. He would have given anything to turn the clock back to that summer's day in 1998 when he and Stella were in the first flush of their relationship and she'd invited him to meet her family 'in one extremely foul swoop' as she'd put it at the time. Stella was just thirty then and already quite a high-flyer at the bank. Nick, by contrast, was a newly elected MP on a relative pittance, so she'd been the major breadwinner. It wasn't until five years ago, when his career had really taken off, that they had taken the mutual decision for her to give up work and be the supportive stay-at-home wife that's such a boost to any high-ranking politician.

His trip down memory lane was disturbed by the sound of her speaking again.

'She must have suspected it wasn't her husband's child before now?'

He pursed his lips. 'Maybe. All I know is that

she only found out for sure when she and her husband had DNA tests to see if their bone marrow was a close enough match to help their son.'

She shook her head, her expression softening with sadness. 'That poor boy, his life has barely started.'

Nick nodded. In truth, he hadn't wanted to consider anyone else's point of view, other than his and Stella's. But the boy kept popping into his head.

Allowing a couple more moments of reflective silence for Ben, Nick cleared his throat.

'Stella, you must believe me when I say that I'd never been unfaithful before this or since. I love you too much.'

But she didn't appear to be listening. She was squeezing her hands together, looking desolate now.

'Life's so cruel isn't it?' she murmured, almost whimsically. 'There I am, trying to get pregnant all these years, then losing it . . . and you have meaningless sex with a stranger and get a son.'

As the last word left her mouth, she made a choking noise and her face crumpled, her eyes filling with tears. She wiped each cheek with her sleeve.

'Don't, please.' Nick leaned forward to try and pat her knee reassuringly, but she twisted her legs slightly so they were out of his reach. 'Do you think you'll ever forgive me?'

She smiled sadly at him, but it didn't reach her eyes. 'It's really not that simple though, is it? There's more to come, more to endure. Unless . . .' Her expression suddenly changed and she looked at him as though he were a stranger. 'You weren't seriously thinking about saying no to helping the boy, were you? Is that why his father turned up at the press conference?'

Nick shook his head. 'James wanted me to –'

'I might have guessed,' she interrupted, visibly irritated.

'– but I had already decided I was going to do it. I asked for more time to think because I wanted to discuss it with you first, but I think Joe Eastman took it to mean I was going to refuse, so he flushed me out into the open.'

'I'd have done exactly the same in his position,' she said resolutely. 'You have to help the boy.'

He nodded. 'Of course I will, but in the meantime, I *have* to know, where does all this leave us?'

She frowned and picked awkwardly at a stud on the leather chair.

'The short answer,' she said eventually, 'is that I don't really know. It's all come as such a shock that I need time to think.'

'Time spent with me, or without me?' He knew he was being unfair by pushing her for specifics, but he couldn't bear the thought of losing her, even for a few days or weeks. He didn't care if she didn't utter a single word to him, as long as he could see her, share the same airspace. He was terrified that if he let her out of his sight for even a moment, she might never come back.

'Without you,' she said quietly.

CHAPTER 16

Pushing his key into the Yale lock, Joe turned it and felt the door yield. It wasn't double-locked, meaning Karen was home, a thought that prompted a somersaulting motion in the pit of his stomach.

She was sitting motionless in the armchair, staring at the television screen. An old black and white movie was showing, but he could tell from her stiff shoulders that BBC News 24 or Sky News had told her all she needed to know about how his morning had been spent.

'He'll never help us now.' She didn't look at him, suggesting anger, but her voice was surprisingly conciliatory.

He meant to sigh but it came out as a frustrated, irritable puffing noise as he threw his jacket on the back of the sofa.

'He'd only said maybe and we all know that's delaying tactics before saying no.'

She swivelled round in the chair to look at him, her expression suggesting that, after three years of marriage, she didn't know him at all.

'Not necessarily. We could have worked on

him . . . subtly. Instead we've publicly humiliated him. Did he really deserve that?'

'By we I take it you mean *me*?' he demanded. 'And since when did his feelings matter? Anyone would think you're still in love with him.'

'I'm going to treat that immature, attention-seeking remark with the contempt it deserves,' she said measuredly. 'Look, I know you did it for all the right reasons, but . . .'

'But *what*, Karen? As far as I'm concerned, I have now put him in a situation where he *has* to do it.' He was saying the bullish words, but inside he was feeling distinctly less assured.

'Maybe,' she shrugged. 'Or maybe he'll think that now his political career is probably over anyway and his wife undoubtedly knows everything, he doesn't *have* to do anything anymore.'

He computed what she'd said and suddenly felt overwhelmed by weariness and defeat, slumping on to the sofa with an air of hopelessness.

'You're right. I've fucked everything up.'

He wanted to be antagonistic towards her, to rant and rail at her for having a son that wasn't his, but he couldn't. Not right now anyway. He knew that, despite all their differences, there was a crucial common aim they still had: getting Ben his best chance of survival. After that, he'd focus on the bigger picture.

Catching the taxi and watching the mayhem unfold behind him, he'd felt a curious sense of elation as the adrenalin had coursed round his body. But within minutes, it had gone, leaving him drained and wretched.

The sofa cushion sank as Karen sat next to him, tentatively placing her hand on his knee. Her touch was so light he could barely feel it.

'Don't be too hard on yourself,' she murmured. 'We'll work something out.'

They sat there, wordlessly, for a few seconds. If Karen knew what the solution was she didn't say so, and Joe certainly couldn't think of one. This morning, storming Nick's press conference had seemed like an inspired idea, but now, with the story splashed over every news channel and Ben's future no more certain, it was looking like an increasingly rash and reckless judgement.

As they sat there, side by side, Karen's hand resting on his knee, he realised he felt confused, torn between his deep anger towards her and his need to have her comfort him through the ordeal he was suffering.

If ever there was an example of how love can both inspire elation and cause intense pain, this is it, he thought miserably. The woman to whom he'd always turned for emotional support, whom he'd trusted so implicitly, was the same one who had betrayed him so badly. The dilemma was tormenting him.

He didn't want to sleep in the spare room, every ounce of his being wanted to cross the landing and feel the warmth of her embrace, to return to how they used to be. But he couldn't. He knew that if he did, it would only be a temporary Band-Aid on a wound that ran so deep he feared it might never heal. So he stayed away, both emotionally and physically, biding his time until he could give proper, measured thought to the situation he now found himself in.

The doorbell rang, its shrill sound making them spring apart, their former awkwardness snapping back into place.

Karen stood up and peered out of the window. 'It's Tania. She said she wanted to come over.'

I'll bet she did, he thought mutinously as he watched her leave the room. He heard the door open and there was a murmured conversation pitched too low for him to hear, then seconds later Karen walked back in followed by Tania.

It was a funny old thing, he mused, the relationship between a man and his wife's best friend. He had to admit he found it pretty disquieting to have someone so intrinsically wound through his and Karen's life, probably knowing more about his wife's inner thoughts on their marriage than he did. But for the most part, he and Tania had muddled along, she not irritating him too much, he giving her a wide berth.

Yet now, as she walked into the living room, he saw his enemy, the woman who, as he saw it, had engineered his wife's sordid little fling and robbed him of a blood tie to Ben. And now she was here with a concerned look on her face.

'Oh look, it's the advance party for damage limitation,' he sneered.

Tania stopped in her tracks, unsure whether to sit down or beat a hasty retreat, but Karen grabbed her arm to propel her forward, glaring at Joe as she did so.

'Cut it out. She's here to help us.'

Already, the closeness he'd fleetingly shared with Karen was a distant memory. There was a distinct two against one feeling in the room and he was most definitely the lone element.

'Tania says we should probably find somewhere else to stay because as soon as the press find where we live we won't be able to move. And with the speed they work, we haven't got long.'

He glanced at Tania who just nodded apologetically.

'So we'll decamp to Mum's,' he shrugged. 'They won't find us there.'

Karen's expression suggested she'd rather decamp to a reporter's house.

'You can all stay at mine if you like?' said Tania. 'It'll be a bit of a squash but I'm sure we'll cope.'

Joe rapidly decided he'd rather live on his own front lawn in the full glare of the media, but as he opened his mouth to speak the doorbell rang and stole his moment.

With the well-practised air of someone used to dealing with the unwanted attentions of the press, Tania sliced a finger down the side of the closed curtains just enough to peep outside. As she did so, a camera flash went off.

'Too late,' she muttered. 'They're here already.'

Gloria pottered around her spotless kitchen, wiping the already sparkling surfaces whilst Ben sat in his highchair munching a banana. Every time a small blob stuck to his mouth or, heaven forbid, fell on the floor, she was at the ready with a piece of prettily decorated paper towel. However much she loved her grandson – and she did wholeheartedly – it didn't transcend the grip that her obsessive compulsive disorder had on her life.

From the moment she woke to the time she lay her head back on the pillow, her day was ritualised, mostly with cleaning-related tasks. She wasn't an obsessive hand-washer like many OCD sufferers and she didn't feel the urge to count everything, but she was preoccupied by straight lines, tidiness and everything having its place. If she saw a wonky picture in a restaurant, she'd be seized with the compulsion to straighten it. And if it was immovably fixed on all four corners then she'd have to sit where she couldn't see it or it would doubtless spoil her evening.

Far from being irritated or hindered by their mother's condition, Joe and Andy had benefited from it, never having to raise a finger to help around the house as children, and rarely so as adults.

Gloria wouldn't let them, always feeling that no

one could complete a task to her own exacting standards, and, besides, as even the most amateur of psychologists could have told her, doing everything was a control issue that made her feel needed.

It wasn't until Joe had met Karen that Gloria had finally found herself confronted by someone questioning her obsessive tidiness. It was after Sunday lunch one day, before Ben was born, and Joe and Andy were in the back garden trying to erect a flatpack bench for their mother, with lots of Laurel and Hardy-style head-scratching.

Rather than sit with Karen enjoying a relaxing, post-lunch coffee, Gloria had busied herself around the room, straightening picture frames and picking flecks of dust from the carpet until her daughter-in-law developed a perplexed frown.

'Do you ever just sit and do nothing?' she'd asked.

'At night, yes. If there's a good film on.'

Karen had stood up and walked across to the mantel-piece above the fire, moving one of the picture frames at a right angle to the others. 'What will happen if you leave that as it is?'

Gloria had twitched, knowing what it was leading to but feeling uncomfortable because no one had ever broached it with her before.

'Nothing. It just displeases me to look at it, that's all,' she'd replied, putting it back in line with the others. 'I don't see the point of making things untidy when they could just as easily be tidy.'

Karen had let the subject drop that day, but not long after Ben was born, she'd returned to it, asking her mother-in-law if she was aware that OCD was controlling her life and whether she wanted to do something about it.

'What do you mean?'

'You know, go see someone about it.'

'Like a psychiatrist?' Gloria was horrified at the suggestion. As far as she was concerned, only people with severe mental problems did such a thing.

'No, a psychotherapist. They'd try to discover why you do it then help you deal with it.'

At which point, Gloria had burst out laughing, loud, theatrical guffaws as if to suggest there was only one mad person in the room and it wasn't her. 'Going to a head doctor because you do a bit of tidying every now and then?' she'd trilled. 'My dear, you really are a scream.'

Karen hadn't mentioned it again, but the seed had been sown and to this day, Gloria would start one of her rituals and find her enjoyment of it diminished because she was doubting her reasons for doing it.

There it was again, that niggling feeling as she scraped her nail across the tiniest fleck of food on Ben's highchair tray.

'All done?' She kissed him on the forehead and lifted him out of the chair, carrying him through to the living room and placing him on the large plastic mat she'd bought specially for his visits.

There was a tap on the front door and through the frosted glass she could see a bulky outline.

'Ooh, perhaps that's Postman Pat with a parcel for you,' she smiled, opening the door.

It was a large, middle-aged man in a dark blue coat, no parcel in sight. He looked a little like a policeman and her heart started to race.

'Mrs Eastman?'

'Yes, is everything alright?'

'Bob Kemp. The *Journal*.' He pulled a notebook out of his pocket and flipped it open. 'I was wondering if you had any comment to make on your son's little outburst?'

Gloria frowned slightly. 'Sorry, I'm not with you . . .' A chill ran down her arms. 'Which son?'

'Joe.' He looked over her shoulder to where Ben was sitting on the floor. 'Is that Ben?'

She followed his gaze, then turned back again, her brow furrowed. 'How do you know his name? Sorry, *who* are you again?'

He looked faintly awkward then raised his eyebrows. 'You really don't know do you?'

She shook her head. 'You're scaring me now.'

'Sorry, Mrs Eastman. It seems that your son Joe turned up at a press conference this morning and accused Nick Bright of having an illegitimate son.' He nodded towards Ben. 'Your grandson, in fact . . .'

She stared at him for a couple of seconds, computing what he'd said, then cleared her throat and inwardly calmed herself.

'Sorry, I have no idea what you're talking about,' she said stiffly, before slamming the door shut and instantly pulling her hand-stitched velvet curtain across the door.

Scooping Ben into her arms, she sat rocking him on her knee as the reporter continued knocking on the door and talking to her through the letterbox.

'Jesus, son,' she whispered tearfully. 'What have you done?'

Joe replaced the receiver, his face pale and pinched. 'That was Mum. They're on her doorstep too. How did they find her so quickly?'

'Same surname as you. Phone book. Electoral register. Whatever. It never takes them long,' said Tania robotically.

The television was back on, with the sound on low. They watched the start of the six o'clock news wordlessly, with Joe groaning when the familiar footage of him at the press conference flashed up yet again.

Tania yawned and peered through the curtains again, sparking a cacophony of flashbulbs.

'Bloody hell, a picture of my eyelashes. That'll sell papers.' She sat back down. 'There are about ten reporters and photographers and a couple of camera crews.'

Joe looked towards the window. 'They'll give up eventually.'

'Don't count on it.'

Karen walked in from the kitchen, her mobile phone in her hand. 'Apparently, the surgery's crawling with press too. I've just had to use up the rest of my holiday allowance.'

She slumped in the armchair and threw her mobile down on the rug. 'My voicemail is full of messages from reporters, wanting to tell our story "sympathetically".' She made quote marks with her fingers. 'Yeah right. And anyway, how did they get the bloody number?'

'Not so wild guess?' ventured Tania. 'Probably someone at the mobile phone company or BT. The world's full of overstretched, underpaid workers who are happy to give the press information for a few quid.'

'Really?' Karen pondered this for a moment, aghast that people could do such a thing. 'Still,' she sighed, 'at least they don't have a picture of Ben.'

Tania nodded and smiled but Joe looked tetchy.

'It's all bollocks though isn't it? Anyone who knows me will know it's him, so he'll still get pointed at in the street, poor little sod, won't he?'

He shook his head in despair just as the doorbell rang for the tenth time in as many minutes.

'Jesus Christ,' he mumbled, 'what *have* I unleashed?'

'And what do they want from us?' asked Karen.

Tania smiled ruefully. 'Nick Bright's head on a plate.'

CHAPTER 17

Stella stood in the bay window of her sister's home, nursing a cup of tea and staring through the net curtains at suburban life. She daren't actually open them again and gaze out, because yesterday there had been a photographer lurking, taking the deeply unflattering picture that was all over this morning's newspapers, of Stella looking puffy and haggard under various lurid headlines alluding to the strain of having an adulterous husband. The sight of it flashed all over the television news had simply compounded her misery.

The woman across the road was loading her children into the car, presumably for the school run. She looked harassed and Stella wondered whether she too ever fantasised about changing her life for something different. If she looked at my life, she mused, with no children, a highly successful, famous husband and a never-ending selection of supposedly glittering social occasions, she'd probably be envious, thinking I had everything. Whereas all I want right now is *her* life, with its predictability and routine stresses and strains of parenting.

The woman's husband came out of the house, clutching a battered briefcase. He kissed his wife perfunctorily on the cheek, waved at his children through the car window then set off walking in the direction of the train station. Judging by his well-worn suit, Stella guessed he was probably a middle manager somewhere who arrived by nine a.m. every morning, took an hour for lunch then pitched up home by six p.m. at the latest to share an early supper with his family. Watching as he shrank into the distance, she wondered whether she could be happy with someone as dependable as that, someone happy to coast along as one of life's flatliners. Or whether the reason she was with Nick, a vibrant sometimes irascible life force, was because she wouldn't want it any other way, for fear she might feel strangled by anything so relentlessly predictable. She let out a world-weary sigh. Right now, predictability was looking very attractive indeed.

Hearing the door open behind her, she turned round to see Nick walking into the dining room, doing his shirt up.

'Jesus that sofa was uncomfortable.' He winced and rubbed the back of his neck.

'Good.' And she meant it.

He didn't react and she was unsure whether he'd assumed she was joking or perhaps hadn't even heard the remark. Threading his tie under his collar, he crossed the room towards her. As he reached the bay window he held his arms out awkwardly, as if to embrace her, but she leaned backwards out of his reach. He dropped his arms back to his sides and smiled briefly.

'I guess you're not ready for that yet.'

Wordlessly, she shook her head and continued to stare out at the cul-de-sac, empty now except for Nick's official government car.

'Right.' He hovered awkwardly for a few moments before extending an arm towards her, his fingers resting lightly on her forearm. This time, she didn't back away. 'I'd better be going. Are you staying here?'

She nodded, giving him the faintest hint of a smile, more to dilute the thick air of awkwardness than out of any sense of feeling even slightly conciliatory.

'Wise I suppose. Until the fuss dies down at least.' He stopped speaking and looked apprehensive. 'So when do you think you'll come home?' He had tried to make it sound off-the-cuff casual, but they both knew it was a loaded question.

'Don't push me. We agreed on that much,' she said quietly.

He nodded, looking apologetic. 'Sorry, it's just that I can't bear the thought of being away from you, even for one night.'

'Except when you're conceiving secret sons.' She felt nasty saying it, but the sudden compulsion to try and hurt him consumed her.

'Ouch.' He picked up his briefcase. 'I guess I deserved that.'

She watched numbly as he walked down the front path and climbed in the back of the car, ignoring a couple of photographers who materialised from nowhere and giving a hesitant wave in her direction. Then he sped off back to London and God knows what.

Only when it was out of sight did she drop to her knees and let out an animalistic howl so loud that Judy heard it from the bottom of the back garden and ran in to comfort her.

The cup of coffee in front of Joe was stone cold, a circle of dark brown film floating on the top. He was staring down at it, his jaw rigid with tension. His head jerked upwards as he heard a mobile ring, then dropped again when he realised it was Tania's not his.

'Hi,' he heard her say in a flat voice, before walking through to the living room and out of earshot.

Karen was sitting opposite him, flicking through one of the ubiquitous property magazines that dropped through their door each week, full of houses they had once loved to drool over but could never afford. Before Ben was born, they would often read them over breakfast, each picking their favourite house and dreaming of the day they won the lottery or invented the next big thing so they could buy it. But there was no time for such frippery these days, their time taken up with injections, blood transfusions and optimistically searching the internet in the hope that, one day, they'd stumble across an article saying 'US doctor finds guaranteed cure for Diamond Blackfan Anaemia'.

Karen's voice broke into his thoughts.

'Look at this.' She pointed at the page in front of her. 'Two million quid for a three-bedroom house. The world's gone mad.'

Joe looked at her blankly then made a scoffing noise. 'What *are* you doing?'

'Sorry?'

'Looking at bloody property magazines?' He reached across and grabbed it, throwing it on the floor where it scattered noisily in to several pieces. 'Our life is in fucking chaos and you're musing about house prices?'

She looked at the magazine sprawled on the floor then slowly raised an eyebrow before turning back and leaning towards him across the table. Her voice was low but menacing. 'You caused the chaos so don't have a go at me. I was just trying to be normal.'

'I caused it?' Righteous indignation propelled him to his feet and he strode across the room, which, considering the size of the kitchen, didn't take long. He turned to face her, his back resting against the work surface. '*I* caused it? I don't fucking think so. You're the one that shagged a cabinet minister.'

'I'm well aware of that,' she replied calmly. 'But we could have contained it, *you* were the one who chose to announce it to the world.'

'Yes, to save Ben's life!' he spat. 'Something *you* don't seem too bothered about.'

As the words left his mouth, he knew he'd overstepped the mark, but it was too late to retract them. Her face had already turned white with fury.

'Don't you *ever* fucking doubt my love for my son!' she screamed, jumping to her feet and flying at him with hands raised. She pounded them against his chest as he flinched with each blow and turned his head to one side.

'That was a cheap fucking shot,' she cried. 'Night after bloody night I lie awake, worrying about what's going to happen to him. I would give *anything*, even my own life, for the knowledge that he could be cured, so don't you *ever* fucking suggest that I don't care.' She stopped thumping him, her hands falling listlessly to her sides as she stumbled backwards and slumped on a chair. Her arms on the table, her head bowed, she sobbed uncontrollably.

Still in shock, Joe stayed where he was, rendered immobile by a feeling of sadness and remorse. After a few more seconds, he tentatively moved forward and stood behind her, his hands hovering above her shoulders. He wanted nothing more than to touch her, to console her, but was unsure how she might react. Even after everything that had happened, he still hated to see her like this.

Placing his fingers lightly on her shoulders at first, he felt reassured when she didn't recoil and started to rub the top of her back.

'I'm so sorry,' he murmured. 'I was completely out of order. I know you love Ben more than anyone in the world.'

She didn't respond but her sobbing subsided to large, intermittent sniffs. Eventually she straightened her back and lightly placed one of her hands over his.

'And I know you do too.'

He felt a wave of relief that she may have forgiven the rash remark fired off in resentful anger rather than rooted in genuine belief. Sighing, he removed his hands from her shoulders and sat down in the adjacent chair.

'You're right. The chaos *is* the fault of me and my bloody big mouth. I fucked up.'

Karen squeezed his forearm and gave him a sad smile. 'You did what you thought was best. No one can blame you for that, including me.'

A slight tapping noise prompted them both to look towards the living-room door where an apprehensive Tania was peering into the kitchen.

'Is it safe to come in?' she asked. They both smiled.

'Yes, I've stopped beating him up now.' Karen pointed to the empty chair opposite. 'Come and join us.'

'I said something extremely twattish,' said Joe sheepishly.

'Surely not.' Tania seemed relieved their relationship had temporarily returned to its usual jokily combative ground. 'That would be *so* out of character.'

He laughed and poked out his tongue, pleased too that the atmosphere had lightened considerably. He was about to suggest making them all a fresh cup of coffee when Tania cleared her throat and looked expectantly from one to the other.

'That was James Spender on the phone.'

'Oh God, what *now*?' Karen looked anxious.

Tania beamed broadly. 'Nick's agreed to go ahead with the preimplantation.'

'Yes!' Joe instinctively leapt to his feet and punched the air, whilst Karen stared wordlessly at her friend as if she might suddenly announce she was making a joke in very poor taste. When she realised it *was* true, she too shot out of her chair and flung her arms around Joe, pressing her right cheek against his chest and holding on for all her might.

At first, startled by the first such intimate contact since her confession, Joe was unsure how to react, his arms raised in the air, hovering hesitantly above her head. Then he lowered them and enveloped her in a quick hug before the adrenalin subsided and they both awkwardly took a step back out of each other's reach.

'That's fantastic news,' he said, feeling close to tears. 'The end could finally be in sight.'

He was talking about Ben's poor health. The fate of his marriage was something about which he still had to decide.

★　　★　　★

'Quiet, *please*!' James raised his hands in the air. He was surrounded by a mêlée of reporters and camera crews, all jostling for prime position and shouting questions at him. They'd been standing outside Portcullis House, the building close to the House of Commons where Nick had an office, for the two hours since the news had been put out via the Press Association that an official statement was to be made at one p.m.

It was ten past now and the crowd was getting extremely restless, in particular the local evening papers grumbling about impending deadlines.

'As soon as you all calm down, the statement will be made,' bellowed James. It seemed to work and an uneasy silence descended to just a backdrop of nearby traffic noises.

'Right. Thank you.' He looked over his shoulder and nodded at a security guard standing by the revolving glass doors. Nick emerged from the building and stood at James's side, his presence prompting the reporters to become excitable again.

'Are you going to resign?' shouted the man from the London *Evening Standard*, but he was steadfastly ignored as Nick consulted the piece of paper in his hand and opened his mouth to speak.

'Sssssh,' a fierce-looking woman chastised her colleagues, pushing her radio microphone closer to Nick and James.

'Of late,' Nick began, speaking slowly and deliberately so he didn't make a mistake, 'my private life has been eclipsing headlines about all the good work my department has been doing to carry on improving a health service that is already the envy of the world –'

'What about the boy?' shouted someone from the back of the throng.

'Quiet!' James scowled in the direction of where the voice had come from, but everyone looked like butter wouldn't melt in their mouths. 'Carry on,' he murmured encouragingly to Nick.

'I take full responsibility for that and, consequently, have this morning resigned from government with immediate effect – in the hope this will allow my colleagues to get on with the important job of governing the country, without distractions.'

An audible gasp went round the crowd as he said it, the reporters scribbling down a verbatim note of his words, the cameramen double-checking their lenses were still firmly trained on him.

'What did the Prime Minister say?' asked the woman from the radio station, but Nick raised his hand to indicate he hadn't finished speaking.

'On the matter of the son I never knew I had, I wish you all to know that I *will* be co-operating with the preimplantation genetic diagnosis and I thank you all for *your* assistance in protecting him from any unnecessary and harmful publicity. I hope for his sake it stays that way. For my part, this is the only comment I will *ever* make on this matter. I can't emphasise that enough. Thank you.'

Folding up the piece of paper, he gave them a twisted smile and turned to leave.

Chaos broke out with immediate effect, reporters bellowing 'Will you stay in touch with your son?' and 'What does your wife think of all this?' to his retreating back.

Nick ignored them and stepped back through the doors of Portcullis House where two security guards closed in on the door to prevent anyone else from entering.

Following him inside, James patted him on the back. 'Well done. That was tough but . . .' he petered out, distracted by the sight of the Home Secretary walking towards the lifts.

'Ah Minister! I need a word . . .'

He scurried off, leaving Nick standing alone.

'Now there's a question.'

Judy nodded towards the television in her living room, where a news bulletin had just shown Nick retreating from the assembled reporters.

'Sorry?' mumbled Stella, still staring at the screen even though her sister had now switched it off.

'"What does your wife think of all this?" I said, *there's* a question.'

Stella didn't answer. Dejectedly, she stood up and walked across to the window where a small group of children were circling the cul-de-sac on their bicycles. Every so often, the net curtains of one of the houses twitched and the face of a concerned parent peered out, checking their children were still visible.

'Well? What *do* you think?' persisted Judy from behind her.

'Thank God it's over. That's what I think.' She turned away from the window and faced her.

'*Over*? Hardly.' Judy's expression was derisive.

'Don't.' Her tone was mutinous because she knew what was coming. All their lives Judy had seen fit to give her opinion on Stella's every utterance or action, whether solicited or not, and it had been the cause of some ferocious arguments between them.

Animated by indignation, Judy leapt up from the sofa and strode behind it, her face clouded with concern.

'What, exactly, does Nick have to do to make you leave him? Knock you about?'

Stella let out a hollow laugh. She knew she shouldn't get drawn into this line of questioning, but as ever, her sister knew exactly what buttons to press.

'For pity's sake, don't be so melodramatic. If every marriage ended because of one affair, we'd *all* be living alone.'

'Not every man cheats. Mike has never been unfaithful to me.'

'You don't know that.'

'Yes I bloody do. And if I even *suspected* it, I'd chuck him out.'

'Well bully for you.'

They glared at each other across the room for a few seconds, the years stripped back as if they were once again two young girls bickering over the ownership of a prized toy. Then Judy's expression softened and she walked round to the front of the sofa, patting the empty cushion next to her.

Still feeling prickly, Stella was reluctant to sit there, but she did so for fear of making matters worse and finding herself with nowhere as discreet to stay that night.

'When we were growing up, I was always so jealous of you,' her sister said. 'You were prettier than me, brighter than me, and he always denied it, but I know you were Dad's favourite . . .'

None of it was true. Stella had always felt like a frump next to her more outrageously 'out there' sibling, and Judy had been every bit as bright at school but had chosen to waste her years chasing boys rather than gain impressive exam results. If anything, their father had favoured his older daughter, secretly admiring her joie de vivre and healthy disrespect for authority.

'. . . you could have married *anyone*,' she added wistfully.

'I married a man who became a bloody cabinet minister!' Stella couldn't hide her disdain. As ever, her sister was displaying what she saw as the rank stupidity that so often sparked their fallouts. 'He's hardly some deadbeat using dole money to buy heroin, is he? I don't get your point.'

'My *point*, is that you gave up everything for him and he gave up nothing for you.'

243

She shook her head slowly. They'd skirted round this issue before and she'd painstakingly explained to her sister that she'd given up work because she'd *wanted* to, feeling it might enhance her chances of getting pregnant. In those circumstances, the suggestion that her husband should abandon a high-flying political career to stay at home whilst she carried on working was palpably ludicrous, yet Judy didn't seem to accept that the current set-up had been a mutual decision.

'So what are you saying?' Stella felt and sounded irritated now. 'That I'm some downtrodden housewife, being forced by my overbearing husband to hide my light under a bushel? Is that it? Am I presumed to be incapable of independent, rational thought on the path my own life is taking?'

She glared at her sister who shifted uncomfortably in her seat.

'No, that's not it at all.' Judy let out a long OK-if-I-must sigh. 'I wasn't going to mention it, but Mum's always thought he wasn't good enough for you.'

Stella stared at her for a couple of seconds, just to check if she was about to grin broadly to illustrate the juvenility of her remark, but she didn't. So Stella threw her head back and let out a loud, theatrical laugh.

'You're actually bloody *serious*! Have you heard yourself?'

Judy tightened her lips disapprovingly. 'Take the

piss if you want, but it's true. Mum says he's a rough diamond and they can sometimes let you down.'

Leaping to her feet, Stella strode to the fireplace then swivelled back to face the sofa, her face twisted with disbelief.

'Well, how *thrilled* you both must be to be proved so spectacularly right.'

'It's not like that –'

'Save it . . .' she interrupted sharply. 'Perhaps that jealousy you were talking about has finally consumed you so much that you think it's acceptable behaviour to bitch about my marriage behind my back?'

She looked inquiringly at her sister who was shaking her head.

'It wasn't like that. We were concerned because we *love* you, that's all.'

'So how come Mum and I have never had cosy chats about you and Mike then?' Stella countered, knowing it sounded childish. 'And as for Mum's view of Nick, I could have married the fucking Pope and she'd think he wasn't good enough for our family. She's so entrenched in her little bubble of twee garden parties and book clubs with fellow snobs, she has no idea of the real world. Give me a working-class boy made good any day.'

'Even if he cheats on you?'

'Cheat*ed*. Past tense and singular.'

They lapsed into sullen silence until Judy took an audible intake of breath.

'You're going to stick with him, aren't you?'

Stella walked towards the living-room door, her hand resting on the ornate brass doorknob. Her tone was cool. 'Actually, I'm not sure what I'm going to do. But when I've made a decision, I'm sure you and Mum will have lots to say about it.'

She walked out into the hallway, then took a step backwards, leaning her head back into the room.

'By the way, thanks for the use of your spare room. I'll be out of your hair as soon as I've packed.'

Halfway up the stairs, she bumped into Oliver careering down the other way, his talking Buzz Lightyear in his hand. 'Auntie Stella, will you play space wars with me?' he pleaded.

'I can't my darling.' She smiled warmly at him. 'I have to go now, but we'll play it another day.'

'Where are you going?' he asked, curling an arm around her leg and squeezing it tight.

'Good question,' she murmured, her eyes brimming with tears.

CHAPTER 18

Joe was lying on his side on the living-room floor, pushing Ben's wooden Brio train around the track and making 'choo choo' noises, much to the little boy's obvious delight.

'Sometimes, I wonder who gets the most pleasure from that thing – him or you,' smiled Karen.

Her attention was diverted by the clattering sound of the letterbox being opened and snapping shut again.

'Christ, how many pizza leaflets do we need?' she muttered. It was too early for the postman.

Out in the hallway, she picked up the standard-sized white envelope with 'Mr and Mrs Eastman' scribbled on the front and wandered back through with it.

'It must have been delivered by hand . . .' Frowning, she tore it open.

'Bloody hell!'

Joe looked up at her questioningly.

'It's a letter from Jake Thompson at the *Post* . . . offering us *two hundred thousand pounds* to tell our story.'

'Very funny.' He went back to playing with the train.

'No, I'm serious. Look.' She handed him the letter.

He read it, his eyes widening. 'Wow. That's life-changing money.'

She nodded, amazed that what they might have to say would be worth that much.

'That would pay for Ben's operation and clear the mortgage on this place,' said Joe practically.

But she shook her head as soon as the words left his mouth. 'It would also mean open season on our family. The minute we open our lives to them, they'll feel they can write whatever they like, whenever they like.'

Sighing, she took the letter from him and pointedly tore it in to small pieces, before placing them in the waste-paper basket by the fireplace. 'I'd rather be poor and anonymous.'

He stared at the bin for several seconds, obviously deep in thought.

'But we're not anonymous anymore, are we?' he said eventually, pointing towards the pile of newspapers on the dining table. 'Today they've written about my antics at the press conference, and let's face it, tomorrow and for many days after they'll write all sorts of conjectured crap about us anyway, so we might as well take the money and put our side of the story. At least then we can control it a little.'

'No. Because then, that lot out there . . .' she

jerked her head towards the window '. . . could hound us forever on the basis that we'd co-operated with them just once.'

'Not necessarily.'

'It's true,' she persisted. 'I remember seeing a chat show once, something like *Parkinson*, and there was somebody famous . . . can't remember who . . . talking about fame and how it's not a tap you can switch on and off.'

'But we're not famous.'

'Famous, infamous, it doesn't matter. The minute you *invite* attention you can't then complain about it when it doesn't go your way at a later date.'

Joe shifted himself into a sitting position, still looking doubtful.

'But haven't I kind of invited attention already?'

She gave it careful consideration. 'I think people will see that you turned up at the press conference out of desperation, to save your son. And they'll sympathise.' Walking to the fireplace, she leant on the mantel. 'But if we invite the media into our home and get paid for it?' She pulled a face. 'I think we'll lose what good faith we have.'

He shrugged. 'Your call. But I still think we should give it a little more thought, because without that money we're going to struggle to find the cash for Ben's op.'

'We could always ask Nick Bright.' She winced as she said it. 'Even if it's just a loan?'

Joe's face was unreadable but his answer was not.

'Over my dead body.'

The cardboard box on his desk had originally housed a printer but now had the word 'rubbish' scrawled across it in black felt pen. Nick smiled at the irony. Was that what *he* was now . . . rubbish? Yet another body on the funeral pyre of politics?

His PA had used the box for the usual collection of letters from mad constituents, the ones written in green ink and capitals about subjects ranging from supermarket trolleys to bus timetables. But she'd finally sent them off to the incinerator and now the box was full of Nick's bits and pieces, most of which were probably rubbish too but he hadn't found time to clear them out. Now he had more time than he knew what to do with.

Picking up the framed photograph of Stella, he studied it for several seconds. Why *had* he cheated on her? It was a question that had tormented him since learning of Ben's existence, but prior to that it had barely crossed his mind.

The morning after his indiscretion he had felt a slight twinge of guilt. But confident that Karen wasn't the kiss-and-tell type, he had swiftly pushed it to the back of his mind as a brief aberration that had meant nothing. He got on with his life, as certain as ever that Stella was the only woman for him, both physically and mentally.

So why, he asked himself again as he stood in his empty office facing an uncertain future, had he taken such a risk for a brief sexual encounter with a complete stranger?

Whenever that night had surfaced in his mind, he'd always hastily pushed it out again, probably more through guilt than anything else. But now he focused his attention on it and the memory came flooding back easily.

That night at the local elections, he already knew he was being lined up for a job in the cabinet, having been secretly sounded out by the Prime Minister. Only he and Stella had known, sworn to discretion because the soon-to-be outgoing minister was still unaware of his impending fate.

So that knowledge, coupled with the euphoria of some excellent results at the local elections, had made Nick feel pumped up and, subsequently, incredibly horny. And Stella was out of town at her mother's.

The first time he'd noticed Karen, she was standing in the corner of the room, surrounded by party workers celebrating their victory. She was blonde and pretty, not the type he normally went for. But there was something about the quiet strength in her eyes that attracted him. And, if he was honest, her great tits.

He toyed with the idea of strolling over to say an idle hello, but then Tania hove into view and dragged her off in the direction of the bar. He'd moved to another part of the room and got cornered by a group of fresh-faced, first-year politics students who all thought they were going to change the world. Wait till you start paying bills like the rest of us, he'd thought, tiring rapidly of their idealistic chatter.

Several drinks and the Taj Mahal of hard-ons later, he decided to call it a night and go home for a spot of self-abuse in front of the first dodgy porn channel he could find.

As he emerged into the cold night air and started trying to hail a taxi, he spotted someone a few yards away fruitlessly attempting the same thing.

'Let's do a deal,' he slurred. 'Whoever gets a cab first shares it with the other.'

'But what if we don't live in the same direction?' the female voice had replied. When she walked towards him and emerged from the shadows, he'd realised it was her, the one with the great tits.

'I'm central,' he said, trying to ignore the twitching in his boxer shorts.

'Me too.' Ten minutes into the cab journey, they'd shared small talk about the party and her friendship with Tania, two drearily safe subjects that had done nothing to abate his erection.

'Actually,' he smiled hazily. 'I noticed you earlier and was going to come and say hello. You have amazing . . . eyes.'

'Thanks.'

He couldn't be sure, but she now seemed to be using those eyes to great flirtatious effect, lowering them slightly so she peered at him through long, downturned lashes.

And then it happened. Almost unconsciously, he moved nearer so his face was just a few inches from hers and waited to see if she recoiled. She didn't, so he tentatively pressed his lips against hers and felt his cock stiffen further as she responded. Within a couple of seconds, the coy kiss had turned into a full-on mêlée of lips and tongues, his stubble grinding against her face. By the time the cab stopped, his hand was inside her blouse and cupping one of the treasures he'd been coveting earlier.

'We're here, mate.'

The cab driver's grating voice sliced through the sexually charged moment and Nick pulled back to look her in the eyes. He knew this was the point he could either get out of the cab alone and forget what had just happened, or . . .

'Coffee?'

She nodded her agreement to the euphemism and followed him out of the cab and up to the door of the Victorian terraced house he and Stella were in the process of flogging to buy something on the river.

The minute they were inside the hallway, the door closed behind them and Nick pressed her against the wall and kissed her again, his hands tugging open the front of her silk blouse whilst she fumbled with the button and zip of his trousers.

As her hand found his cock and clasped it he thought he might pass out from expectation. His sex life with Stella was good, but there was something urgent and explosive about doing it with a stranger.

Cupping her breasts, every bit as spectacular as he'd imagined, he moved his tongue from one to the other as she groaned loudly and started to remove her own skirt. He was disappointed to note she was wearing tights, but she slipped them off with ease and he manoeuvred himself into firing position.

Reluctantly removing his hands from her breasts, he hoisted her skirt up and tugged her pants to one side, thrusting himself inside her. It lasted for two minutes, tops, but he had to admit it was the most exciting sexual encounter he'd ever had. She was attractive, they were both pissed and lacking inhibitions, it had a heady sense of urgency and, for him, the biggest turn-on of all was that he'd fucked her without even knowing her name.

'What's your name?' he asked as he tucked his shirt back into his trousers.

'Karen.' She smiled and picked up her handbag. 'And I have to go.'

He knew he should have offered to call her a cab, but it would have been at least a twenty-minute wait. Twenty minutes of polite chit-chat and post-coital awkwardness. So he'd simply smiled, kissed her perfunctorily on the cheek in a nice-to-meet-you way and let her go it alone in the dark night air.

Since then, however ashamed he was to admit it, the encounter had sneaked into his thoughts several times whilst making love to Stella. But only in an anonymous, porn-film sense, not because he had any feelings for Karen. In fact, until the day she walked into his office, eighteen months later, he'd have struggled to remember what she looked like.

And yet that brief, meaningless encounter had created something he and his wife, the woman he had loved for years, had so far failed to produce . . . a child.

Placing Stella's photograph on top of the box, he asked himself the question again. Why *had* he cheated?

'Because I was pissed and thought I could get away with it. Simple as that,' he murmured to himself, with rare honesty.

Picking up the box, he paused a moment, stopping to take one last look around the office that housed so many memories from his political career. Then he walked out, closing the door firmly behind him.

CHAPTER 19

Karen emerged into the garden carrying a breakfast tray, squinting from the early morning sun. It was a pleasant day, but not warm enough for just T-shirts, so she had her dressing gown on and Tania was wearing one of Joe's sweatshirts. Ben, still wearing his fluffy all-in-one pyjamas, was sitting on a blanket on the grass, playing with brightly coloured building bricks.

'Where's Joe?' asked Tania, as she lifted the two mugs of coffee from the tray and cleared a space for the plates of toast.

Karen nodded towards the back fence that bordered the enclosed garden of another house.

'Our neighbour, a lovely old lady called Jean, has agreed we can jump over the fence and get out through her house to avoid the photographers. He's gone to get the papers.'

Sighing, she took a bite of toast and handed Ben's bottle of juice down to him. 'For the first time ever, I'm actually glad my parents retired to New Zealand . . . away from all the crap.'

'There is no hiding place.' Tania pulled an ominous face. 'It'll have reached there.'

'It has, but more diluted than here thank God. I've had a couple of very awkward phone conversations with them and had to stop Mum jumping on a plane, but I've assured them we're all fine.'

Tania smiled. 'I ran the gamut of the bloody photographers again this morning. A couple of them even called out my name, so they've obviously twigged who I am.'

'They won't write about you . . .' She looked uncertain. 'Will they?'

Her friend shrugged. 'Probably. After all, if I hadn't been working for Nick, you'd never have been at that party in the first place. Tomorrow's headlines will probably be "Tania Fletcher, the MP's Pimp".'

Karen groaned. 'Sorry.'

'I'm *joking*. And stop bloody apologising!' She rolled her eyes then sighed. 'To be honest, I've had other things on my mind.'

'Oh?'

She looked pained. 'I'm pregnant.'

'What? *How?*'

'I'm not *that* bloody ugly.'

Grinning, Karen prodded her. 'My point is that the last time I asked about your sex life you said it was more endangered than a giant panda . . . now you're suddenly pregnant. Whose is it?'

Tania winced wearily. 'James.'

'James?' She looked puzzled at first, then her eyes widened as realisation dawned. 'What, James *Spender?*'

Her friend nodded.

'But you hate him.'

'Alcohol is a terrible thing.'

'Why didn't you tell me you'd slept with him?' She felt slightly wounded that she'd been kept in the dark.

'Shame,' Tania grimaced. 'The very same reason you didn't tell me about Nick.'

'You have nothing to be ashamed of. You're single and so's he.'

'I know, it's not that. More that he's also spoken to me like shit and just because he was nice to me for all of five minutes, I succumbed. I fell for one of the oldest cons in the book.'

'Don't be too hard on yourself.' Karen patted her shoulder, then her expression morphed into one of concern. 'Are you absolutely sure you're pregnant?'

'Positive Predictor-test sure.'

'Ah. So what are you going to do?'

Tania shrugged her shoulders. 'I was hoping you might have a suggestion.'

'Have you seen him again?'

'Only at work.'

'So he doesn't know?'

She shook her head.

'And I take it this isn't going to be the start of something beautiful?'

'Hardly.' She let out a puff of air that rippled the top of her coffee. 'Pregnant from a bloody one-night stand? Abortion clinic here I come . . .'

She glanced over at Ben, then, realising what she'd said, turned puce. 'Sorry, I didn't mean . . .'

But Karen was already shaking her head. 'Don't forget, I thought I was pregnant by Joe. If I'd known otherwise, I might have had a termination myself.'

'Only might?'

'I guess you have to go with your gut instinct at the time.'

Tania nodded thoughtfully. 'I read an article the other day that said two out of ten men are unknowingly bringing up children that aren't theirs.'

'Yes, I'd heard that.' She bit her lip. 'The burning question is: how many of them stick around once they find out?'

Their conversation was curtailed by the sound of a low groan coming from the end of the garden. Joe was straddling the fence, his trousers caught on a protruding piece of wire. Throwing the carrier bag of newspapers to the ground, he managed to extricate himself and jumped off, stooping down to kiss the top of Ben's head as he approached the table. He looked thunderous.

'They've really gone to town on me.' He pulled out the *Post* and tossed it with disdain on to an empty chair.

Sensing this should be a private moment, Tania got to her feet. 'I'm going to head off now. Thanks for the coffee.' She patted the sweatshirt. 'Can I bring this back another time?'

'Of course. Let's speak later.' Karen gave her a knowing look, feeling guilty that her friend was having to leave before they'd even begun to properly discuss the pregnancy and her options. But she could tell from Joe's glowering demeanour that Tania was better off out of it.

As soon as she'd gone, Karen picked up the *Post* under Joe's watchful eye and held it out in front of her. Across it, in giant letters and above a picture of some blonde girl with a gormless expression, was the headline 'Joe was a B-eastman in bed'.

She frowned in puzzlement, her heart beating that little bit faster as she wondered about the timing of this alleged sexual encounter. 'Who is she?'

He shrugged nonchalantly but his face was etched with frustration. 'It's some girl who says I slept with her at college. I don't even bloody remember speaking to her, let alone sleeping with her.'

'So why would she . . . ?'

He rubbed his thumb and forefinger together to indicate 'money'.

'I was single at the time, so it's hardly libellous to say I shagged her, is it? Even if it's not true,' he said bitterly. 'And look at this one . . .' Picking up another paper, he flipped it open at the centre-page spread. The headline read: 'Husband in Nick Bright scandal "Sallies" forth.'

'It's a bloke from my old ad agency who says I enjoyed a close friendship . . .' he made quote

260

marks with his fingers '. . . with Sally. He reckons it prompted your fling with Nick Bright.'

'That *is* libellous. You were married then.'

'That's why they've said "close friendship", because they can't actually prove it, but the phrase leaves the reader in no doubt that something was going on. And besides, it's true isn't it, so I can hardly sue.'

He slammed his fist down on to the newspaper. 'My point is, I don't even fucking *know* the guy. I think I said hello to him once in the canteen.'

They both sat there, he still staring disbelievingly at the stories, she frowning in faint disapproval.

'I don't get it,' she said eventually. 'Why are they having a go at you? I thought I was the villain?'

Not waiting for an answer, she gathered up all the newspapers and marched across to a large black dustbin they used for leaves and grass cuttings. Lifting the lid, she threw them inside.

'Now they're chip paper.'

She could see Joe was struggling to stay calm, his cheek twitching with anger, his mouth pinched.

'Jesus,' he spat. 'All I wanted to do was save Ben's life and now they're *crucifying* me.'

She moved behind him and instinctively put her arms around his neck, resting her head against his. It was a simple gesture, not out of the ordinary for a normal, happily married couple, but given their circumstances it felt awkward, like an embrace between two strangers.

His shoulders stiffened and he didn't attempt to touch her hands, but neither did he move away. She felt strangely reassured by that small crumb of comfort.

Nursing a glass of whisky, Nick moved from the galley kitchen into the living room where the post-match analysis on Sky Sports was blaring out of the television. Scowling, he flicked it on to mute. He liked watching the football, not the endless, turgid waffle that straddled it.

Sitting down on the sofa, he picked up his mobile for the tenth time in as many minutes and checked the screen for any calls. It was on silent because it had been ringing constantly since his resignation and he'd said all he was going to say on the matter to the press. But he was desperate to hear from Stella, other than the perfunctory, daily text she'd been sending to let him know she was OK.

He knew she'd left her sister's house, having learned the fact via an uncomfortably stiff and faintly hostile conversation with Judy, but other than that he had no idea what she was up to.

What he *did* know was that he missed her dreadfully and wanted her back home. Not because she did everything for him or because he craved company: he missed *her* as a person. Her sophisticated conversation, her sense of the ridiculous, her ability to talk him down from angry strops about work, her slightly crooked smile, her cool, soft skin next to him at night. Everything.

He slumped back against the cushions, the dull pain in his chest reminding him of the teenage angst he suffered when his first-ever girlfriend dumped him.

His once precious career was in tatters, but it bothered him far less than the prospect that his marriage might go the same way.

The door entry system buzzed loudly, prompting his chest to pound from both shock and the expectation that it might be Stella.

With the agility of a mountain goat, he was off the sofa and across to the entryphone.

'Hello?' His face dropped. 'Oh. Really? OK, send him up.'

Replacing the receiver, he frowned slightly and peered through the spyhole into the hallway. After a few seconds, he opened the door and raised his eyebrows at the sight that greeted him.

'Have you come to talk to me or rob me?'

Joe was standing in front of him in a black knitted beanie hat, hoodie and black jeans. The hood was pulled over the hat, casting his face into shadow, and he was wearing dark-rimmed glasses. Under his arm there was a small box wrapped in white paper.

'It was the only way I could get past the bloody reporters blocking your doorway. I carried a parcel so they thought I was a courier.'

'Nice one. Drink?'

'Thanks.'

Nick jerked his head towards the living room,

indicating that Joe should follow him. As he poured him a whisky and topped up his own glass at the same time, his mind was racing with thoughts of why Joe was here, particularly as he had said yes to the preimplantation.

It felt odd to be standing just two metres away from his nemesis, the man who had precipitated the chaos his life was now in, but he didn't feel anger anymore. He'd had plenty of time to reflect on Joe's actions and knew that, ultimately, he could only admire him for them.

However, judging by Joe's body language and blatantly cold manner, he could only assume the feeling wasn't reciprocated towards the man who had screwed his wife behind his back.

'So. Why are you here?' He handed him the drink and sat down on the sofa, gesturing towards the armchair. But Joe remained standing.

'The press are hounding us. Can you call them off?'

Nick laughed softly then realised he was deadly serious.

'Look, mate, if I could control them, I'd still be in the cabinet. And they certainly wouldn't be standing outside my building right now.'

Joe frowned. 'But what about privacy laws?'

Placing his empty glass on the coffee table in front of him, Nick leaned back and placed his arms behind his head.

'They'll protect Ben as he's only a child, but I'm afraid you invaded your own privacy when you pulled that stunt at the press conference. You can't use the media for what you want then demand they lay off at a later date, it doesn't work like that.'

Glancing up, he suddenly became worried for his own safety as he saw Joe's face darken, his fists clenched by his sides.

'Sorry,' he backtracked hastily. 'That probably sounded a little pompous. I didn't mean it to, that's what years of being a politician does for you.'

He smiled nervously, hoping to lighten the atmosphere, and it seemed to work. Joe's hands and face relaxed and he finally sat down with a weary sigh, shaking his head in a gesture of resignation.

'I thought that might be the case. Karen said as much when we were offered money to tell our story.'

'How much?'

'It was two hundred thousand but it's gone up to three hundred now.'

Nick let out a low whistle. 'You must be tempted?'

He nodded, looking faintly shameful. 'But Karen's having none of it. She's very principled.'

'Admirable, but principles don't pay the bills.'

'Yes, particularly when we have to *pay* for the treatment to try and save Ben's life. Put that in one of your bloody speeches.'

Nick put his hands up in surrender. 'I don't

think anyone would listen now. I'm already yesterday's man.' He paused, a thought striking him. 'Do you need some money?'

But Joe shook his head almost instantly. 'Thanks, but no thanks.'

He got the impression the refusal had more to do with pride than them already having the money they needed, but the resolute tone convinced Nick not to probe any further.

Joe's scowl dissipated slightly and silence descended. Levering himself to a more upright position, Nick refilled his whisky glass and held the bottle out towards his unannounced guest who declined.

'Actually,' he pondered. 'Thinking about it, did Karen know you were going to turn up at the press conference?'

Joe shook his head.

'In which case, there might be the legal argument that as she hasn't invaded her own privacy, she should be left alone. The same goes for the rest of your family. But you, I'm afraid, are a marked man. Me too.'

Joe let out an almost imperceptible groan. 'What about your wife? How's she taken all this?'

Nick shrugged. 'Hard to say really. She's gone away for a few days and we've not really conversed beyond the initial "you bastard" bit. You?'

'I'm just concentrating on Ben.'

'You're very close to him, aren't you?'

Joe nodded and bit his lip, trying to control his

emotions. 'We've got such a strong bond that I couldn't believe he wasn't my flesh and blood.'

'Does it matter?'

'No. I realise that now.'

He didn't show any signs of elaborating and Nick didn't want to push him. In truth, he didn't really want to know any more, feeling he had enough problems of his own without having to take on board someone else's.

'Stella and I have been trying for a baby.' He stared down at the Persian rug. 'She'd just had a miscarriage when all this happened.'

'It must have been very tough for you both . . . you know, finding out you already had a child.'

'Tougher for her I think. She's desperate to have children.'

'And you?' Joe was looking at him intently.

'Not sure. But I'll probably embrace it when . . . if . . . it happens.'

Joe opened his mouth to speak then paused, as if he was struggling to say whatever was coming next.

'Have you thought about what role you want in Ben's life?' he said evenly.

'He's your son, not mine.'

He seemed faintly surprised by the answer. 'Don't you even want to meet him?'

'To make me feel better about myself?' Nick shook his head firmly. 'No, he's got you, and when he gets older he'll understand that my decision had nothing to do with rejection and everything to do with what felt right at the time.'

'And what about the next one?'

Nick felt it like a punch to the thorax. The next one. There was going to be another. He knew it and yet, until now, he hadn't really humanised it. He'd been thinking of it as a sterile process in some laboratory, but now in his mind's eye, he was picturing a pink-cheeked baby. Yet another one with the wrong woman.

He closed his eyes and fought back the swell of nausea rising from the pit of his stomach.

'My feelings are exactly the same,' he replied flatly. 'Whether you decide to step up to the mark and be "Daddy" is entirely up to you.'

Leaping back over the garden fence with well-practised agility, Joe removed his beanie hat and walked in to the brightly lit kitchen. He could hear low voices in the living room and presumed it was Tania again. She seemed to live here these days.

Unzipping his hoodie, he wandered through and found Karen sitting on the sofa looking strained and red-eyed. His brother Andy was next to her, his arm round her shoulder.

'What's happened?' His heart lurched.

'I nipped out to the chip shop for us and some woman walking past shouted "Where's your little bastard?"' she explained tearfully.

Andy looked up at him. 'I've told her they're morons and to take no notice.'

He nodded vehemently and sat down in an armchair, kicking his shoes off. 'Is Ben in bed?'

She nodded, using the end of her sleeve to wipe under her eyes.

'Why don't you go and have a nice long bath?' he said quietly. 'Andy and I will keep an ear out for little 'un.'

'I think I will.' Kissing Andy on the cheek, she murmured 'Thanks for everything' and left the room.

Waiting until the floorboards creaked above their heads, Joe stretched his legs out in front of him and made a puffing noise. 'I'll tell you what, mate, this isn't getting any easier.'

'I know, I've read the papers. It's brutal stuff.'

'It's *shite* stuff. I've never even met that woman in the *Post*, let alone shagged her.'

Andy nodded sombrely. 'I knew she was bull-shitting as soon as she said you had a big dick.'

Joe laughed. It felt good.

'And anyway, who's interested in a load of old crap about someone they don't even know?' he demanded.

His brother pursed his lips. 'Well someone must be, or they wouldn't print it. Supply and demand I think they call it.'

'Yeah, I suppose so.' He shrugged resignedly. 'I know I brought it on myself, but it doesn't half hit hard when it's *you* they're writing about. No wonder celebrities say they stop reading the papers.'

'They came to my door too. I told them to fuck off,' said Andy with characteristic bluntness. 'But

Mum's finding it harder to deal with them outside her house every day. You know what's she like, torn between telling them to go away or making them a nice cup of Darjeeling so she doesn't appear rude.'

He started rummaging inside his coat pocket, pulling out a crumpled brown envelope.

'Here, I want you to have this.'

Puzzled, Joe took it and started to rip it open. 'Not your Pokémon cards,' he teased.

'Fuck off, you're not getting your greasy mitts on those,' quipped Andy.

Joe peered inside, his eyes widening.

'There's at least a couple of grand here . . .'

His brother nodded. 'Two thousand, three hundred pounds to be precise. I was saving for a motorbike, but I'm a bit old now . . . it seems daft . . .'

He handed back the envelope, his nose prickling with emotion. 'Thanks, but I can't take it. You've wanted one since we were kids.'

Andy shrugged. 'Priorities change. Ben's what's important. Get money where you can, mate, sod the consequences.'

Joe looked at him and nodded animatedly. 'You're absolutely right, but keep your money. As I have absolutely nothing to lose, I've got another plan.'

CHAPTER 20

Nick woke up with a pounding hangover and remembered that, last night, he'd polished off the best part of a bottle of whisky. He'd always been fond of the stuff, but when he'd been promoted to cabinet he'd made a concerted effort to lay off it, particularly because he was Health Minister and in the habit of preaching to others about moderation.

He stumbled into the kitchen and flicked on the kettle, then opened the fridge to look for the fresh orange juice he always started the day with. But the carton was worryingly light and when he poured it into the glass there was barely an inch left and it was fizzy.

Stella kept the fridge and cupboards well stocked with everything he liked and, if he was honest, he'd come to take it for granted that his favourite coarse grain mustard would be there or the special yoghurt drinks he swigged back each day to help his cholesterol. But now the stocks were running low and he was faced with the very real and present danger of having to cross the portals of a supermarket himself.

If ever questioned about her role in his life, Nick acknowledged that Stella was the glue that held him together, both practically and emotionally. It was a well-rehearsed answer that rolled off his tongue effortlessly. But now she was gone, he realised how true it was, how his heart felt as empty as his fridge.

Mr Cheese and Mrs Chalk was how their mutual friends had referred to them in the early days of their marriage, his best man even referring to it in his speech. She came from a well-to-do family headed by her father, Ralph, who had been chairman of a blue-chip company and successful enough to buy a large country home with a swimming pool and paddocks when his daughters were still young. Consequently, Stella had enjoyed a stereotypically idyllic childhood with summer pool parties and gymkhanas.

Nick, on the other hand, was brought up in a small terraced house in Fleetwood, just outside Blackpool. It was a seaside town, so what his family lacked in resources he made up for with summer days spent on the beach or searching every slot machine on the pier for loose change. Money, he now knew, had been tight for his parents Bill and Mary who both worked in the local fish market. But he hadn't noticed then, thriving instead on their tough love and the familiar routine of school, out to play, home for tea and bed by nine p.m. Besides, it wasn't as if he was surrounded by friends who had flashier

272

lifestyles, they were all pretty much in the same boat, their parents struggling to stay afloat financially. He'd craved having a younger brother to kick ball with, but his mother said they couldn't afford to have any more children. So he'd remained an only child.

He hadn't been academic, but his love of sport saw him through school as well as the gift of the gab learned from spending so much time in the company of adults. His parents had never talked down to him, often including him in their kitchen-table debates about the state of the nation. Bill was a dyed-in-the-wool Labourite and when Mary had voted for Margaret Thatcher in 1979 he'd sulked for over a week. He was dead now, from lung cancer, brought on by the forty-a-day habit he'd finally whittled down to ten just before he was diagnosed at the age of fifty-two. He'd lasted another two years.

Mary had fallen to pieces at first. After all, they'd met at seventeen, married at nineteen, and spent the past thirty-five years by each other's side. Their one night apart had been Nick's birth, and even then his father had left the hospital at midnight and returned seven hours later. Suddenly, Mary's life felt empty and Nick and Stella spent most weekends hurtling up and down the motorway to visit her. Then, one weekend eighteen months on, she'd shown them a cutting from a newspaper property section, of a new development of flats on the Costa del Sol.

'I'm torn between wanting to stay in Fleetwood forever, because it reminds me of Bill, and being driven mad by it because he's not here and it's not the same anymore. So I've made a decision,' she'd said.

The decision was to sell up and use the money to buy a neat, two-bedroomed flat in Spain, somewhere completely different to everything she knew in the hope that her life would move on. And it did. To her credit, she was now a 64-year-old woman who looked about fifty-five and had a wonderfully active life full of good friends. Nick had never dared say it to her, but it was almost as if Bill's death had been a release for her, a chance to live in the country she'd always been fascinated by but Bill had refused to go to, citing 'horrible food and foreigners' as the primary reasons.

Knowing the British newspapers were printed in Spain and some busybody was bound to enlighten her, Nick had called to warn her a few hours after the press conference. She had listened very quietly and not made any judgemental remarks, which he was grateful for, but he could hear the disappointment in her voice and it crucified him. After all, here was a woman who'd had a tough life, yet her proudest achievement was her rock-solid marriage and the happy family home she'd created for her only child. And here he was, repaying that legacy by admitting he'd had a sordid one-night stand whilst his wife was out of town and now had a 'love child', as the papers had referred to Ben. *Her* grandson, in fact. It had crossed his mind that she might want to meet the boy, but she hadn't mentioned it and he hoped it stayed that way.

Draining a glass of water instead of his usual juice, Nick sighed and glanced across at the bookshelf where a picture of him and Stella on their wedding day had pride of place. It hadn't been a lavish affair, just a quick register office ceremony followed by a lunch for about fifty friends and family, then off for a fortnight's honeymoon in the Seychelles. Stella had wanted it that way, knowing that otherwise her mother would hijack the entire thing and she'd be dressed in a meringue whilst the London Philharmonic played on the vast lawns of her parents' house and various hideously snooty relatives brayed their way through the day.

But even that hadn't been her parents' greatest disappointment. That was reserved for her choice of husband. They *liked* Nick, they'd told her the day before the wedding – something she didn't reveal to Nick until many years later – but they didn't think he was right for their daughter. Not equipped with the life skills to get on in this world, her mother had said. Stella had told him all this the night he'd come home and sworn her to secrecy about the impending cabinet job, and they'd laughed heartily at the irony. Then two nights later, he'd gone to the local elections and had sex with another woman – both betraying his wife *and* confirming her parents' doubts about him in one fell swoop.

His heart fluttered as he heard a key rattle outside the front door. He knew it wasn't the cleaner because they'd sacked her after catching her rummaging through some of Nick's private papers, probably with the aim of trying to sell some dirt on him. So it *had* to be Stella. His chest tightened as the front door opened and, sure enough, she was standing there with a suitcase in her hand. She placed it down on the floor and closed the door.

'Hello.' He made sure his tone was light and friendly.

'Hello.'

Hers wasn't and he knew immediately that she was still a long way from forgiving him, if she ever did. He looked at his watch. It was 8.30 a.m.

'You're early.'

'I was trying to catch you out.' She smiled thinly. 'Oh sorry, bit late for that.'

She picked up the suitcase and strode through to the bedroom, returning seconds later without it.

'I've got an appointment. Bye.'

The front door slammed shut and Nick stood there for a few moments, wondering what it all meant. Did leaving the suitcase mean she was staying? What was the appointment? Hair? Medical? Divorce lawyer? An icy chill ran down his neck.

Her tone had been distinctly frosty, but she'd

come back, however briefly, and her suitcase was in the bedroom. For now, he was going to treat it as a promising development.

Dragging the iron across the vast expanses of Joe's sweatshirt, Karen hummed along to one of the tunes being played on Steve Wright's Radio 2 show. God knows there were still many question marks in her life, but she was feeling happier than she had in a long time, simply because she knew everything that *could* be done to improve Ben's quality of life was about to happen. She didn't have to fight for it anymore and it afforded her something approaching a sense of calm.

There were many issues to be resolved between her and Joe, but as long as they ignored the elephant in the room, or rather the *spare* room, they seemed to be rubbing along together quite well.

'Ah, the devil, so to speak,' she murmured to herself as she heard a key in the lock.

'I was just thinking about you,' she said as Joe walked into the room. But he didn't return her smile, looking decidedly uncomfortable. Walking across to the mantel-piece, he reached out and switched off the radio.

'Hey! I was listening to that.' She deliberately kept her tone light and conciliatory, whereas prior to recent events she'd probably have snapped his head off for being so presumptuous.

He was pacing now, pointing to the armchair as

he passed it. 'Can you sit down? I need to tell you something.'

She felt a flutter of rising panic, her sense of calm erased. 'What is it?'

A number of possibilities flicked through her mind, but the one she kept coming back to was that he was going to leave her.

'I've sold my story.'

Karen looked momentarily relieved then her features shifted to a frown when she realised she hadn't a clue what he was talking about.

'*What* story?'

'My feelings on everything that's happened.' He shifted nervously in his seat. 'It'll be in tomorrow's *Post*.'

'This is a joke, right?' she said carefully. 'I mean, we discussed this and . . .'

One look at his face told her he was deadly serious.

'How *could* you?' She leapt to her feet and, unsure what to do next, sat back down again. 'After everything I said?'

'A hundred and fifty grand, that's why,' he replied tetchily. 'We've barely got a pot to piss in, and now we can pay for Ben's treatment, give Mum her ten grand back and Andy can buy his motorbike.'

'What happened to the three hundred?'

'That was only if it included you and photos of Ben.'

Shaking her head in disbelief, she looked at him

as though he were a stranger. Indeed he *felt* like a stranger. Nothing brought home their current disengagement more than what he'd just done, going against her express wishes and single-handedly inviting the media spotlight to shine in the darkest corners of their family life.

There was nothing she could say to change his mind. The deed was done. Her husband had spilled his guts about their marriage to a reporter, probably saying things he hadn't yet said to *her*, and she hadn't even been consulted on the matter.

But deep down, what depressed her most of all was that she knew she didn't have a leg to stand on, that the situation they now found themselves in was entirely of her own making. And as far as her husband was concerned, that plain fact had robbed her of any say in the matter.

'The pressure's off, Karen,' he said stiffly. 'You can leave your job, you never liked it much anyway . . . and we can both be here for Ben until he's on the way to being better.'

She nodded resignedly. 'Let's just hope that taking the money doesn't mean we're harassed every step of the way.'

'I will be, but then I was always going to be,' he shrugged. 'But apparently there might be a legal argument that, as you didn't know about the press conference or take part in the *Post* interview, the media should leave you alone. Mum and Andy too.'

'Really?' Her mood lightened slightly.

'Yes. Ben and the new baby will be protected as they're only kids, but I'm going to use a bit of the money to send a lawyer's letter to the papers pointing out that you haven't invited media attention at any point and are still entitled to a private life.'

'Wow.' She raised her eyebrows in surprise. 'If you can pull that off, I'll love you forever.'

They both smiled nervously.

CHAPTER 21

'Look, I'm eating with both hands!'

Karen held up her knife and fork to demonstrate, then sliced through her baked potato, the butter oozing out of the sides. 'I love Ben dearly, but God it's lovely when I get a bit of a break.'

She was sitting in Tania's tiny patio garden, just the two of them and one of those two-chair 'Bistro' sets with floral cushions you see in mail order catalogues aimed at retired people. There wasn't room for anything else. The table was only designed to hold coffee cups but they'd managed to squeeze on two lunch plates and a couple of large glasses of sparkling water.

Karen sighed contentedly. 'It's funny, but although people warn you about how time-consuming babies are, you never really know what they mean until you have one. I'm always eating with one hand, *if* I get to finish a meal at all, and I can't remember the last time I had a bath without little rubber ducks floating around me.'

Tania nodded and looked rueful. 'Food for thought.'

Karen clasped her forearm and gave it a little squeeze. 'Oh God, sorry, I haven't been much use to you, have I? Are you any further on deciding what to do?'

To her surprise, her friend's eyes filled with tears. Tania had always been the stoical, glass-half-full one in their friendship, the one who saw the best in every situation. When Karen had suffered the usual years of teen angst, fretting about spots or moping about boys, Tania had jollied her along whilst coasting through it all relatively unscathed. Later, she'd claimed that to suffer emotional upset, you had to have a boyfriend, and because boys had largely ignored her, she'd never been troubled by the inevitable angst that went with them.

Whilst Karen had been blonde, blue-eyed, buxom and, consequently, popular with the boys at their school, Tania had red, wiry hair and an ironing-board chest, meaning she was destined to be known forever as, in her own words, 'the ugly friend'.

But all that aside, she *still* seemed immune to extreme emotion even whilst watching weepy movies or hearing that her paternal grandfather had died. Karen had accompanied her to the funeral and spent the entire ceremony in floods listening to his friends' eulogies, whilst Tania had remained resolutely dry-eyed.

She had been just ten when she watched her mother slowly deteriorate with breast cancer for two years until she died. At *that* funeral, she was sobbing so violently that Karen had to hold her up, and for weeks afterwards she kept bursting into tears at school and being gently led away from lessons. Karen's theory was Tania's heart had been so broken by her mother's premature death that subsequently nothing had even come to close to upsetting her. She was all cried out.

So the sight of the tears now coursing down her face was indicative of the turmoil she was feeling about this pregnancy.

Karen extracted a tissue from her sleeve and handed it over.

'It's clean.' Like all mothers with young children she felt the need to clarify the matter.

Tania smiled gratefully and blew her nose. 'I think I've decided on a termination, but then I panic and think I might never have another child and talk myself out of it. I'm all over the place.'

'That's natural. It's the hormones . . . and it's a bloody big decision to make on your own.' She put her glass down and grabbed both of Tania's hands. 'Look, at the end of the day, it comes down to a simple choice between going ahead with it in the knowledge that you'll be a single parent and it will probably be a bit of a struggle, or having an abortion and hoping that one day you'll meet someone who wants a baby too and do it as a team.'

'It sounds so straightforward when you put it like that. But I'm not sure I could handle the guilt of getting rid of it just because it's not convenient.'

Letting go of her hands, Karen stretched her arms over her head. 'You're only about three weeks gone, so you've got some breathing space before it's crux time. Maybe you should start by telling James. He might surprise you by saying "Let's get married and have lots more babies . . ." or something like that.'

Tania made a spluttering noise. 'Have you been taking drugs? I wouldn't marry him if he was the last man on *any* of the planets, never mind earth.'

'OK, maybe not. But I still think he has a right to know.'

'Maybe. I'll give it some more thought, though to be honest, I'm thinking about nothing else at the moment.' She topped up Karen's glass. 'Now, can we talk about something else because that conversation's depressing the hell out of me.'

'Depressing? I can give you a run for your money on that one.' She leaned down and picked up the *Post* from where they'd chucked it earlier. On the front page there was a giant picture of Joe looking sombre below the headline, in towering letters, 'MY BABY AGONY'. She flipped the paper open at a spread with the headline: 'Exclusive: "I'll still bring Nick Bright's son up as my own".'

Tania nodded at it. 'You have to admit, though, that's encouraging.'

She shrugged. 'For Ben, yes. But it doesn't mean he'll stay married to me.'

'Course he bloody will. He absolutely adores you.' She stacked her half-eaten plate on top of

Karen's empty one and smiled. 'I remember the night you guys met at that party.'

Karen smiled wistfully at the memory. 'Me too. Like it was yesterday.'

'*I* noticed him first. Ironic now, when you consider how combative we are.'

'He was so good-looking, wasn't he? Still is, but it wasn't just that. We really did connect,' said Karen. 'Mum always used to say to me, "You'll know when you know" and I'd be "Yeah, yeah," but as soon as I saw him I knew *exactly* what she meant.'

'I was so jealous,' said Tania. 'Not because he made a beeline for you rather than me, but because it meant I didn't see as much of *you*.'

'God, yes. In the early days, I would practically sit on his lap whilst he was having a shit. I couldn't get enough of him.'

'It's still there, you've just become a bit side-tracked, that's all.'

Karen groaned, feeling remorse, regret, guilt and most of all, sadness. 'I don't know. I still love him, but it's struggling to breathe under the weight of everything that's happened. And I have absolutely no idea what he feels for me anymore.'

Tania raised her eyebrows. 'Sex?'

'Yes please,' she grinned.

'Is he still in the spare room?'

She nodded. 'I miss him.'

The pattern of their friendship had always been that Tania supported her, no matter what. If Joe ever upset Karen, Tania hadn't needed to know why to be upset with him too. And even when she was told the details, and probably felt there was sometimes a little blame on both sides, she *still* supported her friend. It was the rule of their girly code.

So when Tania let out an impatient grunt, her face clouded with irritation at Karen's last remark, it was highly unusual. Unheard of in fact.

'I'm not being funny,' she said, placing her elbows on the table and leaning towards her friend, 'but I've seen you and Joe together from day one and he has *always* done the chasing. That's your little routine . . . you're a bit of an ice queen and he works hard at warming you up.'

She paused, but Karen was too startled to reply.

'Whatever floats your boat and all that,' she continued, 'but don't you think it's time to break with the old routine and perhaps chase *him* for a change?'

She stopped speaking and stared at Karen challengingly. 'In other words, if you miss him, then stop bloody whingeing and *do* something about it.'

Joe studied Karen as she paced back and forth in the kitchen, clearing the supper plates from the table and loading them into the dishwasher. She had cooked a home-made lasagne, not altogether successfully given her culinary skills, but he'd waxed lyrical anyway knowing she was at least making an effort.

He could see that she'd put in a little time on her appearance too, with her hair brushed and loose, the way she knew he liked it, and enough make-up to enhance her features but not look overdone. She was wearing a little vest top that just covered her breasts when she was standing upright, but revealed rather more of them when she stooped down to fill the dishwasher trays. Against his better judgement, he could feel himself getting a hard-on. Undoubtedly, he still found her attractive, but he wondered whether this was because he now felt more emotionally detached from her, increasing his desire in a sex-with-a-stranger kind of way, rather than the gentler 'making love' with someone you're married to. Or perhaps it was sexual starvation: after all it had been some weeks now since he'd pounced on her in the bath.

From the minute he'd first laid eyes on her at a party, he'd known that she would become someone significant in his life after a succession of momentarily exciting but ultimately meaningless encounters with women of all shapes and sizes. Joe loved sex, but by the time he met Karen, he'd grown tired of the empty version and wanted something a little more heartfelt.

Her kooky-looking red-haired friend had been the one to make eye contact with him first, but she wasn't his type, too boyish and eager to please. She was like a stick of rock with the word 'desperate' running down the middle.

Karen had been an entirely different proposition, blonde and slightly icy, with pale blue eyes that had coolly scanned him and rapidly moved to someone else. The chase was on. He'd used Tania's eye contact to approach them both, then left her flailing in the shadows as he'd turned his spotlight on Karen, regaling her with anecdotes or observations about the people in the room.

The breakthrough had come when Tania had muttered something scathing about the hostess boasting there might be a 'celebrity' coming to her party.

'I've just seen Stuart Little in the kitchen. Does that count?' Joe had quipped, and Karen had burst out laughing. The pale eyes turned warmer and she shifted her centre of gravity so she was facing him. That night, he'd managed to eke her telephone number out of her, then retreated, knowing he shouldn't push his luck and satisfied he had a line of contact with her in the future. But it had taken several phone calls and a couple of chaste coffees in public places before he'd convinced her to go on a proper date. During one drink-fuelled confessional on their honeymoon, she'd admitted that she'd fancied him from the minute she saw him but felt he was the 'shag and go' type and didn't want to be another meaningless conquest.

Joe let out an unconscious sigh of lament at the memory.

'Penny for them?'

He looked up to find her hovering by the dish-washer, smiling at him questioningly.

'Sorry?'

'That was a big sigh. What were you thinking about?'

He flushed slightly. In normal circumstances he could have told the truth with impunity, a happily married man reminiscing wistfully about the day he met his wife. But Joe's brain was whirring through the possible outcomes if he answered truthfully. Would she take it for what it was, an idle thought process that had no bearing on their current situation? Or would she read something more into it, perhaps that he was close to forgiving her and starting afresh?

He held her gaze for a couple of seconds then came out with it, his body stiffening with all the anticipation of jumping into a pond without knowing how deep it was going to be.

'I was thinking about the night we met.'

A look of surprise flashed across her face, but she composed herself quickly and smiled warmly.

'That's nice. Not regretfully I hope?'

'No, because then we'd . . .' He stopped imme-diately, as soon as he realised he was about to utter the knee-jerk response that many couples give in such situations but which in his case was wholly untrue.

'Because then we'd what . . . ?' She looked at him expectantly, not having guessed what he'd been about to say.

He thought about lying, coming up with some trite explanation of why he'd clammed up, but he couldn't think of one.

'I was going to say . . .' he continued quietly '. . . because then we'd never have had Ben. But then I realised that wasn't the case.'

Her smile withered before his eyes. She turned to face the work surface and hung her head, her back to him. He heard her sniff, but her hair was obscuring the side of her face.

'Are you alright?'

She nodded but didn't turn round.

'Sorry. But you *did* ask.'

Straightening her back, she turned round. He couldn't tell if she'd been crying but her eyes looked shiny and her body language was apprehensive. After a couple of seconds, she walked over and grabbed a chair, pulling it closer to his before she sat down.

'You look tired,' she said softly, resting her hand on his knee. The move had seemed casual but the expression on her face suggested she'd just crossed the Grand Canyon of emotional divides.

'How about,' she murmured, 'you go and lie down on our bed and I'll give you one of my special massages with warm oils.'

He felt a ripple of nerves in his stomach, whether through excitement or uncertainty he wasn't sure. His overriding emotion was one of surprise that Karen had made the first move, something she had rarely done throughout their relationship. It had never bothered him in the early days because he had enough sexual self-confidence for the two of them, but when Ben had been born and they'd both matured more, it had started to rankle a little.

When they'd first met, she would often treat him to a sensual massage, but the last time had been just after they'd learned she was pregnant. Since Ben, she'd always said she was too tired, or that she'd spent the whole day tending to the needs of the doctors and patients at the surgery and didn't want to spend her nights tending to the needs of her husband.

Now, here she was, moving close to him, offering him a massage which would probably, if he wanted it, lead to sex. One month ago, even in the midst of the stresses and strains surrounding Ben's illness, he'd have jumped at the chance to relieve the pain they both felt, even for just a few minutes. But that was a *shared* pain, as parents of a seriously ill child. This new pain, knowing another man had fathered his 'son', was his alone and he was struggling to even comprehend it, let alone deal with it.

He glanced down at her hand, resting on his leg. Tellingly, his erection had gone.

'Thanks, but I have heaps to do. Paperwork, that kind of thing . . .' He stood up and her hand fell back to her side, listless. She looked startled by the rejection and her eyes filled with tears. But whilst, in the old days, any sign of her being upset would have prompted him to scoop her in his arms and cocoon her, this time he did nothing. More tellingly, he *felt* nothing.

As he left the room to head upstairs, he didn't even look back.

'But *why*?'

Stella sounded calm, but Nick could tell that underneath lay a dogged determination that wouldn't let the matter rest until she felt she had a satisfactory explanation.

'I've told you. I was pissed. You were away. I was feeling sorry for myself . . .'

He knew it made him sound as weak as he felt.

'Are you really that pathetic?' She didn't sound derisive, it was more the quiet disappointment that he found so much harder to take.

'It was once, that's all.' He let out a sigh and immediately tried to suppress it . . . unsuccessfully.

Her eyes flashed with irritation and she glared at him. 'You're in no position to sound hard done by. Do you have any idea how much this has hurt me?'

'I know, I know.' He stood up from the sofa and walked across to the TV. It was on mute but still distracting, so he switched it off. 'But what's done is done. I wish I could change it but I can't, so we need to work out how we can move on from it.'

'*I'll* decide when I'm ready to do that, not you.'

She was sitting at the dining-room table where she'd been for the past half an hour. 'It might suit you to move on, but until I can reconcile in my mind why you slept with someone else, I can't make any decisions about our future.'

'Slept is too strong a word.'

As soon as he said it, he regretted it, knowing he had crossed a line from which there was no turning back without hurting her further.

'By which you mean?' Her eyes didn't leave his face.

'That it wasn't an all-night thing in the same bed,' he hedged, hoping she'd accept the explanation but knowing full well that he wasn't going to get off *that* lightly.

'So where did you have sex then? I've been meaning to ask,' she said sarcastically.

His mind raced with possible answers, but was there such a thing as the perfect reply to your wife's question of where your infidelity had taken place? He opted for the truth, consoling himself that at least he wouldn't have to spend a lifetime editing his every utterance on the subject.

'The hallway.'

'Her hallway?'

He felt nauseous. 'Stella, do we have to do this?'

'Whose hallway, Nick?' she said flatly.

'Ours,' he mumbled, hanging his head. 'At the old house.'

'I see.'

She stared out of the window for a few seconds,

looking desperately sad, and he wanted to rush across the room and hold her, to take away her pain. But he'd *caused* the pain and the knowledge left him floundering, unsure how she'd respond.

'I suppose I should be grateful it wasn't in our bed.'

Her tone was icy and he realised it had been the right call not to try and comfort her at this juncture. In fact, the embrace of Pol Pot might have been more welcome. He wasn't sure whether he should feel comforted that she hadn't exploded with rage, though with Stella you never knew. Aside from her palpable distress over her failure to have a baby, she was always in control of her emotions. Even during the few marital arguments they'd had over the years, she had rarely lost her temper, opting for a tone that was at best, measured, at worst, menacing.

This, of course, made her the perfect politician's wife, practical, unflappable and stoical in the face of the nation's television cameras when required to accompany her husband to a high-profile event. But right now, Nick rather wished she *was* the emotional type, then he might better assess where he stood.

'So you were so overcome with lust for each other that you barely got inside the front door?' She asked the question as one might inquire if someone found the weather temperate for the time of year.

Nick closed his eyes, wishing this could all go

away. 'As I said, I was pissed and wasn't really thinking straight, but I suppose I just wanted to get it over with and get rid of her.'

'Oh the irony of it.' She wasn't smiling.

Standing up, she walked across to the kitchen where she'd left her handbag on the worktop and picked it up, hooking it over her shoulder.

'Where are you going?' He tried to keep his tone casual, not wanting to pressurise her, but anxious to know if her visit to their flat was merely temporary. Her unpacked suitcase was still in the bedroom.

'None of your business.'

'I just want to know you're OK, that's all.'

She was walking towards the door, but stopped and turned slowly to face him. He might have imagined it, but she looked slightly conciliatory.

'I forgot to ask. How did it go this morning?'

His eyes widened almost imperceptibly, surprised she'd even mentioned it. When he'd told her about the appointment with Pickering and asked her to go with him, she'd flatly refused.

So he'd sat alone in a cubicle, with just a porn mag and plastic pot for company, and produced the sperm that would create another life.

'Fine.' He shrugged. 'It will be frozen until they need it.'

She looked thoughtful. 'What happens to any embryos that aren't a near perfect match?'

It was the question he'd been dreading she'd ask and he felt a stab of pain shoot through him as she said it.

'I suppose they'll be destroyed.'

She blinked rapidly, but not before he saw the glint of a tear. This time, he didn't hesitate, moving swiftly to her side and wrapping his arms around hers, pushing her head into the nape of his neck.

'Darling, I'm so, so sorry. The last thing I wanted to do was hurt you.'

She extricated herself from his embrace. 'I know. But you did.'

'Irrevocably?'

'I really don't know, it's still all so raw.'

He nodded. 'I understand, but I need to know something. What upsets you most, my weakness or the consequences of it?'

The shadow of a frown crossed her face as she considered his question.

'I'm not sure I can separate the two.'

Two seconds later, she was gone.

CHAPTER 22

Spanning her thumb and forefinger across her forehead, Tania rubbed her temples. There was a dull ache between her eyes which was making it impossible to concentrate. She just wanted to go home and disappear under the duvet, refusing to emerge until her life had taken a turn for the better.

She flinched at the sound of hands being clapped together close to her right ear.

'Come on, chop chop.' It was James in full barking mode. 'Where's that poll on waiting lists I asked for?'

She stretched an arm out and handed him the documentation without looking up.

'Thanks. I need to show Colin. He's doing *Question Time* tonight so I'm cramming him.'

Colin Burton was the new Health Secretary, in the job for two months now and making the impact of a feather landing on concrete. He was a mild-mannered and consequently deeply uncharismatic man who found James terrifying. Consequently, his senior aide was running the department unchecked, making the atmosphere more unbearable than ever.

Raising her head, her eyes narrowed with discomfort, Tania said wryly, 'Political life goes on, eh?'

He looked at her derisively. 'What are we supposed to do . . . resign because our previous boss fucked up?'

She didn't respond, lowering her eyes again then closing them tight in obvious pain. It was out of character enough for even James to display concern.

'Are you OK?'

No, I'm not, I'm bloody pregnant, she wanted to scream.

'Sort of. I have a lot on my mind, that's all.' She deliberately kept it vague because she couldn't trust herself to venture anywhere near the truth in case she burst into hot, self-pitying tears, but her evasiveness had clearly backfired.

'Don't we all, dear,' he drawled, looking over his shoulder towards Colin's office, distracted by work again. 'And it's most inconvenient that you're taking the afternoon off. Do you have to?'

'Yes, I'm afraid so,' she muttered. 'Actually, I need to talk to you before I go. In private. Have you got five minutes?'

He looked at her as if she'd suggested they go backpacking round the Baltics for a year.

'As long as it *is* only five minutes,' he intoned self-importantly, rolling his eyes. 'Is it another secret? Don't tell me, you've discovered Colin's a transvestite . . .'

If only, she thought. 'No, I want to ask your advice about something.'

Placing his hands on her desk, he leaned over her, his eyes squinting. 'Are you leaving? Because if so, you can fuck right off. Does it say careers adviser here?' He ran a finger along his forehead.

'No, sadly I'm staying,' she sighed. 'Just a quick coffee, that's all.'

He glanced at his watch and started walking towards Colin's office. 'OK, there's a brief hiatus at twelve thirty. I'll meet you in Vito's at twenty to one.'

She remembered something she thought he should know.

'By the way, one of the fertilised eggs is a perfect match for Ben. It's being implanted today.'

James didn't even break his pace, merely turning his head so he could speak over one shoulder.

'You're mistaking me for someone who gives a shit.'

Vito's was virtually empty, except for a couple of middle-aged women surrounded by John Lewis carrier bags and a homeless man enjoying a cup of tea and reading one of the pile of *Big Issues* he had in a bag.

Tania chose a table for two, positioned out of earshot, and hung her coat over the back of the chair before going to the counter and ordering two coffees.

Hers was a cappuccino, his black with no sugar,

much like his personality, she thought. She felt overwhelmingly nauseous, but wasn't sure if it was a side effect of the pregnancy or merely the thought of telling James.

Walking back to the table, she chose the chair that faced the window and watched the world go by. There was a flurry of junior office workers on their lunch break and eagerly heading to one of the many bars and cafés nearby.

Not for the first time, she wondered why she didn't get herself an uncomplicated clerical job, where your duties started at nine a.m. sharp and ended at five, with no work problems bleeding into your spare time. They probably didn't earn much less than her, yet her life seemed to be consumed by her job, with twelve- to fifteen-hour days and, sometimes, phone calls in the middle of the night when a particular newspaper hit the streets with a bombshell political story.

But deep down, despite her regular misgivings, Tania knew she thrived on the unpredictability of life at Westminster and that the safe, same-old same-old of a small office would drive her insane with boredom.

Perhaps it's the same with my love life, she pondered. Perhaps that's why I'm drawn to men who present me with some challenge, however bizarre.

There was Bill, the 'surf dude' who'd rarely ventured outside his home town of Birmingham yet felt compelled to live in boardwear and wore a beanie hat permanently fixed to his head (even in bed). She'd met him shortly after starting her first-ever job, at Birmingham's Central Office of Information, and mistook his dress sense as a quirkiness of character. Unfortunately, he turned out to be a 24-carat bore and, as she discovered after he had to remove his beanie hat in the shower, balding with a comb-over.

Then came Rick, the delivery driver who appeared at her door shortly after she'd moved to London, with a microwave and kettle she'd ordered over the internet. He'd asked to use her loo, she'd offered him a cup of tea, and he was cute. By the time he was draining the dregs of his mug, they'd swopped numbers and arranged for him to show her 'the sights' the following Saturday, which turned out to be his local pub and Indian restaurant.

Rick's future, he told her, was as a rock star. He was only delivering electrical items until his musical genius was discovered. Six weeks and several shags later, she finally persuaded him to play her some of his 'demos' and clamped on a beatific smile as she listened to what she could only describe to Karen later through tears of laughter, as two dustbin lids being run over by a trilling ice-cream van.

And since then, no one except her brief, ill-advised liaison with James who was now ten minutes late for their meeting.

Having discovered she was pregnant so early on,

she'd had weeks now to um and ah over whether to tell him about her condition. Some days, she'd arrived at work determined that she was going to tell him, only to slope off home again having got cold feet. Other times, she'd composed long letters, telling him how sorry she was that it had happened but how she felt he needed to know, only to throw them away in fear and frustration.

Time was no longer on her side. A decision *had* to be made and, despite wishing she could simply forget she and James had ever even kissed, she knew that morally she had to involve him.

Glancing at her watch, she noted with growing irritation that he was now fifteen minutes late. Reaching for her mobile, she was about to call him when he burst through the door looking flustered and cross, plonking himself in the chair opposite and glancing distastefully at the cup of now cold coffee in front of him.

'Couldn't we have dealt with this in the office?' he grumbled. 'Colin hasn't got a fucking clue what he's doing. I can't even go for a piss without him popping up beside me to ask some puerile question about the NHS that even the dimmest Big Brother contestant would know.'

Tania winced. 'Sorry. Do you want another one?'

She nodded towards the cold coffee, but he shook his head and undid the button on his jacket, seeming to relax a little.

'So what's all the secrecy about?' he smirked. 'Are you after second helpings?'

Another wave of nausea swelled in her abdomen. 'No, I've had my fill thanks. But that *is* why we're here . . . indirectly anyway.' Knowing James's attention span she felt it wise to come straight to the point.

Having realised her motives weren't sexual, his expression had already clouded with boredom and he started to look over her shoulder at the other customers. She knew there was no point sugaring the pill.

'I'm pregnant and I thought you should know.' She felt a rush of adrenalin as she said it, followed by blind panic that someone so indiscreet now knew her innermost secret.

He looked at her blankly. 'Why, are you leaving?'

She recoiled in disbelief, briefly wondering if he was feigning ignorance. But instinctively, she felt he wasn't.

'No, I'm telling you because it's yours.'

Snorting, he picked up a teaspoon and idly stirred his cold coffee. 'Very funny.'

'James.' She said his name calmly and quietly. 'I'm serious.'

He narrowed his eyes, scrutinising her face. 'Jesus, you *are* fucking serious! But I used a condom.'

'Obviously a faulty one.'

He let out a grunt of despair and slumped on the table, laying his head on his arms. She stared at the back of his head, wondering what to say next, but then he rose back up again, his look of arrogant defiance restored.

'How do you know it's mine?'

Frowning, she pursed her lips and breathed deeply, trying to resist the urge to lunge across the table and impale the teaspoon in his forehead. He realised he'd overstepped the mark.

'OK, OK. But you're not keeping it are you.' The rhetorical delivery was absolute.

'No need to ask your opinion on what I should do then,' she said flatly.

She wasn't sure what she'd expected him to say, but felt stung by his obvious assumption that she'd be having a termination, as if it was a decision akin to getting rid of an old sofa which had served its purpose. She'd known he wasn't going to go gooey-eyed and suggest a trip to Mothercare, but she'd hoped he would have shown some degree of under-standing that she was in a very difficult situation.

'Look, I'm happy to help out . . . if you need it,' he ventured, looking awkward.

Her heart lifted slightly as images of James changing nappies and pushing a buggy through a park flashed into her mind.

'You know, to pay the clinic bill.'

The image evaporated.

'Gee thanks,' she muttered sarcastically. 'I'm overcome by your support.'

He looked briefly taken aback by her tone, as if he didn't understand it.

'Well what did you expect?' he demanded, not waiting for an answer. 'You didn't seriously think I'd be thrilled, did you?'

'No,' she sighed. 'And I'm not either. But I'm the one who's got to deal with it and, believe me, it's not been an easy decision.'

'But you *are* getting rid of it.' He looked at her intently.

She nodded. 'That's why I asked for this afternoon off.'

He flopped back in his chair, clearly relieved. 'Believe me, once it's done you'll soon forget about it,' he said with characteristic insensitivity.

'Why? Had a lot of experience of this kind of thing have you?'

'No, but I read a lot about it when we were thinking of amending the abortion bill.'

He picked up his mobile phone from the table and she could see he was about to leave, considering the matter closed. His casual attitude to the situation irritated her and she didn't want him to get off that lightly.

'Actually, the clinic says I need someone to come and pick me up afterwards. You know, in case I'm still a bit woozy or *upset*,' she said pointedly.

He squirmed uncomfortably, pressing buttons on his mobile. 'What about your mother?'

'She's dead.'

'Karen then.'

'I told you. She's having the fertilised embryo implanted today.' The irony of their two situations didn't escape her.

He looked up disapprovingly. 'You're not suggesting *I* come and collect you?'

'Why?' She let out a hollow laugh. 'Out of the question is it?'

'Look.' He put his face close to Tania's. 'Number one, what if I get recognised and we end up in some media diary? Can you *imagine* the repercussions? Secondly, I have the afternoon from hell at the office.' He stood up and walked around the table. 'I doubt I'll have time for a shit, let alone an outing to a clinic.'

'I see.' She stared fixedly out of the window, trying not to cry. He was studying the screen of his mobile phone again.

'How about if I organise a car to collect you and take you home?' he said over the top of her head.

She nodded wordlessly, then stood up and pulled her coat from the back of the chair, throwing it over her arm. She turned to face him.

'I'll text you the clinic's address,' she said miserably. 'All things going well, I should be ready to leave by six.'

'Fine.' They were standing close to each other. Neither moved.

'This isn't going to make things awkward in the office, is it?' he added edgily.

'No more than usual, no.'

He turned to leave and she followed him out of the café, feeling as soiled and discarded as the old chocolate bar wrapper that lay at her feet.

CHAPTER 23

Perched on the edge of the hospital bed, Karen looked pale and apprehensive, studying Joe's back view as he stood at a discoloured window, one of its corners taped over with cardboard.

A minute passed before he walked back to the bed, picking up the clipboard that held her notes and reading them.

'Don't pretend you know what it all means,' she teased.

'Actually,' he countered, 'we probably know more about it than any of them. We've researched it enough.'

Karen scraped her foot back and forth along a line in the pattern of the floor.

'*Please* come in with me?' she beseeched, not looking at him as she said it. She heard him sigh, more in faint frustration than resignation, so she knew what was coming.

'We've been through this. It just doesn't feel appropriate.'

'Appropriate?' She felt weary, drained from spending two hours the night before trying to persuade him. 'This is the twenty-first century not some bloody Jane Austen novel. You're my husband and I want you there, isn't that enough?'

'Put like that, yes,' he acquiesced. 'But add in the cold, hard fact that you are about to be impregnated with another man's baby and I think anyone would see my point of view.' He chewed at his thumbnail. 'I'm not sure I could just sit there and watch it happen.'

'I know, I know,' she said sympathetically. 'But isn't everyone going to think it a little odd you're not in there holding my hand?'

'Pickering won't.'

'Yes, but he's the only one who knows the circumstances. What about the others?'

Joe shrugged. 'They'll probably assume I'm squeamish. Besides, I don't really care what they think.'

The familiar creak of the door opening stopped him from saying anything further. He smiled welcomingly at the young hospital porter who was standing just inside the room looking hesitant.

'Come in, mate.' Joe put the notes down and looked at Karen with an expression of faux jollity. 'Hop on.'

With a leaden heart, she duly obliged and he busied himself fluffing her pillows whilst the porter fumbled with the wheel mechanism of the bed.

'It seems a bit dramatic sitting on this,' she mumbled. 'Can't I just walk there?'

Joe made a pooh-poohing face. 'It's important

you're relaxed. Now's not the time to be worrying about appearances.'

'Oh, I don't know.' She gave him a loaded look. 'Right now, keeping up appearances is very important to me.'

He smiled weakly, though she concluded it was more for the benefit of the porter who had sensed the tension and was looking awkward. He kept his head down and edged the trolley through the door and out into the corridor, with Karen perched on top feeling at best daft, at worst a complete fraud.

Outside, Joe tucked her trailing dressing-gown cord behind her back and kissed her chastely on the forehead, like he would an aged aunt in her death throes.

'Good luck,' he murmured.

Jesus, she thought, he sounds like a parent about to see his offspring compete in an egg and spoon race, but she didn't feel derision, only an intense sadness.

She smiled wanly as the porter pushed her down the corridor, one step closer to the procedure that would hopefully save her son's life but would probably destroy her and Joe forever.

Quickly glancing over her shoulder, she saw him standing like a statue, watching intently until she turned the corner and he was out of sight.

Facing forward, she slumped down on to one elbow, fighting back tears. She knew she shouldn't have pressurised him, knew that what she was asking him to do would have fazed even the most emotionally resilient of men, but she desperately wanted him there, *needed* him. The thought of going it alone made her feel frightened, stripped back to the vulnerability she'd felt as a child when being wheeled in for her tonsillectomy and the nurses had insisted her mother stay on the ward.

They turned another corner and reached a bank of lifts where a group of visitors impatiently pressed the call buttons. As Karen's trolley pulled up alongside them, they all stared at her with a mixture of sympathy and morbid fascination, wondering what life-threatening condition had immobilised her. The temptation to hop off and do a jig was overwhelming.

She heard it faintly at first, then it grew louder. A feeling of warmth flushed through her.

'Wait for me.'

Joe ran round the corner, slightly red-faced from the exertion, and stopped in front of her. Panting, he bent forwards and placed his hands on his knees.

'You're right,' he gasped. 'You can't go in alone.'

The waiting room had been fuller than Tania expected, with five other women already there. They'd been casually reading magazines but she knew that, like her, the words about beauty regimes or celebrity parties would be swimming before their eyes, their minds full of less appealing images of what was about to happen.

The timetable of events so far had been a bit of

a blur. There'd been a last-minute chat with a doctor to confirm she truly wanted to go through with it. She'd nodded enthusiastically as if accepting a competition prize, worried that showing even the slightest reluctance might have led to her being sent away for more time to think.

Then she had changed into a hospital gown, followed by more reassuring words from the nurses, and now she was lying on a trolley in an anteroom, waiting to be anaesthetised and feeling sick with nerves and indecision.

'OK?' The anaesthetist looked down at her with a kind smile.

She just nodded, not trusting herself to speak. She wanted to fast-forward through the platitudes and wake up back at her flat, minus her pregnancy and with selective amnesia.

'Right, we're going to put you to sleep now, then push you through to theatre,' said the anaesthetist.

She felt the needle in her flesh, remembered the feeling of wooziness washing over her, then nothing more until she came round, aware of a crying sound. As she tried to lift her head, a nurse appeared at her side.

'Stay lying down a minute, Tania,' she said softly. 'You're still a bit disorientated.'

Lying facing the wall, she blinked a few times with confusion, before her memory kicked in and she remembered why she was there.

The deed was done. Although she felt an intense sadness, there was also a sense of relief

311

that there was no decision for her to agonise over anymore.

After a couple of minutes of staring at the same stretch of wall, she gingerly turned over, pleased to note there was no soreness. Surveying the room, she saw there were two other women alongside her, both clearly coming round from the same or a similar procedure. One was sobbing hysterically.

'Is she OK?' she asked with concern.

'Yes, love. It's just a reaction to the anaesthetic,' the nurse reassured her. 'It obviously doesn't affect you as badly. Come on, let's get you out of here.'

The nurse pushed her through to a large room full of Parker Knoll-style chairs, partitioned off by curtains.

'Hop on to one of these.' She smiled. 'You seem fine, but you'll need to stay around for another couple of hours just to check there are no after-effects. If you feel up to it, there's a little canteen down the corridor, or I can go get you a cup of tea and a biscuit.'

'I'll wander down, thanks.'

She was surprised by how unaffected she felt, both physically and emotionally, though she suspected the latter was in abeyance, to be unleashed later. Pulling on her clothes, she strolled down to the canteen and helped herself to a coffee from an automatic machine.

The room was empty and she had the choice of four small Formica tables. As she sat down, the door opened and a woman she recognised from the waiting room walked in. She smiled and gestured at Tania's table. 'Mind if I join you?'

It transpired she was a married mother of three who had fallen pregnant accidentally with her fourth child.

'It was a disaster,' she explained. 'My other children are all at school now and I had just started to get my life back. I'd got a part-time job and, for the first time since we got married, my husband and I actually have a bit of money instead of having to struggle every month. Life was good. Then . . .' She paused and looked uncomfortable. 'Well, you know what.'

Tania nodded sympathetically, thinking what a gut-wrenchingly hard decision it must have been for the woman to terminate a natural sibling to the children she already had and by the man she was happily married to.

'What about you?' the woman probed.

Although this mother had confessed all about her situation, and although they had a shared empathy from the procedure they'd gone through, Tania still couldn't bring herself to tell a stranger about her situation. Well, not the truth anyway.

'There was something seriously wrong with my baby,' she mumbled, 'so I came here rather than wait for nature to take its course.'

She knew that, given the woman's story, she should feel less inclined to judge *herself* so harshly, particularly as the 'father' wasn't interested and there was never going to be a happy-ever-after scenario.

But there was still something that stopped her being kind to herself: a deep-seated moral code which made her feel wretched about ending a life, however small and unformed it had been. It made her feel better to pretend the termination had merely been an easy way to dispose of a baby that would never have developed, rather than face the truth she found so unpalatable, that neither she nor its father had wanted it.

Later, when tucked up in bed at home, an advert came on for Pampers, showing lots of healthy, bouncing babies laughing with their mothers. She switched it off and cried herself to sleep, feeling the loneliest she'd ever been.

Joe walked into the bedroom carrying a tray laden with a cup of tea and a plate of buttered brown toast. Laying it down on the bedside table, he flicked on the reading light and walked over to draw the curtains.

'How you feeling?'

Karen smiled wanly. It was the umpteenth time he'd asked her the same question since arriving home from the hospital a couple of hours earlier.

'Just fine, thanks.'

In fact, she felt physically normal, probably able to get up and repaint the living room if she so wished. It was mentally she was struggling, because she still had no idea what was going on between them and the feeling of limbo was killing her.

When she'd heard his breathless voice as he ran to catch up in the hospital, her heart had soared with the expectation that *this* might finally be the breakthrough she'd been waiting for.

If he was agreeing to be present when the IVF took place, she thought, then perhaps it was a sign that he was reconciling himself to the idea of bringing up the second child as well as staying very much a part of Ben's life. She could only hope.

But even though he'd been there in body, dutifully holding her hand in front of the theatre staff and responding to their general, well-practised chit-chat about the traffic or the weather, in spirit he'd been somewhere else. His hand had been lifeless in hers, his look distant. To her mind, his message had been very much 'I'm here to help you save face, but please don't read anything more into it than that.'

Now they were back home and he was fulfilling his caring duties admirably, as instructed by the doctor. He'd run her a cool bath, vacating the room so she could undress, and was now insisting she try to eat something before going to sleep.

She lifted a piece of the toast and bit into it, chewing mechanically before taking a sip of tea to wash it down. Out of the corner of her eye, she noticed him step out of his jeans and throw them over the chair in the corner, something he'd always done when they still shared a room.

He then walked round to his side of the bed, peeled back the duvet and climbed in.

'Pickering said I needed to keep a close eye on you,' he said casually, switching off the light on his side of the bed and lying down with his back to her. 'Sleep tight.'

Karen sat rigid, her mouth frozen mid-chew, staring ahead of her as the enormity of this development sank in. Her heart was pounding so much she thought it might erupt from her chest.

Sure, he'd made it clear he was here under doctor's orders – although he could still have heard her from across the hall if there was a problem, couldn't he? she pondered – and he was still wearing his T-shirt and boxer shorts and he hadn't even kissed her goodnight.

But, as she saw it, it was another breakthrough which had brought him back in from the cold of the spare room. And for that small mercy she was immensely thankful.

Finishing her mouthful of toast, she switched out her own bedside light and lay staring at the ceiling, shedding quiet tears of hope and relief.

NINE MONTHS LATER

CHAPTER 24

Karen waddled into the living room, feeling like her swollen belly had arrived ten minutes before the rest of her. She didn't remember being this big with Ben, but perhaps it was the lack of stomach muscles this time round, she thought ruefully.

Her first pregnancy had been a joyous one, with her and Joe equally thrilled to be expecting a baby and even Gloria fussing around and attending to her every need. Friends sent cards and gifts at the news then rang regularly to see how she was feeling, which, in truth, was pretty damn good. She'd had no morning sickness to speak of and in the latter stages the only physical manifestations aside from her vast abdomen had been a propensity to cramping in her calves and a spot of late-night heartburn.

But this pregnancy was an altogether different story.

Joe was around, she knew that because she occasionally saw him across the room, or giving Ben his injections, or sitting next to her in bed reading a book. But as far as him engaging with the bump,

319

or even acknowledging it beyond helping with something heavy, there was nothing.

And her mother-in-law was chilly, to put it mildly. She inquired about the health of 'it', as she always referred to the baby, clearly worried that any potential problems might affect Ben's treatment, but other than that it was as if the pregnancy didn't exist.

Similarly, other than an enthusiastic 'Auntie' Tania and Karen's parents' regular missives from New Zealand, friends rarely referred to her ever-increasing size, patently embarrassed by the circumstances surrounding it. Her pregnancy had become the elephant in the room. Rather fittingly, she thought, as she was beginning to resemble one.

Absent-mindedly, she rubbed her swollen abdomen, comforted by the thought that whoever lay inside might hold the key to Ben having a healthier future. Thanks to the regular tests she had had to undergo as part of her 'unusual' situation, as Pickering always referred to it, they already knew the baby was a boy. Karen was secretly thrilled, wanting a little brother for Ben to play with and feeling that because they shared a gender, perhaps the bond formed by one giving prolonged life to the other would be even greater. But Joe had only smiled in a non-committal fashion when she'd told him, failing to make any comment at all on how he felt about the life growing inside her.

For her part, her feelings were exactly the same as when she'd been carrying Ben: overwhelming love and protection towards her unborn child. The stark difference was she felt she couldn't share those thoughts and feelings with her husband. Every day, there was a moment, if not several, where she was about to mention a symptom or a twinge but would stop herself, fearful that any mention of her blindingly obvious pregnancy might hurt Joe. On the very few occasions where she forgot and brought it up, he would smile quickly or make a small grunt of acknowledgment, but beyond that, nothing.

The only positive point in all of it had been that, following the legal letters, she had pretty much been left alone by the media, spared the sight of her swollen shape splashed across the newspapers. In the early days, the occasional, opportunistic freelance photographer had taken her picture as she left the house, but finding no market for the photographs they'd eventually given up.

Lowering herself on to the sofa, she smiled uneasily at Gloria who was helping Ben to do a jigsaw. He was jabbering away to himself in a combination of toddler gobbledygook and the occasional word.

Poignantly, the first proper word he'd uttered had been 'Daddy' whilst sitting in his highchair watching Joe make a sandwich.

'That's usually the first word they say anyway,' Joe had said at the time. 'It's easier to say than

"Mummy".' He was underplaying it, but Karen could tell he was secretly thrilled.

These days, Ben's vocabulary was expanding rapidly, with 'more', 'want' and 'ta' in general use as well as 'bollocks' after an unfortunate outburst by Karen when she'd stubbed her toe on the corner of the dining table.

But physically, he looked younger than his age, the relentless regime of injections and transfusions taking an inevitable toll on his body. His skin was faintly sallow and his arms and legs seemed puny next to the more robust boys of his age they sometimes encountered at the local swings.

'Nana, want,' he said now, pointing at a piece of jigsaw equidistant between Gloria's hand and his own. She reached across and gave it to him with an indulgent smile, always happy to jump when her grandson demanded it. Karen and Gloria's relationship was as tricky as ever, but she had to admit she secretly admired her for the way she'd handled finding out Ben wasn't her biological grandson. As far as Karen could see, it hadn't altered her feelings to him one little bit.

'Ready?' Joe appeared in the doorway looking pensive, an overnight bag in his hand.

Karen nodded and edged her way off the sofa and on to her feet, ruffling Ben's hair as she did so. 'Bye, soldier. See you later.'

She smiled quickly at Gloria. 'Thanks for holding the fort. We'll see you la—' She stopped

322

talking, her attention diverted by the television that was on mute.

'Quick, turn it up!'

Gloria obliged and the three of them stared at the screen as the newsreader read out a bulletin with a large picture of Nick as the backdrop.

'The Prime Minister has just announced that Nick Bright, the former cabinet minister who resigned after admitting an affair, is to *return* to frontline politics as Health Secretary, the position he stepped down from. He will replace Colin Burton, who has been sidelined to Transport. It's a return from the cold for the man who was always predicted to achieve great things . . .'

Joe switched it off, a look of disgust on his face.

'Unbelievable,' he muttered. 'Eleven months. Is that all political penance takes these days?'

'They must rate him highly.' Karen stared at the blank screen, stunned at seeing Nick's image again after so many months of media silence.

There had been a few articles here and there, penned by acerbic commentators questioning his whereabouts, and a couple of paparazzi photographs of him and Stella strolling through a Tuscan village – not hand in hand she'd noticed – but other than that Karen had assumed Nick had opted for the relatively quiet life of a back-bench MP. There had been absolutely no contact between them and he had gone to ground to such an extent that even Tania was unclear what he was up to. His return to the top end of politics had taken her completely by surprise and she wondered with dread whether it was about to reopen the floodgates of media attention for her and Joe.

'Here we go again.' He voiced her fears.

'Hopefully not.' She was trying hard to remain optimistic. 'Apart from the stuff already in the public domain that they keep repeating over and over again, they will probably still lay off me and the kids at least. They don't really have any grounds to do otherwise because I've kept a very low profile.'

'We'll see.' He didn't look convinced. 'Right, let's leave for the hospital before the first reporter knocks on the door to ask our reaction.' His expression and tone were sarcastic. 'Needless to say, Mum, if there's a knock at the door, don't bother answering it.'

Gloria nodded. 'Good luck with everything.'

Karen noticed she directed the comment solely at Joe and couldn't bring herself to refer in specific terms to what was about to happen.

'Thank you, Gloria. I'm sure the birth will go well,' she said pointedly.

She stared at a damp patch on the ceiling as she felt Mr Pickering tugging at her abdomen. Ben's had been a natural birth, an unpredictable mix of blood, sweat and tears in the early hours of the morning. So far, an elective Caesarean seemed a lot more civilised.

She and Joe had arrived at the hospital at nine a.m. and now, after being wheeled down to theatre, here she was at eleven a.m., numb from the chest down and strangely numb from the neck up too. It was supposed to be one of the most exciting days of her life, but she felt desperately flat, anxious that the baby was healthy but dreading what the future might hold for them all. Unlike Ben's birth where her feelings had taken precedence over Joe's, this time she felt acutely aware it was the other way round as she privately fretted over his every expression and utterance, trying to read what was going on inside his head.

A large screen just inches from her chin was protecting her from whatever was happening on the other side, which, as far as she could tell, was Pickering rummaging for his car keys somewhere around her lower intestines.

She felt no pain, but she knew from Joe's pale, almost green face that there was probably a lot of blood and gore the other side of the screen. He had taken a quick look a few minutes ago at Pickering's instigation, but had so far resolutely resisted any urge to do so again.

Suddenly, she felt an intense dragging sensation then heard the medical staff's voices intensify in urgency before the sound of a baby crying filled the room.

Pickering poked his head round the screen, his mouth obscured by a surgeon's mask.

'Everything fine so far,' he mumbled. 'We just

have to preserve the umbilical cord for our needs, then he's all yours.'

Karen smiled up at Joe who smiled back, but she noticed it didn't reach his eyes. He quickly returned to looking troubled and she wondered whether it was concern for the health of the new baby and his usefulness to Ben, or simply for the unusual situation he found himself in, standing by his wife's side as she gave birth to another man's child.

Ever since he'd climbed into bed with her after the implantation, he'd stayed there, gradually moving back his things from the spare room. First his alarm clock, then a couple of books he had on the go, followed by clothes and finally, his favourite pillow.

But any hope Karen had that his reappearance in the main bedroom might spark a return to other aspects of their relationship was short-lived. A week passed and he simply pecked her on the cheek and turned over to sleep every night. Then a month.

Again, Tania had advised her to make the first move, but on the few occasions she'd mustered the courage to do so she'd been politely rebuffed. He hadn't even tried to mollify her by pretending it was in case they harmed the baby in some way: he'd frozen her out with an awkward movement or glance. Eventually, as her tummy grew visibly bigger, she'd stopped trying, feeling so awkward that she started undressing in the bathroom.

'It's driving me mad,' she'd lamented to Tania one night. 'On the one hand I don't want to make a big deal out of it because it might drive him back to the spare room, but on the other, it's so hard having him next to me and not being able to touch him, even just affectionately . . . he avoids that too. Perhaps I should just ask him to move out and put us both out of our misery.'

'Don't you bloody dare,' Tania had chided. 'Things might improve after the baby's born . . . don't forget there's a ruddy great lump stuck to your front that reminds him you were unfaithful. So if you genuinely want things to be how they were, you have to give him time and just wait and see.'

Right now, watching Joe as he stared at the midwives and doctors checking the new baby, she wondered if things ever *could* be the same again. With relationships falling by the wayside for something as trivial as one or two arguments, the odds didn't look good for a marriage that had endured the infidelity of both sides, two children who weren't biologically the husband's and one of whom was seriously ill. But here he still was, her strong, indomitable Joe, standing by her side and looking, for all the world, like a supportive husband. But deep inside, she wondered, was he still the same man she'd fallen so desperately in love with? Or had he disappeared forever?

On the few occasions she had become tearful during the pregnancy, panicking about the future, he had held her hand in a buddy kind of way and reassured her that everything was going to be OK.

'I'll be there with you,' he'd always said about the birth, but beyond that he wouldn't be drawn, sidestepping any attempts she made to talk about the future with the remark 'let's just concentrate on getting Ben well first.'

And now, here was the key to everything, being handed to her by Pickering. A small, red-faced creature with a fiercely furrowed brow, wrapped tightly in a blanket and squinting in the light. She took him and gently laid him across her chest, his face towards her.

'Look, Joe.' She twisted her head to try and see his face.

Moving forward into her line of vision, he stooped down to peer at the baby. 'He looks exactly like Ben did.'

'Do you want to hold him?' Every bone in her body beseeched him to say yes.

'Don't worry.' He took one step back. 'He looks very comfortable where he is.'

Karen looked up at Pickering and caught a shadow of concern pass across his face, but he swiftly buried it under a professional smile.

'Well, he's a very strong, healthy chap and the umbilical cord was in good shape, so he should be very useful to us.'

Karen wished he wouldn't refer to the baby as if he was a commodity, but she let it pass. It was something that played on her mind constantly, how she was one day going to have to explain to this child the circumstances surrounding his birth, whilst simultaneously making him feel he was very much wanted and not just born out of medical necessity. Again, it hit home to her that the conception and birth were just the start of a long, hard road along which there were still likely to be some horribly rocky moments, not only with the media but with her children's peer group ultimately finding out the truth and questioning them about it, or worse, teasing or bullying.

Pickering had moved back behind the screen to check the work of the assistant surgeon stitching her up. Satisfied, he nodded at one of the midwives.

'You can take Mrs Eastman back up to the ward now.'

As they wheeled her out towards the lifts, the baby lying by her side, Karen swivelled her eyes from side to side trying to locate Joe.

'Is my husband here?' she asked the midwife walking alongside her.

'Yes I am.' He emerged from behind the trolley, looking perplexed. 'Sorry, but will you be OK on your own for a little while? I think I need to get some air.' He held up his mobile phone. 'I'll call the usual suspects to let them know everything went well.'

'Sure, see you later.' She smiled bravely, but inside she felt like curling up in to a tight ball and sobbing. There was none of the euphoria that followed Ben's birth, when Joe had stayed glued to her side, staring in wonder at the small bundle beside her. This time, she felt deflated, depressed and gut-wrenchingly alone.

'I felt nothing.'

Joe stared miserably into his pint, watching an air bubble float aimlessly around the top of it.

He was feeling like a total heel for abandoning Karen at such a vulnerable time, unable to shake the image from his mind of her sitting alone in the hospital room with just the new baby for company, but he'd had to get out of there. The pressure of having to look like the doting father, when he felt like anything but, had been too great.

As he'd been leaving the operating theatre, following in the wake of the trolley carrying Karen, one of the midwives present had smiled warmly and unwittingly offered her congratulations, oblivious to the soap-opera shenanigans surrounding the new arrival. Strangely, her ignorance of the situation also comforted him, reminding him that despite weeks of newspaper stories about everything from his supposedly 'gaunt' appearance through to intimate details about his past sex life, there were still some people on the planet who didn't read that kind of stuff and had no idea who he was.

Joe had attempted to smile at her, but it had withered on his face as he'd felt a swell of emotion in his chest and tried to choke it back with a staged bout of coughing. She'd looked at him with concern.

'Are you alright?'

'No,' he'd wanted to shout. 'My wife has just had another man's baby. Another son, to go with the son at home who's also not mine. And I'm bloody devastated.'

But instead, he mumbled 'Fine, thanks,' and ducked out of the room, quickening his pace to catch up with the trolley.

Staying a few paces back, he'd stared ahead of him at the supposedly blissful scene of mother and healthy newborn child, an event that is arguably the best day of any new father's life. But he'd felt as if he were viewing the happiness of a complete stranger, a woman unknown to him who just happened to be passing in the corridor. He'd felt horribly excluded from the bubble of bliss and became consumed by the urge to get away for a couple of hours, to wait for the uncertainty and, if he was honest, anger to subside.

He didn't want to sit alone in the pub, a nobby no-mates. So he'd called Andy, knowing his brother would happily drop whatever computer he was tinkering with in favour of a couple of pints. He was right.

'I *tried* to feel something, I really did.' He let out a heavy sigh and gave Andy a wistful look. 'And I know she was desperate to see me become involved in it all. But I just couldn't.'

His brother shrugged. 'It's early days.'

'I know, but when Ben was born I fell in love with him *immediately*. No question. I couldn't wait to hold him, even his smell was like a drug to me. It still is.'

'These are very different circumstances. Not just because you actually *know* the baby's not biologically yours, but also because you're not sure of your feelings for Karen anymore.'

Andy was a man of few words, but the ones he did utter usually made perfect sense. He'd never had Joe's success with women, preferring the less demanding company of circuit boards and the satellite channel Granada Men and Motors, but whenever questioned about the lack of a relationship in his life, he'd always claimed he was happier alone. Gloria had confided in Joe that she suspected his brother might be gay, a concern that had made him burst into laughter.

'He's far too badly groomed. No self-respecting gay man would touch him with a bargepole,' he'd scoffed.

When he'd mentioned it to Andy, he'd rolled his eyes and muttered that just because he didn't choose to enlighten his mother on the few occasions he'd got his leg over, it didn't mean he was struggling with his sexuality.

In fact, the first ever time Joe had introduced him to Karen, Andy had waited for her to go to the ladies before growling, 'Lucky fucker. She's bloody gorgeous.'

The pair had forged a close bond, with Andy

using his best man's speech at Joe's wedding to wax lyrical about Karen's beauty and wonder what on earth she saw in his brother.

'Another pint?'

His thoughts were dragged back to the present by the sight of Andy holding his empty glass aloft.

'Half, thanks. I'd better not go back to the hospital stinking of booze.'

As the pub was virtually empty, give or take a couple of solitary drinkers who looked like they didn't have homes to go to, Andy was back with the order within a couple of minutes.

'I was just thinking . . .'

'Bloody hell, alert the media.' Joe grinned.

Andy pulled a ha-ha face. 'About when you first met Karen. You couldn't stop talking about her and when I met her, I could see why.'

Joe simply nodded, a tight knot in his chest at the memory of better days.

'So what's changed?'

'What, you mean apart from the two children that aren't mine?'

His brother frowned. 'Come on, you're bigger than that. Let's look at the cold, hard facts here. You had a proper affair, she had what was probably an ill-judged retaliatory one-night stand. She got pregnant and thought it was yours and she's now having another baby by another man, not because she wants to, but because she *has* to. Have I missed anything out?'

Joe shook his head disconsolately. 'I know what

you're saying, and yes, put like that, I should be trying to rise above the finer details and remember why I first fell in love with her . . .' He paused and stared at the floor. 'But I can't. I don't know if it's a dented ego because the boys aren't mine or whether I simply don't love her anymore.'

'In my humble view?' Andy placed a hand on his broad chest. 'It's the former and you need to get over yourself. Happiness is where you find it.'

'Have you been reading a psychology book or something?'

'Fortune cookie at my local Chinese.'

Joe smiled. 'That happiness lark is easier said than done, mate. Every single night, I lie there next to her, willing myself to just lean over and show her the affection I know she's desperate to get back, but I don't because her belly is swollen with another man's child and I can't get round that. I hate her for it.'

'No you don't, you just think you do. And society expects you to . . . it's what shite like that Jeremy Kyle show relies on.' Andy took a glug of his pint and stared at his brother thoughtfully. 'OK, put it this way . . . let's assume that she didn't have her one-night stand and Ben is biologically yours . . .'

Joe nodded, wondering where this was going.

'Picture the scene. Everything in the garden is rosy, then you get a call out of the blue from that bird you had the affair with . . .'

'Sally.'

'That's it. Sally. Saying that she had a child nine months after your affair but thought it was her husband's –'

'She wasn't married.'

Andy glared at him. 'OK, thought it was some *other* bloke's she shagged around the same time as you. But that it turns out it must be yours because they'd had to have a DNA test because he's ill and, well, blah blah blah . . . you know what I'm getting at.'

'Yes, you're saying that Karen would stand by me.'

Andy was gulping down his pint but made a thumbs-up sign.

'I'm not so sure she would. And besides, the comparison is flawed because she wouldn't have brought the baby up thinking it was her own. And she also wouldn't have to live with the new one knowing it wasn't hers.'

His brother rolled his eyes. 'I give up.' He looked at his watch. 'I'd better get back to work. I have a pain in the arse customer who's insisting he needs his computer back by tonight or, apparently, the world will end. What a thrilling life I have.'

Right now, brooded Joe, I'd take it over mine.

Following a quick glance over his shoulder, Nick swivelled away from the dinner table, his food still half-eaten on the plate. Picking up the remote control placed next to his wine glass, he pressed his finger on the volume button and stared intently at the television.

'We missed the beginning,' he muttered to Stella, who stayed resolutely in the same position, carving her steak and ignoring the forty-inch screen that was the bane of her life.

A reporter for BBC1's six o'clock news was standing under an umbrella outside the House of Commons, flinching slightly as the rain lashed against his face.

'It's fair to say that, despite today's weather, the Health Secretary's future is looking bright again,' he intoned, before handing back to the studio.

'God, how original.' Stella raised her eyes heavenward and faked a yawn. 'Your surname is a pun writer's dream.'

He grinned. 'Think I might change it by deed poll to Nick Forprimeminister and see how they get round that.' He turned back to the table and started eating again. 'Still, at least he sounded upbeat. I doubt tomorrow's papers will be as forgiving.'

Stella didn't respond, reluctant to start up a conversation about politics. She had other matters on her mind. Topping up his wine glass with his favourite Barolo, she felt a flutter of anticipatory nerves.

'Karen had another son today.'

He stopped fleetingly mid-chew, his eyes hardening slightly, before carrying on and swallowing his steak with an expression that suggested it was a lump of rubber.

'So I heard. Now we can all get on with our lives.' He took a large mouthful of wine.

'He seems to be healthy.'

'Fit for purpose then.' He gave her a wintry smile.

She wanted him to ask how she knew, to engage with her and instigate further conversation about it. But she knew he wouldn't. Nick's way of dealing with a subject he didn't like was to avoid it, to act like it simply didn't exist.

She stayed quiet, studying him intently, waiting for even a small flicker that might suggest he'd attempt to fill the awkward silence. But nothing. In the past, she would probably have let a matter drop if it was clear he didn't want to elaborate, but not now. Not after what he'd put her through. She knew that from now on, the ball was always going to be in her court, because he genuinely loved her and had been terrified at the thought of losing her. And now his political career had taken off again, the stakes were even higher.

'Aren't you even the *slightest* bit interested in getting to know your sons?' she asked firmly.

He let his cutlery drop on to the plate with a loud clatter. 'Stella, don't. We've been over and over this.'

She looked stern. 'Not to my satisfaction we haven't. You say you don't want a relationship with them, but I need to understand *why*. If I had two children and never saw them, I couldn't sleep at night.'

'Men and women are emotionally different. And this situation is different. If you had two children, it would be because you had made the decision to go ahead with the pregnancy and birth. I didn't get that choice, so I feel no commitment to them.'

Elbows on the table, he placed his head in his hands and rubbed his hand back and forth through his hair. 'I want my children, *if* I have any, to be with the woman I choose to have them with, the woman I love . . . you.'

He reached out and clasped her hand, giving it a small squeeze. 'It's better for all concerned if we just leave things as they are.'

This was the most in-depth explanation she'd heard him give, particularly for Nick who had never been the type of man to discuss his emotions or fears. He'd always seemed infallible, a strong head on broad shoulders, a man's man but without the chauvinism. That's why she'd first been attracted to him, feeling he was as mentally strong as she was and would never feel intimidated or emasculated by her forceful personality and highly successful career.

She'd needed someone like that after a string of 'right on' boyfriends who, she now realised, had bored her, lacking the gumption to challenge her when she made all the decisions or criticised them. They had pandered to her, validating her spoilt behaviour and prompting more of it, becoming continual victim to her aggressor.

Then she'd met Nick, a bulldog among the poodles. On the first date she'd objected to his

338

choice of restaurant; he'd ignored her and booked the table. When she refused to go, he had fixed her with an icy stare, growled: 'Call me when you're hungry' and left. She'd been hooked from that moment on by a man who might not have had her education, but who was her undeniable equal in intellect and strength of character.

In the months since she'd learned about his betrayal, she had played over and over in her mind how the man she thought was so strong, both in personality and morals, could have allowed himself such a moment of weakness. It would have been easy to flounce out of his life, leaving him high and dry both emotionally and politically. But she knew the satisfaction of revenge would have been short-lived, replaced by the sobering realisation that she still loved him deeply and had thrown a good marriage away on the basis on one mistake. As she saw it, leaving Nick might have made the press, not to mention her sister Judy, happy. But once the spotlight had moved on, they'd get on with their lives and she'd be left coping with miserable solitude and desperately missing her sexy, witty powerhouse of a husband.

So she'd made the decision to stay put, to wait and see. And she was glad she had, for the past six months had been like the early days of their marriage, with both of them making time for each other and rediscovering the joys of morning sex without the coitus interruptus of James Spender calling.

If Nick's brief infidelity had been just that, it would now be resting in some far recess of her mind, never to be accessed again. But there were now *two* significant reasons why it was at the fore-front again.

'What if *they* want to meet you when they get older?' She looked at him questioningly.

He shrugged slightly and looked faintly lost. 'Then I suppose I would have to afford them the respect of doing so. But the approach won't ever come from me.'

'Even if we never manage to have children?' She felt a well of nausea in the pit of her stomach as she voiced the thought that haunted her.

'Yes. Even then,' he replied firmly. He reached over so both his hands were clasping hers. 'Look, this new job is going to mean lots of attention focused on us again . . . you know, interviews about health policy where they sneak in a question about our marriage . . .'

She nodded silently, unsure where he was going with this.

'So I guess I'm asking . . . are we OK now?' He looked pained. 'Everything *seems* fine, but I don't want to presume anything.'

He stopped talking and smiled hesitantly, his eyes beseeching.

Leaning across the table, she pushed the tip of her nose against his and stared fixedly into his eyes.

'Nice tie,' she remarked, glancing down.

'Thanks. A woman I love more than anything in the world bought it for me.'

She started to kiss him, sucking his lower lip.

'Is that a yes to my question then?' he murmured.

Nodding, she grabbed hold of his tie and pulled him towards the bedroom.

CHAPTER 25

'Tania, meet Charlie. Charlie, this is your Auntie Tania.'

Karen smiled warmly as she watched her friend lift Charlie from his cot and take one of his tiny hands in hers. 'Gorgeous, isn't he?'

'He's the absolute *spit* of Ben when he was born.'

'That's what Joe said,' she murmured, gazing at the baby.

When she snapped out of it and looked at Tania, she noticed her friend's face had flushed pink, her eyes watery as she stared down at Charlie.

'Are you OK?'

'Fine.' She nodded, a solitary tear spilling on to her sleeve. With her spare hand, she brushed a sleeve across her face. 'I'm still a bit emotional after you know what.'

'Listen to me, madam.' Karen's tone was firm but caring. 'One day, you are going to meet a man who deserves you and have a baby. You have made the right decision, no question.'

Tania didn't acknowledge the sentiment, circling her thumb over the back of Charlie's hand.

Shortly after the café meeting with James, where

he'd shown scant interest in the pregnancy, Tania had rung Karen in floods of hysterical tears. She'd felt horribly guilty at not being able to rush across town and comfort her friend, particularly as she'd been the one urging her to tell him, and worse still for not being able to accompany her to the abortion clinic that same afternoon because she'd been undergoing implantation a few miles away.

Friendships don't often come under more intense pressure than that, she thought, yet here was Tania, still congratulating her on the new baby and proving herself to be a loyal, enduring mate.

'How are things with James?' she asked tentatively.

'The same really. In other words, he treats me like a piece of shit.'

'Hasn't he even asked how you are?'

'Nope.'

'What an unfeeling wanker.'

'Can't argue with you on that.' She placed Charlie back in the small, perspex cot at the side of the hospital bed. He didn't even open his eyes.

'He's drunk on breast milk,' said Karen, glancing towards the door then dropping her voice to a whisper. 'But he'd better not get used to it, because the minute I leave the watchful eyes of the midwives, he's on the bottle. My boobs are killing me. They're cracked and bleeding.' She winced and gently rubbed her chest.

Tania seemed to have composed herself and was

inspecting a grape from the fruit bowl. 'So where did the name Charlie come from?'

'*Charlie and Lola.*'

'Sorry?'

'Ben's favourite TV programme. We said he could choose his brother's name.'

'Bloody hell, good job it's not the *Teletubbies*. Hello everyone, meet our new son Tinky Winky Eastman.'

They both laughed at the thought. It was pleasing to see her friend show a bit of her old spirit and humour.

'How's your wound?' Tania peered dubiously at Karen's abdomen.

'Not bad. Another couple of nights and I should be able to go home, provided there's someone there to keep an eye on me.'

'Has he said anything?'

They both knew who she was referring to.

'Not much. He comes, he goes, he smiles when he feels he should, rather than actually wanting to. The usual,' she shrugged. 'I know he won't do anything drastic whilst I'm like this, but once I'm fully recovered . . .' She petered out and stared at her hands. 'I haven't got a bloody clue what's going to happen.'

'And what about little cutie chops over here?' Tania jerked her head towards the cot. 'What happens next with him and Ben?'

Karen let out a long, controlled sigh, feeling an invisible weight bearing down on her shoulders at the mere thought of what lay ahead.

'They're testing the blood taken from his umbilical cord, just to check he's as good a match as they thought he was when they chose him for the PGD.' She paused a moment, briefly sidetracked by the terrible possibility that he might not be, before rallying herself to carry on.

'Then we have to wait a few months to see if he's got the same condition as Ben . . . It's highly unlikely because it's not hereditary, but they have to double-check anyway and it can take a while to show up,' she said wearily. 'If he hasn't then we can go ahead with the transplant using the blood cells from Charlie's cord which they're stored.'

She had discussed this in great detail with the medical team and played it over in her mind a thousand times, but now she was actually explaining it to someone in layman's terms, the unpredictability and ensuing stress of it all winded her. She started to pant slightly, her throat restricting and preventing enough air intake to fill her lungs.

'Shall I call someone?' Tania looked sick with concern, her hand hovering near the alarm cord.

Karen shook her head and placed a palm against her chest, trying to calm herself. She closed her eyes and attempted to regulate her breathing. 'Sorry. A little panic attack I think. I'm alright now.'

'We'll change the subject,' said Tania softly.

'No, don't. I *need* to get emotional about it. With

345

the doctors, it's all very professional and with Joe, well, we *talk* about it, but only like strangers discussing the practicalities. It's almost a relief to break down a bit and admit I'm finding it hard to cope.'

Tania leaned down and enveloped her in a tight hug, both of them sharing a little weep. After a few seconds, she straightened up and sat down in the chair by the bed, peering through the end of the cot.

'It's amazing to think that someone as small and helpless as this can save another life.'

Karen nodded, calmer now and dabbing the corners of her eyes with a tissue. 'Pray he can. The alternative doesn't bear thinking about. It will have been all this trouble for nothing.'

'Except you have yet another gorgeous baby boy,' smiled Tania.

Karen nodded tearfully, her eyes filling again. 'Yes I do. Any tiny doubt that I was having him for the wrong reasons has disappeared completely. I love him so much.'

They both stared thoughtfully into the cot, before Tania tucked her hair behind her ears and said 'Right' in the brisk, efficient manner that people use when they're about to change the subject.

'So where's Joe now?'

'He's taken Ben to Gloria's. He said he'll be back after lunch, in body if not in spirit,' she said despondently. 'I was hoping all the blood, sweat and emotion of the birth might bring him round a bit, but if anything it's made him even more distant with me.'

'Give him time.'

Karen let out such a heavy sigh it was as if every last breath had left her body. 'That's what I keep telling myself. But every day that there's no intimacy between us feels like another nail in the coffin of our marriage. It's bloody hard to fight your way back from that.'

'You will.' Tania looked at her watch. 'Bloody hell, I'd better get going. Nick starts back today.'

'Will you say anything?'

'Do you want me to?' Tania was apprehensive, as if she'd rather boil her own eyeballs in oil.

Karen shook her head, her nose wrinkled. 'Don't worry, no point really.'

'OK, I won't,' she said, clearly grateful for the let-off. 'For once, I'll be more than happy to keep my mouth shut.'

She bent down and gave Karen a quick peck on the cheek. 'Ciao, baby.' Then she turned and ran her finger across Charlie's cheek. 'And goodbye to you too, you little miracle.'

Lobbing her handbag under her desk, Tania's backside had just touched her chair when Nick walked back into the office for the first time in nearly a year. He was carrying a cardboard box and she noticed instantly that his demeanour had changed.

The Nick of old had been a strutter, someone who filled the room with his charisma, compelling everyone to look at him. This Nick was a humbler presence who looked as if he'd prefer it if no one noticed him at all. Tania realised it must have been tough as hell for him to walk back into a building where just about everyone knew his innermost secret and were probably whispering behind their hands.

Thanks to the set-up at Westminster, where she, James and the others in the office were employed by the Civil Service and not the party in power, it was impossible for a politician to surround himself solely with his own people.

'Nick, hi, lovely to see you!' she enthused, leaping to her feet and walking over to give him an awkward peck on the cheek. 'How have you been?'

He smiled ruefully. 'Not bad. Could have been better.' He nodded towards the cardboard box. 'I didn't even bother to unpack this from the last time. It's just been sitting in a cupboard at home.'

'Well, saves time I suppose,' she replied breezily, aware she was now talking vague rubbish in her bid to appear normal and not mention the 'Charlie' word.

Gesturing towards the door of his old office, she was about to accompany him across its threshold when the double doors to their right swung open and a pinstriped whirlwind materialised.

'Ah Nick, you're back!' James clapped his hands

together like a primary school teacher rallying his pupils. 'I knew it wouldn't be long.'

'You knew more than me.' Nick's tone was clipped and let everyone present know, in no uncertain terms, that he now found James intensely irritating.

After Nick had resigned, Tania had composed a long letter telling him how much she had enjoyed working for him and how sorry she was to see him go. Despite his initial refusal to help her friend, she'd ended up feeling enormous sympathy for him and the position he'd unwittingly found himself in. She had also felt his qualities as an employer should be regarded separately to whatever was going on in his personal life, and she'd always found him to be an excellent boss.

But when she'd asked James if he too had been seized with the urge to pen a message to his retreating minister, he'd looked at her as if she had a 'Danger: Do not feed' sign around her neck and muttered: 'Why on *earth* would I do that?'

Although she'd not heard back from Nick, she felt her letter had a lot to do with his friendly demeanour towards her now, and clearly James's lack of correspondence was contributing towards the distinct chill in the air between them.

James obviously sensed it too and immediately snapped into brisk-and-efficient mode.

'Just so you know, I have double-checked that the newborn child is protected under the same legal ruling as Ben, and it's all in place.'

'I know. My lawyer sorted it out months ago,' said Nick witheringly. 'Now if you don't mind, I'm going to get on with some work.'

He stepped into his office and partially closed the door behind him, letting James know that he wasn't to attempt to follow him.

Tania was about to walk back to her desk when Nick poked his head round the door and smiled engagingly at her.

'Tania, can you bring in the latest NHS waiting-list statistics for me? Thanks.'

He disappeared, leaving James glaring at her as she scurried off to the appropriate filing cabinet.

Burying her head in the drawer, she swore she could feel the burn of his resentment on her back, so she took her time finding the file in the hope his perilously low boredom threshold would prompt him to move away.

When she tentatively lifted her head and peered behind her, he had indeed disappeared from sight, but overconfident, she swivelled round to find him standing in front of the spare office desk, currently home to the latest work-experience student, a tall willowy blonde in her twenties.

'You'll go far here,' he boomed at a volume clearly designed to reach Tania's ears. 'If you have some spare time after work, I'll take you for a drink so you can pick my brains about politics.'

'That shouldn't take long,' Tania beamed at the girl before fixing James with a hard stare. 'Now if you'll both excuse me, *I* have work to do.' She tapped the top of the file she was taking to Nick.

The work-experience girl looked terrified, unsure why James was suddenly expressing such interest in her career ambitions after ignoring her for the previous two weeks.

'Darling, don't big up your part,' James called after Tania. 'You're taking in a bloody file then coming straight out again, that's all.'

Striding self-importantly to Nick's office, she tapped on the glass and walked in, handing him the paperwork.

'Thanks,' he smiled, in a 'That'll be all' manner.

But she hovered uncertainly, glancing back at the open door and praying James wouldn't come in and see that his summary of her task had been right.

'Anything else?' asked Nick with a slight frown.

'Look, I know this sounds daft,' she mumbled, 'but do you mind if I just close the door and sit here on your sofa for a little while, as if we're having a really important, secret meeting that James isn't involved in?'

He looked perplexed then burst out laughing. 'I get it. Please sit down.'

He gestured towards the two-seater leather sofa and walked across to the door, poking his head out to address the office in a booming voice.

'Hold all calls. I'm having a very important meeting.'

Closing the door, he walked back to his desk and grinned.

'Anything that makes that little shit feel excluded is fine by me, because that's how it's going to be from now on.'

Tania smiled and picked up a copy of *Private Eye* to flick through at her leisure. She knew it was a small, silly victory against James, but after the way he'd treated her over the pregnancy she felt she'd regained *some* dignity, however inconsequential. And it felt damned good.

Picking Ben's card up, Karen looked at it again for the third or fourth time that day. It was homemade, a sheet of A4 folded in half, with a yellow blob in one corner, presumably the sun, and some blue scribble at the bottom, meant to be the sea. Opening it, she saw the words 'Congratulations Mummy, all my love Ben xxx,' written in the same spidery, inept style that all adults adopt when feigning a child's writing. She noticed Joe hadn't signed his own name.

She tried to stand it back on the bedside cabinet but it kept falling over. So she leaned it against the back wall, next to one of the many newspapers where a small report had appeared stating that the woman who had had an affair with Nick Bright had given birth to their 'designer baby' but not naming her or Charlie. Inevitably, it was a label that would be stuck to the poor child all his life, she pondered sadly.

As she turned back, she jumped when she saw a woman in the doorway to her room.

Tired, she had to squint a little to make out her features. She seemed familiar, then she felt the small hairs on the back of her neck rise up.

'You're Nick's wife.'

Stella nodded, hanging back with an uncertain expression. 'I hope you don't mind.'

Karen shook her head numbly, not knowing what to say, and gestured towards the empty chair at the side of the bed. As Stella walked towards it, she passed the cot and peered in.

'He's called Charlie.'

'Can I?' She placed her hands six inches apart, parallel to each other, suggesting she wanted to pick him up.

Karen nodded slowly, unsure how to react. She hadn't expected this visit, so there'd been no time to read the 'What to do when the wife of your baby's father pays a visit' handbook. 'Go ahead.'

Gently, Stella lifted a sleeping Charlie from his cot and cradled him in the crook of her arm with the skill of someone who had done it many times before. She looked totally at ease holding a baby, smiling down at him and making clucking noises.

Given this brief hiatus, Karen's mind was racing, one particular question taking precedence over the rest.

'Why have you come?' she asked gently, anxious not to sound accusatory or aggressive.

'I don't really know. I just found myself hopping in a cab and instinctively heading here,' she said, dragging her eyes away from Charlie and glancing across at the framed picture of Ben.

'Is that . . . ?' She petered out, as if afraid to say his name.

'Ben. Yes it is.'

'He looks like you.'

Karen nodded. 'I know. That's why I didn't realise . . .'

She stopped speaking, cowed by the enormity of the situation between them, embarrassed by its sensitivity.

'I'm so sorry I slept with your husband,' she blurted out.

Stella smiled sadly. 'Not as sorry as he is.' She placed Charlie back in his cot and perched on the arm of the chair.

'At first, I felt I should hate you,' she said matter-of-factly. 'But then I realised that you and I didn't even know each other so it wasn't really your betrayal, it was his.'

She looked down and traced a finger along the arm of the chair, giving Karen the opportunity to take a good look at her.

The skin on her face was crêpey, giving her a careworn look, and she clearly worked hard at making her fine, flyaway hair look as immaculately groomed as it did. But her large, heavy-lashed green eyes made up for these drawbacks and she was undoubtedly a very stylish women, dressed in a classic white shirt and beige chinos and looking a million dollars.

'Did you know he was married?' she asked idly, her eyes suddenly studying Karen's face intently.

'No, he didn't mention it.'

'They never do, do they?' Her expression was weary, suggesting she too had encountered a married man at some point in her life.

'But in fairness, I didn't ask either.' Karen felt her left buttock going numb and shifted her weight on to the other. 'My husband had an affair so I had no-questions-asked sex with someone else to make myself feel wanted. That's all it was . . .'

'And now parenthood,' said Stella ruefully. 'Twice.'

She stood up and walked around the bed, pausing in front of the framed photograph of Ben. Picking it up, she brushed a speck of dust from the glass and stared at it.

'We've been trying for a baby for years.' She didn't sound accusatory or resentful, just melancholy.

Inwardly cringing, Karen wondered what to say.

'Motherhood is nice,' she ventured. 'But it's not the be-all and end-all. It's exhausting . . . your own life sort of gets swallowed up.'

Stella smiled benevolently. 'That's what my sister and friends tell me, but of course they all have children too. I know they're trying to make me feel better, but the truth is that I've had forty years of a selfish, childless existence and it lost its appeal some time ago.'

A thought hit Karen and she tensed up.

'Do you want a relationship with them? Is *that* why you're here?'

But Stella had started shaking her head halfway through the sentence. 'No. I was just curious, that's all.'

'And what about Nick? Will he want to see them?' She doubted it, judging by his reaction when she'd tried to show him the photograph of Ben, but she had to know for sure.

'No.' Stella shook her head again, this time more vehemently. 'Men are funny creatures aren't they? They can separate nature and nurture in a way that we can't.'

'This case is a little unusual though, isn't it?' She was keen to back Nick's decision to remain uninvolved. 'Ben already has a "dad" in Joe and Nick was forced to father Charlie, so I can see his point of view.'

'Maybe.' Stella shrugged. 'But my point is that few women in the same situation would give up their right to see their children, whatever the circumstances in which they were conceived.'

Karen nodded, unsure what to say next. She hadn't expected to like Stella, assuming she would be a typically privileged type who had brayed her way through secretarial college with the sole intention of finding herself a rich company director as a husband. She also assumed she'd be rather sexless, a woman whose prime years were well behind her and whose husband made a habit of bedding other women to get his kicks.

But she was clearly bright, funny, and far more attractive in the flesh than the occasional grainy newspaper photograph Karen had seen of her. She also realised, for the first time, that Nick's infidelity probably *had* been a brief, one-off drunken aberration by a man who undoubtedly loved his wife very much and would do anything to keep her.

She felt a sudden rush of envy, aware it was ironic. She wished she could be as sure of Joe's feelings for her.

'Are you still trying for a baby?' she asked.

Stella held the question for a few seconds, looking as if she was about to cry. Whether it was emotion about her infertility or a reluctance to share intentions with a stranger, Karen didn't know.

Eventually, she wrinkled her nose and sighed. 'I'm not getting any younger, so I doubt it's going to happen to be honest. And they think my miscarriage might have been because of a condition that would prevent me from carrying *any* pregnancy to full term.'

She stood and picked up her handbag from the floor. 'Adoption from abroad might be a better option. Let's face it, there are a hell of a lot of children out there who could do with a loving home.'

Karen nodded and smiled, extending her hand towards her. 'Well, whichever it is, I wish you luck.'

Stella shook it. 'Thanks.'

She walked over to the door and turned around briefly, her eyes moving from Charlie to the picture of Ben.

'But I think you might need it more than me.'

Putting her Banham key in the door, Stella was surprised to find it unlocked.

'Hello?' she shouted tentatively, wondering if the apprehension she felt at leaving for her unscheduled hospital visit had prompted her to forget to double-lock it.

'Hi.' It was Nick's voice.

A look of surprise on her face, she walked into the living room tapping her watch. 'Either you've resigned again or there's a fire drill going on at Westminster.'

'Thank you for your sarcasm,' he smiled. He was sitting at the dining table, surrounded by paperwork. 'But this is the new me, back early and doing here what I used to stay and do in the office. If they get rid of me, so bloody what?'

She raised her eyebrows. 'Wow. I'm honoured.'

He looked at her beseechingly. 'Put the kettle on will you? I'm parched.'

'Suddenly, I'm *not* so honoured,' she muttered, thinking that perhaps the long days of old when she'd had the apartment to herself weren't quite so bad after all.

Returning five minutes later with two mugs of tea, she placed them on the table and sat in the chair adjacent to his. He was still scribbling away, but within seconds he signed a document with a dramatic flourish and put his pen down.

'Done. Working day over.' He took a sip of tea. 'Why don't we catch an early movie?'

But Stella had more pressing matters on her mind. 'I went to see Karen today.'

'Sorry?'

'Karen Eastman. I went to the hospital.'

Previously, he would have gone ballistic, not only because she hadn't discussed it with him, but because she'd risked being spotted by a passing photographer who would have flogged the picture to every national newspaper in the country.

But this Nick was a new, less inflammatory one, knowing he was on the back foot and in no position to question *anything* his wife might choose to do.

'Why?' he asked calmly.

'I wanted to see what my husband's sons looked like,' she shrugged. She knew it was a cruel thing to say, but she couldn't help herself.

His expression remained impassive at first, but then he started to blink rapidly, a tear escaping and rolling down his cheek.

Stella's eyes widened in shock. The last, in fact the *only* time she'd seen her husband cry had been at his grandfather's funeral, the man who had believed in him more than anyone else.

'Oh my God, darling I'm so sorry.' She stood up and wrapped her arms around his back, holding him tight. They stayed that way for several seconds, she stroking the back of his head, he burying his face in her chest. Then he broke away.

'You don't have to apologise.'

'I do. I shouldn't have made that crass remark. I should have realised you'd be more affected by the birth than you're making out.'

He sighed wearily. 'That's not it.'

'Oh?' She was perplexed, feeling nauseously apprehensive that he might be about to deliver yet another bombshell. She wasn't sure how many more she could take.

'I'm upset at the thought of you seeing a baby fathered by me but belonging to another woman. I can't imagine how painful that must have been for you.' His brow knitted at the thought.

'You know what?' She gave him a half-smile. 'It actually wasn't anything like as bad as I thought it was going to be.'

She sat on the chair next to him, kicking off her shoes and stretching her legs out in front of her. 'I think I had built up this chocolate-box picture in my mind of a radiantly attractive woman, glowing with pride and happiness alongside her new sons, the babies I will probably never have. But what I saw was a tired, lonely woman who doesn't have any of the answers in life. In other words, I got closure.' Shuddering, she pulled a face. 'Yuck, I can't believe I've just used that word.'

She had always scoffed at the mushrooming self-help industry, believing it turned people into self-obsessed bores who'd do better if they solved their problems themselves via talking to friends and family.

'Really?' He clasped her hands and looked at her intently. 'Because I couldn't bear to think of you suffering in any way. You mean more to me than anything else.'

Not given to emotional outbursts, this was the equivalent of Nick reading her love poetry.

'And my main concern is *you*,' she said softly. 'I don't want you brushing all this under the carpet because you think that showing your feelings about it will upset me. It's *OK* to show interest in them. Really.'

Nick let out a huge sigh which rippled a piece of paper on the table in front of him. 'That's very sweet of you, but it doesn't change what I've said before, that my interest in them extends only to how they affect my relationship with you. No more.'

'It's just that you've always wanted a son.' She searched his face for a hint of emotion as she said it.

'With *you*.' His expression remained impassive.

She brushed away a wisp of hair from his eyes. 'I think I'm finally coming to terms with the notion that it might not happen.'

Still holding her hands, his thumb and forefinger played with her wedding ring, twisting it one way, then the other. 'We have each other. That's what's important.'

She nodded, consoled that he felt that way. But

she needed to say more, something she had broached once before, a couple of years before her doomed pregnancy. At the time, he'd been vehemently opposed to it, but now their lives had moved on, mistakes had been made, and her forgiveness of him meant he owed her.

'There's always adoption,' she said lightly.

His eyes darkened and he let go of one of her hands to rub his hair. Her insides turned over, anxious that he was about to refuse, knowing it would lead to an almighty argument in which she would tell him that, for once, her wishes took precedence over his, and that for her it was a deal-breaker.

But to her surprise and delight, he started to nod slowly.

'Yes,' he said, with a look of surprise at his answer. 'Yes, there is.'

CHAPTER 26

Humming quietly to himself, Joe picked up the towel that had been placed to dry on Ben's bedroom radiator about a week ago and walked along the corridor. Folding it in half, he pushed open the bathroom door and stopped in his tracks as he saw Karen lying in the tub, her naked breasts visible above the soapy water.

'Sorry,' he mumbled awkwardly, placing the towel on the loo seat and starting to step backwards out of the room.

'Don't be daft,' she smiled. 'You've seen me naked loads of times. In fact, why don't you join me?' She sat up and shifted backwards, patting the space in front of her. 'There's plenty of room.'

'Thanks, but I've just had one with Ben.'

'That wasn't my point.' She smiled again, her eyes giving him a come-hither look.

Joe wanted the ground to open and swallow him up. He didn't want to embarrass her with an outright rejection, but there was no way on earth he could cross the emotional and physical chasm between them by undressing and getting into the bath with her as if everything was normal. Looking over his shoulder, he pretended something had distracted him.

'I thought I'd got Ben off to sleep, but I can hear he's still whimpering a bit. I'd better go check him.'

She nodded, but he could tell from her expression that she knew it was a blatant lie. She looked so sad and lost that for one fleeting moment he was seized with the urge to rush over and take her in his arms, to reassure her that everything was going to be alright. But he didn't, because he couldn't. Almost as soon as he felt it, it was gone again, crushed by an overwhelming exhaustion and the feeling of numbness that rarely left him these days.

Closing the door behind him, he walked back down the landing and into Ben's bedroom, as if justifying his excuse to himself.

The boy was fast asleep, just as Joe had left him five minutes ago. Slumping on to the chair next to his cot, he rested his elbows on his knees and stared ahead into the landing. He knew the time had come to break the impasse.

Sinking back down into the now lukewarm water, Karen closed her eyes and tried to ignore the tight knot forming in her chest. Save actually climbing out of the bath and dragging Joe in, she couldn't see what else she could have done to let him know she wanted to make amends, wanted to try and restore some sense of normality between them.

She felt like she wanted to cry. But the tears wouldn't come, just an all-consuming rush of loneliness and a lump in her throat. Now she knew what people meant when they said that actually being alone was better than feeling the loneliness of a failing or long-dead marriage. Trouble was, for her, it *wasn't* dead, just struggling for air under the pressure of everything that had happened.

Her body was now starting to reclaim itself, her stomach returning to its normal size, her nipples now healed from her short, unsuccessful stint at breastfeeding that, as she'd predicted to Tania, had ended as soon as she left the hospital.

She'd hoped that when the bump which tormented him had gone, he'd gradually come back to her, one small step at a time. A hug here, a kiss there, even just raw sex without any manifestation of love. But the latest rebuff brought it home to her that their problems were far from over.

Standing up, she reached for the towel he'd left on the loo seat and wrapped it round her body, staring at herself in the mirror as she did so. The lighting wasn't terribly flattering in the bathroom, but even so, she couldn't believe how much she'd aged in the past two years. The whites of her eyes, once crystal clear, were now faintly yellowed with exhaustion, and the lines around them were more noticeable now, not from laughter but from more than a year of worry and sorrow.

She'd been coasting along in the four weeks since Charlie had been born, trying to ignore the obvious tension in the house, hoping that if she avoided confronting it then it might dissipate. But if anything, it was getting worse.

On the surface, Joe was friendly enough, inquiring about Ben's day if he hadn't been with him, or asking her whether she'd seen some lost shoe or umbrella he was searching for. But other than that, it was as if they were existing in two parallel universes. He would always politely turn down her offer of a meal, preferring to snack from the fridge later at night, and rather than watch television downstairs with her, he would potter about or view a different channel on the portable upstairs.

His relationship with Ben was as strong as ever and he did virtually everything for him. At times, Karen felt the outsider. But with Charlie, it was a different story, as if the child had an invisible fence around him that Joe couldn't, or rather wouldn't, cross. He'd pick him up if he was crying and occasionally change his nappy if Karen was busy with something else, but with the dutiful detachment of dealing with other people's children rather than his own.

Sighing with the dread of what she knew she had to do, she towelled herself rigorously and grabbed the dressing gown hanging behind the door. She was tired of brushing everything under the carpet, weary of waiting and hoping that everything was going to be OK. She *had* to know what was going on.

As she opened the bathroom door, she heard him reaching the bottom of the stairs and going into the living room. This time, there were going to be no excuses, no slippery explanations that allowed him to disappear to another room and leave her thwarted yet again.

He looked surprised as she walked in just two paces behind him, her hair dripping on the rug. She pulled her dressing gown closer to her, but her eyes never left his face.

'Everything alright?' He looked edgy.

'No, not really.' She was about to launch into the showdown she'd been planning in her head for some weeks now, but her desire to see their relationship survive was still overwhelmingly strong. She had to test him one more time, just to be sure.

'I need a hug.'

His expression suggested she'd just asked him to bungee jump off the Grand Canyon. 'You're a bit wet,' he said apologetically, staying exactly where he was.

She flopped into the armchair with a heavy sigh. 'I remember the days when you actually climbed into the bath with me. They weren't that long ago . . .'

'That was before . . .' He stopped, hardly needing to state the obvious.

'What's going on, Joe? I need to know.' There,

she'd said it. The showdown had begun and, like the outcome or not, she was determined to keep going until she had answers.

'Sorry, I don't know what you mean.'

She fixed him with a determined stare. 'Yes you do.'

His expression was pinched. 'Ben will have the transplant and I'll be there every step of the way.'

'That's not what I meant.' Her tone was patient but weary, letting him know that she knew he was trying to hedge the real issue and she wasn't going to tolerate it.

Standing up, she moved from the armchair to the sofa, patting the cushion next to her. 'Please sit down. There's something I want to say.'

He did as asked but with the reluctance of a teenage boy being dragged to the opera. The space between them was enough to accommodate a third person, but Karen shifted along a few inches and took his hands in hers. He didn't pull them away, but they rested there limply, screaming reluctance.

Taking a deep breath, she closed her eyes briefly, then opened them and verbally jumped, her pulse quickening as she heard herself saying the words she'd been rehearsing for some time.

'Now that we know everything is being done to help Ben, I've been able to give some proper thought to other things – mainly you and me.'

She paused, expecting some kind of reaction, but none came. He stared at her unblinkingly.

'Everything's that happened has made me realise

how much I love you, *need* you in my life. I was so hung up on your affair with Sally that I couldn't see past it . . . couldn't see the damage my bitterness was doing to our marriage.'

She let out a long sigh of relief as she felt the release of saying the words.

'You're an incredible father, you always have been,' she said softly. 'But you're also an incredible *man*. I haven't said that enough.'

'Or indeed at all,' he smiled ruefully.

She felt heartened by this display of humour, taking it as a breakthrough. Her spirits soared and she felt emboldened.

'From now on, I'm never going to let you forget it,' she laughed, her eyes shining with hope. 'You'll be bored sick of me telling you, I promise.'

But her laughter wasn't reciprocated, her stomach lurching as she noticed the unmistakable skew of discomfort on his face. She ploughed on regardless, hoping her optimism might win the day.

She smiled warmly at him. 'I was thinking that maybe, in a few months' time, once we know everything is fine with Ben, we could perhaps try for a baby of our own?'

She couldn't believe she'd actually dared to speak the words out loud, but a nagging sensation in the pit of her stomach made her feel it was now or never.

Looking down at their entwined hands, he gently removed his and stood up, shaking his head slowly as he walked across to the window, turning round to face her with a furrowed brow.

The hope she'd felt just seconds ago had now shrivelled to nothing, replaced by a deep thump of dread.

'I'm leaving.'

His tone was faintly apologetic but firm, and she knew immediately that this wasn't an attention-seeking, empty threat: he meant it. There'd be no cajoling or prevarication or change of mind. But she couldn't help herself anyway.

'You can't. You love Ben too much.' Her voice came out small and shaky.

Joe shook his head. 'It's not about me and him. I'm leaving *you*.'

She felt a stab of raw pain in her chest as she realised she'd finally lost him. She knew he'd been emotionally distant for some time, but as long as he'd been living under the same roof, she'd held hope that things might change, that one day she'd find a way to make him love her again. But now he was moving out, she felt any chance of them reconciling slipping away from her.

'When?' It was all she could think of to say.

He shrugged slightly. 'I'll probably stay at Andy's for a while, until I can find somewhere to rent nearby. I still want to see Ben every day . . . if that's OK?'

She blinked back tears. '*OK?* Of course it's OK. Joe, this is madness . . . we've come through so much, we can't give up now.'

'I'm afraid I have.' He stared down at his feet. 'I'm not doing this lightly, believe me. I've been thinking about it for a long time, making one decision, then changing my mind, back and forth, back and forth . . .' He waved his hand from side to side to illustrate the point.

'So surely that tells you there's still something between us,' she beseeched, a tight knot in her throat.

'The dilemma was about leaving Ben, not you,' he said matter-of-factly. 'But I figured he won't notice much difference, provided we keep it friendly.'

Karen stared miserably into space, devastated by the sight of her husband talking so calmly about the arrangements for their separation.

'We can be like we were again,' she said plaintively. 'It'll just take time . . .'

But he was already shaking his head. 'It won't work.'

'How can you be so sure?' She was crying soundlessly, tears running into her already wet hair.

'Because I've thought of little else since Charlie was born.'

'And what made you come to this conclusion?' She tried not to sound bitter, but it was hard.

Joe pushed himself away from the window and walked to the armchair, perching on the arm just a metre away from her.

'You have to admit that even before I found out about Ben, things were patchy between us . . .'

She shook her head. 'It was normal marital stuff. Don't rewrite history, Joe.'

'Some of it was, and I take the blame for a lot of it because of what happened with Sally. But whatever the cause, it sometimes felt we were just coexisting under the same roof, purely because we wanted to provide stability for him.'

She made a puffing noise to show her intolerance for what he'd said. 'Isn't that what *all* married couples do at some time or other, soldier on through a rough patch for the sake of their children? We're not alone in that. And don't forget, we have a *sick* child. That puts a terrible strain on a relationship.'

'True,' he nodded. 'But ours isn't a rough patch, Karen, not from my point of view anyway, and certainly not now. It feels irreparable.'

'Why?' She felt and sounded defeated.

'God, there's a question.' He smiled sadly. 'If it was a case of simply dealing with the whole Ben bombshell, I might have been able to get past it. But it isn't, is it? Upstairs is yet another son who's not mine and I'm sorry . . .' his voice cracked slightly '. . . but I just can't handle it. I thought I might be able to, but I can't.'

'It's only been a couple of weeks . . .'

He shook his head. 'I loved Ben unconditionally from the day he was born and that will never change. But it's *different* with Charlie. Much as it shames me to say so, I just don't feel I can love him in the same way . . . and I don't feel I love

372

you enough anymore to stay and play at happy families.'

She started to sob noisily, wiping her eyes and nose on the end of her sleeve. 'Now you've said all this, can't you give me a bit longer to try and make it right? I promise I'll do whatever you want . . . we're a *family*,' she pleaded.

He leaned forward and took her hand, idly stroking the back of it with both his thumbs. It was the most intimate he'd been with her in weeks.

'Sorry, but I just can't do this anymore. It's too late. I need to move on with my life, and so do you.'

Dropping her hand, he stood up.

'I'm going upstairs to pack a few things.' He shifted awkwardly from one foot to another. 'I think it's best if I go to Andy's tonight, but I'll be back in the morning to take Ben to nursery.'

She nodded miserably, her chest so tight with pain that she was struggling to breathe. Her feelings veered between wanting to wrap her arms round his legs whilst begging him to stay, and flying at him with fists flailing for abandoning her. But she did neither, paralysed by the shock that from now on, she was on her own.

EIGHT MONTHS LATER

CHAPTER 27

Aiming the key fob at the car, Karen waited for the familiar beep of the locking device. Shifting Charlie on to her other hip, she grabbed Ben's hand and checked the road before they crossed to the house opposite. Wrestling with the latch on the rotten, splintered gate, she walked through and closed it behind her, taking one last glance at her car and praying it would still have all its tyres by the time she came out.

She and Joe had been living apart for eight months now, six of which he'd been renting this godforsaken place where her heart was in her mouth every time she brought Ben here. It was a vast, sprawling council estate where most of the residents were charming people who worked hard at trying to retain some level of community spirit. But there was a hard-core group of yobs intent on making life difficult for everyone else, who ruled the streets by fear and, consequently, made every ordinary, law-abiding person batten down the hatches after seven p.m.

The house was split in two, with Joe thankfully in the flat upstairs. It meant fewer break-ins, though he'd still suffered a couple of broken windows from well-aimed rocks in the early hours of the morning.

The doorbell had been vandalised so many times, he'd now given up having one, so every time Karen visited she had to call him on his mobile to let him know she was five minutes away. Sure enough, as Ben ran up the pathway, Joe opened the door and scooped him up into his arms, showering him with kisses.

Sometimes he invited Karen in, sometimes he didn't. But today he smiled broadly and jerked his head towards the stairs. 'Coming up a minute? I've finally finished the *project*.'

This was his secret code word for Ben's bedroom. Joe had been planning to spruce it up ever since he moved in, but with the painting and decorating work he did for other people to earn money and then the outgoings of buying household items he hadn't managed to beg or borrow from others, he hadn't had the time or the resources.

The first time Karen had left Ben here to stay the night, she'd driven off out of sight and parked in a layby, sobbing her heart out. They were tears of pain and regret at the finality of Joe renting himself somewhere to live, but also at having to leave her baby son to sleep in a dingy box room in a house more than a mile away from hers. But in fairness, Ben never shed so much as a tear when she left him. As long as Joe was there, that was all he needed.

Climbing the stairs, she tried to ignore the yellowed, peeling woodchip on the walls and think positively. Joe had already worked wonders with the inside, slapping on a batch of white paint left over from a recent decorating job at a local accountancy firm. But he wanted to make Ben's room special, somewhere he would feel was unique to him.

'Right, young man.' He winked at Karen over Ben's head. 'Take your shoes off and put them in your room please.'

Joe hovered behind Ben as he opened the door to his bedroom and stood wide-eyed, taking it all in.

The walls were now Thomas the Tank Engine blue, with red skirting boards and a Thomas duvet cover on the bed, which had four painted cardboard train wheels attached on each corner.

'Wow!' Ben threw himself on to the bed, burying his face in the pillow before sitting up and grinning.

'What do you think?' Joe asked her.

The truth was that the colours made the room look even smaller than it already was, but regardless, Karen knew it was every little boy's dream bedroom.

'It's wonderful,' she smiled warmly.

Charlie started to wriggle in her arms, arching his back so she had to tighten her grip to hold on to him. 'I take it you want to get down,' she gasped, struggling to contain him. 'Just for a minute then.'

She placed him on the floor and he crawled over to Ben, who lifted him on to the bed with him. He chuckled with delight when his brother started to tickle under his arms.

Karen watched them wistfully. The boys were incredibly close and it felt so odd to tear them apart every Wednesday night, Ben staying with Joe whilst Charlie always returned home with Karen. But that was the arrangement they'd come to once Joe had found this place and was no longer kipping on Andy's sofa. Before then, Joe had turned up at the house each morning to take Ben to nursery, sometimes popping in for a quick father/son rough and tumble around teatime before starting the injection routine and heading off once Ben was asleep. Karen knew Joe's main reason for getting his own place was so Ben could stay the night, so she couldn't complain about the once-a-week routine, but she didn't have to like it.

'Mummy, can Charlie stay?' Ben asked plaintively, his arms wrapped round his little brother's waist, manhandling him across the room.

'No darling,' she said breezily. 'He has to come home with Mummy.'

'Why?'

She wanted to scream 'Because your father doesn't love him like he loves you.'

'Because he's too young. He's not a big boy like you.'

She sneaked a quick glance at Joe who was

staring steadfastly ahead, watching Ben and Charlie wrestling on the carpet.

'Usual plan?' she asked. 'You drop him at nursery, I'll pick him up?'

Joe nodded. 'Sure. I –'

But he was interrupted by the sound of Karen's mobile ringing in the depths of her handbag. Rummaging, she retrieved it and took the call.

'Karen Eastman . . .'

'It's me, Mr Pickering.'

'Oh hi.' Her heart missed a beat every time she heard his voice, wondering what fresh hell it brought.

'I have some good news for you.'

'You do?' She looked expectantly at Joe who frowned back. Realising it was an important call, he stood rooted to the spot, staring intently at her.

She could hear Pickering rustling some papers at the other end of the phone. 'Charlie is clear of the disease. We can go ahead with Ben's transplant.'

Karen made a small gasping noise and clamped her hand over her mouth, stifling a sob. The relief was so intense that her legs felt weak, as if they might buckle from under her. She put her other hand against the door frame to steady herself.

'What is it?' Joe's face was etched with worry.

Glancing across at the boys who were still rolling around on the floor, she smiled widely. 'Charlie is in the clear,' she whispered.

Joe closed his eyes tight shut. 'Thank God.'

'I'll call you back later,' Karen told Pickering. 'Thank you sooo much.'

She ended the call and she and Joe stood smiling at each other, united in their relief and joy that not only was Charlie going to avoid being plagued by the same crippling condition, but he could now finally help to save Ben's life.

'This is it. It's finally going to happen.' He let out a long, slow breath. 'Fingers crossed, no more injections, no more transfusions . . .' His voice cracked slightly and he bit his lip.

She squeezed his forearm. 'We've waited so long for this. Please God it works.'

Nodding his agreement, he straightened his back, clapping his hands together as he did so.

'Right, I'd better get the tea on. It's Brussels sprouts on toast, Ben, is that OK?'

Ben wrinkled his nose. 'Urrrgh.' Clasping Charlie around his ample girth, he lugged him over to the doorway where Karen and Joe were standing. '*Please* can Charlie stay?'

Karen raised her eyes heavenward. 'I've already said no. You'll see him again tomorrow.'

She leaned down and attempted to lift Charlie, but both of the boys resisted her, the younger one bursting into hot tears at the thought of being separated from his brother.

Joe kneeled down and tried to reason with Ben. 'Come on son, he has to go home to bed. He doesn't get to stay up a bit later like you do. We can play a game when he's gone.'

Slightly mollified, Ben reluctantly let go of a screaming Charlie and watched sullenly as Karen picked him up and headed for the front door.

'God he's beautiful.' She stared down at Ben. 'He looks so peaceful.'

Joe nodded, his eyes bloodshot from lack of sleep. 'It's as if his body knows the worst is over.'

Ben made a little snuffling noise and moved his head slightly. They both leaned forward expectantly, but his eyes remained closed.

'He's zonked, poor sod.' Karen stroked his hair.

When Charlie had been declared clear of Diamond Blackfan Anaemia, progress had been swift.

A week later, Ben had been given chemotherapy to stop his blood production, then the sample from Charlie's umbilical cord had been transplanted to Ben in the hope it prompted him to start producing his own healthy bone marrow. That had been two hours ago and he had yet to wake up, although Pickering had assured them he was functioning normally and simply tired.

Joe rested his chin on Ben's arm and stared at him. 'A general anaesthetic is a big deal when you're this little. I reckon he'll be kipping for at least another hour or so.'

She glanced at her watch. 'I'm starving. Shall we go to the canteen in shifts?'

Pursing his lips, he pondered for a moment. 'I'll come with you. The nurse can call us back if he wakes up, which I doubt. It looks like a deep one.'

Five minutes later, she was sitting at a small Formica table in the hospital canteen whilst Joe queued to pay. He'd left his mobile lying in front of her and it made a loud beeping noise, indicating a text message.

She resisted the urge to pick it up, but glanced at the screen. It was upside down but she could clearly make out the words 'New message: Em.'

Her insides lurched. Who the hell was Em? There was no one in their social circle called Emma or Emily and her mind raced to think whether he had mentioned anyone by that name, only to come to the conclusion that he hadn't.

It's happening again, she thought. He's having an affair. Although, of course, as they were separated he was ostensibly a free man, able to date who he wished with impunity.

Her lip trembled and she bit it, trying desperately to control herself. Amid all the angst she'd suffered over his leaving, it had never once crossed her mind that he might start another relationship. She thought he was as confused and generally worn out as she was, too exhausted and mixed up to even think about starting fresh with someone new. But now the evidence had flashed in front of her, she felt naive. After all, why *wouldn't* he? Their sex life had all but ground to a halt ages ago, so now he was living alone, with most of the week to himself, it was fairly obvious he'd take the opportunity to see or shag who he damn well pleased. She felt sick.

He appeared at her side, carrying a tray laden with two cups of pale coffee and some tired-looking beef sandwiches.

'I know red meat is supposed to be bad for you, but where do you stand on green meat?' His lip curled as he lifted the top slice of bread and stared at the contents.

Karen took a bite. 'You know what? Because it's the first thing I've eaten since Ben has been cured, it feels like a bacchanalian feast.'

He smiled but it seemed hesitant. 'Steady. We've a way to go yet.'

'But Pickering said it had gone well . . .'

'True. But complications could set in.'

Karen was the optimistic one, taking every situation as read unless told otherwise, whereas Joe was a cautious soul, mulling over every possible option and taking the view that if you considered the worst then you'd be equipped to deal with it *if* it happened. For the most part, it made them a good combination, but there were times throughout their relationship when she'd longed for him to throw caution to the wind and jump with both feet into something like she did, particularly when it came to booking holidays. She'd happily book the first supposedly great deal that popped up on the internet; he'd order brochures, research TripAdvisor, ask friends for their experiences and make such a song and dance about it that sometimes she felt all the spontaneity had gone out of their trip. But then one year, she'd persuaded him to do it her way, and they'd turned up at two a.m. to a Spanish 'villa' that resembled a cowshed with wall-to-wall cockroaches. From then on, she'd appreciated his fastidiousness a little more.

Slowly chewing his sandwich, he let out a long sigh. 'It *is* looking good though, isn't it?' His tone and expression suggested he needed to hear her validation.

'Yes, absolutely. Pickering said there was a slim chance it might not work, but then they always have to say that, don't they? I'm 99.9 per cent sure he's going to be fine.'

'I can't believe we're nearly there. After all this time –' He broke off and stared in to the distance. 'Life starts here.'

She smiled, but inside she felt an overwhelming rush of sadness. It might be the start of Ben's normal life, but it also marked the end of their marital life which now consisted of pickups, drop-offs and snatched conversations in hospital canteens.

Nothing else had changed. She hadn't been to see a solicitor and, as far as she knew, neither had he. In fact, the 'D' word had never even been mentioned. They still had their joint account to pay all the bills and the house was in both their names.

Before she could stop it, a tear fell from her eye

and plopped on to the table. Joe saw it and looked concerned.

'You OK?'

She nodded, not trusting herself to speak without breaking down even more. She was unsure whether she was crying with relief or for what she'd lost, or maybe both, if it was possible to weep from happiness and sadness at the same time.

'I know I help out, but it must have been tough on you these past few months,' he said quietly.

Indeed it had. Since Joe had moved out, she'd often had to give Ben his injections and it had taken its toll on her nerves. Somehow, Joe had always managed to console himself with the thought that what he was doing was for Ben's own good, but she didn't have that psychological strength. She felt she was causing her son pain, rather than protecting him from it, and it went against every fibre of her being. Most nights, as Ben quietly sobbed himself to sleep as the post-injection pain subsided, Karen would sit and watch him into the small hours, wondering and worrying how such a little body could endure so much. These days, she slept four or five hours a night, tops. Although Tania would often ring and try to drag her out to dinner, invariably she would end up visiting Karen's for a takeaway whilst Ben and Charlie slept safely upstairs. On the nights Ben was with Joe, Karen would get Charlie settled early and treat herself to a long bath before collapsing into bed in the hope of catching up on the week's lost sleep. Now, in direct contrast to her own stale social life, she was imagining Joe spending long, fun nights having rampant sex with someone called Em.

She closed her eyes, fighting against the tight knot in her chest and willing herself not to break down. 'I'll be alright in a minute,' she whispered.

Karen started slightly as she felt his hand encircle her forearm and squeeze it. It stayed there.

'Remember when you told me what an amazing dad I was?' he murmured.

She opened her eyes and looked at him, her eyes brimming with tears she knew it was hopeless to try and resist. 'Yes,' she nodded, making no attempt to hide her wet face.

'Well you're an incredible mum. Ben may have been unlucky in some respects, but he's very lucky to have you.'

Her stifled sob drew the attention of two women sitting a couple of tables away, but as soon as they had glanced across to where the noise was coming from they looked away again, realising it was a private matter.

'I suppose hospital canteens see a lot of tears,' she said, accepting the tissue Joe was passing her.

'Yep. And a good few will be because of bad news, so we're the fortunate ones.' He was still holding her arm, stroking it reassuringly.

'Just think, he'll be able to play football without

getting breathless,' she smiled, trying hard to lighten the mood. She knew she should be feeling euphoric about Ben's operation, and she was, but she also felt abject despair at the thought that he would leave hospital to face a life of dipping between his parents' separate homes.

'And he can watch the CBeebies bedtime hour without it triggering a panic attack because he associates it with injection time,' said Joe with a relieved sigh. 'Life isn't just going to get better for him, it will for us too.'

He removed his hand from her arm and she felt the small shiver of solitude again.

She nodded. 'And for Charlie.'

It was true. Charlie was growing sturdier with each passing day and it was blindingly obvious that in a year or so, he would have overtaken his more sickly brother in physical strength. When a child is ill, everyone's attention focuses on him, but Karen knew it could be just as hard for a healthy sibling, constantly relegated to the side-lines during hospital visits and having his head snapped off by parents irritable from stress and lack of sleep. She was pleased that, all things going to plan, Charlie wouldn't have to endure much more of that.

'Did you say he was at Tania's?'

Karen nodded, wrinkling her nose as she pulled a suspect piece of lettuce out of her sandwich and placed it on the side of the plate.

'Who's looking after who?' he grinned.

Actually, Tania had been a godsend these past few months, stepping in to help out with Charlie whenever Karen needed a break. She was indebted to her friend, but she knew that Tania was also getting something from the arrangement, in fact she'd said as much herself.

'Since the abortion I've been thinking a lot about whether I really want to have kids,' she'd said over a takeaway and a bottle of wine at Karen's kitchen table one night. 'I'd never really thought about it before, never had to.'

Looking after Charlie, she said, would be a good way for her to find out if she *was* cut out for motherhood. Clearly she was, as she kept coming back for more and they'd developed an especially close relationship.

Karen was pleased because whilst Ben had both Joe and Gloria at his beck and call, Charlie had no one other than her. Her parents were in New Zealand, Nick wasn't involved at all, and Joe was distant at the best of times. So her youngest son having a devoted 'auntie' all of his own was comforting to know.

Draining the last of her coffee, Karen looked at her watch. 'It's been half an hour. Hadn't we better go back up?'

Joe nodded and picked up his mobile. 'I'll be up in a few minutes. I've just got a couple of calls to make.'

To *her*, she thought miserably as she walked out of the canteen and towards the main bank of lifts.

Her oldest son was recovering from an operation, his future still uncertain, her younger son faced a lifetime of infamy and scrutiny, and her husband was sitting just metres away from her, probably on the phone to another woman.

As she stood waiting, surrounded by other hospital visitors, she'd never felt more alone.

CHAPTER 28

'Now *that* was good. I'm officially bloated to the point of explosion.' Andy laid his hands on his stomach and pulled a painful expression, stretching his legs out in front of him before clasping his arms behind his head.

Gloria scowled at him. 'Andrew. Sit up straight at the table please.' She always used his full name when admonishing him, which was often.

Joe had been such a well-behaved child that Gloria had wondered what people meant when they said babies were a hand grenade thrown into your life. Then Andy had been born and she'd understood completely.

Joe was serene and insular, perfectly able to amuse himself for long periods of time with a painting or jigsaw puzzle. But Andy made a gnat with attention deficit disorder seem focused, throwing himself to the floor in floods of hot tears if he didn't get his mother's attention at all times. Of the two, Gloria was convinced her younger son would have blazed a high-octane trail through life whilst Joe would stay in cruise control, keeping his head below the parapet.

So no one had been more surprised than her when it turned out the other way round and Joe had headed for the highly sociable cut and thrust of the advertising world, whilst his brother had become increasingly withdrawn, preferring to lead a fairly solitary existence and work from home.

Andy coming to his mother's for Sunday lunch had been a ritual for many years, mainly because his lack of a girlfriend meant it was come here and eat a wonderful, home-cooked meal, or stay at home and feed himself – and Pot Noodle hadn't yet produced a Sunday-lunch range. He also arrived with a bag of washing most weeks, but Gloria didn't mind, in fact it made her feel wanted.

And now, since all the 'shenanigans' as she called it, Joe had been joining them every Sunday, often with Ben in tow.

Watching her sons and grandson sitting around her dining table, she felt a swell of happiness. What was that old saying? 'A son is a son until he gets a wife, a daughter's a daughter for life.' She knew she was lucky to have two sons with whom she still enjoyed regular contact and a relatively close relationship, but she also knew the reasons for that didn't bear scrutiny. Much as she loved having them visit, she would still rather have seen them both happy within their own marriages and family life, with her popping in on them when asked.

Even though she'd rarely seen eye to eye with Karen, Gloria could see she'd made Joe very happy in the early days of their relationship and she'd been ecstatic when Ben had been born. She'd always wanted a grandchild and because Karen's parents had emigrated to New Zealand, she'd had a clear run, spending many wonderful afternoons with him whilst his mum and dad went to afternoon cinema or early supper. Then his illness had been diagnosed and life had never been quite the same for any of them again.

If anything, it had brought her even closer to her grandson, at times her protective instinct overwhelming her. She would happily have given up her own life as a trade-off for his full recovery.

At first, in the days after Joe had delivered the heartbreaking news that he wasn't Ben's biological father, she had wrestled with her conscience, digging deep within herself to see if there *were* any misgivings or question marks over her love for her grandson. But she found none, just a strength of love for him that remained unchanged simply because it wasn't Joe's blood coursing through his veins.

'Nana?' Ben's voice broke in to her thoughts.

'Yes sweetie?'

'Can I have ice-cream please?'

She smiled and nodded, about to stand up and get it. But unusually for him, Andy beat her to it.

'Come with me, big boy.' He rubbed the top of Ben's head. 'I fancy some too.'

'I thought you were about to explode?' Joe raised an eyebrow quizzically.

'My savoury stomach was. The sweet section is empty.'

Grabbing Ben's hand, he led him out to the kitchen as Gloria looked on, smiling.

'He's thriving isn't he?'

'He's a fat bastard,' Joe quipped.

'I was talking about Ben, not your brother,' she stated, rather obviously. 'And please don't swear.'

He smiled and took a sip of his post-lunch coffee. 'He's doing brilliantly. Beyond our expectations.'

'Yes. Two weeks now isn't it,' she said rhetorically. 'At what point can they say the transplant has definitely worked?'

'It varies really, and obviously there's always a danger he could suddenly suffer a setback, but given he's already putting on weight and showing no signs of breathlessness . . .' He made a small gulping noise, the bad memories filling his mind. 'Well, let's not tempt fate.'

Gloria nodded and patted his knee, realising it was difficult for him to even hope that Ben might finally be able to lead a normal life, let alone say the words.

Andy walked in carrying two bowls of ice-cream, placing them on the table and flopping back into his chair. Ben stayed standing, a fixed smile on his face.

'Nana. Telly?' He looked across to the far end of the lounge, to the child-sized desk and chair he often sat at to watch TV.

Gloria hesitated. Normally, she was very strict about food only being eaten at the dining table, but she'd been breaking a lot of her rules since her beloved grandson was born.

'Go on then,' she beamed. 'Just this once.'

They all watched him as he carefully carried the bowl to the far end of the room and placed it on his little table before picking up the remote and pressing the 'On' button.

Gloria shook her head in wonderment. 'Kids these days. I'm still trying to work out how to use that thing!'

'Why doesn't that surprise me,' muttered Andy to his brother.

Joe grinned. 'Charlie used the remote to series-link the *Teletubbies*.'

'Oh my God, that's incredible.' Gloria was open-mouthed.

Behind her, Andy had inserted his finger into the corner of his mouth to suggest a fish flailing on a hook.

'I'm joking, Mother.'

'Oh.' She was completely unfazed, used to her gullibility being the regular butt of her sons' humour. 'Anyway, how is Charlie?'

Joe shrugged. 'He's great. Karen reckons he's going to be a rugby player. He's got legs like tree trunks.'

Despite the biological details of Charlie's birth, Gloria had been looking forward to being involved in his life, to having a young baby around the place again. She'd seen him a couple of times, whilst dropping Ben off at Karen's, and he seemed a charming little chap, someone she was eager to spend more time with. After all, she thought, how could you not a love a baby?

From the moment he was born, she'd been inviting Joe to bring him to her house at the same time as Ben, but at first he'd always made excuses that Charlie was still too young or needed his afternoon sleep.

Eventually, he stopped coming up with reasons and would just mutter wearily, 'Leave it, Mum'.

She contemplated calling Karen direct about it, sure she could do with the occasional break, but something about Joe's reluctance to become too involved with Charlie prevented her. After all, her first loyalty was still to her son.

As Andy scraped the last vestiges of strawberry icecream from his bowl and pushed it away from him, Gloria took it and stood up.

'More coffee anyone?'

They both nodded and she left the room just as she heard Andy clearing his throat.

'And how are you and Karen getting on?' he asked idly.

Gloria froze in the hallway, rooted to the spot with the bowl in her hand. She wouldn't have dared to ask the question, but she was thrilled Andy had and rather hoped she'd learn something if she stayed quiet and eaves-dropped.

'Not bad.' Joe's voice was low and she had to

cup a hand round her ear to heighten her
hearing.

'Admittedly it still feels a bit weird, but we're
getting used to it.'

'Don't you miss her?'

'Sometimes. Although I'm not sure whether it's
her I miss or just the company. It's hard to tell.'

'Well let's put it this way . . . if I came to live
with you, would you still miss her?'

'Yes. I can't have sex with you.'

Gloria frowned from her hallway outpost. She
didn't like to hear such vulgarity, but made no
attempt to move out of earshot.

'Ah, so it's sex you're missing?'

'Don't we all?'

'I wouldn't know, mate. The last time I got my
leg over King George was still on the throne.'

Joe made a snorting noise. 'What I *meant* was,
I miss having sex with my wife. Mind you, it
wasn't exactly a regular occurrence by the time
I left.' His voice turned serious. 'I guess what I'm
saying is, I miss what we were, not what we
became.'

'But you became that way because of circumstances. They say changing jobs or moving house
puts stress on a relationship, but surely it's nothing
compared to dealing with a sick child?'

'Particularly if you then find out he's not yours.'

'Ah, the ego problem again. I thought you might
have gotten over yourself by now.'

'Don't be like that.' His tone was injured.

'Well someone needs to tell you. Look Joe, I appreciate it's been hard for you and I'm sure I would have been devastated too, but I kind of get the impression you're still forcing yourself to be angry with her, and I just don't get it. You say you left because you were unhappy, but from where I'm standing you seem more miserable than ever.'

Joe started to reply, but his voice was so low that Gloria had to take a step backwards, closer to the room, in an attempt to hear. She winced as a floorboard creaked and started to walk towards the kitchen, but Joe was out in the hallway in a flash. He glared at the empty ice-cream bowl still in her hand.

'Did something keep you, Mum?' he asked softly, his eyes teasing.

She was shamefaced. 'I'm sorry, son, it's just that I heard Andrew ask questions I wouldn't dare ask and . . . well, I just wanted to know the answers, to know you're alright.'

He looked at her, then took the bowl from her hands and placed it on the sideboard just inside the kitchen door.

'Make us that coffee and come and join the conversation. I'll give honest answers to whatever you ask.'

Five minutes later, after placing a tray of coffee on the table, Gloria rejoined them as Andy was mid-flow about the benefits of the latest iMac. Her spirits sank a little as she feared the conversation had moved on too far to be dragged back to more serious territory.

But to her surprise, as their chat came to a natural lull, Joe turned to her with an expectant look.

'Now then, Mum, what would you like to know?'

She baulked slightly, unsure how to deal with this more confessional side of the son who would routinely use avoidance tactics rather than talk about anything personal. But she knew it was now or never, or 'Shit or get off the pot' as Roger had rather vulgarly said in his more drunken moments.

'Um, well, I was interested to know how you felt about . . . um, Charlie,' she faltered. 'He's such a lovely child.'

Joe nodded. 'He is. A great kid.' He let out a long, low whistling noise.

'I take it there's a but?' said Andy softly.

'Yes.' Joe almost look relieved as he said it, as if sharing the burden was what he needed. 'My natural instinct is to get involved, but there's something stopping me and I'm not sure what it is.'

'We already know that,' countered his brother quickly. 'Ego, because he's not yours.'

Gloria tutted at him, anxious his simplistic reasoning might stymie the conversation before it had started. 'I'm sure there's more to it than that –'

'No,' interrupted Joe wearily, rubbing his face. 'He's probably right. I know it's pathetic.'

'It's not pathetic, dear.' Gloria lay a reassuring hand on his forearm.

'Yes it is.' Andy's expression was serious. 'It's not the kid's fault is it?'

'I know that, it's what I tell myself over and over again. But every time I see him I think of Nick Bright.'

'But not when you see Ben?' asked Gloria.

'No. Because my love for him is bigger than anything else. But I don't love Charlie like that.'

'Because you won't allow yourself to,' interjected Andy matter-of-factly. 'He's hardly unlovable is he?'

The two men lapsed into silence, Joe staring at the table, Andy glancing over towards the television, pretending to be interested in the fact that Teletubby Tinky Winky had lost his handbag. Gloria studied them both, her mind racing with all the things she wanted to say. But she knew she should choose her words carefully if she wanted to break through.

'Perhaps you should just approach it differently?' she ventured eventually.

'Sorry?' Joe's expression and tone were defeatist.

'Well, from what you're saying, it seems you're looking at the Charlie situation from your own point of view and no one else's.'

Andy's attention was back with the table and Joe was listening but looking baffled.

'Why don't you try it from his perspective?' She nodded towards the far end of the room where Ben was engrossed in the television. 'He and

Charlie are blood brothers, just like you two. Think of how *he* must feel every time they're torn apart from each other because you don't allow yourself to show an interest in his brother. And believe me, it will just get worse as they get older. Right now, he's too young to question all the excuses you come out with, but one day he'll twig the real reason, and how will he feel about you then?'

She hadn't intended to sound so harsh, but once she started voicing the fears she'd held ever since Charlie was born, the words kept coming. Pleasant listening or not, she thought, at least I have been honest.

Joe was looking slightly stunned, but Andy was nodding his head.

'She's right. Rather than keep banging your head against the same brick wall down the same psychological dead end, try a different route,' he shrugged. 'You love Ben so much? Then do it for him.'

Both Gloria and Joe stared at him as if he'd just announced he was taking hormone tablets and from now on wanted to be known as Andrea.

'That's very deep,' said Gloria, resisting the urge to add 'for you'.

'*What?*' he grunted, looking from one to the other. 'I'm not a complete moron you know.'

'Going back to what we were talking about,' said Gloria pointedly, determined not to drift away from the subject. 'I know Karen and I haven't always seen eye to eye on many things and I will never excuse her for being unfaithful to you . . . but, that aside, she *had* to have Charlie, she didn't choose to, and any mother in her situation would have done the same. You can't punish her for putting Ben's life first.'

'I'm not punishing her, Mum, truly I'm not.' He sighed. 'That's not what it's about at all. I just think we've been through so much that I'm not sure there's a way back.'

'I know you've been through a lot, but don't you think you left too soon, without waiting to see if things would get better once Ben's health improved?' she questioned.

He shrugged. 'Who knows?'

There was a clatter as Ben appeared at the table and heavy-handedly placed his empty bowl on it.

'Gone!' he said triumphantly, his mouth smeared with pink ice-cream.

Joe lifted him on to his lap and wiped his mouth with a napkin, before kissing his forehead. 'Come on, give Nanny and Uncle Andy a kiss, it's time to go see Mummy.'

'And Charlie!' said Ben excitedly, leaping to his feet at the thought.

Joe glanced over his head at his mum and brother and smiled ruefully.

'This is Mila.'

The social worker carefully extracted a small photograph from the file and placed it in front of them with a warm smile that suggested she was as pleased as they were that the months of assessments and paperwork were reaching fruition.

She was called Rita and she'd been alongside Stella and Nick from the start of the adoption process, guiding and reassuring them through many frustrating moments as the Russian judicial system cranked its way slowly towards their goal. Now, with a little girl called Mila to actually look at, they were almost there, give or take any more last-minute 'paperwork errors' that meant yet another official had to be financially induced to sort it out.

Stella held up the picture in front of her but could barely see it through the haze of tears filling her eyes. It was the first time she had cried through the long, arduous process, one that had involved their friends and family being interviewed about their suitability as potential parents. She knew it was necessary, but it felt unjust when a young girl could have a quick knee-trembler behind some bike sheds and become a single mother nine months later without the same scrutiny.

But now she had a face and a name for the little girl, *their* little girl, nothing else mattered and emotion finally overcame her.

'She's beautiful,' she whispered, running her thumb over the girl's cheek.

She was dark-haired, with a cute button nose and chocolate brown eyes that shone with mischief. Despite a year of virtually never leaving her cot, she still looked spirited and cheerful.

'Look, darling. It's our daughter.' Stella passed the photograph to Nick who looked at it and smiled.

But unlike his wife, he felt nothing. As far as he was concerned, he was holding a picture of someone else's child. He didn't know her and had no feelings other than wishing no harm came to her. But he knew this little face staring back at him meant everything to Stella and that, final stages going to plan, she would shortly be sharing their lives and calling them 'Mummy' and 'Daddy'. So he faked it.

'She's lovely,' he smiled. 'I can't wait to meet her.'

'You will. Very soon,' beamed Rita, who began explaining that when the final paperwork was passed by a Russian court, they would be able to fly out and bring her home.

Stella hung on her every word, but Nick tuned out slightly, glancing at the photo and wondering about this cute little bundle soon to shatter their established routines.

He'd always been against adoption as an option for him, feeling parenthood was a big enough lottery without hoping he had the capacity to love a child that wasn't even biologically his. And if truth be known, the fact that he'd felt nothing for Ben or Charlie – not even the curiosity of wanting to see a photograph – had scared the living daylights out of him. Perhaps he wasn't cut out for fatherhood in any shape or form.

An added concern was the onward march of his political career. Things were going really well with Health and the Prime Minister was already making noises that he might consider him for Foreign Secretary in the next reshuffle. That would mean plenty of trips abroad and even longer hours, hardly conducive to a relaxed new parenthood. But the one time he'd tentatively mentioned it to Stella, she'd pooh-poohed him, saying it didn't matter as she would be a stay-at-home mother, holding the fort whilst he earned the crust. She'd pointed out that thousands of army families coped with fathers being away for inordinate lengths of time, so why couldn't they?

He'd also mentioned the highly public element of his job, wishing to discuss all pitfalls before they embarked on this life-changing course. The child, he cautioned, would be coming to a life under the spotlight, where photographers would dog her every move or mistake.

Nonsense, Stella had countered, using her knowledge of the privacy laws to point out that as long as they didn't use their new child to create a cutesy family image with the media, then she would be largely protected from prying eyes. 'Besides,' she'd said, 'it can't be worse than sitting in a cot all day long, with barely any interaction with other human beings. She'll be loved here and that will conquer anything.'

Nick still had his doubts about that, but he knew his love for Stella was cast iron. He also knew he was in no position to dictate that her wants and desires would have to tally with his own. So here he was, sitting with a social worker and being shown a photograph of a child that was about to become his whether he liked it or not.

'What do you think?' Stella was looking at him questioningly.

'Sorry, I was miles away. I can't stop looking at her picture,' he blustered.

The look Stella gave him was so full of love, delight and admiration that he knew he'd managed to say the right thing.

'Rita was just asking if we wanted to change her name, and I said I thought Millie might be good as it's so close to her real name.'

He nodded enthusiastically. 'Yes, Millie Bright has a certain ring to it.'

'Good.' Rita closed the file and tucked it under her arm, indicating the meeting was drawing to a close. 'Well, hopefully, provided the last phase goes smoothly, Millie should be home with you for Christmas, if not, February at the latest.'

As Nick and Stella waited for the lift in the depressingly gloomy, faintly grubby corridor of their local council's social services department, she linked her arm through his and squeezed it, nuzzling her head into the crook of his neck.

'Thanks,' she murmured. 'I know this is really hard for you and I know you'd rather not do it. I also know that you're frightened witless you won't ever love her.'

She paused and lifted her head to look at him directly, her eyes soft with understanding. 'But I know you better than you know yourself, and I promise you that you'll fall in love with her and be the best daddy in the world.'

Nick let out a long, measured sigh of relief. She understood. It was going to be alright.

CHAPTER 29

At the sound of the tinny door chime, slightly warped from too much rainwater, Tania's heart soared.

Grinning from ear to ear, she tore down the stairs and flung open the door, her arms outstretched.

'Come here, gorgeous.'

He grinned with delight as he saw her, his arms stretched out, his fingers grabbing the back of her hair as he clung on for dear life, squeezing her so tight she gasped for breath.

'Time for a coffee? Or would that take up too much of your "me" time?' She looked at Karen quizzically, morphing into a wince as Charlie grabbed roughly at a chunk of her hair and started to eat it.

'Love one.' Karen smiled and followed her through to the kitchen. 'My me time consists of a haircut in precisely one hour. Other than that, it'll be spent doing the poxy paperwork I never get time to do when I have a child hanging off each leg.'

Tania pulled a face. 'I hate paperwork, but luckily I have a father who's a frustrated accountant. He does most of it for me, though I keep one credit card secret for things like vibrators and KY jelly. Can you imagine it? "Tania dear, it says here you've purchased a rampant rabbit? Couldn't you have bought a kitten like everyone else?"'

She grinned, amused at her own joke, but her friend wasn't responding.

'Joe used to do all our paperwork.' She let out a sigh of such velocity that Tania wondered if there was any air left in her body.

In the months after Joe had walked out, their conversations had been about little else, analysing every tiny detail about his behaviour, Karen's emotions, his relationship with the boys and whether there was any hope of a reconciliation.

But as the months had rolled by, they'd exhausted every nuance and mentioned it all less and less, their chats revolving around the more routine subjects of what they'd watched on telly, the weather and Tania's latest date with whichever unsuitable man had come her way via an internet dating website she'd joined a couple of months ago.

Unusually, the last one had been gorgeous and Tania had been full of it, saying he was too good to be true. She was right. By the third date, when she couldn't hold out any longer and fell into bed with him, she'd discovered that at the point of orgasm he made a squeaking noise like a dog's plastic chew toy when it's trodden on.

'It put me right off,' she'd lamented to a squirming Karen the day after. 'He might be sexy out of bed, but in it he's like a forest animal in pain.'

Karen had urged her to persevere, advising that the high-pitched climax might have been a one-off owing to nerves. But no. Two nights later, he'd done it again.

'Why don't you tell him you find it off-putting and perhaps suggest a more acceptable noise for him to make?' suggested Karen, before they'd dissolved into giggles and spent the rest of the night making what they deemed to be 'acceptable' orgasm sounds that had ranged from muted grunts to leonine growls.

But aside from providing them with laughs, Tania's various dates had been next to useless, leaving her with the depressing feeling that, as in the age-old adage, all the good men were either gay or taken. She now considered herself the typical woman that magazines like *Cosmo* and *Glamour* wrote about each month: someone who had wasted the pre-cellulite years on working too hard, before hitting her thirties and realising that her 'career' was a fickle, thankless beast and that all the nice men she had ignored for it had since gone and found themselves lovely young wives. Leaving her with the dregs of the dating pool, men like Mr Wounded Bushbaby and James Spender.

But then, something wonderful had happened, completely out of left field. Something she had been bursting to tell Karen about during their phone chats but had saved until this face-to-face moment.

'I've met someone. And he's great.' She couldn't help beaming like a Cheshire cat, still unable to quite believe it herself.

'Another internet date?' Karen removed Charlie's mini baseball boots and placed them on the floor next to her chair.

'No, that's just it. Someone normal, someone I've known for a while through work.'

Karen looked sceptical. 'Tania, there aren't any *normal* people at Westminster.'

'I know. He doesn't actually work there. He's a self-employed ergonomist.'

'Sorry?'

'Plans offices, makes sure your chair is the right height and distance from your desk, that kind of thing. He's been overseeing the redesign of the Health Department for a while now but he paid particular attention to my "workspace",' she said euphemistically, making quote marks with her fingers.

'And now you're dating . . . what's his name?'

'Ian. Yep, we've had one date so far, with another tomorrow night. Assuming he doesn't shout "Geronimo" in bed or bray like a donkey we might even see Christmas. I like him a lot.'

Karen smiled warmly. 'Good. It's about time you met someone who deserved you.'

'That could be taken as a threat,' she laughed.

'True, but it wasn't meant as one.' Karen looked at her watch. 'I'd better leave in a minute. When do you need me back by?'

'Take all the time you need. Charlie and I are going to feed the ducks, then we're having a picnic and perhaps taking in a *Teletubbies* episode or two. I'll get him ready for bed, so all you have to do is pick him up.'

Karen looked as if she was about to cry. 'I don't know what I'd do without you. I really don't.' She gulped a little. 'I'd have gone crazy by now.'

'You and me both.' Tania smiled. 'This little chap keeps me sane, so the favour works both ways.' She kissed the top of Charlie's head and he chortled with delight. 'I adore him.'

'And he clearly adores you. I wouldn't be surprised if his first word wasn't your name.'

Tania wrinkled her nose to indicate that she was doubtful, but secretly she was thrilled to bits.

'How's Joe?'

She always asked it as a matter of course, and invariably Karen would simply say 'Fine' before they moved on to something else, but this time she looked slightly pensive at the mention of his name.

'I think he's got a girlfriend.' She looked like she might be sick.

'Really? What makes you think that?'

'Because when we were at the hospital for Ben's operation, he got a text message from someone called "Em" but I didn't see what it said. I thought it might be a girlfriend, but then I told myself not to be so stupid,' she garbled, the words spilling over each other in her rush to share her worry. 'But when I dropped Ben with him yesterday morning, there was a note on the kitchen table that said "Speak later, Em x". She must have left when he was still asleep,' she added miserably.

Tania raised her eyebrows, weighing the evidence. She had to admit, it didn't look good.

'There could be a simple explanation.'

'Like what?' Karen looked at her expectantly.

'Like . . .' She racked her brains. 'Like . . . I can't think of one off the top of my head, but there *will* be one.'

'No.' Karen slumped in her chair. 'I'm right.'

'If you *are*, how do you feel about it?'

'In a word, wretched.' She sighed and stood up. 'I'd better go or I'll be late for my appointment. I think I might do a Britney and shave it all off, then go and have a lie-down in a clinic for a while.'

Tania placed Charlie in the high chair she'd bought from a charity shop and stood up, clasping her friend's arms and staring straight into her eyes.

'Now look here. You've stayed strong all through your son's illness and the preimplantation thing-ummy, and you've even managed to survive your husband walking out. Don't crumble now just because he may or may not have a *girlfriend*. Even if he has, she's probably just some fly-by-night fling.'

'I know,' she said, not looking terribly convinced.

'It's just that I suppose I still harboured some hope he might come home, but if he's shagging someone else it seems unlikely.'

After she'd gone, Tania sat cuddling Charlie on the sofa as he gawped at the Teletubbies and occasionally dragged his gaze away from the screen to stare at her.

As she smiled back at him, raining kisses on his fleshy cheeks and never once feeling stupid or fearing rejection, she marvelled at the unconditional love between babies and those who adored them. Seeing Karen so emotionally churned up by her separation from Joe, Tania was beginning to understand why some women went ahead and had babies alone, either from a one-night stand or a sperm bank. It was easier in a way, because you were the one in sole control, able to do as you liked without taking into account another adult's desires or demands. There was still someone to cuddle, but he or she was unquestioning and loved you come what may, with no fear of infidelity.

Her burgeoning relationship with Charlie had given her some much-needed perspective on life, made her realise that, for her, work was an interesting distraction but her main event was going to be motherhood.

When she'd had the termination, she'd been unsure if she'd want children in the future, but now she was approaching thirty-four she knew unquestionably that she did. *That* was the gift

Charlie had given her and she knew that however many children of her own she ended up having, he would always hold a special place in her heart.

Quite when she'd have children or who with was up in the air. Despite the obvious attractions of sole parenting, she was a hopeless romantic desperately wanting to meet the right man and do it all traditionally.

Perhaps Ian would turn out to be that man. She'd have to wait and see.

CHAPTER 30

'Waaaaaaa-hhhh!' Charlie arched his body as she tried to pick him up, throwing his head backwards, his face bright red from the exertion of crying.

After a night of little sleep for either of them, thanks to his persistent, rattly cough, Karen was physically and emotionally exhausted, worn down by two such energetic young boys and their constant demand for stimulation.

Charlie had always been a bruiser, and since his operation Ben had gone from a small, slightly weaker boy to almost full strength, eating for Britain and careering around with the raw energy of his most robust classmates.

She felt constantly frazzled, as if every waking moment was spent against a backdrop of a brass band, all banging drums and crashing cymbals. She ached for peace.

Charlie's latest tantrum was because he'd seen her getting Ben ready to go out and, realising his feet were still bare, instinctively twigged that he wasn't going with him. She wanted nothing more than to slope off back to bed for an hour or two,

417

before relaxing in a piping hot bath and pottering about doing odd jobs in isolated splendour, but she knew her afternoon would be swallowed up taking Charlie to the local recreation ground, endlessly pushing him back and forth on a swing to stop him crying at his brother's absence. If she was lucky, he'd doze off for an hour later that afternoon and she'd fall into a deep, grateful sleep beside him, but as always she would be rudely awakened all too soon by his post-nap grumblings.

Realising this current tantrum wasn't going to be resolved any time soon, she gave up and placed him back on the floor where he writhed in apoplectic anger at the injustice of seeing his older brother suited and booted for a day out with Joe whilst he was left behind with dull, predictable old Mummy.

She looked out of the window at the gloomy skies and resigned herself to an afternoon of her and Charlie getting wet in the local park before coming home and hearing Ben's excited gabblings about his infinitely more interesting day at the zoo or local swimming pool. Admittedly, she could do the same with Charlie, but because he was so much younger it was still a fairly lonely, insular exercise and she could get that for nothing down at the local swings.

It was weekends when being a single parent hit her most, seeing seemingly happy families wherever she went, spending precious time together before rejoining the hamster's wheel of the workplace on Monday morning. Mundane tasks they may have been, but she missed the adult conversation of planning the shopping list or deciding which was the least dreadful show to watch on TV that night.

The joy of partial parenting, like Joe was now experiencing, was that you had the chance to regularly recharge your batteries, approaching the days spent with your children with the energetic enthusiasm of an indulgent godparent. The less thrilling aspects of parenthood – the bathtime routine with a fractious child, the never-ending cycle of dirty washing, the painfully early wake-up calls – were left to the main carer.

She heard the slam of a car door at the bottom of the path, and pushed her hair from her eyes with a heavy sigh.

'Come on, Ben, I think that's Daddy.'

Sure enough, a few seconds later the doorbell rang and Ben rushed to the front door, straining to reach the latch. Karen opened it for him and smiled wearily at Joe as he winced at the sound of Charlie's shrieking.

'Welcome to my world,' she grimaced.

Joe didn't get a chance to reply, as Ben launched himself into the air, wrapping his legs around his dad's waist and causing him to recoil breathlessly.

'Daddy!'

Karen smiled warmly at the sight. It always gave her such pleasure to see the closeness between Joe and Ben, despite everything that had happened.

She knew he could have walked away and have no one blame him for it, but his love for the boy was too powerful.

'You look nice,' panted Joe, lifting Ben on to his hip. 'You've had your hair done.'

'Have I?' Karen played with her hair and felt her face flush. 'I mean, yes I have,' she blustered. 'I treated myself.'

'Quite right too. You should do that more often.'

'It's finding the time to be honest.' She jerked her head back to where Charlie was howling in the living room. 'What with the Little Emperor dominating my every waking hour.'

'Why's he crying?'

'Because Ben is going out,' she answered matter-of-factly, before suddenly realising that it might sound a little accusatory. 'He'll be fine. By the time you've got to the bottom of the road, he'll have forgotten what he was making such a fuss about.'

She looked past his shoulder and down the pathway, to where Gloria was waving enthusiastically from her little red Ford Ka. It was at least five years old, but as it so rarely came out of her garage, it looked conveyor-belt pristine.

Karen waved back. Strangely, her relationship with her mother-in-law had moved on to easier ground since the separation and she'd found her to be a valuable support with Ben.

'I see you have wheels. Going far?'

Joe shrugged. 'Not sure. Mum's packed a picnic

in the car . . . well, a feast for the forty thousand actually.' He grinned.

'One of those "Let's see where the road takes us" trips, eh?' said Karen wistfully. She loved those.

'Actually . . .' Joe looked apprehensive. Her heart leapt into her mouth, wondering what he was about to say, *hoping* it might be an invitation for her and Charlie to join them.

But at that moment, her younger son emerged from the living room on all fours, reaching her ankle and clamping himself to it for all his might. He stopped crying at the sight of Joe and gave him a gummy grin.

'Hello big boy.' Joe bent down and tickled him under the chin. He stood up again and grinned at Karen. 'What *are* you feeding him on?'

'Just a couple of antelope a day.'

By now, Charlie had let go of her leg and clamped himself to Ben's, hauling himself up on to his podgy feet and wobbling precariously from side to side. As Karen tried to pick him up, he let out an ear-piercing scream.

'You two just go,' she panted, trying to wrestle Charlie away from Ben. 'I'll deal with himself.'

But as she prised his little fingers away, she noticed Joe wasn't moving and the apprehensive look was back.

'Um, would Charlie like to come too?'

She stopped wrestling for a moment and straightened her back to look at his face, trying

421

to assess whether the offer was genuine or forced. From his impassive expression, it was hard to tell.

'Honestly, you don't have to,' she smiled. 'I know he's making a scene now, but he'll get over it. He always does.'

'I know I don't have to. I'd *like* to. I was about to ask you before he appeared.'

Karen noticed her heart was racing faster than usual. Perhaps it's the thought of that long, hot bath and afternoon of peace, she thought ruefully.

'Are you sure? He can be a bit of a handful.'

'Absolutely sure. Besides, a few aeroplane games and tickle sessions should wear him out.'

She felt a wave of relief and pleasure flood over her at the thought of Charlie finally getting some rough and tumble with a man, rather than her exhausted, half-hearted efforts at horseplay. He was such a boy's boy he was crying out for inter-action with a male role model, and the lack of one had been playing on her mind. She wasn't sure if this invitation was a one-off, but if not, it would improve Charlie's life immeasurably.

'Will these shoes do?' Joe was pointing at Charlie's blue sandals in the hallway.

She nodded and handed them to him, watching as he expertly slotted them on to Charlie's feet and buckled them up. A calm had descended on the child, as if he sensed he was now involved in Ben's plans and had no further need to play up.

'He creates merry hell every time I try to put his shoes on,' she murmured.

'They're always better behaved with people they don't know as well,' he reassured her, standing up and resting Charlie on his hip. 'Anything I need to know?'

'Same as Ben was really. He'll probably fall asleep on the way to wherever you're going and he likes cheesy pasta or ham sandwiches for lunch. Other than that, he's pretty uncomplicated.'

She tweaked Charlie's cheek, but he was too busy staring at Joe and twirling his finger through his hair. She was about to say 'He likes you' but stopped herself, fearing it might sound too suggestive and desperate.

'He's an affectionate little chap, isn't he?' laughed Joe, as Charlie pushed his nose against his.

Karen smiled warmly. 'He's gorgeous.' She resisted the urge to add 'and I hope you think so too'.

'Right.' Joe placed a hand behind Ben's neck and steered him out of the door, before picking up Charlie's rocker-cum-car-seat. 'We'll be back about six I reckon, if that's OK?'

'Fine.' A thought suddenly struck her and she lowered her voice, squinting towards the car. 'Won't Gloria mind about you taking Charlie along?'

'No. I discussed it with her on the way here.'

He started to walk down the path when Ben suddenly piped up.

'I wanna sleep Nana's.'

'Another night, son. I think Mum wants you home tonight.' He looked questioningly at Karen over Ben's head.

She shrugged. 'He can if he wants, as long as Gloria doesn't mind. But *he* needs to come home.' She nodded towards Charlie. 'I wouldn't wish a night with him on anyone right now!'

'Yay!' Ben ran down the path to tell Gloria the good news.

'OK. Then it'll be just Charlie and me back here at six,' said Joe.

As he turned to follow Ben down the footpath, Karen felt a lump of apprehension in her chest as a thought popped into her mind, one that if she didn't say now on the spur of the moment, she knew she probably never would.

'I'm cooking a casserole later.' She managed to sound admirably casual. 'You're welcome to stay and have some when you drop Charlie off.'

Between friends or relatives, it was the kind of innocuous invitation uttered thousands of times a day all over the country, the kind you don't think twice about saying.

But in their situation, Karen felt utterly exposed, shivering at the mere thought of a 'No thanks' that would feel like the most extreme of rejections. He probably had plans with 'Em', she thought mutinously.

'Actually, I . . .'

He looked hesitant and that was enough for her to trample awkwardly over the rest of his sentence.

'Don't worry. It's just that I'm making it anyway and you might have been hungry and it would have saved you from cooking when you got home . . . that's all, no problem at all that you can't,' she rambled nervously.

'I was about to say "I'd love to",' he continued, looking bemused.

'Oh great, good then! See you then then!' Any feeling of elation at his acceptance was overtaken by her embarrassment at the ham-fisted way she'd handled it.

She couldn't believe that she'd been married to this man for nearly five years, sharing their most intimate secrets, and yet here she was behaving like the class nerd asking the school soccer star if he wanted to accompany her to the end-of-term party.

'Yes. See you then then,' he parroted, setting off down the path with an enthralled Charlie still playing with his hair.

She knew he was mocking her, but she didn't care. She'd take anything that wasn't the cold detachment of the early months of their separation.

Shutting the door behind her, she placed her back against it and closed her eyes, a small smile playing on her lips.

Wiping her hands on the apron, she glanced at the clock for the fifth time in as many minutes. It was 5.45 p.m. and the casserole was cooking nicely, a couple of beers were chilling in the fridge, and she'd been careful to ensure the kitchen table looked like it always did. She wanted to give the impression of no fuss and no frills, but the reality was she'd spent most of the afternoon in a state of high anxiety, flapping about and getting little done except a very short, lukewarm bath and experimenting with various make-up 'looks'.

'Christ, what *are* you doing?' she'd muttered to herself at one point as the overpainted image favoured by lap dancers stared back at her.

He'd seen her without make-up first thing in the morning and piggy-eyed and puffed up after various long nights spent weeping herself to sleep over Ben, so anything would be a step up from that. And besides, she didn't want him to *see* that she'd made an effort, preferring him to marvel at her natural radiance rather than wonder which bottle it came from.

So in the end, she'd opted for the 'natural' look of light mascara, a faint brushing of Bobbi Brown blusher and a smudge of Elizabeth Arden Eight Hour Cream which looked liked lip gloss but could be explained away as a medical necessity for chapped lips. It was important to her that Joe didn't *know* she'd made an effort, because she was worried sick that if he did, it might alter the delicate balance of their relationship, which seemed recently to have moved on to easier ground.

She wanted him to feel comfortable sitting back at the kitchen table with her, to spend enough time there that he started to realise that he missed family life and, please God, missed her. She didn't want to rush him.

The blight of 'Em' had popped into her head several times during the day, and she wondered how she could casually broach the subject. It was too soon to ask him outright about his love life, yet she couldn't fathom any other way of doing it without sounding like the desperate, estranged wife who wanted him back more than anything in the world. Which, of course, she was and did.

She glanced again. 5.47 p.m. Removing the apron, she stuffed it in a drawer and smoothed down her skirt. It was a casual cotton one from the local ski-and-surf-style shop, but it clung sexily to her bottom and was topped off with a lace-edged singlet she knew he liked. The overall effect was pretty but not seductive.

Noticing the wine rack sitting on top of the work surface, she contemplated for the umpteenth time whether to offer him wine with his food, to loosen him up a little. She wanted to stay in control of her emotions and knew that the wrong side of a couple of glasses made her confessional and maudlin, so she would have to trust herself to only sip whilst he swigged.

Grabbing a couple of bottles, she lay them in the fridge to chill and opted to make a decision later.

The casserole simmering, not to mention herself, she sat down to watch the six o'clock news, but wasn't really taking it in until the item about a celebrity couple announcing their separation after ten months of marriage because of 'work pressures'. She made a loud scoffing noise, marvelling at how easily some people drifted in and out of marriage as if it was merely a tiresome interlude in their lives and had little or no perception of what *real* problems were.

Just as the news finished at 6.30 p.m., she could hear a thudding noise against the front door. Frowning, she walked out to the hallway, feeling a little wary. Joe knew there was a doorbell.

'It's me,' a voice hissed.

It was certainly him, so she opened the door to find his arms trapped by the leaden weight of Charlie, fast asleep and lolling to one side.

'I tried to press the bell with my nose but ended up having to boot the door,' he grinned.

'Bring him straight up.'

Karen ran up the stairs and led him to the old spare room which was now Charlie's, pulling back the blanket so he could lie him down.

'I changed his nappy about half an hour ago, so he should be fine,' he whispered, gently placing Charlie's beloved bunny by his right cheek.

As they walked back down the stairs, Joe leading the way, she watched the back of his head and remembered fondly the many times she'd done this when they'd still been together. It was just another of those mundane things that you took for granted when you were living with someone, the mere sight of them a reassuring presence.

She gestured him through to the kitchen where he hovered awkwardly by the cooker until she pulled out a chair.

'Sit here. Beer?'

'Lovely, thanks.' He sat down and looked around the room, paying particular attention to the notice-board where Ben's many squiggles had now been joined by Charlie's.

'I see there's another artist in the family,' he smiled.

'I can't bear to throw them away, but I suppose I'll have to have a clear-out soon or I'll have to take a storage unit to accommodate them all.'

'The little 'un is a great kid.'

'He is. Demanding though.' She raised her eyes heavenward.

He shrugged. 'Or perhaps he's just normal. Don't forget, we're only used to Ben who was pretty sickly at the same age.'

She nodded, ladling the casserole into two large bowls with huge chunks of buttered French bread on the side, just how he liked it.

Placing them on the table, she noticed he had almost finished his beer. 'Do you want wine?' So much for the dilemma about whether to open a bottle or not, she thought ruefully.

'Love some, thanks. I'll get it.' He stood up and opened the fridge, reaching across to the cutlery drawer for the opener before grabbing two wine glasses from an overhead cupboard, all with the practised ease of someone who knew the house inside out.

'And he's so close to Ben, isn't he?' he chatted, continuing the Charlie theme. 'I know all brothers have a bond, but theirs seems stronger somehow.'

'Well, Charlie did save Ben's life. So I suppose that counts for something.'

'Yes, but they don't know that yet.' He took a mouthful of casserole and made a dreamy face. 'When do you think you'll tell them?'

'I don't know really. When do you reckon?' She was careful to involve him in any decisions relating to Ben.

He shrugged. 'When the time feels right I suppose. Certainly when they're old enough to understand the whole concept of PGD.'

'Tania *still* hasn't grasped it,' she laughed.

'How is the old bag?' he asked affectionately.

'She's good. She's met a nice man called Ian who's an ergonomist.'

'A what?'

'That's what I said. He plans office space I think.'

'And does he know he's dating a woman who needs donkeys to get from one side of her desk to the other?'

'Apparently, yes. And he *still* asked her out, so that's promising.'

She stopped speaking but noticed he was chewing a large chunk of bread. Anxious to fill a silence that would have been comfortably commonplace in their marriage but felt awkward in their separation, she carried on.

'She's still working with Nick Bright.' She could never bring herself to use just his Christian name. 'Apparently, he and his wife are in the process of adopting a little girl. I saw there was a little bit in the paper about it the other day, but it didn't give much detail.'

Joe shook his head, his eyes narrowed in disbelief. 'To the day I die, I'll never understand how he could have two kids of his own and barely acknowledge they're even on the planet.'

'Because I suppose it's about the time you put in more than the biology of it all,' she ventured, aware she was veering into sensitive territory and anxious not to preach.

'Maybe.' He turned down the corners of his mouth before shovelling in another mouthful. 'God this is good. How did you suddenly learn to cook so well?'

'Necessity,' she smiled, thinking to herself, because the cook of the house left me.

Taking another sip of wine, she then refilled her glass to the top at the same time as his. She could feel her anxiety subsiding as the alcohol hit her system.

'So,' she said brightly. 'How's life with you?' She meant 'Who are you seeing now?'

'OK.' He didn't look convinced. 'I've tried to make what I can of that flat, but it doesn't feel like home. I don't think I'll stay there long term.'

431

More wine. 'Where will you go? Any thoughts?'

'Somewhere not quite as rough. I came home the other day and even my dog was on bricks,' he grinned.

'And you don't even *have* one!' She was aware she was laughing a little too enthusiastically at everything he said, but the wine was lifting her spirits to an excitable level.

She drank some more. They were halfway down the second bottle now and she knew she'd matched him glass for glass, meaning she was approaching the grey area, where history proved she veered between general hysteria and vomiting her stomach up through her eyeballs.

She knew she could easily be about to commit emotional hara-kiri, but she couldn't help herself.

'Can I ask you a question?'

He looked faintly amused. 'Course you can. Though I'm not very good on world capitals, apart from the obvious ones.'

She ignored his attempt at a joke, determined to stay as focussed as she could manage after nearly five glasses of wine.

'Who's Em?'

Now he looked puzzled. 'Er, the bloke who makes all the gadgets for James Bond?'

She scowled, displeased that he was trying to avoid telling her about his new girlfriend.

'Do I win a prize?' he grinned.

'Stop being bloody faceshhhh . . . facetiousssh,' she muttered. 'Who is she?'

'*She?*' He pursed his lips. 'Well I only know one and you wouldn't know her.'

'So who is she? The one I don't know?' Her brow furrowed with the effort of trying to establish whether her sentence actually made any sense.

'Hang on, before I answer that, how do you know the name of the woman that you don't actually know?' His eyes were mocking her.

Her shoulders sank and she made a small humphing noise of defeat, knowing she would just have to come clean and be damned with it.

'The name Em was a caller ID on your phone at the hospital . . . you left it on the table, I wasn't snooping,' she said plaintively. 'And then I saw a note from her on your kitchen table.'

'I see.' His expression turned serious and he gazed out of the kitchen window, scratching his head. 'I didn't really want to have to tell you as it's very early days.'

She felt the thump of disappointment hit her chest so hard that she fell back in her chair, the alcohol making her veer violently from high-octane laughter to wanting to grab his leg and plead 'Dump her' through a veil of angst-ridden sobs.

'How long have you been seeing her?' she managed to mumble.

'Since I moved into the flat,' he replied bluntly.

'That's not early days, that's nearly seven months!' She was aware her voice sounded shrill.

'Depends how you view these things.'

Karen lapsed into a self-pitying silence, staring

at the floor with a sadness in keeping with realising the end of a dream was nigh.

'Are you in love with her?'

She managed to keep her voice steady as she asked, but it belied her emotional fragility. She knew it was a loaded question. She willed herself not to cry as she looked up at him for the answer.

'Am I in love with her?' he debated, narrowing his eyes. 'Let's see . . .'

She hung on his every word, sobered by quiet despair.

'Well, she's blonde and slim, and she does this cute little thing with her nose when something displeases her . . .' He twitched his own from side to side and smiled fondly.

Karen felt nauseous.

'She's also sixty-five and a complete pain in the arse.'

'Sorry?'

'Em is my landlady,' he laughed. 'The calls, the visit . . . they were about the rent. I've been late paying it a couple of times recently.'

A wave of relief washed over her, then humiliation at realising he'd been stringing her along and enjoying the ride.

'Bastard.' She poked her tongue out.

'Idiot,' he smiled. But it didn't reach his eyes.

She felt horribly exposed, not to mention daft. He now knew that she'd been paying rather more attention to his new life than she'd been letting on, and she wasn't sure where the realisation left their fledgling, uneasy 'friendship' of cosy, shared casseroles.

'I'm flattered that you care though,' he added.

'Of *course* I care.' She knew the alcohol was loosening her tongue and she felt slightly out of control. But she'd already gone this far, so she figured she had nothing to lose. 'You're the father of my . . .' she paused, panicked about what to say next '. . . child.'

He nodded, a glimmer of a smile playing across his lips. The air suddenly felt thick with the things she wanted to say, but she didn't want to put him under pressure and risk frightening him away.

'So,' she said with fake breeziness, desperate for distance from what had just happened. 'How did you find it with Charlie today? Did he behave himself?'

He shrugged. 'Yeah, he was great. No trouble at all.'

'Ah, it's only me he plays up for then.'

'Always the way.' He shifted in his chair. 'Actually, it was easier having the two of them because he kept Ben occupied a lot of the time.'

'And what about Gloria?'

'She was quite well behaved too.'

She punched him playfully on the arm. 'You know what I mean. How did she get on with Charlie?'

'Really well. She kept saying he and Ben reminded her of Andy and me, so apologies, but there's every chance Charlie might grow up to be a computer geek with a personal hygiene problem.'

Karen laughed. It felt so good to be sitting at the kitchen table with Joe again, chatting and joking over a bottle of wine like they used to. Her expression turned serious again.

'Thank you.'

'For what?' He looked genuinely baffled.

'For taking Charlie out today. It meant a lot to me.'

'I figured it would give you a bit of a break, but I did it for Ben really. He loved having him along.'

He took another sip of his wine and stared back out of the kitchen window. The sun was setting, casting an orange glow across the garden.

'I miss that view,' he murmured.

Her heart felt like it was going to burst from her chest with the overwhelming urge to take the emotional baton and run with it, but she knew she needed to curb it for fear of spoiling things.

'Well, if you come for supper more often, then you'll see more of it,' she said lightly.

'True.'

She was hoping he might be seized by a compulsion to take her in his arms and declare that, actually, the missing-the-view comment was really a smokescreen for missing *her* and that he wanted to move back in with immediate effect. But he stayed resolutely where he was, his arms resolutely folded, his face impassive.

She drained the last of the second bottle into each of their glasses and lifted hers in a toast.

'This is nice. It's been too long since we've just sat and chatted.'

He looked wary at first, then smiled. It seemed genuine. 'It has.'

'I miss you.'

The thought popped into her mind and she instinctively blurted it out before she could change her mind. It hung there between them for a couple of seconds, a heartfelt remark that crossed a line.

After what seemed an eternity, he gave her a quick smile. 'I miss what we had.'

She wasn't sure what he meant by that, whether it had the unsaid, bitter aftertaste of 'and I don't think we can ever get it back'.

She waited to see if there was more coming, but he was staring at his feet and showing no inclination to elaborate.

'Do you still feel the same as when you left?' she asked softly. 'You know, that you could never love Charlie like you love Ben?'

He gave her a measured look then closed his eyes, letting out a long sigh. 'Karen, I've taken him out *once*, that's all. I really can't say at this point.'

'And what about your feelings for me?'

It was written all over his face that he didn't want to have this conversation right now and she knew she was risking driving him away when he'd only just taken a tentative step back over her threshold. But this was the man with whom she'd shared the most emotionally searing, publicly exposed heartache and it was difficult to rein herself in and pretend she didn't still feel a raw hope that they might reconcile. Particularly with several glasses of wine coursing through her veins.

She didn't take her eyes from his face, waiting for his answer.

'I'm still really mixed up about it all,' he said, his tone and expression reluctant. 'But I'm getting there.'

He stood up and removed his jacket from the back of the chair, placing it across the crook of his arm. Leaning over, he kissed the top of her head.

'Let's just take it one casserole at a time, eh?'

She smiled apologetically and nodded.

He paused by the kitchen door. 'I'll do another day out with the boys same time next week, if that's OK. And if supper is on offer when we get back that'd be nice too. I've heard you've finally learned to do a mean shepherd's pie.'

'Best in town.'

'Adios then.'

And he was gone.

Karen sat there for the next hour, staring out at the view he said he'd missed and replaying the evening over in her mind, flashes of quiet delight occasionally illuminating her eyes as she remembered his affable teasing.

She wasn't sure where the next part of their journey was going to lead. All she could do was hope, be there for him and wait and see.